Downeast Ledge

The town known as Ashton, Maine, in this book does not represent
a real community in Maine or any other New England state, but is merely a construct of the
author's imagination. Similarly, no character in this work of fiction depicts any actual person,
living or dead.

Published by NEMO Productions
P.O. Box 260079
Madison, WI 53726-0079

Publisher's Cataloging-In-Publication Data
(Prepared by The Donohue Group, Inc.)

Gilliland, Norman.
Downeast ledge : a novel / Norman Gilliland.

p. ; cm.

Interest age level: 12 and up.
ISBN: 978-0-9715093-6-8

1. Dementia--Patients--Maine--Atlantic Coast--Fiction. 2. Caregivers--Maine--
    Atlantic Coast--Fiction. 3. Self-actualization (Psychology)--Fiction. 4.
    Social perception--Maine--Atlantic Coast--Fiction. 5. Atlantic Coast
    (Me.)--Fiction. 6. Black humor. I. Title.

PS3607.I4455 D69 2013
813/.6 2013904698

Library of Congress Control Number: 2013904698
Printed in Charleston, South Carolina
For information about quantity discounts,
please call NEMO Productions at (608) 215-4785,
email us at: normangilliland1@gmail.com,
or visit our website at www.normangilliland.com

For Amanda,
who, like her name, conjugates beautifully

Downeast Ledge

A Novel

Norman Gilliland

NEMO Productions
Madison, Wisconsin

CHAPTER 1

Was there something new in the air that summer? Ashton had its usual fragrance of the fishmeal plant in Eastport, a tincture of tar and creosote from road repair out on Route 1, and brush smoke wafting in from cleared fields. At high tide you could smell the salt in the cold bay. At low tide there was a whiff of kelp and moss and devil's apron strings baking in the afternoon sun and the unyielding scent of the evergreens that stretch across ninety percent of the state.

But all of that had been with us for generations. Something different must have blown into the air the summer I met Dr. Walter Weston Sterling.

Because the clutch in the Dodge had given out again, Brian ran me out to my new job at the Sterling cottage in the Boston Whaler. *Spank-spank-spank*, we slapped across the tidal churn like a skipping stone because he liked to make every trip as fast and ass-battering as possible, and by the time I got a foothold on the steep stone steps to the yard, my Nikes were soaked and my self-confidence was shot. So instead of going straight to the porch door, I put my backpack down by a rattan throne in the corner and stalled around, hoping to regain a little poise.

Leaning over the rail, I looked past the widening wake of the Whaler to my side of the river, the Dunning side, where sunlight flashed on the picture window Pop and Brian were installing in our living room. I followed the slope of our lawn past our forsaken sailboat, which jutted up among the dandelions like a planter, and traced the gray granite jags of the far shore, where I could pick out familiar shingled walls and sagging roofs and the occasional chimney shimmed up with a little know-how and a lot of promises.

Progress has been hard on Ashton, Maine.

Past the last house out there, the pines and spruces rose up unbroken, except for the occasional timbered-off acre, all the way to Dunning's Point County Park, a neglected clearing that boasted a few fire rings, some picnic tables, trash, and a perpetually tipped-over Porta Potty.

Beyond the point is the Cauldron, a place so frightening that, most of the time, even the cormorants avoid it. For the few minutes a day when the tide is high, dead high, the Cauldron is deceptively quiet. You could float right into it on water wings. But as soon as the tide begins to drop, a row of rocks rises up like crooked teeth with the water boiling around them barring the way back out, and a granite wall blocks all but a few yards at the far end. Crazy as he is about risking dismemberment, Brian says that the only reason to go into the Cauldron is to kill yourself because, one shift in the wind or one wrong turn, and you'll get ground into fish food.

I was thinking about the Cauldron when Geneva opened the door and startled me into the business at hand. She was slender, fortyish, silver blond, and casually dressed in clothes that had cost a bundle back in the day. That was the quickest way to spot summer residents with old money—faded clothes with a pedigree. She was wearing a pale blue satin long-sleeved blouse––Gucci, I'm guessing—with a pale yellow cashmere sweater thrown over her shoulders, white pressed Capri pants, and—an exception to the rule—new blue dime store sneakers. She was pleasant but cool. As she adjusted the sweater to cover her shoulders better, a slender gold bracelet slid away from her wrist.

"Amber, all you all right?"

No, I wasn't all right. I felt like a complete doofus, standing there with wet feet and no idea how I was going to tackle the job at hand. I turned away from the rail and edged toward the shadow of the rattan throne in an effort to keep my feet out of sight. I started to put my hands in my pockets, but my jeans were a little too tight for that, so I just let them dangle at my sides, which was equally lame. I couldn't help thinking of the time I went into Eastport to have my senior picture taken. The photographer sat me in front of a plastic fence with my body twisted sideways as I looked into the camera and tried to smile.

"That Amber," Brian said when he saw the pictures, "for once in her life, she's got her head screwed on straight but the rest of her is crooked."

Brian's mission in life is to humble me, and he excels.

I did my best to put past and present embarrassments out of my mind. "Oh, I was just so taken with your view," I said, assuming that she was already starting to take me for some kind of airhead. "It's so nice to see you again," I gushed, sinking deeper into apparent idiocy. I wanted to vault over the rail and run into the woods, but instead I motioned toward my backpack, which was stuffed with a week's worth of clothes. "I brought some things in case you want me to go ahead and stay tonight. I know that this came up kind of suddenly."

We had talked once, over gyros and Greek salad at a waterfront place in Eastport. I regretted ordering the salad because, indecisive in matters of etiquette, I wound up talking with a mouthful of olive pits. I suspected that mine was the only response to her classified ad in the *Quoddy Tides*.

She was a little pasty for a summer person and she looked tired, but her blue eyes sparkled with amusement as I stumbled trying to pick up my pack and hide my feet with it. "Oh, your references spoke so highly of you that I thought we could skip the formality of another interview."

My first reference was the only relevant one. I'd been dog-sitting and doing errands for Mrs. Townsend from the time I was old enough to drive and she was more than old enough to *stop* driving. Pop is a man of great courage, but after he lost the driver side mirror on the Dodge to one of Mrs. Townsend's middle-of-the-road fly-bys, he urged me to do whatever I could to get her off the road. So I volunteered my services, and even when I was away at college in Machias, I came back every weekend to chauffeur Mrs. Townsend and her demented shitsu Peach.

My next two references were kind of a stretch, but they were very enthusiastic. There was the president of the Eastport Marine and Merchants Bank, whose pneumatic tube device Mrs. Townsend had knocked out of action twice as she careened past the drive-up window in a shortcut to the beauty parlor. His recommendation was a little vague but it was on this letterhead that dripped with credibility.

For my third reference I used Hal Foley. From a slightly illegal age, I had waited tables at his restaurant, Foley's Food Mill out on Route 1. With a lifelong loan from the bank, Hal had bought the old Blacktop Diner when the owners moved to Sarasota. He classed it up by pitching out the plastic accessories-- table cloths, chandeliers, and rhododendrons—and replacing them with what he called the real thing. He also upgraded the menu. Out went the gut-buster burgers and limp French fries and in went a dizzying array of hand-crafted entrees and sides. Something for everybody, he said.

And the place began a long slide toward oblivion.

I had stuck with Hal through a few payless Fridays and his letter puffed me up into a full-blown Wonder Woman.

Not that I would've looked that great in the costume.

"Poor Mrs. Conditt," Geneva was saying. "She's been doing so much for our family for so many years it's a wonder she didn't need physical therapy sooner." She went on to explain that her husband had just gone upstairs for his nap, so I'd have to wait about a half hour to meet him.

"I'm sorry," I said. "I'm not usually late. In my two years at the restaurant I wasn't late once and never missed a day." No way was I going to unload the whole sorry bundle about the bum clutch on the Dodge and Brian's teeth-rattling ride across the river.

Geneva put me at ease with an understanding smile. "You'll get to know him soon enough. Your mother tells me you're saving for grad school. Tell me more about yourself."

What can you say about yourself when you're twenty-three years old and you've lived practically all your life on the Dunning side of Ashton, Maine? I wanted to say that I was a world traveler and an Olympic gymnast, but the truth was that I had spent most of those twenty-three years going to and getting through the consolidated school in Hixton and getting a B.A. in Family Relations at the University of Maine in Machias. I pretty much sucked at sports. Up until the age of twelve I did some horseback riding, and then Roger Winthorpe's mare ran away with me, causing me to promise God that if he would spare me just this once, I would never again entrust my life to a large irrational animal. Just as I was promising to become a nun— quite the offer for a lapsed Congregationalist—the horse lurched to a jerky halt and pitched me off, which I figured invalidated the devotional part of the contract, but I was true to my vow about animals.

I wasn't even much for the water. I had gone out in our sailboat with Pop and Brian, poking along the river and into the open water, one time venturing all the way past Eastport, where the islands scatter like stepping stones across the Bay of Fundy. Pop had tried to make a sailor of me, but the whole business made me nervous and the boat had sat in the yard ever since he and Mom had a hair-raising homecoming in it. Hair-raising for Mom, that is, because she was the one who had to jump overboard and haul it in to shore while Pop steered. Once they were dried off and warmed up, he spoke casually of the boom dipping into the water as he pinched into a wind gusting to fifty. But that was it for Mom, and she and Pop never went out there in that terror again. That made sense to me. Anything that tries to tip over to get where it's going is not my chosen mode of transportation.

I wanted to tell Geneva that I could pack some incredible number of sardine cans in an hour, but wooden counters had put the sardine factory out of business long before I came along.

For about a month each summer when I was little, we raked blueberries at some fields down toward Machias. I was pretty good at it and the money wasn't bad when the Indian kids didn't steal my berries. Maybe I should say the *other* Indian kids because I myself am a sixteenth Penobscot through Pop's side of the family—part Scot, part Penobscot, and all good intentions, as Pop says. The blueberry picking dried up when the owner hired this guy with some kind of combine that could scour the whole field clean in about four seconds for a hundred bucks. After that, I took in sewing and sold eggs until I was old enough to work at Foley's Food Mill. Hal put a lot of sweat equity into the place but he had made a fatal error. The food was too diverse and upscale. The menu was confusing and the special deals were too complicated. I was trying to save up for some vague plan to attend grad school, so when the place went belly up I wasn't any happier than Hal. He went to work at the particle board factory in Woodland and I put all of my efforts into making wreaths.

All right, here it is. The wreaths were so simple. All I had to do was get some wire, some string, and some hay and make these round forms that upscale boutiques could whip into the most darling and pricey little Christmas decorations you ever saw. I figured I could turn out about nine hundred of the little bastards and be in pretty good shape for a year of grad school. But, damn were those things messy. Even the fresh hay was so full of dust that after a few wreath forms my snot turned black. I stuck with the job, though, wrapping and tying while my toes went numb, wiring and stacking with frozen fingers till the shed was bulging at the seams with the things. Then I waited for the day when the truck was scheduled to come and pick them up and pay me. When the big day passed, and the next, and we found out that the wreath company had gone bust, I cried black tears.

Of course, I didn't tell Geneva any of that. I just told her what I thought she wanted to hear, that I was trying to save some money for grad school, that I liked old people, and that I had taken some first aid and CPR courses through the Eastport Square Dance Club, AKA, the Romping Squares. Some of the club members are pretty far along in years, and our president-for-life thought that some CPR know-how might come in handy some night. I had won an honorable mention for bringing a child-size manikin named Lulu back to life, at least in theory. The truth is, Lulu's mouth reeked so of grain alcohol and rotting rubber that I applied my lips with gusto just to get the resuscitation over with before I puked.

A few days later, my intimacies with Lulu ended for good when the Squares updated their techniques and did away with the mouth-to-mouth business.

My recap of my meager qualifications seemed to satisfy Geneva. She sat down on the rattan throne and motioned for me to sit down on a more modest chair nearby. A diamond in her wedding ring caught the blue of the sky and the river. She seemed a little on edge as she ran a finger over her delicate gold bracelet. At the time I thought she was just concerned about whether I'd be able to take care of her husband for the next two weeks.

I would soon find out that she had a lot more than that on her mind.

She continued to rub the bracelet, as if to get out a stain. "Dr. Sterling can get around pretty well," she said. "In fact a little too well. We really should put one of those childproof gates upstairs. He's inclined to wander." She glanced nervously toward the door as if he might even then be teetering on the top step. She went on to explain that he was self-sufficient in the bathroom—a great relief, you might say—but that he might need a little help getting there.

"Don't worry," she added. "You'll know when it's time because he starts to fidget and then he tries to wander off. I'm not sure he knows exactly where the bathrooms are anymore, but there's one upstairs and one downstairs, so he's never far from one or the other. She went on to tell me about his mealtimes, his nap time, and his bedtime, so that I began to wonder if she'd ever be around. "In a minute," she said, "I'll get him up for an early lunch, and then I'll be gone until about six." After an awkward silence she added, "I do volunteer work in the county."

I thought she would explain, but she didn't. The only volunteer work that I knew of was driving the Bookmobile, but Geneva looked a little too refined to do that because the job required the frequent changing of flat tires, adding oil about every hundred miles, and a good deal of swearing.

She looked at her watch and changed the subject. "As I said the last time we met, you'll need to fix lunch, keep Dr. Sterling entertained until he goes down for his afternoon nap, maybe walk him around the garden a bit, and keep an eye on him while you're getting dinner."

I had practically memorized the classified ad in the *Quoddy Tides*. I had a copy of it in the back pocket of my jeans. I knew what came next.

"It's just for the two weeks, till Mrs. Conditt is completely mended and can come up from Boston." After hearing a little thud in the back of the house and dismissing it, she went on. "You'll be staying here in one of the upstairs rooms. It's possible that we'll have to call on you during the night."

That wasn't in the ad, and it sounded kind of foreboding, but I had come this far, and I'd have to find a large low-tech blueberry field to make the kind of money she was offering.

She shoved the bracelet onto her wrist and stood up. "Well, Amber, your references had only the best things to say about you, and I'm so pleased that you'll be helping Dr. Sterling."

I gave one of my drippy feet a little shake and assured her that I, too, was excited about the arrangement. She smiled and stood and stuck out her slender hand and I smiled as I got up and shook it. Then I followed her inside with my pack and waited in the living room while she excused herself to go upstairs and check on her husband, which was the first time that she had actually referred to him that way. I fiddled with my hair, which I had tied back with an elastic band. In my effort to be tidy, I had gotten it so tight that my eyes felt like they were slanting. Brian called it my Chinese position. I undid it and started all over again, but the elastic went shooting across the room and bounced off a bookcase. As I crawled around looking for it, I saw a book by Walter Weston Sterling, something about gene splicing. It turned out that most of the bottom shelf was by Walter Weston Sterling and several books on the shelf above it, thick books about medicine, physics, and chemistry. There was even a million-seller paperback that boasted about some kind of science fiction award.

"Look who's up already."

I jumped to my feet and smoothed my hair as best I could.

The stairs creaked, and down came Geneva leading the great man, step by step.

CHAPTER 2

E ven hunched over, Dr. Walter Weston Sterling was big. His thick white hair, neatly parted on the left, fell across his forehead as he lowered his foot. Only when he was all the way down did he take his eyes off the carpeted steps. Arm in arm with Geneva, he shuffled into the living room, where I stood frozen beside the bookcase like a burglar caught in a spotlight.

Geneva steered him by the elbow. She spoke in the kind of loud, deliberate, overly cheerful voice you might use with a toddler or a dog. "Walter, this is Amber, Amber Waits. She lives across the river in Ashton and she'll be staying with us until Mrs. Conditt comes back."

He nodded—I think—and looked at me with the bluest eyes I had ever seen. He was wearing a flannel Pendleton shirt buttoned all the way up to his Adam's apple. Formless gray pants hung from a belt cinched above his waist. His shoes were old mossy-looking soft-soled things that were double tied. I wanted to turn around and look at the books again to be sure that this was the same Walter Weston Sterling.

I couldn't tell if he was taking in what she was saying or not. He seemed to take *me* in with those blue eyes of his though, and he nodded slightly, maybe just because he was trying to keep from lunging forward. As I stood there, self-conscious about my frizzy hair, Geneva maneuvered him over to the sofa and plopped him down. He put his hands on his knees, looking like he might well settle there for the entire two weeks.

Geneva sat at the far end of the sofa and talked about him as if he couldn't hear her.

"As you can see, he can get around pretty well. But he's like a two-year-old. If you turn your back, he can get to all kinds of places that are dangerous."

As my gaze drifted from Geneva to Dr. Sterling, I kept expecting him to zing her with some kind of comeback, the way Pop would if Mom made a crack like that, but he was staring at the floor in front of the coffee table. The rug there looked like one of those flying carpets, colorful, intricately woven, and expensive, full of such loving detail that it probably took some arthritic Persian woman a year to pull it together, but I don't think he was really looking at it. I wondered what was going through his mind. I wondered if his head still contained all the stuff he had written in those books. I wondered if he was just putting on an act to avoid having to deal with Geneva, if he wasn't pulling a fast one, pretending to be out of it when she was around, but secretly tapping out his next brilliant book when she wasn't looking.

"Dr. Sterling began developing Alzheimer's about two years ago," Geneva was explaining. She had told me that at our first get-together, but now she went into detail. "You know, they say that it comes on slowly, but to me it seemed that one day he tied his tie and put on his jacket and drove to his office and the next we were leading him around like a child. He was a brilliant man, brilliant, who laughed at off-color limericks, liked dark beer, and could look at impressionist paintings for hours. And more than anything else, he loved sailing. Said it was nothing but a lot of physics and a dash of determination."

To me it was more like gut-grabbing fear that bubbled up from the will to survive, and I admired sailors who dared to go out on rough water knowing that if the boat could do it, they could do it. Now here was one of them who had withdrawn into himself, whose life was contained in this house or the walls of his skull, and I wondered how far the confident, fearless, seafaring Walter Weston Sterling had gone.

His appetite was still there. I discovered that right off the bat. Before she departed in a clanking yellow stick-shift Mercedes for public service unknown, Geneva gave me the lowdown on the care and feeding of her husband. The upshot of it was that he could down just about anything once it had been run through a blender. She didn't seem to care too much what it was, and she rattled off a long list of things that sounded more like punishment than food. But I came up with something that would be good for him and for the local economy. I made him a sardine sandwich, chopped it up and put it in the blender with a little oil and vinegar, churned it up till it was all a blur, poured it into an I-Heart-Maine mug, and topped it off with a sprinkling of parsley flakes. He seemed to like it just fine. He was most of the way through it when the mug slipped from his hand and spilled all over his lap. I steered him into the downstairs bathroom and cleaned him up as well as I could, but he had to get into some clean clothes, and I told him in short loud words to stay in the bathroom while I went upstairs to look for some. I was poking through the dresser drawers in the master bedroom when I heard the water running in the bathtub. I was in such a hurry to get back downstairs that I knocked a picture off the dresser—a photograph of a girl about twelve years old smiling atop a white horse. She was wearing a helmet and holding a trophy and she was very pretty. A little gap between her front teeth made her particularly charming, even though I was looking at her through broken glass. I stuffed the picture under the dresser and beat a path downstairs in time to find Dr. Walter Weston Sterling stark naked except for a pair of sagging navy blue socks. He was climbing into the bathtub.

It was one of those deep old claw-footed tubs and I could just picture him falling in there and breaking his neck, so I ran up and grabbed him by the shoulders, but he was strong and he damn near pulled me into the tub with him when he sat down, his wet skin squeaking against the porcelain sides. The water was ice cold. He let out a howl and started climbing back out, but he was sliding all over the place, and down I went, right into the tub with him and he wound up on top of me. Now *I* was the one howling, partly because the water *was* cold and partly because I had this large seventy-something nude man falling all over me. We flopped around like a couple of mackerel in a bait box and then I untangled myself and stood there dripping on the bathroom floor, gasping, my face cherry red to the roots of my soggy hair.

The funny thing was that I hadn't started laughing, which is what I usually do when almost anybody touches me below my neck. From the age of about ten I've been so ticklish that just the slightest contact will set me off. It was funny when I was a kid, but when I started going out with boys my little quirk was not so amusing. Anything more than a quick hug and I doubled up rolling on the ground. When they're feeling amorous, boys have no patience with that kind of thing. My latest boyfriend, Fred Archer, was very patient—for a while. Somehow we made it through the senior prom—which, fortunately, had very few slow dances—and off and on through my four years at Machias, and then we had a big fight about nothing—about eating the frosting before the cupcake—and he also gave up on me. We weren't all that well suited anyway. He loved his truck far more than he loved me and he could touch it anywhere he wanted to.

I finally got Walt dried off and put back together and managed to get my clothes changed without letting him out of my sight and then we settled down to a fairly civilized afternoon. At first it was a little strange being alone with Walt because I couldn't tell whether he was aware of me or not. I had done plenty of babysitting, but this was different. Even with babies no bigger than a wad of gum you could get a reaction. They'd squirt and giggle and wiggle around and play peek-a-boo till your eyes crossed. And they'd cry when they wanted something and they'd look at you kind of soulfully when they were sucking on the bottle or just lying there trying to figure out who the hell you were.

I had taken care of some old folks too. Mrs. Townsend for one, whose depraved dog, Peach, would yap at anything that moved. Practically every week, my mother or I would drive Mrs. Townsend into Eastport to have her hair done. She didn't have much hair and it sure didn't grow very fast, but she had to go in every Tuesday afternoon anyway to have it done by this guy named Maurice from Quebec who was really Todd Flink from a mobile home near the Dennysville dump. I took care of Mrs. Townsend by lying to her—by telling her that her hair looked fantastic even though it reminded me of whipped potatoes, by letting Todd go on with the Quebec deception even when he used this dumb French accent that sounded like somebody had him by the throat, and by being nice to Peach despite a secret desire to pop him into one of those pumpkin guns and blast him into orbit.

Well, none of that worked with Walt. I couldn't play peek-a-boo with him because he wouldn't keep eye contact. Most of the time he'd just stare at the floor or out the window, and if something actually came into his field of vision, he seemed not to notice it. And you sure couldn't tell him lies to perk him up because he wouldn't react even if you told him he had a clam stuck to his ear.

At least that's the way I started out. But after a couple more days of feeding him blender lunches and putting him down for his afternoon nap and whiling away the afternoons with him, I found it harder and harder to ignore him. At first we'd sit there on the sofa, me on one end and him on the other, while I combed through cookbooks trying to figure out what in the world I was going to fix for the three of us—Walt, Geneva, and me—when our food preferences were so out of sync. The first couple of nights I got away with some simple stuff—an omelet and a tuna quiche. With a pinch of strategically placed parsley and some thyme, you can make a hot dog seem classy—once. Once is charming, but after that you've got to get serious, so I was poring over Geneva's cookbooks when I realized that I was treating Walt like a piece of furniture. So I started talking to him as I looked at the pictures of all the fabulous entrees I could make.

The funny thing was, I not only didn't tell him any lies, I told him exactly what I was thinking. I figured how often do you get a chance to let it all out with another person and not have to worry about what you say coming back to you?

I looked over just to make sure he was okay. He was sitting with his elbow on the arm of the sofa. His feet were side by side, unmoving. He seemed to be looking at the dust motes that were drifting in the sunlight that came through the porch windows.

I folded my arms and stared at a streak on one of the panes. "You know, Walt, I hope you and I both survive this relationship. If you don't drown in the bathtub or croak from my cooking, you'll be doing fine. And if I don't get run out of town for abusing the elderly, *I'll* be doing fine, too. I'm in over my head and I just want to get through this thing. I'm starting to think that just getting to grad school is going to be hard enough. I sure hope that once I get in, grad school itself doesn't take this much out of me. I probably should've let somebody else take this job, but to tell you the truth, I can sure use the money. Nothing personal. You're a very charming guy. But I *am* in it for the dough."

That seemed kind of harsh so I rambled on some more. "It's for a worthy cause, of course. You'd have to agree with that. I mean, you probably have about sixteen graduate degrees. Me, I'll settle for one and then I'm out of here. I'll get a real job somewhere, not waiting tables in some pathetic restaurant on Route 1. And not just hanging around, riding shotgun in somebody's loud pickup truck and getting my knee squeezed." I was really talking a blue streak and I knew it, but it didn't matter. It wasn't bothering Walt any. No matter what I said, he wasn't going to keel over dead. I felt a lot better afterward, too. I was almost sorry when I heard the raspy old Mercedes coming up the driveway. I kind of wished that Geneva had stayed away longer.

After supper I took Walt out on the porch and talked his ear off some more. I told him all about the people on my side of the river, pointing toward each house. Out toward Eastport it was starting to go dark, but as I looked back in the direction of Ashton, a glow the color of a rare steak streaked the sky, and the scattered lights coming on twinkled like jewels.

"You see back there, Walt? You see those two little islands there? Well, just beyond them is my house. I've only been away from it a couple of days and already I miss it. What do you think I'm going to do if I ever go off to grad school? U-Maine in Machias was far enough. Grad school would be all the way down in Orono. I'd probably even miss my brother for crying out loud. He knows boats like the back of his hand. He's only twenty-one and he's got an interview down on Mount Desert at one of the boat works, as a *designer*. Can you believe that? He didn't even go to college, just two years at a technical school. You just wait. One of these days you're going to see a sign that says 'Boats by Brian' and that'll mean he's made it. My mom and pop, you'll just have to meet them. Only time I ever saw my mother scared was when she and Pop were out in the sailboat and a headwind built against them out there at the mouth of the river. It took them half an hour to get out into the bay, two seconds to decide to turn around, and two harrowing hours to get back in. And ever since, that boat's been doing nothing but grow weeds."

For some reason, I'd been thinking about that story a lot lately, a story about brave and capable people reaching their limit.

I looked over to make sure that Walt was okay, that he hadn't died of boredom or something. But he was about as perky as usual, staring out across the pink tint of the water, so I went on. "Now that next house to the left, that's the house of my friend Cherie Gillespie. Years ago, Mr. Gillespie was a professional golfer and he was in Northeast Harbor to play the course there when he met the future Mrs. Gillespie. She was working at that big hotel in Northeast, the Asticou. Anyway, he took to her at first sight and the two of them came up here so he could meet her family. The two of them were standing outside the house just chatting or something when this can of shingling glue fell off the roof and hit Mr. Gillespie on the head. When he got out of the hospital he didn't seem to care about golf anymore. He left the circuit and got a job marketing sardines for a while, and he's been up here ever since. At least that's how my mother tells it. I wonder about her stories sometimes, but she swears it's true. He's kind of gruff except when he's been drinking. Then he cheers right up, but that's not an option anymore because his liver's toast."

I wasn't sure if I should tell Walt the next thing on my mind, but I couldn't see what harm it could do, so I went ahead.

"Now out there toward the point is the Archers' house. Fred and I were kind of going out for a while there. He's a sweet guy, I guess, but I'm not sure he'll ever grow up. He used to make up little songs and poems as if they were right off the top of his head, but I could tell that he had written them down and memorized them because they came out a little too fast and easy. I suppose you'd have to call them love poems though they were kind of funny. We were okay for a while there till a couple of things came between us. He'd been saving up for a truck and when he finally got it he was the happiest guy on the planet, you know, and suddenly I came second. If that truck needed a new head gasket or the clutch needed to be bled or some damn thing, well, doing anything with me could wait. Not that I cared about him spending all his money on it. It was the time and attention that I was jealous of. And I don't even think of myself as the jealous type, you know, Walt? And if we went somewhere in that truck and I put my hand on it somewhere, you know what he'd do? He'd go over and polish the affected area. That's what he called it, *the affected area*. Walt, that truck was eight years old when he got it. Don't you suppose it had plenty of *affected areas* when he got it? I mean, it's not like rust was going to come blossoming out of the finish just because my hand had been there."

To be fair and honest, I had to tell Walt about the other reason Fred and I had broken up. I didn't go into it in great detail because it was so personal, but I did mention how, late in our relationship, Fred had gotten pretty fed up with my being so ticklish. Fred was as red-blooded as any other buck around Ashton, and that pickup must've seemed like a great platform for frolicking under the stars, which is not exactly sublime when one of the frolickers is doubled up snorting with laughter.

Farther out on the Dunning side of the river I showed Walt the light at Roger Winthorpe's. "He raises hogs and sells antiques," I said, watching the light flicker slightly through the dusk. "Nobody seems to know how many kids he and his wife have. Some of them may be strays that came in from relatives. It's the same way with the antiques. If you've got something you want to get rid of, all you've got to do is declare it an antique and dump it on Winthorpe's front porch and it gets absorbed into the jungle of junk. It gets looked after. I don't know if he's ever actually sold anything. I think he just barters. His wife does a fair job of fixing the stuff up, you know, scraping it down with shards of glass and sanding it and varnishing it and all that. I think she's trained every one of those kids to do it, too. Whatever they're doing in that house, at least they're all in it together as a family."

The next one out was Mrs. Townsend's light. "She may be a little stick of a woman and kind of bent over," I said, "but she's got the best-done hair in town, in all of Washington County. She still dotes on her first husband, who's been dead longer than anyone can remember. She's always talking about Paul this and Paul that. Sometimes I think that dog of hers, Peach, is kind of a replacement for him except that he's so dumb. Every time you step into the house he's got to get to know you all over again. He'll snap and bark his fool head off at you until he finally figures out who you are and that you're not going away. Then he's just as bad when he's your friend because he'll jump all over you and run his sloppy spotted tongue all over your face and try to get you in the mouth with that thing or have sex with your leg."

Past Mrs. Townsend's house things got pretty dark. The woods went on for a while, broken by a small cemetery and some timbered-off acres, then the blacktop disappeared into the trees, turned to gravel, and ended at Dunning's Point Park.

"Every summer there's a picnic out there at the point," I said. "A bunch of us families have been going out there since who knows when. Fred's grandfather on his mother's side has been going out there for seventy-five years they say. He's been pretty sick though, so he may miss this summer, for the first time in all those—"

Off the end of the point I saw a light that was unfamiliar. I got up and went to the edge of the porch as if that would give me a better look at it. It was good and steady so I could tell it wasn't a boat. It was kind of faint and yellow, a house light sure enough. I couldn't imagine anybody building out there, but nothing else made sense. It was something I never would've seen from my side of the river.

For the next few evenings, I spent time on the porch with Walt, telling him about my family and friends and how I didn't know what I wanted to do with my life. I told him about my doubts and worries and he always looked just as interested at the end as he did at the beginning. I had no clue as to whether he was taking in any of it, but I could be sure that he wasn't going to make fun of me behind my back or tell my secrets to his friends.

And I became more and more aware that after talking to Walt, I felt better. I was glad when Geneva made herself scarce because then I had him all to myself.

CHAPTER 3

I was comfortable. I had fallen into a smooth routine with Walt, and in our way we had become good friends. Geneva got him dressed in the morning. The three of us had a simple breakfast in the kitchen. Walt's Cream of Wheat didn't have to go through the blender because I had taken to getting up early and pouring milk on it ahead of time so that when he shuffled up to the table and eased into his chair, the stuff had gone to mush anyhow, and he seemed to enjoy it a little more when it came out of a cereal bowl, even if it was messier. We went through a lot of napkins keeping him mopped up, and once he even got a dollop of cereal in his ear somehow. But I had things under control. A few times after Geneva left, I walked him all around the yard, by the cedar trees, along the edge of a rough patch that jutted toward the worn slate stepping stones among the raspberry bushes, and right up to the drop-off overlooking the river. When the fog came in, we sat on the porch and I read to him or we listened to his treasured LP of a guy named Thomas L. Thomas singing Welsh ballads or we worked on a jigsaw puzzle. We didn't have the original box for the puzzle, so for a while I wasn't sure what it was a picture of, though it gradually took the form of a ballerina in a pink tutu, standing tiptoe.

The comfort didn't last. One morning, Geneva informed me that she wouldn't be coming back until the morning of the next day. Suddenly we were way beyond volunteer work in the community. We were into having another whole life out there somewhere while I stayed alone with Walt overnight. I wasn't about to complain, but I was plenty uptight about all the trouble he could get into. I wanted to call Mom to ask for her advice, but I had made my mind up to do this two weeks on my own, kind of like a spirit quest, a rite of passage, and so I was determined to take what came head-on and deal with it.

On my side of the river we never locked our houses, even if we went away for a day or so, but I figured that I'd better not take any chances with the Sterlings' cottage and so I bolted the door to the porch and turned the key in the kitchen door before I went to bed, and I made sure that the yellow light above the kitchen door was on. Fortunately, Walt seemed to be doing okay on his own in the bathroom, so I left him alone in there, and I didn't get too fancy about getting him into his PJs. I tucked him in good, but I was still worried about him taking a dive down the stairs, so I rigged up a cowbell on a string that I ran from his doorknob to mine. That way, the minute he tried to leave his room, I'd get a jingle, and I could get to him before he could even get out of his room.

To tell you the truth, though, being alone with him in that house was a little creepy somehow, and every stray pop and squeak in the woodwork gave me a jolt equivalent of about half a can of Red Bull. I had been given Mrs. Conditt's room at the head of the stairs, from which I had a shadowy yellow view of the driveway and the woods, and as I lay in bed, I glanced out there about once a minute. But the air was so mild and delicious that after a while I opened the window a crack, settled under the down comforter, and drifted off.

Something rattling the kitchen door brought me to my senses and I sat up so fast that I knocked my head on the reading lamp. I took a quick look out the window. No car. Geneva always parked the Mercedes in the driveway. I stuffed myself into my jeans and grabbed the closest weapon at hand, a paperweight, and yanked open the bedroom door, which, of course, set that stupid cow bell to ringing like a damn car alarm. Now I had to run the risk of Walt breaking his neck on the stairs while I did battle with the intruder.

My blood was up, and down I went, stopping only once to glance back at the top of the stairs. As I burst into the kitchen, paperweight held high, I heard a little click, and, half-blinded in the fluorescent light, I found myself face to face with a tall, slender strawberry blonde in a navy blue windbreaker and tan slacks. Her wavy hair was tied back behind her ears in a long pony tail that flashed when she turned to close the door.

"Who are you?" I asked, lowering the paperweight to shoulder height.

She stepped toward me as if to back me out of the house. "I'm Karen goddam Sterling. Now who are *you?*"

"I'm taking care of Wal—of Dr. Sterling until Mrs. Conditt comes. She's in Boston."

"Well, do you have a name?"

"My name is Amber Waits. I live across the river."

"Never would've guessed. Do you always sleep in your bra?"

Well, I don't usually, but I was kind of on guard, still, at the Sterlings' house. I wasn't about to tell her that, though, so I ignored the question and came back with one of my own, not very well put.

"So you're, like, Geneva's daughter or something?"

She laughed. She had mauve lipstick that matched her nails. "Or *something*. Walt's daughter, too, or so they say. What were you planning to do with that—weigh down some particularly threatening paper?"

Suddenly the paperweight seemed hot in my hand. I set it on the kitchen counter, noticing only then that it was clear glass with what looked like a humongous scorpion inside it.

Karen brushed past me on her way into the living room. When I followed her, she flipped on the overhead light. "Now that you're disarmed, tell me, how is Walt? Not talking your ear off, I hope."

Up close she looked even younger, not much older than I was. She was pretty and, except for the lipstick, she wasn't even wearing makeup. She had hazel eyes, a slightly oversized mouth and full lips, the kind that guys seem to find enticing. She had a few freckles across the bridge of her nose.

That question about Walt seemed a little harsh. And calling her father by his first name struck me as a putdown.

"God," she said, looking around, "some things never change, do they? So how *is* Walt?"

Did she really give a rip? I couldn't tell. But he was her father, so I figured she deserved some kind of answer.

"I'm not the best one to ask," I said, "but if you want to come back in the morning—"

She laughed. "No, thanks! I've come up all the way from Logan tonight, with the top down at that. I'm beat. I'm here for the duration." She started peeling off her windbreaker, one of those expensive heavy ones with a fleece lining. She had broad shoulders and her face was wind-burned. She yawned. "Well, don't just stand there. Make yourself at home."

Something about her smile made me realize that she was the young girl in the fallen photograph. She was the girl on horseback posing with the trophy.

She moved around the living room, looking at the books as if to confirm her declaration about some things never changing. She was light and graceful, like a deer, and there was something vulnerable about her too, as if at the slightest flash of light she would bound away. She reached the end of the bookshelf, turned, and looked right at me.

"So what do you think of Geneva?"

"Geneva?"

She rolled her eyes toward the crown moulding. "Geneva. Geneva. My mother."

I wasn't ready for the question. The best I could come up with was, "She dresses very nicely."

Karen laughed so loud that I glanced nervously at the top of the stairs. "Well—what's your name again—Amber? You sure have a way with words. She didn't mention me?"

I was a little faster this time. I made up something tactful. "I'm sure she did. But I've been kind of overwhelmed."

She raised a finger. "Oh, I don't doubt it! But you don't have to cover for her. She's good enough at covering for herself. I suppose you've met Jack."

I shook my head. "Just your mother and—Dr. Sterling."

"Oh, for God's sake, just call him Walt. Everybody else does. So just where do you live?"

"Over there." I pointed toward the porch. "Across the river on the Dunning side. Do you know Ashton?"

She shrugged her broad shoulders. "I've only been coming here every summer for my whole life. Though I can't say that I've ever spent much time in town."

"There's not much reason to," I said. "I mean, there's nothing to see, nothing to buy."

She was looking around the room as if taking inventory. "You live here year round then."

"So far. But I want to go to grad school in Orono next year. I just need to save up enough money."

"And that's why you're here."

"Well, and to help out with Walt."

A frown puckered her chin. "Oh, no doubt."

I felt that in a small way Walt belonged to me, too, and that I had a right to my opinion about him. "He's sweet," I said, "and he's patient. He's a good friend." I couldn't resist adding, "He knows how to keep a secret."

She gave me a strange look. "I would think so. Look, I really am ready to crash. And you must be ready to keel over after spending a day with Walt. I'm going to bring in my stuff and go to bed. I suggest you do the same. And if you hear any loud noises during the night, better batten the hatches. Things can get pretty lively around here. Summer fireworks! No need for a sweet thing like you to get burned by them. Well, I won't keep you up." She headed for the kitchen. "Better get some shut-eye while you can and lose the bra. You'll sleep a lot better."

Of course, I didn't. I lay awake most of the night waiting for whatever fireworks she was talking about. I listened to her walking to and from her car, to the quiet popping of the stairs as she came up, and to the soft click of her bedroom door. I heard the eerie warble of a loon, the distant breaking of water on rocks as the tide pushed into the river, and what sounded like the bark of a fox. I heard a car sometime during the night and footsteps in the gravel driveway, but I was too sleepy to think about it, and the house was quiet. The next thing I knew, the gray light of morning was brightening my room—or the room I had come to think of as mine.

As the woods came to life, I dressed quickly, thinking it would be poor form for the hired help to stumble down to breakfast after everyone else was up, but Geneva was already back, and she had beaten me to the kitchen. Worse than that, she had Walt up. He sat staring at the floor from his place at one end of the Formica-and-chrome table.

"Sorry I'm late," I mumbled. "I guess I didn't get much sleep last night." I patted Walt on the hand and smiled, thinking that he was smiling back just a little.

Geneva was pouring herself a cup of coffee. She turned just long enough to give me a friendly smile. 'I'm sure tonight will be better. This place takes some getting used to." She sat down at the other end of the table and said without apparent interest, "I suppose you met Karen last night."

I cleared my throat, not knowing what I should say. "Yeah, I did. I'll bet you're excited to have her here."

She looked out the window. "Oh, I was excited all right. She left school two weeks before she was supposed to graduate. Four years in Paris—and for what? Apparently not everyone is as eager to go to grad school as you are, Amber."

Karen hadn't said anything about *that*. Paris? Not Paris, Maine, either, I was sure. With just two weeks to go? I couldn't imagine getting that close to anything and letting go, but I did my best to smooth things over. "We've got some people around here that don't care if they ever do anything after college," I said. I was thinking of Fred, who had no plans whatsoever, except to get some kind of construction job and put away enough money to keep himself in Moxie and beer and truck wax. Even Brian, who has a bright streak a yard wide, was going to settle for his two-year degree, latch onto the boatyard job, and spend all his money before it could go "stale" as he put it. That's not saying that either one of them was grad school material, but I couldn't see Karen settling down that way. She seemed like someone who was going places.

Geneva took a sip of coffee and went on. "She seems determined to take whatever advantage she has and throw it away. I think she does it to spite us—or at least to spite *me.*"

Suddenly Karen was standing at the kitchen door. "For God's sake, Mother, think outside yourself for once. Do you really believe I'd screw up my life just to spite you?"

The coffee cup stayed right where it was, screening Geneva from her daughter. Her voice was soft as steam. "It may be your life, but *we're* paying for it."

Karen charged into the kitchen. She had on the same tan slacks from last night, but she had changed into a tight V-neck sweater that showed off a pretty figure just a few pounds past gorgeous. She poked a mauve fingernail at the tabletop to emphasize what she was saying.

"What was it all for, Mother? For me? If so, I had a good hard look at it and said *enough*. For you? If so, *you* should've been the one sitting through those stuffy lectures." She threw her hand toward Walt, who continued to stare at the tile floor. "Was it for *him?* Somehow I don't think so." She stooped down beside him. "Do you give a damn if I bailed out of college, Walt? I don't think so. The defense rests."

Geneva set down her coffee cup. The spoon clattered as she stood up and put the heels of her hands on the edge of the table and leaned forward, looming over Karen and Walt. "You will not treat your father this way. You will not treat *me* this way. You will not treat *yourself* this way."

Karen rolled her eyes and stood up. "Oh, for God's sake, Mother, you sound like a grammar exercise. That place was driving me *crazy*. They were all a bunch of pompous twits—and that's the students. I'm not even going to talk about the faculty. I'm not about to live the rest of my life with people lisping about expositions and auctions."

The table creaked as Geneva leaned harder on it. "And just what *do* you propose to do with your life?"

Karen threw her hands into the air. "I don't propose to do *anything* with it. I'll let it take care of itself."

I had been lingering back around the sink, trying to think of an excuse to slip out of the house, perhaps an urgent need to go digging potatoes in Aroostook County, but Geneva pulled me into the fray. "You're young, Amber. You have goals and ambitions. You're saving money for grad school. You have some kind of career in mind I suppose. How much sense does this make to *you*—putting in three years and all but two weeks of a fourth and then *dropping* out, just throwing it all away at the last minute?"

I was stuck. It seemed crazy to me, all right. I would've pushed right on through those last two weeks even if I had to do it walking on my hands, and then I would've blasted out of there to find a job of some kind. But Karen had a cerebral quality about her that made me believe she had a reason for what she had done, a reason bigger than just finishing her degree for the sake of finishing it. Fortunately, she interrupted her mother's question.

"Don't drag Amber into this. You hired her to handle Walt, not to be a referee."

"That's another thing," Geneva said. "Why do you insist on referring to your father that way? *Dad* was perfectly good for the first twenty years. Why shouldn't it be good now?"

Karen went limp. She'd had enough arguing. "Oh, what difference does it make?"

Walt had been sitting quietly at the head of the table the whole time, staring at those floor tiles. I went over and put my arm around him. "You must be getting hungry by now. I know I am. Are you ready for some blender magic?"

"I'm going out," Geneva said quietly. "I have some pro bono work to do in Eastport and then I'll probably go up to Saint John to get some things. I don't expect to be back until about six." She wrapped her silk scarf around her throat, swiped her car keys and sunglasses from the counter, and headed for the door.

"We may or may not be here," Karen said, not caring whether her mother heard.

I thought she was just being defiant, but she had something specific in mind, something dangerous.

CHAPTER 4

After breakfast, Karen announced that she had a mission of her own in Eastport.

"Fine," I said. "I'll hang out here with Wal—with Dr. Sterling." I wanted to work on the ballerina puzzle with him. Foolish as it was, I hoped that watching me put all those pieces together would miraculously reawaken Walt's intellect.

But Karen had something else in mind. "No, we'll go together, you and I and Walt. Just call him that, will you? Geneva refuses to understand that I use that name to distinguish him from the person that was my father."

I wanted to ask, then, why she called her mother Geneva, but I was already in deep enough.

And suddenly there we were, flying down the Woolsey Point Road, the three of us, packed into Karen's red Mustang convertible, which she drove like an ambulance, with squealing rubber and swirling dust. I hung onto the door handle, trying to keep my hair out of my face. Walt was wedged into the backseat so tight that he wasn't going anywhere. We were a fine can of sardines, hurtling toward this destination of Karen's, whatever it was.

I didn't ask where we were going. For one thing, in a way it was none of my business. I was sort of a domestic, and if the Sterlings wanted to pay me for careening around the State of Maine, that was up to them. For another, I didn't want to play too much into Karen's hands. When someone's trying to impress me, I'm usually pretty cool. Fred would try to impress me by doing doughnuts in his truck, but I didn't want to encourage that kind of thing, so I just sat back and ignored it until he got it out of his system. I figured, let Karen get this out of her system and I'll just play along. Anyway, at the rate she was driving, we'd be there before I could get the question out.

On the outskirts of Eastport she hooked a left turn into a gravel parking lot and came to a halt in front of Skipper Kip's Marina. I pried myself off the door handle, helped Walt out, and followed her to the slips. Before long she stopped at a classy old wooden boat called *Sea Clip*. It was maybe thirty-two two feet long, low to the water, tapered at the stern, and all squared away, but in need of a fresh coat of polyurethane and spar varnish, and when the light was right I saw a spectacular cobweb arching from the mast to the boom. Whoever had taken it out of mothballs had missed a few things.

"It's beautiful," I said, trying to restore it in my imagination.

Karen didn't waste any time. She hopped aboard and started pulling the cover off the mainsail.

"A birthday present from Walt. Long ago, before he started slipping, he signed it over to me for my twenty-first birthday."

Before he gave up on me, Pop had taught me a few things about sailing, so I knew enough to help out. I sat Walt down on the cockpit bench while Karen unlocked the cabin hatch and went below. I didn't bother to ask her what she had in mind because I could tell that she was getting ready for a cruise. She was a little hesitant, though, a little uncertain in the way she went about things. She was putting on a pretty good show but she was no salt, I could tell that much.

She came up with some life vests and had a go at starting the engine. She fiddled with the choke and pressed the starter and the engine wheezed and coughed and then settled back down to sleep. She glanced over at Walt as if he would give her some tips, but he might just as well have been back at the cottage staring at the kitchen floor. I looked back down the pier so as not to seem too concerned about Karen's struggle with the engine and saw a couple of men standing there enjoying the show. As Karen turned and caught sight of them, I noticed that the stop switch was sticking out. I rammed it with the heel of my hand, and when

Karen tried the starter again, the engine caught and settled into a steady *putta-putta-putta* wreathed in enough blue smoke to clear the doubters from the pier. After I pulled off the bow and stern lines and the spring line, Karen backed us out of the slip and we pushed through the foul cloud toward open water.

I put a life vest on Walt and we plugged along under power as the *Sea Clip* stretched herself over the light chop. It was low tide and all kinds of rocks and ledges broke up the bay, but Karen didn't seem concerned about them. She steered across the deepest part of the water, swung wide of a point, and moved us toward the mouth of the river. The tide and the wind were with us so the crossing was smooth, and within half an hour we were passing that now familiar cottage on the bluff at the end of Woolsey Point. It looked like little more than a green and white matchbox set on a shelf. I was surprised to see Walt looking at it—or at least looking toward it—and I wondered what he was thinking. Karen was watching him too, and for a moment I had the feeling that I should be somewhere else.

She pushed on past the bluff and edged along the Woolsey side of the river until some rocks forced us out into deeper water. Ahead I saw the two little islands—Benbow and Rush—that were a kind of gateway to my house and I felt strangely homesick. I had been on the far side of the river for only a few days, but I felt as if I had been on the other side of the moon for a month. I wanted the comfort of my parents, who were so outspoken and at ease with each other. I missed my brother despite his juvenile habit of twisting my ear. Even sloppy, scruffy old Fred would be a welcome change from the friction that ran like an undertow beneath everything I had seen of the Sterlings.

Once we were back out into the bay, Karen steered us into the wind and dropped the engine down to idle, and we hoisted the sails. She pulled up the main while I fed it into the slot and she ran up the musty old jib by herself while I tossed the sail ties and the cover into the cabin. We weren't graceful but we got all the lines cleated and squared away without losing anybody. Karen cut the engine and there we were, heeling gently, with just the wind and the wash against the wood and canvas. I thought she would sail back toward Eastport, but she eased the tiller over and let out the sails until we were moving dead downwind and billowing out in that way that looks so beautiful from a distance but puts me on pins and needles because a shift in the wind can throw everything from one side to another and spin you right over on your ear. One time I saw the sails start to pucker and I just knew that the boom would swing across and kill one of us, but at the last second Karen steered us out of it. When a puff came up, she let the mainsail out so fast that we jerked upright and I fell down. She tangled the tiller in the line that controlled the boom.

I was nervous. The mast looked as tall as a steeple and the sails loomed as large as the side of a barn.

I kept trying to read Walt for some sign of response—pleasure or fear—but he just stared at the flaking varnish of the deck or occasionally raised his gaze to the chipped blue water of the bay. When the boat heeled, he rolled with it until his back was against the rail, and there he sat as his driven daughter bore down on an island near a neck of land to the south.

"Don't you suppose we ought to sail back toward the river?" I asked, watching the jagged shoreline grow larger until its granite fangs rose up out of the water.

She smiled and brushed the hair from her face. "That wouldn't be the Sterling way." She glanced over at Walt as if he would explain. He was bracing himself against the rail, but otherwise he had no response.

Karen threw a leg over the tiller and re-tied her hair. "The Sterling way is to make the most of any situation, to push the envelope. It's a corollary to that great cliché—*suck out the marrow of life*—live it to the fullest.*"

"I'd settle for living life to the *longest*," I said.

"Oh, don't worry. Sterlings have been sailing through that slot for half a century. I've been through there plenty of times myself."

"Just not at the helm until now," I ventured.

"So you're about to see something historical." She gave the tiller a shove and we headed right for the rocks. She looked from the granite outcroppings to the slot between the islands to her father's face, stretching for a better view of what was ahead. Her knuckles were white on the tiller and her mauve lips lost their color. She was nervous, no doubt about that, and she was doing her best to bluster her way through it. I wondered if that was part of the Sterling way too.

The rudder kicked and the mainsail snapped, but Karen steered us through the snag and took us right through that slot to deeper water.

"There's one for Walt," she said cheerfully. When I looked back toward the bay, I heard her let out a breath.

I wasn't quite so glad because I was wondering how we were going to get back through there with the wind practically on our nose. Karen pulled the tiller and tightened the mainsail and we scooted off with the wind coming from the side. I knew enough to take the slack out of the jib and we heeled over good until we loosened things up a little. I didn't think she liked having the boat at a tilt any more than I did, but she pretended to be having a good time. She whistled a jaunty little tune over and over, and I got the idea that she was doing it absentmindedly as a way to keep up her courage.

When we got to the far side of a rugged outcropping, I recognized it as the Cauldron and I had no desire to go any farther.

"There's water back here you don't want to get into," I said. I had seen the Cauldron plenty of times from the rough little clearing at Dunning's Point where people came to picnic and watch the water boil on the rocks when the tide changed. Even from a couple hundred yards away, I could tell that the water was just starting to crease and pucker. I could hear it wash past broken granite and fallen trees and I knew that it would soon be whipping into a deadly rush and that the only thing to get us out would be that colicky old engine. I didn't question Karen's nerve, but I did doubt her good sense.

"Don't worry," she said, letting the mainsail out some more as she steered us broadside to the wind. "It's a little too early to go through there. With a little more water you can do it though. I just wanted to have a look at it."

She hove to and held us out there, watching the water in the Cauldron buckle and slap until I thought we'd get sucked into it by the incoming tide. She was having some trouble keeping the boat in position, which made me all the more nervous, but I figured I had already used up my quota of warnings, and since we had somehow cheated death so far, I bit my lip and waited to see what she would do. We were drifting, I could tell that. The tide had grown stronger than the wind and I could see the details of the shore, right down to the picnic tables in the park and the shattered remains of a dinghy above the high tide line.

Suddenly I realized what she wanted. She wanted me to lose my nerve before she lost hers. She was pulling us into a dangerous game of daring. If I gave in first and asked her to turn back, she could run for safety and not have to admit that her courage had failed. Of course, she had my common sense working on her side. In a round of chicken the more sensible person always loses.

I considered jumping ship, diving into the water and striking out for the park. That would certainly impress her, but I already knew how strong that tide was, and the water temperature was all of fifty degrees or so. I had a pretty good crawl, but not that good. And then there was Walt, of course. I wasn't above letting Karen run herself onto the rocks on a dare, but what would happen to Walt?

I gave in and told her that I wanted to go home.

She smiled as if at some secret joke and steered us out. The hissing Cauldron fell away behind us, and we moved back toward the slot between the islands.

I was more right than I knew about how hard it would be to get back through there, but I wasn't about to gloat since, as the saying goes, we were all in the same boat. The wind was picking up again and going through there dead on the nose, so that we didn't have room to zigzag our way into the bay. Karen tried it a couple of times, but we were pinching something fierce. The sails couldn't hold the wind and, with a great deal of noise, we went nowhere.

"We'll have to go around," I said. Courage had nothing to do with it. There was no other way. "It's going to cost us a couple of miles," I told her, "but at least we'll have power."

Karen had already come to the same conclusion. She dropped off to a more easterly course and we took off again.

Now I couldn't resist taking the high road. "Were you planning to get back before your mother comes home?"

Her voice was husky as she fought the tiller. "We'll get back when we get back. My mother can go fly a kite."

It was windy enough that she just might enjoy doing it. I raised my voice to be sure Karen got my meaning. "Well, I'm saying, she'll probably be worried."

Karen steered into a puff and fell off again as it let up. "Sweetie, you don't know Geneva. She may be annoyed because you aren't there to fix her dinner, but she certainly won't be worried about *us*. And if something happens to Walt, well, she'll have the luxury of blaming me forever."

I looked at her father, who was apparently unaffected by all of our hardships on the high seas. Karen had hooked a nylon cord from his life vest to the cabin door latch. He flopped around occasionally as the *Sea Clip* heeled and righted itself, but otherwise he might just as well have been back in the living room, gazing out past the porch.

"She already blames Walt for not writing his last book—the one that he started just before the Alzheimer's got him. His publisher offered him a hefty advance for it, but he only got two chapters done before his brain turned into a big Etch A Sketch. Geneva kept hoping that he actually finished the manuscript and stashed the rest of it somewhere. But she's turned the cottage upside down—and the house in Boston—and *no book*. She was rather put out. As you may have gathered, she could use the money."

I took Walt by the hand. "That's so sad. The last things you had to say."

"So you can imagine how heartbroken Geneva would be if we all hit the rocks and went to the bottom out here, leaving her nothing but a nice insurance payoff."

The wind shifted again, forcing us even more to the east, and getting back to the house by six was no longer an issue. Getting back before dark was. I suggested that we abandon sailing and fire up the engine.

"If it would make you happy," Karen said, giving me the impression that I had lost another round of chicken. She brought us into the wind, and while the sails flapped and snapped, she tried her hand at firing it up. It smoked and wheezed but wouldn't turn over. We fiddled with the throttle and punched the stop until I was coughing and wheezing too, but it was no go.

"I suppose Walt knows something about getting it started," I said.

"You got it," Karen said. "He knows—or knew—a lot of things. Looks like we sail after all."

It was past seven by the time we got back into the bay, where we had a straight shot at Eastport. The wind was still shifting to the east and we had to tack a good deal to stay on course. We became a fairly efficient team, so that I knew when Karen was going to come about and I had the jib sheets ready to change over. If it hadn't been for the darkening sky in the west and the chill coming into the wind, the trip might actually have been fun. I wrapped a blanket around Walt and we beat our way along feeling fairly secure.

Then, out of the scattering of traffic in the bay, a white powerboat came toward us at full throttle. I could make out two people, one of them a man standing behind the windshield, the other huddled in the back. Both of them were wearing sunglasses.

Karen muttered an obscenity and threw her leg over the tiller in an effort to look relaxed.

The person bundled in the back came forward. It was her mother.

The powerboat kept coming at us even as the man turned to say something to Geneva. If this was a dramatic approach, it was getting a little out of hand. He was going to have to slow down or turn hard to avoid us, and we weren't fast enough to get out of the way. Staring in disbelief, I shouted and started waving him off, but by the time he looked back around it was already too late. He cut the throttle and threw the wheel over, but the powerboat struck us a glancing blow and came to a stop in a welter of wake about six feet from our windward side.

I came forward to look at the damage, a long white scrape in our hull.

Geneva shouted over the blow and the water and the droning of the motor.

"Thank God you're all right, baby! I couldn't imagine where you could be until Jack thought of calling the marina!"

The man at the wheel of the powerboat smiled and doffed an imaginary cap. He worked the wheel a little more than was necessary. Black hair whipped across his eyes. He was zipped to the throat in a blue and white parka.

"Piece of work, isn't he?" Karen said to me. "Jack Crystal. Crystal and Sterling. Kind of a joke. She folded her arms and gave the tiller a little push with her leg so that the *Sea Clip* fell away slightly. "Everything's fine, Mother, or it was until somebody rammed into us. Why don't you go to your favorite restaurant for dinner—you and Jack, of course—and the rest of us will continue on home."

With more over-steering, Jack Crystal brought the powerboat in closer. Karen's mother leaned a little farther forward and raised her voice. "Look, we were really terribly worried! I can't believe you would go off like this—all three of you—without so much as a note!"

Sea Clip heeled in a puff but Karen didn't stir. She still steered with her leg. "Oh, how quickly we've gone through the worry stage to the inflicting guilt stage," she told me. She had her back to her mother.

"We want you to motor back," Geneva called through cupped hands.

Karen stayed where she was. "Can't, Mother! The engine's on the fritz."

"Then let us tow you in."

Karen called over her shoulder. "Not very bloody likely."

The powerboat putted in a few feet closer. Geneva began consulting with Jack, who stood with one hand on the wheel, looking like the cover of a men's wear catalogue.

Karen used the opportunity to jerk on the mainsheet. The *Sea Clip* heeled over and took off. As specks of light began to come on at the edge of the bay, I looked back and saw the new unfamiliar one off the end of Dunning's Point. When I turned around again, Geneva and her Jack had fallen back, but as we crossed and re-crossed the bay in what was left of the daylight, the powerboat was never out of sight.

We were lucky. Coming into the marina we had a light crosswind, so that with just the main and a lot of nail-biting, we were able to edge up to the pier without breaking anything.

The night was tense and grim. When we got back to the house, Geneva's friend Jack did his best to lighten the crisis with jokes and digressions. Geneva wasn't having any of it though, and when Jack finally left, I was afraid that she and Karen would go at it good, and they did. They squared off in the kitchen, so I went into the living room and sat on the sofa with Walt. Karen came in after me, her mother followed, and there I was in the middle again.

"I couldn't believe you would try to take that leaky old boat all the way over there."

"I didn't *try*, Mother, I *did* it. And it's not all that leaky. I pumped the bilge. It sails fine. Or it did until somebody ran into it."

"Well, if it's not one thing, it's another, isn't it? Are you trying to drive me crazy?"

Karen was standing with her back to the porch door. She crossed her arms and cocked a brow. "I'm not *trying* to drive you crazy, Mother."

"Oh, then—"

"If you'd stop being so self-centered for half a minute you'd realize that I'm not trying to do anything to you at all. I'm just doing what I do."

"And dropping out of college two weeks before graduation is *doing what you do*?"

Karen shrugged. "Apparently."

"You gave me no warning about this when we talked on the phone."

"I didn't know about it when we talked on the phone. Maybe I should've sent you a letter."

That last was pointed like a dart.

Geneva passed her hands over her forehead, brushing back her silver blond hair. "I don't even want to get into this now. Look, what about your father? What if there had been an accident?"

"Jesus Christ, Mother, don't you suppose Amber and I would've been in it too? Anyway, wouldn't you say he's already *had* his accident?"

Walt gazed at the usual spot on the living room rug while his wife and daughter argued about him like he was a piece of furniture.

Geneva looked up at the ceiling for a moment. "We're getting nowhere fast, as usual. Just tell me what's on your mind for tomorrow. Another—never mind—I won't even call it an escapade. Just tell me what you have in mind."

Karen shook her head. "Not a damn thing, Mother. I'm just taking each day as it comes."

"All right." Geneva lowered her voice in resignation. "Tell me, Amber, what would *you* suggest? What's there to do around here that would engage the mind of a bright, imaginative, restless girl of twenty-three?"

I had been looking past Karen, to that distant light off the end of the point. I wondered if people were arguing over there or if their night was peaceful. It crossed my mind that we could all become great friends if we just went over to Maurice's and had our hair done. I imagined us all with frosted French twists. Maurice was a diabetic, and rumor had it that whenever he got an urge for the forbidden pleasure of ice cream, all of his hair-dos came out looking like twist cones. There's nothing like having really weird hairdos in common to build camaraderie. But I didn't say that. I told Geneva in so many words that I couldn't think of a thing in Ashton that would hold Karen's interest for the blink of an eye.

"Well, what do your friends do? You have friends your age, don't you?"

"No ma'am, not exactly. My best girlfriend, Cherie Gillespie, moved away last month to go to secretary school in Woodland. It's been kind of quiet since then."

"All right then. You must have a boyfriend. What does he do?"

I made a face. "*Ex*-boyfriend and you don't want to know about *him*. The less said the better. I'm sorry to say that, aside from an occasional fire, the most excitement we get is at the summer picnic."

I shouldn't have said it, shouldn't have breathed a word about the grubby down-home doings out on Dunning's Point, and of course, Geneva latched right onto it. She wanted to know all about the picnic, but I clammed up because I could not in my wildest pineapple pizza-driven dreams picture Karen at the Dunning's Point picnic. And of course, the more I held back, the more fascinated Geneva and Karen became because they wanted a way out of the corner they were in, and they wanted me to provide it.

CHAPTER 5

As Karen swerved the Mustang around the potholes on the Dunning's Point Road, I tried to figure out where I had gone wrong. I told Karen that my side of the river was the most boring place in all of Maine. I told her how dull the yearly picnic was, that I went to it out of sheer habit and lack of imagination, that the food consisted mostly of gooey canned creamed peas, carrot Jell-O, and dangerously warm potato salad. I told her that anyone who had spent most of the last four years in Paris, for crying out loud, would be bored numb by a hodge-podge of locals swigging cheap beer in a poorly-kept park at the outer edge of Ashton's dreariest neighborhood.

I pretty much believed it, too.

"I like canned creamed peas," Karen said with a toss of her ponytail, and when the day came, there we were—she and I and Walt—scattering gravel on our way down the road that ran along the Dunning side of the river.

Karen looked over and smiled through the dust. She had thought to wear a scarf and sunglasses. "You know, I'm a lot more open-minded than you seem to think. I'm not going to pass judgment on your friends—or is it that you think *they'll* disapprove of *me?*"

I started coughing, not from the dust but at the notion that anyone could take issue with Karen's cosmopolitan poise and meticulous prettiness.

We passed my house, neat and white, overlooking the river where it opened up and split our scattered town in two. We passed the tall, narrow, chaotic hovel where Fred still lived with his parents and their big black soulful mutt, Blip. We passed fields gone to bracken that covered up old cellar holes and tumbledown rock walls and rail fences. But we did *not* pass the hand painted sign advertising antiques at the shingled cottage of Roger Winthorpe. Karen wheeled the Mustang hard into the rocky driveway. "Does he have good stuff?" she asked as she hopped out of the car. She hurried onto to the creaking porch, much of which was occupied by an ornate black and gold pedal organ.

Winthorpe had seen her coming and he was out there to greet her with his gap-toothed grin. When he saw me he waved and called out. "You on your way to the picnic, Amber?"

I climbed out of the car, made sure that Walt was secure in the backseat, and followed Karen up to the porch. I stuffed my hands in my jeans pockets in an effort not to look too enthusiastic. "Looks like we're going to check out the inventory first," I said, I watched Karen trace a mauve fingertip across the gold lettering on the pedal organ. I introduced her as "my friend from across the river." I gave Winthorpe the benefit of the doubt and he became an antiquarian, hog farmer, and part-time constable.

"How much for the organ?" Karen asked, running her fingers over the uneven keys.

Winthorpe ran his fingers through his beard. "Don't know! Didn't cost me nothing. When I got up today, there it was on the porch, like the morning dew."

Karen pushed her sunglasses into her hair and looked at me as if to ask if he was putting her on. I knew he wasn't. Things were always turning up on Winthorpe's doorstep, although usually it was dogs and cats and the occasional stray child. A parlor organ was an unusual arrival.

"Well, then," she persisted. "How much do you want for it?"

Winthorpe ran his thumbs along his suspenders. He's bulky and he has a habit of testing his suspenders, especially after meals or a pitcher of beer. "Let me think about that some. It'll be here for you in the meantime. I don't suppose anybody's going to snatch it up today."

Just then one of his brood squeezed through the screen door and started pumping the pedals and another pulled a few stops and played a passable, though winded, "Heart and Soul."

Karen found the performance perfectly charming. "Maybe the price just went up," she said, smiling.

"Guess I'll have to put them on the payroll," Winthorpe said. He patted the player on his blond head and then gave him an affectionate shove on the behind with the toe of his work boot.

"If you bought it, how would you get it to the house?" I asked, trying not to sound too much like a wet blanket. Walt was starting to look a little restless. I tried not to imagine him starting the Mustang and taking off for parts unknown.

"Oh, one thing at a time," Karen said as she ran her hand over the scrollwork above the keyboard.

"By the way," I told Winthorpe, "over there in the car is Dr. Ster—Karen's father, Walt."

With a gentle thump on the back of a blond head, Winthorpe broke up a wrestling match that had broken out between the organists. "And these two are Zero and Knocker—at least that's what I call them." He waved to Walt. "How are yuh?"

"Oh, he's uh—" I couldn't finish before Winthorpe jumped down from the porch and strode up to the car.

As a law enforcement official he was supposed to be observant, and he figured out at once that Walt was a little different. He said some friendly words, patted him on the shoulder, and asked him if he was on his way to the picnic.

"He wouldn't miss it for the world," Karen said.

Winthorpe called over to us. "I'm on my way back out there. I've got a pig in the cooker and I came home just to get the barbeque sauce. Amber, have you heard about Fred's granddad?"

He had been ailing for a couple of weeks. But since I hadn't seen Fred lately, I was out of the loop. "I hope he's gotten better," I said.

Winthorpe shook his head. "It's going the other way. But then at eighty-five you don't have much left on the warranty. Last I heard, he was vowing to make it to the picnic, but it don't look like that's going to happen. Ain't that a shame?"

I wished I could call Fred and offer him my sympathy, but since we had broken up so recently it didn't seem like a good idea.

Winthorpe gave Walt another pat on the shoulder and flicked a rock from the driveway with the tip of his steel-toed boot. "It's a particular shame since he's our senior picnicker. Been going out to the point every summer for seventy-four years. Can you believe that? This was to have been his diamond jubilee."

Karen made the disappointment her own. "His diamond jubilee. That *is* too bad."

It struck me as strange that she was so much more sociable on my side of the river. But I was sure that things would get a lot stranger at the picnic, and it turned out that I was right—all too right.

It began well enough. Somebody had done a great job of making the point look respectable. The Porta Potty was back on its feet, although its garble of graffiti was still there; the broken bottles and squashed cans were gone; and the rusted rims of the fire-pits sat straight for once. Most of the neighborhood was already out at the park by the time we got there, including my parents and Brian and his scruffy friends.

Brian and his friends were always getting into what they called mud ball. It was a kind of so-called touch football played in the worst terrain available. By "touch" they meant that you touched the guy with the ball until he fell over, preferably facedown in the mud. It was Brian's favorite way to get rid of his old clothes. He'd go through a set every time he played. Buttons popped off by the handful and cloth shredded by the yard. By the time I introduced him to Karen, his shirt was torn half off and his flinty chest was sweaty and heaving. He looked like he had just walked off the cover of a romance novel, but he smelled like a gym sock. Karen took to him right away.

"Brian has an interview at a boat yard down on Mount Desert next week," I said proudly of the throbbing shambles slobbering down a beer. "For a designer job. He's got a knack for making them sail smooth."

"Only I don't sail them," Brian said, licking the foam from the top of the can. "I *run* them. Why waste time with all those acres of polyester when all you need is a motor?"

With a well-placed throw of the football, one of his friends knocked the beer can from his hand and Brian spun around, snatched up the ball, and threw it back so hard that catching it nearly knocked the culprit off his feet. He grabbed his beer and ran back into the fray.

My parents were over at a picnic table with Mrs. Townsend and Peach, who had wrapped his leash around the foot of the bench three or four times because he went wild whenever anyone came around. He barked at me even though he'd known me since he was an embryo.

"Count your blessings," I told Karen. "He's worse when he likes you. He jumps all over you and tries to stick his tongue in your mouth." I didn't mention his sex-with-your-leg trick.

"Amber, you're always exaggerating." Mom introduced herself to Karen and tugged at Pop's sleeve. He was talking pork with Winthorpe's wife, who had brought down three or four of the kids.

"He got that fire going back about four-thirty this morning," Pop was saying. "And I'll bet that aroma has been driving Peach crazy the whole time. It's not just noise that sets dogs off, you know, it's—well, who's this? Here come two girls and one of them looks familiar."

"I haven't been gone *that* long," I said, although it did seem as if I had been at the Sterling's house for a month.

"Your dad thought you'd give us a call," Mom said. Her smile showed that she knew better. "I told him you'd go the distance," she said. "*I* didn't expect to see you before the picnic."

Pop wasn't going to hear any more of that. He finished his beer and set the can on the table in order to shake hands with Karen. "Rumor has it that I'm Amber's dad."

I thought I saw Karen blush. "I would have guessed," she said. "She has your dark eyes."

"That's the Penobscot shining through," Pop said, putting his arm around my neck. "That's how I get to claim her. None of her mom's other boyfriends have those Penobscot eyes."

Mom smiled indulgently. "He's at it again. Wouldn't you be surprised if I *did* have a man or two hiding in the closet?"

"Not in *our* closets. There's not room. You up for the summer are you, Karen?"

She cocked her head as if to appraise him. "Oh, I'm just taking one day at a time."

"Me too," Pop said. "Well, I hope you can take *this* day all right."

Mrs. Townsend finally got Peach to stop yapping. I think she had a move all her own that she resorted to sometimes. He'd give a little *yip* and that was all you'd hear from him for a while.

After all the introductions, we fell into a conversation about Fred's grandpa, how sick he had been and what a shame it would be if he'd have to miss the picnic for the first time in seventy-five years.

Pop cracked a new beer. "The time's going to come sooner or later."

Mrs. Townsend sighed. "For poor Paul it came too soon, for my second husband, a little too late." Looking past Karen, she saw Walt sitting in the Mustang. "Who's the cutie in the car?"

"That's Karen's father, Walter," I told her.

"*Dr. Sterling*," Karen said. I never knew where she was coming from. Whatever I made of her father, she always changed it.

Mrs. Townsend's inaccurately painted mouth gaped. "What's the matter with him?"

"He had a bad year," Karen said.

Pop went over to Walt and offered him a beer.

"He only drinks food that's been through the blender," I said before I could think better of it.

Pop gave me a disapproving glance. "This beer's been through the blender and then some."

Walt took the can in both hands and drank.

"What do you make of that?" I asked no one in particular.

Pop took the beer back and raised it to Walt in a salute. "If you get thirsty, there's more where this came from. We'll have some roast pork in a little while, too. Hope you brought your blender."

"Oh, Frank—" My mother turned away to suppress a laugh.

Winthorpe and a few more of his kids came rattling up in his four-by-four, setting Peach off like a fire alarm. When the dust and racket died down, one of his towheaded boys jumped out of the back and described in lurid terms the way Winthorpe had waylaid and butchered the pig that very morning and consigned it to the cooker, a fifty-five gallon drum cut in half and fitted with an oak handle and a thermometer. Winthorpe wasn't about to open the lid to see how the pig was doing, though, because it would be bad luck. "It ain't but pig and fire and time," he declared, pulling part of a wristwatch from his hip pocket. "And the time ain't for another twenty-two minutes. Then we'll eat pork."

I got Mom to keep an eye on Walt while Karen and I walked through the cedar trees to see the Cauldron. We found a little outcropping with a couple of trees you could hold onto and watched for a while as the water surged over the rocks, met the outgoing current, and boiled up. It was about halfway to its full power and plenty impressive already as everything circled and snapped between the point and the island. I was glad to be watching it from solid ground, and I grabbed a little cedar tree to make sure I stayed there. I'd never heard of anyone sober falling into the Cauldron and I wasn't about to be the first. Karen seemed unconcerned though. She stood free at the edge of the outcropping, one hand on her hip, as the water gushed just a few feet below.

"They're lovers, you know." Without moving away from the ledge, she turned and looked back at me. "In most matters my mother doesn't have very good taste."

I began to picture Geneva and Jack together in some romantic place, like the honeymoon suite at the Economotel in Machias. There was Geneva in her yellow cashmere sweater, pale blue satin blouse, white pressed Capris, and dimestore sneakers. And there was Jack Crystal, looking at her with sleepy eyes, standing stiff and smiling faintly as he flipped a switch that made the purple heart-shaped Jacuzzi start burbling. When he started taking his parka off, I blinked hard several times to stop the video.

"I suppose that, after my father, she wanted somebody easy," Karen was saying, "somebody that didn't require her to think. Of course, they've been at it off and on since before I was born. In my worst nightmares I dream that Jack's my father. If I ever have the guts, I'll get my DNA checked."

I shook my head in disbelief. "He really doesn't seem her type. He doesn't seem *anybody's* type."

Karen smiled down at the Cauldron. "My father used to say that there's *somebody* for *everybody*. There's somebody for you, somebody for me. Of course, there's no guarantee that you'll ever find that person. It's so much a matter of chance. That was one reason I let my parents send me to Paris. I figured what are the chances that I'll find that person—or even the second best or third best—in Boston? It would be too easy."

I'd never thought about love that way. But she seemed to have a point. If I hung around Ashton for the rest of my life, how likely was it that I would find my one-and-only? I looked through the cedars at the boys grubbing in the dirt with the football and suddenly *I* wanted to go to Paris, or at least to Bangor.

Karen pushed her toes past the ledge until she tottered over the swirling water. "You've probably noticed that my mother is a lot younger than my father. She was twenty-two when they married. He was forty-five. His parents thought she had tricked him into marrying her so she could get her hands on the Sterling money."

"Nobody on my side of the river has *that* problem," I said. "What could his parents do about it?"

She laughed and turned toward me. She was so close to the edge that she seemed to be standing on air. "They *spent* the fortune, of course! Or at least as much as they could before they died. They had the power of their convictions—and talent, apparently, when it came to spending money."

I was still hanging onto the little cedar tree even though I hadn't ventured nearly as close to the edge as she had. "It's too bad they couldn't just work it out."

She came toward me a little. "Well, maybe my grandparents had a point. Geneva hasn't exactly been standing by her man in sickness and in health. The minute my father was stricken, she picked up where she left off with Jack. He knows how to work the angles. I'll say that for him, and so now she has someone after *her* money, what's left of it."

"Well, it must be tough with your father the way he is," I said. "Your mother seems like a lonely person to me."

"Amber, sweetie, if she is, it's her own fault. She can always join the damn Rotary Club or something."

"I know it may be hard to tell, "I said, "but I'm sure she was glad to have you home, even if she was bent out of shape because you quit school."

"Oh, sure, because at least I wasn't with Maturin."

"Your one-and-only?"

"Maturin? God, I hope not. But Geneva was opposed to our liaison. She and *Jack* were opposed, and that, of course, made him all the more delicious."

Far out past the island, a dark blue boat bucked the whitecaps. At first I imagined that it was Karen and me, during our trip to the edge of the Cauldron, but this boat was sheeted in and heeling over hard. Karen and I hadn't sailed with that kind of confidence.

"So what did make you come home?" I asked.

She shrugged and poked around in the pocket of her windbreaker and came up with a cigarette, something exotic, I believe, because it was pink. "We broke up," she said. "I went to the house in Boston and ate and drank too much for a week and then broke down and called him to try to get back together, but he'd already gone home to Nigeria." She pulled out a lighter, cupped her hands away from the wind and got the cigarette going. "I never could get him to tell me he loved me."

The boat turned sharply and came toward us and now I could see the sailor, small against the distant tree line and open water. Karen saw the boat, too. She watched it cross a sparkling swatch of water, took a deep breath, and flipped her unsmoked cigarette off the ledge.

"Did you ever have a dream so real that you thought it *must* come true?"

I thought for a moment. The best I could come up with was the time in high school when I dreamed about my diary turning up in the boys' locker room. I told Cherie about it and a few days later, after we had a fight, she turned the dream into reality. To this day there are boys I can't look in the eye. I skipped all of my high school reunions.

Karen kissed me on the cheek. "Sweet Amber. I had a dream one time, maybe more than once, that I was sailing out there in the *Sea Clip* and I ran onto a ledge and the water was starting to pound the boat apart when someone sailed up to save me. I could see right away that he was a pirate, but I didn't care. I let him sweep me into his boat and sail away with me."

"Was that before you met Maturin?" I asked.

"Oh, sure. I had given up on the dream by then. In the daylight it seemed kind of silly."

The blue boat kept coming. The tide and the current were starting to clash. We waited for the boat to turn back toward the islands and the bay, but instead of swinging around, it turned toward the Cauldron and went straight for it.

Karen was fascinated. I could tell that she was imagining herself in that boat, imagining the way she would work the tiller and the sails, when the wind and tide were right, to carry herself over the rock lip of the Cauldron. The boat we watched was smaller than the *Sea Clip*, nothing special in itself, but the way it moved was something else. Instead of a jib it had a big genoa that swept it along on the beam, so low that I thought the water must surely be curling into the cockpit. The bending sails blocked our view of the sailor as the boat creased the chop at the mouth of the Cauldron and shot into the froth. The boat dropped slightly and went in deeper, making me think that it would surely be rolled over and swept onto the rocks. Karen was out on the ledge again, completely unaware of the danger as she watched the boat. It was beating into the wind now, flying toward the Cauldron, on and on, turning only at the last instant before the granite spikes roared out of the crashing water. The sails snapped around and the boat rolled onto its other side, righted itself, and rushed back toward the rock lip.

As it came out, we had our first good look at the sailor, slender and dark-haired, in loose-fitting gray pants and a loud green Hawaiian shirt. He seemed perfectly at ease with the wind and the water and the boat, and completely unaware of us as he wove his way through the rocks, scattering cormorants that lingered off the end of the point. As fast as he had come at us, he sailed away and shot back toward the distant islands, showing on the stern the name of the boat, the *Paul D.*

Peach's barking broke the spell. Karen and I walked back through the trees to the picnic just as Mrs. Townsend was returning from the Mustang.

"That your father?" she asked Karen in that smoker's voice of hers. She sounded as if she had just discovered mayonnaise or something. "We had the most wonderful talk. He's wonderful. The way he looks at you has such meaning, such significance."

Karen was looking at Mrs. Townsend, too, with skepticism and suspicion, but I could tell that Mrs. T was sincere.

"He reminds me of my first husband, Paul," Mrs. Townsend continued, trying to elicit some verbal response from Karen, but just then a familiar station wagon sped past and turned toward a side clearing favored by some of the old-timers. Not far behind it, the all-too-familiar red pickup truck slid to a halt. Yapping away and jerking at the end of his leash, Peach made their arrival seem all the more urgent.

"Now what?" I asked Pop as he walked toward Winthorpe's cooker.

"It's the rest of the Archers," he said, unfazed by the drama of their arrival. He picked his way over crisscrossing roots. "You know *them*," he said, "They never go at anything halfway. I wonder how the old man's doing."

At first I thought he meant Walt, and I looked back to make sure that he was still safe in the car. Mrs. Townsend had returned to the Mustang. She was kneeling beside him, her hand on the top of the door, in a posture of confidence or confession. Karen glanced back, gave her head a toss, and quickened her step. I could tell that she was becoming more and more annoyed by the attention Walt was getting.

As we waited for Winthorpe to raise the lid on the roast pork, I watched the Archers move about in the clearing, spreading out picnic blankets and unloading baskets while Fred and his father lagged behind, helping a third person whose feet dragged on the ground between them.

"It's Fred's grandpa," I said to myself. "I can't believe they brought him to the picnic when he's at death's door."

My father's keen hearing has been my undoing more than once. He looked toward the Archers and said that they were probably just following the old man's wishes. "He wasn't about to miss his diamond jubilee," he said. "And they weren't about to let him."

A few of the male Archers had gotten there early to stake out some prime real estate, and they had made themselves comfy in the clearing. They had set up a pyramid of beer cans that they were trying to knock down with apples. The preliminary emptying of the cans had apparently affected their aim.

"If this picnic gets too dull for you, you can go over there," Pop told Karen. "The Archers really know how to whoop it up."

Fred and his father seated Grandpa Archer against a pine tree a safe distance from the target practice. One of the apples came a little too close to Fred's precious pickup and he drove it to the edge of the clearing, well out of harm's way.

It occurred to me that the pickup was probably his one-and-only and I wished them a happy life together.

Mrs. Townsend was talking to Winthorpe's mother, who went over and paid Walt a visit.

"What do you suppose is going on with Walt?" I asked Karen.

She shook her head. "Your side of the river is a world unto itself."

"They enjoy talking to him," Mom told us. "Most of us stopped listening to Mrs. Townsend so long ago that she probably wanted somebody new to unload on, and Walt doesn't seem to mind. Guess it can't do any harm."

A few minutes later, she tapped me on the shoulder as Winthorpe's father went over to Walt and struck up a one-sided conversation. "Look, there's another one," she said. "He's told all of his fishing stories so many times that we know every one of them by heart. We know which one we're going to get just by the way he takes his first breath to tell it. Now he's got a new audience and nobody's going to interrupt him. Karen, I think your dad's turned into the life of the party."

And so he had. On my side of the river, little half-forgotten tiffs have kept some of us from talking to each other for years. You might run into some neighbors all the way over in Machias or even up in St. Stephen and they'd just look the other way because they had a vague notion that once upon a time someone in your family had slighted someone in theirs. The McCluskys and the Flinks had been going on that way ever since Merlin Flink tricked Bud McClusky into eating a loon egg at the firemen's pancake breakfast. But Walt, everybody could talk to him. He held no grudges and no contrary opinions and he paid one person about as much attention as the next. He played no favorites. And as I already knew, you could tell him your innermost secrets and he'd keep them to himself.

Finally the big moment came for Winthorpe to raise the lid on the pork. Everyone gathered around the cooker and admired the creator's handiwork all over again, even though the thermometer obviously wasn't working too well because it read fifteen hundred degrees, which was impossible. Winthorpe's oak handle hadn't worked out too well either because it had burned off.

"It's probably the treated lumber," he suggested. "They put so many chemicals in the wood these days." As everyone except Walt gathered around licking their chops, Winthorpe doubled up a couple of work gloves and raised the lid.

When the smoke cleared, there was nothing resembling a pig in that cooker. We saw a large cinder with a contemptuous finger of flame coming out one end.

"*Sheew!*" That seemed to be the collective response.

Mom leaned over the item, whatever it was, and fanned away the smoke. "It looks like something blew up in there."

Pop wiped an ash from his eye. "That pig's had a hell of a bad day. Got up in the morning expecting the same old roll in the mud and by afternoon she's a goddam cinder."

One of Winthorpe's younger boys started crying. He really had his heart set on roast pork.

Even Peach seemed to know that something was wrong. He broke into a barking fit and jerked right out of his collar. Shouting and clapping her hands, Mrs. Townsend toddled after him.

In the meantime, the Archers' part of the picnic was also heating up. The beer can pyramid had finally been demolished and now the apples were seeking another target—the tree where sat Grandpa Archer.

"The Archers like their firewater," Pop said as he turned his back to the smoldering pork relic and got in the car to go pick up some hot dogs. "That's probably how they got Grandpa cranked up for the picnic. I wouldn't be surprised if some of them land in the drink before they're done."

It might have been better if they had. Karen couldn't resist a closer look at the goings-on in the clearing, and I followed her to the edge of it with a kind of grim curiosity. Grandpa Archer was certainly being very composed as the apples whizzed past him on one side and the other.

"Maybe he knows what lousy shots they are," I said.

Karen didn't answer. She had a slightly better angle on the action and she was seeing something that I wasn't.

"He doesn't know that or anything else," she said at last. "He's dead."

Suddenly his clumsy arrival made sense. Grandpa Archer had apparently passed away a few hours before the picnic and his family had fulfilled his final wish to attend it.

And suddenly there was Fred, standing in the clearing with his arm cocked. He let fly with his apple and the clapping of the clan proclaimed that his aim was true.

It struck me then that Grandpa Archer and Walt had something in common, that each of them had become what those around them wanted him to become, but I had a hunch that in that regard Walt had just begun his service.

CHAPTER 6

Mrs. Conditt arrived right on schedule, two weeks after my first day with the Sterlings. Jack Crystal drove her all the way up from the Bangor airport in his vehicle, which was some kind of replica of a vintage sports car. He had her stuff crammed into the back and Mrs. Conditt was wedged into the passenger side with her voluminous overcoat stuffed around her like bubble wrap. When she got out, she was carrying a big black purse and a bouquet of violets and geraniums and dusty miller that had somehow survived the trip. As I watched from my upstairs window—her window now—I cried. I'm not sure why. Maybe it had something to do with my relief at getting out of that pressure cooker. Maybe I was sorry to be leaving Walt behind with someone who probably wouldn't care about him as much as I did, though I know it was selfish to think that way. Maybe I was just wrung out from keeping up with the Sterlings for two weeks. Or maybe it was just the stage of the tide and the phase of the moon, but it felt good to wring myself out.

Mrs. Conditt was pleasant enough, even though she was obviously frazzled and her spine hurt. By the way she moved I could see how she could have thrown her back out dealing with Walt. She shuffled into the living room kind of hunched over, as if she had a clothespin pinching her tailbone. She was short of breath and left a trail of wadded Kleenex and atomic fireball wrappers. According to Karen, she was so addicted to hot candy that she often blushed from it.

Walt was there on the sofa in the living room, gazing toward the river. To him Mrs. Conditt didn't register any more than the shadow of a cloud crossing the sun.

Geneva wrote me a check, folded a fifty-dollar bill around it, and patted my hand. "You've been very special to all of us, Amber. I hope you'll come back soon. I'm sure Karen would like that."

She was more right than she knew. Early the next morning, my first in my own bed in two weeks, I was roused by the sound of a car in the driveway. I got up and stuck my head out the window and there she was, standing beside the Mustang. "It's gorgeous out. What do you say to another boat ride?"

"I'd kind of like to have breakfast," I said.

There was no stopping Karen. Before I knew it, I was munching a granola bar as she sped down the road toward the marina.

She was more confident this time out, maybe because the wind was light. We still had some trouble getting the engine going, so I sprayed some WD-40 on the stop and got that smoothed out while Karen adjusted the throttle and checked the fuel, and we got into the bay as if we actually knew what we were doing. I missed Walt. The boat seemed kind of empty without him braced against the cabin, gazing out over the water.

Karen could tell what I was thinking. "Geneva got me to promise not to take him out on the water again." She hooked her leg over the tiller. "As if it makes any difference whether he's out here with us or sitting in the kitchen with Mrs. Conditt."

"You don't think he'll ever get better?"

She put her foot down and leaned forward, propping her elbow on the tiller. "You've spent the past two weeks with him. What do *you* think?"

"But your mother thinks—"

"Geneva thinks all kinds of things, and sometimes she doesn't think at all. Our little family is like a boat without a rudder. How about that for an apt metaphor?"

"Were you and your mother always at each other like this?"

"Well, not when I was *in utero* so far as I know, though she never gave up smoking and hot curry." She shot me a quick look. "That was a joke."

Now that I was no longer employed by the Sterlings, I felt freer to say what was on my mind. "So what's the problem between you and your mother? Did you get along with your father when he was—when he was all there?" It was a painful thing to say, but I didn't know how else to put it.

"When he was around," she said. "I know. I sound like a neglected brat, all of whose problems stem from inattentive parents. Right? Am I right?"

I could hear her anger rising again and I felt cold. I pulled my hands into the sleeves of my oversized sweatshirt and folded my arms across my chest. "Karen, I'm sorry I asked. It's none of my business."

"Tell me about the Archers, Amber. Tell me about what happened at the picnic."

I didn't have an answer for her. I looked across the bay toward the point. The sunlight skipped across the flat blue water and lit up the pines and cedars to the south. "They're from my side of the river," I said. "People have a different way of thinking over there. No doubt you figured that out pretty quickly."

"So tell me about your boyfriend. Fred. Does he often throw apples at dead ancestors?"

"He's *not* my boyfriend," I insisted. "He's my *ex*-boyfriend. And even that's hard to believe now. And no, I've never known him to do anything even remotely like that. It just goes to show you, in the end, how unpredictable people can be."

"Oh, we're all beasts, Amber. Under our clothes, we're all beasts."

We sailed all day, back and forth across the bay, as Karen built up her confidence. The quirky puffs that rolled through the breaks in the shoreline and socked the sails no longer intimidated her. She took the *Sea Clip* through the slot between the islands without effort and threaded her way through the rocks along the shore opposite the Cauldron. I had never been out there, and it struck me as a wild and dangerous place. We came to a remote, rugged island topped by a solitary house, hardly more than two stories of weathered shingles and peeling paint perched on a crag above the water, and I thought Karen would turn back, but she had none of my misgivings. She pushed on, farther and farther out, until I feared that she'd break into the open Atlantic. The wind had been building all afternoon and shifting, and Karen had learned from her mistakes. Instead of waiting for the wind to turn against her completely, she swung back toward the bay, feeling her way along the water path. We had misjudged the tide though, and in front of that lonesome house the *Sea Clip* struck rock and stuck fast.

The tide was going out, and we could tell that we weren't about to sail off of that ledge, so I started cranking the engine, but it wouldn't turn over. I went through the motions of adjusting the throttle and checking the oil pressure. I even tapped the fuel gage several times even though I knew the tank was practically full. All the while, we were taking a beating from the wind, so we brought down the sails and there we sat.

"Ideas?" Karen stood with her feet spread and her hands in the pockets of her khakis.

I had nothing to offer. We couldn't put down the anchor and try to kedge our way off because we didn't have any power for pulling. I poked an oar over the side and hit bottom without getting a budge. "We sure can't sit here all night waiting for the tide to come back in." I said, looking up at the house on the island, hoping that someone would come out and offer to help, although I saw no sign of life up there.

"All right." Karen sounded as if she had been debating a solution in her mind. She untied the sweater from her shoulders and tossed it into the cabin.

Suddenly I knew what she was up to. "Are you sure this is the best way out?"

Right there, without a pause, off came her clothes, underwear and all, except that she put her sneakers back on. She had a figure to die for, and she wasn't shy about showing it off. No tan line either, making me wonder what all had been going on back in France.

She climbed onto the side of the boat and sat down. "Right now it looks like the *only* way," she said, and over the side she went. She gasped as she sank shoulder deep in the cold water. Her voice became low and husky. "If we get off, just don't let the boat get away without me."

I moved to the back of the boat to make the bow as light as possible. With the oar I tried again to push us off the ledge, but I couldn't get a good angle, so I settled for backpaddling as Karen put her shoulder to the bow and pushed. "Damn!" she sputtered. "How can it be so stuck?"

As she was resting, I slid over the side in my clothes and joined her. The cold water took my breath away and my legs went numb as I swished my way toward the bow. I grabbed onto the bow line because the last thing we needed was for the boat to leave both of us. We braced our feet against the hard bottom, put our shoulders to it, and pushed, but the outgoing tide was against us, and with each passing minute, the *Sea Clip* settled more heavily onto the ledge.

"Damn!" Karen propped her back against the stubborn bow.

I stood up shivering, wet to the shoulders. "At this rate, you won't get back before your mother."

"Screw my mother. And if she and that gigolo of hers come out looking for us again, I swear I'll...."

She stopped and I realized that Karen didn't *know* what she was going to do or what she wanted to do, today or for the rest of her life. She was as stuck as the *Sea Clip.*

There was nothing to do but get back on the boat and dry off and wait for the next passer-by to help haul us off—or wait through the night for the tide to come back in. The *Sea Clip* was a musty old tub, but at least she was well provisioned. Before Alzheimer's got him, Karen's dad had kept his boat in good order. Since then, though, stuff had been chucked into the cabin by one person or another, and so sails and lines and tools and just plain junk lay helter-skelter on top of Walt's good order, and it took us a while to find the dry clothes that he had packed. They had been down there bagged up for a couple of years, and so they smelled like a cellar with a leak, but they were dry, and now it was my turn to peel down, except that, being wet, my clothes stuck to me like skin, and I had to ask Karen for a hand in getting them off. By then, I was more than ready for Walt's baggy khakis and flannel plaids. "I look like I ought to be painting houses," I said. I had nothing on underneath, of course, but not wanting to look like a total dweeb, I decided not to do up the top button of my shirt. The result was, by my standards, a saucy décolletage.

Karen laughed. "You look very comfortable. Clothes can be such a nuisance, don't you think?" She gestured toward the sun-bleached house overlooking the ledge. "Maybe we should, you know, jump up and down and wave to get their attention."

Something in the way her eyes caught the light made me think so much of Walt that before I knew it, I had asked her just what had happened to him.

She turned and looked out the porthole behind her as if expecting someone, a rescuer from the island maybe. "Didn't Geneva give you the gory details? I suppose not. Would you like for me to tell you that he was reading a paper to his distinguished colleagues when he suddenly put his hand to his forehead and fell mute into the arms of a Nobel laureate?"

I wrapped my shirt tighter and backed toward the companionway ladder. "I'm sorry I asked. I was just, I don't know, concerned or something."

She picked up a gaff and tossed it onto a cluttered bunk. Some of the tension left her voice. "Well, it came home to me the first time he forgot my name. If you want the messy specifics, why don't you ask Geneva? Geneva will tell you plenty once you get her talking."

I went topside and tried starting the engine again, mostly just for something to do, but hoping that it would miraculously spring to life.

Karen came up and hooked her arm around the boom and the folded mainsail. "Poor Amber. I'll bet you rue the day that you crossed the river and got mixed up with the Sterlings, the tarnished Sterlings. My father was a charming man, a brilliant man, maybe even a nearly perfect man. I wish you could've known him. What you're seeing is like the end of a shipwreck, like the bow of a great ship as it's about to slip beneath the waves forever, and sometimes I wish that it would hurry up and go down. Is that awful of me?"

I gave up on the throttle and sat down beside it. "I don't know. No."

"What you're seeing is some of the passengers getting sucked down with the boat. If I were you, I'd swim away fast and hard before you go down with—"

We saw it at the same time, the boat coming bare-masted around a turn in the shoreline, dark blue against the gray rocks and pointed fir trees.

"Thank God!" I stood up and waved with crossing arms, little knowing how much that moment was going to change Karen's life and my own.

It didn't take me long to recognize the boat as the one that had flirted with the Cauldron, the *Paul D*, and as it came closer I could tell that the sailor was the same too, right down to the loud green Hawaiian shirt. Karen and I stood side by side at the boom as he came toward us.

I waited for him to speak as he came near. When he didn't, I finally broke the stillness.

"Are we ever glad to see you!"

He was thin and sinewy and his clothes flapped loosely in the breeze. His long, dark, curly hair fluttered about a boyish face. He moved easily about his boat and tossed over a coiled line.

I fastened my top button.

With a hand on the backstay, Karen leaned over the stern. "Where are we?"

"Tie on," he said, as if we had been planning this operation for weeks in advance.

I didn't know anything about knots, so I put about four tight twists around one of the stern cleats and watched the line go taut as he revved up his outboard motor and headed for deeper water. I had no idea whether I had done the right thing or not, whether the cleat would go popping off, ripping a hole in the boat, or if we'd be dragged over at some awkward angle. Our rescuer hadn't said anything one way or the other. So there we were, about to take whatever he gave us. The *Sea Clip* shuddered and wrenched sideways a foot and then refused to budge another inch. He brought his boat back through its own wake and threw his end of the line to us.

I watched him head toward the deeper water again. "Is he giving up on us?"

Karen had been paying close attention the entire time. "Not on your life," she said.

Some yards out, he stopped and threw his anchor. He backed toward us, letting out anchor line that streamed from the blue fiberglass bow of his boat. When he was a few feet from us, he stopped.

"Throw me the line," he said at last, holding his hand out for it.

When we were tied to his stern again, he throttled up his motor until the noise made me cover my ears and the water was a welter between his boat and ours. Just as I was about to duck to avoid a blast of exploding engine parts, the *Sea Clip* slid gracefully from the ledge and settled down into honest depth. He kept on pulling until we were well clear of the ledge. Then he hauled in his anchor and towed us until our bow turned into the wind.

Karen seemed to come out of a dream. She tied down the tiller and we hoisted the main. The second it was up, the towline came flying back onto our foredeck.

"Where are we?" Karen asked again.

I cupped my ear to hear his answer as he turned away.

"Downeast Ledge."

By the time we had the jib up and trimmed, our rescuer was too far away to thank. We were so intent on steering a course home and staying clear of more shelves that we were a good mile away when we looked back and saw him tie up to a mooring on the other side of the island.

"That house must be his," I said, looking over my shoulder as I cranked another wrap in the jib sheet. "Maybe we should paint it for him."

I was only kidding, but I should have known by then that Karen would have a plan of her own.

The next afternoon, as I was helping Mom to hang clothes, Karen pulled up in her Mustang and asked when I would be free.

Even through the sunglasses I could read mischief in her face, but at least she looked cheerful, more cheerful than I had ever seen her, and I hated to discourage it. "We have about two more bushels to hang up," I said. "The dryer needs a new belt or something and Pop hasn't had time to fix it."

Karen came to the line and started pinning things up. I was surprised that she knew how.

"How are things over your way?" Mom asked. I could tell by her smile that she was hoping for a tidbit of gossip.

"Oh, affairs as usual," Karen said with deliberate ambiguity as she hung up a pair of Brian's briefs.

My mother looked over at me, smiling at the double entendre. Behind her, the river widened and flowed out to the deceptively pretty bay.

"How's your father?" I asked, strangely formal.

"You know *him*," Karen said. "Steady."

"Has he made any more friends since the picnic?" Mom was so direct that I figured in one visit across the river she could find out all there was to know about the Sterlings. No innuendo and no beating around the bush. She'd go over there and clean out all the secrets in a hurry and tell everybody just to straighten up. That was my mother. *I* couldn't bring myself to take people head-on that way. I always let them unfold slowly through a thousand little hints and acts.

"It's nice that you can spend your summer together," Mom said. "This may be the last one for the four of us. Brian's likely to be going down to Mount Desert and Amber's going to get a job somewhere and then be off to grad school. I hope you're making the most of your time with your family."

Karen looked over and smiled sweetly. "Oh, I have been. This morning I baked oatmeal raisin cookies."

At first I thought she was kidding because I couldn't imagine Karen standing still long enough to bake anything, but from the tone of her voice, it was clear that she was serious. Then I began to feel uneasy.

"You baking for a boy?" Mom was not so much asking as making a statement.

Karen dropped a clothespin and started digging into the basket for it. "I wouldn't put it that way exactly, just returning a favor."

My mother had on her knowing smile again. "Baked goods are useful for returning favors, especially if there's a boy involved." She let it go at that. She wasn't nosy, but she sure knew how to work with whatever information came her way. Rarely did anybody put anything over on her.

"Are you free to sail then?" Karen asked me as we hung up the last things.

It was a pretty day for it, with a soft northeast breeze and just enough clouds to keep the sun from being too bright. Karen was comfortable with the boat. She was learning quickly and she seemed to have more of a sense of purpose. Instead of zigzagging around according to the wind, she used it to good advantage to take her where she wanted to go. And she wanted to go back to the house off Dunning's Point.

CHAPTER 7

She took us right to it. We looked for the sailboat, but it was gone. A rowboat was moored around the point, though. We tied up to it and doused the sails.

"Now what?" I said. I thought she might borrow the rowboat, but it had no oars, and the one we had was way too long for it. "How are you going to get up there—with your baked goods as my mother would call them?" I imagined her swimming naked, with her clothes and the cookies in a dry bag balanced on her head.

She went down into the musty cabin and hauled up a blue and yellow inflatable raft. "We'll both go. As soon as we get some air into this." She pried the folds out of it and began to blow air into it with a little hand pump. Fifteen minutes later, slightly winded, we lowered it over the side and climbed in. After a minute or two of rowing, we were on the island, threading our way up a path that wound through blueberry bushes and sumac. The house was more forbidding up close. Some of the shingles had fallen off the walls and others dangled by a nail. The flaking white trim of the windows and eaves revealed weathered gray cedar. A lot of the glass was cracked. A door at the front had long since been hammered shut. One at the side stood open. Farther back, two sheds huddled against the house, their sliding doors clearing the uneven ground by most of a foot. Karen walked the rest of the way around the cottage and rapped on the windowpane in the side door.

I couldn't help laughing. "Standing at the door with those cookies you look like a Girl Scout, just a little less innocent."

She smiled briefly and rapped on the windowpane again. Then, gently, she eased the door open. "Hello?"

The inside of the house smelled like wood smoke and kerosene. "Why don't we just leave the cookies and go?" I suggested.

With the back of her hand she pushed the door open farther and went in.

"Karen, this is not a good idea. We don't know this person at all."

"Hello?" She moved farther into the room, a crude kitchen, and set the foil-covered plate of cookies on the coarse plank drainboard.

The linoleum floor sagged and squeaked beneath my feet. A mouse ran into the next room. Light came into the kitchen through the glass panel of a door set sideways, a poor man's picture window above the sink. Some twisted and wormy apple trees behind the house blocked the view of the water on the backside of the island. Sharp damp air wafted up from the cellar.

Karen was fascinated. Despite my advice, she went into the living room, which was bare except for a wooden sofa with split vinyl cushions that spilled their foam rubber guts. Flanking it was a set of chipped veneer end tables topped by old bean-filled table lamps with shades that had burn holes in them. In front of the sofa was what I at first took to be one of those lobster trap coffee tables, but what turned out to be, pure and simple, an actual trap that smelled like it still had the lobster in it. The yellow walls had been recently repainted with broad brush strokes that slopped onto the window frames and baseboards. Above the little brick fireplace was a smallish trout mounted on a hunk of barn board.

That smell from the cellar came up through an oversized grate in the middle of the plank floor. I put the back of my hand to my nose. "I'm glad he sails better than he decorates," I said. I tried to escape through the front door, forgetting that it was nailed shut.

As I doubled back toward the kitchen, Karen followed me, giving me the idea that she was finally ready to leave, but she stopped at the foot of the stairs.

"Oh, no," I said. "Look, if you want to stay, go ahead and I'll go down there to the boat. Just give me a holler and I'll come back and get you if I haven't already sailed away to get help."

"Oh, come on, Amber. We're just having a look around. What harm can it do?"

I put my hand on the wall to block her way. "Karen, dropping off some cookies is one thing, Trespassing is another. Going up there is trespassing. People get killed trespassing."

She placed a reassuring hand on my shoulder. "It's just a visit. And anyway, his boat's not even out there. It's not as if he's going to sneak up on us. We can look out those windows any time and see what's out there. If we see him coming, we'll go out and wait for him in the yard. You want to wait here? Go ahead. But aren't you just a little bit curious?"

No, I wasn't. I was nervous, that's what I was. But I went up with her, up the steep, narrow stairs.

At least the house smelled better up there. The low ceiling sloped sharply in the gabled room to the right of the stairs. It was hot and dry. The brass bed was neatly made, but looked as if it had been unused for ages. The spread was faded and dusty and we could see our footprints as we circled a stack of flattened cardboard boxes in the middle of the floor.

Karen leaned across the bed and looked out the milky window. "You can see all the way up the river from here. You can see my house."

It was hard to believe, but it was true. We seemed to be at the edge of the solar system. From out here, our house and the Sterlings' looked like neighbors.

The room across the short, cramped hall was different. The floor was cluttered with boots and shoes and clothing, candy bar wrappers and boxes of cereal and crackers. The corner at the foot of the bed was stacked waist high with spotty old books. Carefully, Karen picked one up and opened it. "'Jonathan Dunham. Xmas 1858.' The Waverley novels. I wonder if he's reading these or using them for insulation."

I headed for the stairs. "I think we've seen everything now, unless you want to put on a hazmat suit and plunge into the cellar."

She came with me, but veered away again. After all, we had overlooked what was probably the third bedroom, maybe because the door was closed.

"Just one more and then we'll go," she promised.

"I wouldn't if I were you," said a voice below us.

When we stopped screaming and untangled ourselves, I saw him framed by the light from the front windows, standing halfway up the stairs, his hands in his pockets. He was taller and thinner than he had looked on the boat, but he was wearing the same Hawaiian shirt and loose gray pants. He came up a couple of steps and I could tell from his dark sparkling eyes that our predicament amused him. Under the circumstances, he could've shot us and gotten away with it. Fortunately his hands were empty.

Karen steadied herself against the doorjamb of his bedroom. "We just came to say thank you for pulling us off the ledge yesterday. We left some cookies in the kitchen."

He put a hand on the wall. It was a casual gesture, but it blocked our way out. "You're kind of off course, aren't you?"

To my amazement, Karen responded with the truth. "We were just curious to see the rest of the house. Out here on this little island, it was so intriguing."

"Intriguing." He weighed the word as if to evaluate its credibility. "Have you already gotten the full tour then?"

Karen put her hands in her pockets, looking more at ease. "Oh, no. We just saw the old books and—"

He came up some more and stopped just a step or two from the top. "You haven't been into that room then?" He glanced over his shoulder at the closed door.

"No, we haven't," I said, not wanting to risk my safety on Karen's answers. "And we don't want to. We just got a little carried away with our thank you visit."

The way he studied me made me feel like a bug on the end of a pin. "How you doing, Amber? You don't remember me, do you?"

I didn't and I said so.

"We went to the consolidated school together for about three years. Well, you were there more than I was, I guess. I clocked that freckled kid that pushed you down."

Now it was my turn to stare. "Robbie? Robbie Dunning? My God, have you changed. Didn't you used to be kind of short and wear black all the time?"

He smiled, showing white teeth that were just a little crooked. "I go by Robin now and I've changed my clothes since then. And added a few inches. Seems to me somebody was always trying to knock you over."

"Well, I was kind of outspoken. I used to think it was healthy to say whatever I thought was true. It's a wonder I survived the sixth grade." I was beginning to remember some other things about Robin, but I thought it better to keep them to myself. "What are you doing out here?" I asked. "Don't you live in that house by the spring?"

He shook his head. "Not since my parents died. I'm sort of taking care of this place. My grandparents used to live out here in the summer. After their time, we kind of let it go. I thought it would be worthwhile to put it back together." He patted the plaster wall. "It's sturdy enough, just needs some shimming."

All the while, I was trying not to look at the closed door, and I think Karen was too. "It's kind of isolated, isn't it?"

"I like it that way. I can always get back over to the mainland if I want something."

I was getting eager to leave. I felt uneasy at the top of the stairs, under that low ceiling with only smudged windows to let in the light. I didn't belong there and I knew it. But Karen didn't seem to have that sense. The more uneasy I became, the more relaxed she looked. I said that I had to be home in time to clean the garage before my father came back from Machias. It was an exaggeration, but I made it sound convincing.

Robin walked back downstairs and Karen and I followed, exchanging looks. I couldn't tell what Karen meant by hers, but mine meant *you got us into this, now I'm getting us out.*

When we got to the kitchen I glanced over at the drainboard. He had peeled back the foil on Karen's plastic plate and helped himself to a cookie.

"You'd better push off or this wind will give you bigger problems than your garage," he said as we finally got back outside.

I was glad to see that the *Sea Clip* was still anchored out front. His boat was nowhere in sight, but for the first time, I noticed an overgrown path that wound down the backside of the island. That was how he had sneaked up on us. He had another mooring that was good regardless of the tide. Robin Dunning knew how to take care of himself. Even in grade school he had been good at that. No one seemed to know him well, but he had a reputation for winning any fight he couldn't talk his way out of.

"Did you get your engine fixed?" He took a pack of cigarettes from his hip pocket and offered one to Karen.

She put it to her lips and got it going on his lighter.

"I'll bet you don't smoke," he said, holding the pack out to me.

"Not right now," I said. Not *ever*, but for some reason I didn't want to tell him that. Well, I had smoked about a third of a cigarette on Cherie Gillespie's thirteenth birthday. We took a rowboat out to Rush Island and lit up, and the way she made such a ritual of it, you'd think that she was losing her virginity, which she didn't get around to for another year and which, by her account, was about as big a deal as cracking open a can of beer. The smoking thing, I didn't get. I was careful and sophisticated, inhaled slowly and let out a stream of smoke between pursed lips and held the cigarette loosely—between my middle finger and my ring finger no less—while Cherie coughed herself blue. So for poise, I had her beat all hollow, but two packs of Trident and half a tube of chewed toothpaste would not get that ashy taste out of my mouth.

Now Karen was standing there, smoking a cigarette with Robin and apparently enjoying it. "They looked at the engine at the marina," she said, inhaling deeply. "Apparently they didn't look at it hard enough."

"If you're talking about Skipper Kip's, you're lucky it didn't blow up in your face," Robin told her. "What they don't do and what they can't do add up to robbery."

"My father dealt with them for years, and *he* was nobody's fool," Karen said.

"That must've been when Kip ran it." Robin's words rode on smoke. "He sold out to Ed Pike three years ago and it's been downhill ever since."

Karen shrugged. "Then apparently I'm stuck. I can't exactly sail it to Machias to get it fixed."

"Oh, Brian can probably fix it," I said, "or my—"

Robin made a better offer. "Take your boat off the mooring and anchor it out back and we can fix your engine right here."

He towed us out back to the deeper water where he kept his boat and wedged himself into some tight places for a look at the cooling system and the fuel system and the lubrication. He had pieces spread all over the cockpit and the seat cushions, but, one by one, he put them back into that complicated puzzle that had confounded us, and when he finally put the cover back on, I wondered if he would prove a master of the thing or just another goof-up. Karen had sat cross-legged on top of the cabin all the while, but as Robin set the throttle, she stood up with one hand on the mast as if waiting for the dead to come back to life.

I'd never heard such a sweet sound in my life as the purring of that engine. It gave out just one wisp of blue smoke and then settled down to a steady rhythm that made me think it could take us across the Atlantic.

Karen came closer. "I've *never* heard it sound like *that.*"

Robin gave the hatch cover a swipe with a cloth as if to say that this miracle was one of his lesser ones.

"What's this?" I asked, picking up a washer big enough to go around my ring finger.

"Part of the problem," Robin said. He threw it overboard. "One of those pencil dicks over at the boatyard probably thought he needed that to hold a wire down. When he tightened it, he broke the wire. That's why she worked all right when she'd been running for a while, but was murder to start. When the wire got hot, it conducted through the break."

Karen came down off the cabin and fished a twenty-dollar bill out of her hip pocket. "Here, it's worth a lot more, but this is all I have."

He looked into her hazel eyes as if the money didn't exist. "You've already given me the cookies, remember? Let's just say I was being neighborly. Maybe someday I'll ask a favor of you."

At the time, I couldn't imagine what that favor would be. But then I was only beginning to know Robin Dunning.

CHAPTER 8

When we got back to Karen's house, I expected to see Walt sitting at the kitchen table, gulping down one of Mrs. Conditt's concoctions. She had a recipe for blended liverwurst that whipped into a kind of pungent froth rich in iron, which was one of Walt's deficiencies. She went heavy on garlic, which was good for his cholesterol but murder on his breath, and she added a quarter cup of red wine, which was good for his heart. Then she threw in a couple slices of pumpernickel, which may have been good for his morale. I thought, if only she could come up with an ingredient that was good for his brain, she'd really be onto something. But at least Walt didn't seem to mind the stuff and nobody was going to fight him for it—that was for sure.

But when we got back to Karen's house, Walt was *not* in the kitchen. Geneva and Mrs. Conditt were getting ready to sit down to supper, but Walt was nowhere to be seen.

"He's on the porch," Geneva said, picking a fleck of white cashmere from the elbow of her green silk blouse. "He has a visitor."

"Dad has a visitor?" Karen was so surprised that she forgot to call him by his first name. She sat down on one of the captain's chairs and hung her sweatshirt over the curved back.

"Someone he met at the picnic apparently." Satisfied with the perfection of her garments, Geneva started eating. "There's meatloaf if you want some. We didn't know what time you'd be coming back, as usual."

The *as usual* brought Karen back to her usual edgy self. "The engine broke down *as usual*," she said. "But we got it fixed once and for all. Those people at the marina are dolts."

"Your father seemed to think enough of them." Geneva cocked her chin as if she had just played a trump card in bridge.

"Mother, that was when Kip ran the place. He sold it and it's gone downhill—or underwater—ever since."

For a second there, she sounded just like Robin.

"That's one more reason not to take that boat out," Geneva said. She had already lost interest in the engine, little knowing that its revival had led to all kinds of interesting complications.

Karen brightened. "But the engine works fine now. When you come back from sailing there's always a story as Dad used to say."

"Well, you'll probably want to clean up and change if we're going to have people coming into the house. The phone's been ringing off the wall. Just what happened at that picnic anyway?"

The visitor was Winthorpe. I could imagine him skipping across the river in his aluminum v-hull and tying up at the foot of the stone steps. Why he had come to see Walt was anyone's guess. I followed Karen out to the porch, where Winthorpe was chatting away as if Walt had just said something exciting. Actually, come to think of it, if he had said *anything* it would have been exciting.

"Well, hi, girls. Just came by to see how the old gent is doing. He's a pip, ain't he?"

Karen sat down beside Walt's rattan throne. "How can you tell?"

Winthorpe rubbed his beard and smiled jovially. Somehow the gap where he'd lost an eyetooth made him look all the more cheerful. "Oh, you know. There's just something about him. You can tell you're getting through. He's real quiet about it. You have to read him. But he's taking it in. He's laughing at all my jokes, in his way. A second ago he even said a word or two."

"Is that so?" Karen seemed unimpressed.

"You bet. " Winthorpe winked. "You know, I think Mrs. Townsend wants to run away with him."

I burst out laughing. The very idea was so ludicrous. "What's she going to do," I asked, "have somebody drive the two of them over to see Maurice, alias Todd Flink, so they can get perms together?"

Even Karen smiled.

"Seriously, he's all right," Winthorpe said. "You feel better just talking to him. Was he always this way?"

Karen sat up. "What way? I can tell you, we never had people come across the river to visit us before. But we certainly did in Boston. My father was a distinguished scientist. He had people coming to see him all the time, important people, but never anything like this."

"Then they were missing something," Winthorpe said, adjusting his belt where it was cutting into this beer gut. "He's got something about him. Once you get past his breath, I mean."

"That's the garlic," I said. "It's good for his cholesterol."

Karen rolled back the cuffs of her oversized flannel shirt and folded her arms. "If you've come about the organ, the offer is still open."

Winthorpe folded his arms too, but I don't think he was making fun of her. "Well, actually the kids are having such a ball with it I'd hate to give it up. Takes two or three of them to play it, but once they get her going, they're not half bad. And their little dispositions have improved too. They're not knocking each other over the head so much as they used to. It all started that day you and your dad came by on your way to the picnic." He hoisted himself out of his chair. "I'm taking off. Got to get back across the river. The missus gives me the what-for if I'm out in the boat after dark."

The next day, when Geneva was off as usual, Karen and Walt came over to see me. It was one of those cool breezy days that we get in Ashton in early June, and I was glad that we weren't out sailing because I could imagine the boat heeled over hard and the water curling over the rail in that way that always made me think that we were about to capsize. Karen was up to something though. I could tell by that smile of hers, the one I had seen when she was getting ready to take cookies to Robin.

I had been in the garage, clearing out some of my junk furniture so that Pop could actually park the car in the intended place. Collecting junk furniture is a habit that I inherited from my mother and from *her* mother. Pop says that the impulse to hoard junk furniture is probably carried on the same gene as witchcraft and baldness and is supposed to skip a generation, but in my case it landed right on top of me.

When I saw the red convertible coming up the driveway, I pulled off my work gloves and waited to find out what Karen had up her sleeve.

"Just a visit," she said, as breezy as the weather. "I thought Walt could use some fresh air, and I know *I* can."

"You *always* can," I said, putting up a defense before she could start working on me to help her with some dangerous scheme. "What do you do in the winter? You must get cabin fever something fierce."

"Couldn't say, sweetie."

The more cheerful she sounded, the more concerned I became.

"Because no two winters have been alike for as long as I can remember. You know, in France we'd go to the Alps, and in Boston, we made the social circuit or hopped up to Stowe. Walt was a great skier."

"I'll bet he was," I said. I figured that Walt must have been great at just about everything and I suppose that's why Karen was so mad at him for coming down with Alzheimer's and losing all of his gifts. I wondered if Mrs. Townsend and Winthorpe would have liked him as much then as they did now.

"He taught me everything I know," Karen said, "and I'm not half bad on the black diamond runs."

"Walt, how are you?" I gave him a pat on the shoulder, hoping to see what Mrs. Townsend and Winthorpe had seen, but he didn't look up. His gaze was fixed on a frost heave in the driveway.

"So what do you suppose is in that room?" Karen asked.

It took me a second to realize what she was talking about. I had made an effort to put Robin and his house out of my mind. "Karen," I said, "whatever it is, you don't want to know. Just forget it. And forget Robin, too, if you have any sense. He did us a favor. We thanked him. Let's let it go at that."

"Did us *two* favors," she said. "Three if you count not assaulting us for breaking into his house."

"We did not break in. We just went a little too far. Anyway, he's out there and we're here and let's leave it that way."

She was perched on the hood of the Mustang. She got up and started poking through my junk furniture as if she hoped to find some kind of evidence. "Do you know what's in that room, Amber?"

"No, I don't. I had no idea that we were even in Robin's house. He used to live over by the spring near Route 1. But that was...."

Karen pulled open a drawer to an ancient dresser. The knobs had been replaced by hemp loops, but the glide still worked beautifully and the drawer slid forward without a sound. "But that was *what?*"

I closed the drawer. "That was before he went to prison."

She had stooped down to look at an old cast iron stove, a toy that was modeled after the real thing, right down to the ornate trim and the spring handle. She turned and looked up at me. "Prison? Why didn't you tell me?"

"I don't know. I suppose because you were in such a good mood. I hated to spoil it."

She stood up. "Interesting. So what was he in prison for?"

"I don't know exactly. Receiving stolen goods, something like that. I think first they charged him with going out and breaking into the cottages of some of the summer people."

"Really? By boat I suppose. That sounds so, what, so romantic."

"Yeah, well, the locals had another name for it. They said he'd go along the shoreline at night without lights, tie onto a mooring, go in with a rowboat, grab what he could, and slip away. It's pretty easy around here in the off-season. The houses are far apart and the best ones are secluded. Even if they had alarm systems, it would be half an hour before the police could get to them. There was quite a rash of those burglaries a little over a year ago."

"And Robin did them?"

"How should I know?"

"Come on, Amber. You're a *local*. I'm sure you hear things through the grapevine. You've known Robin since, when, elementary school? You've got to have an opinion at least."

"Karen, they never proved it. In fact, they couldn't make the stolen goods charge stick. He did a few months in Thomaston and then got himself off."

"Got *himself* off? You mean he read up on the law and found a flaw in his case?"

"Something like that. They didn't have a valid warrant when they found some of the stuff overhead in the garage of a house he was renting. So he only did a few months of his sentence. Then they had to let him out."

The more details she wrung out of me, the more fascinated Karen became. "So it's quite possible that he didn't do any of what they accused him of. In fact, *he* may have been the wronged party. Maybe the system is guiltier than he is."

That was more of a twist than I could stand. "Look," I said, "that was just the stuff they tried to pin on him after he turned eighteen. Before that they got him for vandalism. He and some friends were into burning summer homes. That was their form of entertainment around here during the fall and spring. In the winter they were too damn lazy to go out in the cold and slog through the snow. But otherwise, on a good moonless night, they were howling around the bonfire."

Karen wiped some soot from her hands. "And you know this because—"

"Because that time they caught him. Somebody tipped off Winthorpe and he told the sheriff and Robbie and his friends all did some juvvie time down in Portland. He'll probably be paying off the damages for the rest of his life."

She weighed something in her mind for moment. "Well, I can imagine how he might have been bored," she said. "There's little enough to do around here in the summer. The fall must be murder. So do you suppose that the room over the stairs is full of stolen goods?"

Before I could answer, a dark green Honda Acura with a bad muffler turned into the driveway. By the racket alone I could've identified that car anywhere as belonging to Hal Foley of the hapless Foley Food Mill out on Route 1. He pulled up behind the Mustang and sat there quaking for a while because he always did have trouble with the idle on that vehicle. Finally it quit and he got out, all smiles. He had lost weight, which usually is a bad sign for a person in the restaurant business. As he came toward us, he dropped his car keys and stumbled picking them up. He was kind of a klutz, which was also bad in his line of work. During my two years at the Food Mill I had seen more than one boiled lobster dive to the floor. That took its toll on the dishes too, of course. From what I could tell, he was always so eager to get on to the next idea that he made a hash of the thing at hand. Whenever he was around he made me jumpy.

"I couldn't help seeing that the old guy was here," he said, stuffing in the shirttail that had come out when he bent over. "I thought I'd stop by and extend greetings."

I don't know where he got that *extend greetings* business. Hal was always talking that way, as if he wanted to avoid saying what most people would say in any given situation. Some people didn't like it because they thought that he was putting on airs, but I had always found it kind of charming, clumsy with dishes, graceful with words.

"Well, there he is," I said. "Extend away. How have you been, Hal?"

"To tell you the truth, I've been a lot better. I had to let the house go because I couldn't keep up the payments." He was smiling as he said it. That was another thing I liked about Hal. So far as I could tell, he remained cheerful no matter what. He always seemed to feel that everybody else's problems must be worse than his.

I introduced him to Karen. I don't think she knew what to make of him. It was as if somebody had come up to her, chipper and full of sunshine, with an arm lopped off.

"How did you happen to know about Dr. Sterling?" I asked, feeling awkward because anything I called him sounded either too formal or too familiar.

Hal grinned. "Walt? Why, everybody knows about Walt. We don't need a radio station around here because we have Mrs. Townsend. When she's got something on her mind, she makes sure that everybody else gets it on theirs." He picked up Walt's limp hand and shook it and gave him a friendly pat on the shoulder. Then he bent over and had a good look at his face. "You know, it's true what they say. He does have something about him."

Was I missing something? Was I the only person on the Dunning side of the river who didn't see Walt's gift? Maybe I had been ruined somehow because I had met him over on the Woolsey side, where nobody believed in him. It seemed far-fetched, but then so did the notion that he was somehow magical. Sure, I had liked talking to him on the porch that time, and I had felt better after doing it, but I still thought of him as your pretty typical Alzheimer's victim. It seemed to me that the excitement over Walt was getting a little out of hand. In fact, it seemed to me that the entire summer was starting to come unglued.

Okay, I *was* jealous. Gift or no gift, I wanted him to myself. I thought he was *my* discovery.

Karen started walking toward the front of the house, where the yard slanted down to the river, past Pop's forgotten sloop sitting high and dry in the grass. I had a feeling that she wanted nothing to do with her father's newly-found celebrity. When we got to where the view really opens up, she pointed down the river, past Benbow Island to Woolsey Point, then to the right, across the bay. "You can see his light from the porch, you know, out past the last light on the mainland."

She was right, of course. It was the new light that I had seen the first night when I was on the porch talking to Walt. Robin had moved into his grandparents' abandoned summer house and put that light up there to make it easier to come and go after dark. Just what he was doing was anyone's guess. Some people enjoyed sailing at night, though it wasn't a particularly good idea out among all of those rocks and ledges. Then again, for a couple hundred years, some people had been sailing those waters at night because there was profit in it, whether it was running rum or tonks coming through Canada—or pilfering goods from summer homes.

I touched her shoulder, trying to bring her back to Ashton and reality. "Karen, this is your wake-up call. Robin Dunning no doubt has a lot of good points and it's very—what—humanitarian of you to see some of them. But he has some bad points, too, and whatever's in that room probably represents one of them. How bad I don't know, whether he murdered his grandmother and stuck her in there or just has it packed floor to ceiling with inlaid end tables from summer cottages all around the point, I don't know. But I do know that he's had plenty of time to build up his résumé. You know what I mean? We're not talking eating salad with the wrong fork. We're talking—"

"Piracy." She turned and pinned me with her hazel eyes. She was smiling. "He's a pirate, isn't he?"

My thoughts ground to a halt. It was her dream, her stupid dream of being rescued at sea by a pirate. As far as she was concerned, getting hauled off the ledge by Robbie Dunning was the dream come true. All I could think of was that time when I was twelve and Winthorpe offered me a ride on his long-legged chestnut mare and she took off down the road like a missile with me on her bare back and nothing but a dumb bitless hackamore to hang onto, just charging blindly down the Dunning's Point Road, regardless of what might be coming at us over the next hill. That's what Karen reminded me of, that mare, throwing her head forward and stampeding down the road without the least thought of the danger. Winthorpe's horse had pitched me into the hay field across the road from the Archers' house. Cost of the ride—one broken arm and a bruised backside. What Karen's stampede would cost was anyone's guess.

I was starting to think that Geneva wasn't all that bad after all. Here she had a husband who for all practical purposes had pulled up his tent stakes and a daughter who was as wild and willful as a nor'easter. Maybe Geneva was entitled to her diversions with Mr. Jack Crystal. And who could say? Maybe he had more to him than met the eye.

Well, maybe not.

Hal had been kneeling beside Walt. He got up and shook Walt's limp hand again and I knew that Karen and I needed to go back over there to be with Walt, plus I was curious to find out what Hal had gotten out of the visit. But first I had to hammer home my point about Robin.

"Let me just get in one more word," I said as we walked back toward the cars. "I think that *pirate* is probably a far too glamorous word for what Robbie does." I called him Robbie deliberately because it made him seem less like a pirate and more like a boy I'd known in grade school.

"You're starting to sound like Geneva," Karen said. "Whose side are you on, Amber?"

"*Nobody's* side. Nobody's, if such a thing is possible. Or maybe I'm on the side of the greatest good for the greatest number."

Karen laughed, breaking the tension. "Now you're starting to sound like the Mayflower Compact or something. Poor Amber! Always trying to do the *fair* thing. Don't worry. I'm not going to throw myself at *the pirate*. I'm through with throwing myself at men. I went way too far for Maturin."

When we got to the cars Hal was smiling even more than usual. "That settles that," he said, spanking the dust from his hands. "I feel a hundred percent better!"

Walt was still staring at the frost heave in the driveway. If *he* felt any better, there was no way of telling it. "Settles what?" I asked.

"I'm going to turn that restaurant around and I'm going to do it right. I'm going to open the place all over again and make it a place that everybody can go for—great ingredients and great cooking, but with a theme, a focus. That's where I went wrong before. The old place was too diverse, neither fish nor fowl. This one's going to have an *identity*. It'll be something for the tourists and the summer people but with common-sense prices for the neighbors. It's going to be Scots-Irish. I'm going to call it The Brogue 'n' Burr."

He was so excited he took my breath away. "Walt made your mind up to all of that?" I asked, falling back into bad habits where Dr. Sterling's name was concerned.

Hal was positively beaming. You could even see that gold filling way back in his molars. "He sure did! To look at him from a distance you wouldn't think it possible. I mean coming up the driveway I felt kind of foolish, but what they say is true. When you get close up, there's something about him. This was just what I needed to turn everything around."

All I could do was repeat myself. "Walt put you on to all of *that?*"

A few days later, Karen and I thought it would be a good idea to take Walt for a haircut. He had that great head of thick white hair that would've been the envy of many a younger man, and by the second week of June it was starting to curl behind his ears. I figured that we could save a trip and take him and Mrs. Townsend into Eastport at the same time. We could drop her off at Maurice's and leave Walt down the street with the barber while we hauled Peach around the block a few times to work some of the beans out of him.

I had no idea how far Walt's fame had carried.

CHAPTER 9

The minute Maurice laid eyes on him, he went into a kind of rapture. He brought his skinny white hands together and looked up at the ceiling. "You must be the famous *Walt.*" He was so excited that his French accent slipped. "I've heard so much about you!"

Walt, of course, said nothing at all. He had tripped over a piece of loose linoleum and we were all grabbing at him to keep him on his feet.

"We're on our way to do an errand," I said, not wanting to hurt Maurice's feelings by letting him know that we were taking Walt to a barber.

"Oh, but I would be *honored.*" Maurice was practically dancing around Walt, eager to get his hands on that thick white hair.

Karen and I looked at each other as if to say *how much harm can he do?*

"You think he'll be okay?" I whispered.

"I don't see why not." Karen looked around the room, perhaps for life-saving equipment. It was just the usual old place you'd expect from a pet store that had gone bust and turned into a beauty salon. I think a Wiccan discussion group met in there at night. How Maurice kept up on the rent I have no idea. At the moment, Mrs. Townsend and Walt were the only customers.

"I've been training for this all my life," Maurice declared. "I am so familiar with Mrs. Townsend's coiffeur that I can attend to her and still have the honor of serving Dr. Sterling." Bowing, he swept up a pink sheet and made a grand gesture toward the front chair.

We guided Walt to the chair and sat him down.

Maurice pressed his hands together. "I'd like to do something really special for him." His own hair was short and perky, with just a little chemistry added to make it stand on end and show gold highlights.

"Just be reasonable," I said, eager to get Peach out of there before he disgraced himself.

Karen glanced at the weathered storefronts and clapboard houses across the street. "Where do you suppose Geneva does that pro bono work around here?"

It was hard to imagine Geneva spending an afternoon in any of those structures. She might be afraid of snagging her cashmere.

When we were outside Karen asked, "Haven't you ever wondered why we have our summer house way up here and not on the cape or on Mount Desert?"

Peach stopped suddenly at a fire hydrant. I nearly jerked him right out of his rhinestone collar for the sake of finding a more discreet location. I had kind of wondered. "To get away?"

"For my parents to get away. From Jack."

"From *Jack?* Karen, how long has their relationship been going on?"

"I wasn't kidding. Since before I was born. Since before my parents were married. Geneva and Jack met when they were in college and working at a restaurant called the Jordan Pond House down on Mount Desert. Walt came along and swept her off her feet, but I think Jack's been waiting for her ever since."

"Can't he just get himself a girlfriend, for crying out loud?"

"Some people have trouble letting go, in case you hadn't noticed."

"Why did your mother marry your father in the first place?"

Karen shrugged. "He was one hell of a guy—remember? And he was a competitor. What he went after, he got, whether or not it was best for everyone in the long run. The Sterlings are competitors, Amber."

I couldn't imagine growing up with my mother having a boyfriend in the shadows and having to spend my summers in Ashton, Maine, just to get away from him. My parents had been high school sweethearts and had always seemed made for each other. Their occasional sniping was just part of the friction that held them together. I was beginning to see why Karen was so unsettled, having to wonder from the get-go if her family might fly apart at the seams if her mother strayed.

We walked up as far as the corner where Hal had his first restaurant, a sandwich shop in a building that had been a Laundromat. He hadn't done well there, partly because the sandwiches smelled like lint. We turned and went down toward the water. I saw a sheltie and steered Peach across the street before he caught the scent. "So what does your mother see in Jack, do you think?"

"Devotion maybe. My father wasn't the most devoted person."

What did she mean by *that*? I still hadn't gotten used to hearing someone evaluating her own parents. I never thought of my own parents as devoted to each other, even though I knew that they were. It just would've been strange to say it out loud. It wasn't the kind of thing we talked about. Who had eaten the last fudge bar or who had clogged the john—*that* we talked about. Devotion? Never.

Peach caught sight of a Labrador retriever down at the boat ramp and put on a show of straining at his leash and barking. When the lab—about four times his size—barked back, Peach retreated into hasty little circles that wound my legs together.

"Let's forget about Jack," Karen said. "I've spent way too much time thinking about Jack."

When we got back to Maurice's, Mrs. Townsend was standing on the front step having a smoke. As usual, I managed to compliment her hair, even though there was only so much that Maurice or a magician could have done with it. It looked shorter and curlier and it wasn't blue. Maurice was a stickler for color. I said that she looked nice. Karen complimented her texture, whatever exactly that meant. Mrs. Townsend didn't catch what we had said, though. She was looking back into the salon with a worried expression.

Maurice and Walt had their backs to us. Maurice was waving his arms and saying something enthusiastic. We first saw Walt in the mirror, but we didn't recognize him until Maurice swung the chair around.

I laughed out loud.

His white hair glowed with gold highlights. Maurice had ornamented it with little spikes that shot out in all directions like sunbeams. Walt's furrowed forehead suddenly seemed twice as high, tan just above his brows, white where his hair had swept down. His ears seemed half again as big. His blue eyes gazed down at the warped linoleum.

Maurice brought his skinny hands together in a gesture of finality and waited for us to praise his masterpiece. His smile seemed to reflect the light of Walt's new radiance.

Karen stood with the back of her hand to her mouth, weighing the seriousness of the situation. She turned away for a moment, coughed, and said quietly, "Isn't that something? I think you really have a gift, Maurice."

"Do you *think* so?" Maurice was beside himself with joy. He forgot his accent again.

Mrs. Townsend tapped her cigarette over one of the pink sinks. "Sure. She wants you to do her hair too, don't you, dear?"

When we got back to Karen's house, Geneva hit the roof. "How could you allow your father to become such a *mockery?*" She saw no humor in the situation at all. Walt sat on the hassock looking a little like the Statue of Liberty with those spikes sticking out of his hair. But he didn't look upset. I don't think he was unhappy about what Maurice had done. At the same time, I don't think he was busting a gut with pride either. It seemed to me, though, that if he had made Maurice so happy at no loss to himself, well, why *not* allow his hair to be jazzed up a little just this once? Maybe Mrs. Townsend was onto something. Maybe what all of us needed was to have our hair done over good. I mean really wild. It might help us to see ourselves fresh. And at the very least, we could all have a good laugh.

The evening was about to get even more exciting. Karen talked me into staying over for supper, probably because she thought it would help to tone things down with Geneva or at least delay another blowup, and though I felt partly responsible for what had happened to Walt and thought that Geneva held it against me, I agreed to stay, thinking that maybe I could help to smooth things over. So there I was, sitting on the porch with Karen and Walt of the beaming hair when a certain dark blue boat rounded the point and made for the mouth of the river.

We had been talking about Mount Desert and how I was planning to go down there and look for work waiting tables for the balance of the season. Karen was turned toward the sunset, so she didn't see the boat right away, but she saw me glance out that way and turned around just as the orange-red rays caught the sails. At that moment, with the light catching it and the darkening shoreline behind, it could've been a tugboat and still have been as pretty as a petit four. It glided toward us quiet as a moth, sails sheeted in tight to catch the daylight's last breath of wind.

I knew right away that it was Robin, and from Karen's look I could tell that she knew, too. As the boat came on, she smoothed her hair and absentmindedly rubbed at a stray crease on the knee of her khaki pants.

"You don't think he's coming *here.*" Her voice broke into a girlish giggle.

"I'm sure he's been in wilder places," I said, trying to keep her from getting too excited.

We watched silently as he crossed the river. By the time he drifted up to the mooring, we just happened to be in the yard, just happened to be at the top of the stone steps. Without bothering to lower his sails, he climbed into his rowboat and rowed up to the foot of the steps. He dropped a loop over an upright and climbed toward us. Karen started to retreat into the house but thought better of it and stood her ground as he came up the steps and smiled.

"I wasn't expecting this visit," she said, glancing toward the door as if she had a roomful of guests waiting for her inside.

He came up to the porch without making a sound. He was wearing another Hawaiian shirt, a yellow one that stood out against the subdued grays and greens of the Maine coast. "Then we're about even," he said, "because I wasn't expecting yours either. Of course we'd be more even if I was to turn up in your bedroom like you did in mine."

Even in the sunset glow I could see Karen blush. "Well…" she said, at a loss to finish.

"Amber knows why I've come, don't you, Amber?" Smiling, he reached into his shirt and pulled out the plastic cookie plate.

"Around here we always bring back plates," I explained. "It's the best way to get a refill."

Still blushing, Karen accepted it and held it shield-like to her breasts. "Now that you're here, how are you going to get back?" she asked. "It's almost dark."

"I'm pretty good in the dark," he said, without any apparent double meaning.

"I suppose you are." She looked out toward the mouth of the river to make it clear that she, too, was talking about sailing.

He followed her gaze and then surveyed the lacy cedar trees and the sloping lawn. "It's pretty over here, a world away."

Karen nodded in the direction of the darkening islands to the east. "Oh, it's just as pretty out there. A little wilder maybe, but pretty."

He took a pack of cigarettes from his shirt pocket and offered her one. She glanced toward the house again and then took him up on his offer. They both lit up, wreaths of smoke following the movements of their hands.

"You've never been over here before?" Karen let out a long stream of smoke that shot out toward the river and faded.

"Not since I was a kid. My old man used to work up here sometimes."

"Working on boats?" Karen blew the smoke through flared nostrils.

Robin smiled. "Nope. Working on *yards*. He gave up on the water after he got caught out there in a blow."

"You mean he lost his nerve?"

"His *hand*. Caught it in a winch wrap when the boat went over. Had to cut it off himself. He took to driving a gravel truck, did some carpentry and plumbing. He wasn't afraid to go out, just figured one hand is enough to feed to the cod."

He was very matter-of-fact about it, *off-handed* as Pop would say about a tall tale told straight. I wasn't sure if it was true or not, but Karen bought it, maybe because she wanted to.

"Damn," she said, staring out at the bay, which was almost as flat as glass. I believe she was thinking about some of the things that could've happened to *her* out there.

"Your dad still in the plumbing business, Amber?" I wasn't sure if Robin was trying to include me in the conversation or draw me out by dismissing my father as a plumber when he was a consulting engineer for three water districts. He must have read my face because he smiled through the smoke and said, "You know I'm just pulling your leg, right?"

Robin was like that. He'd get you worked up and then he'd go out of his way to smooth you down. I remember in school he made a lot of friends that way.

"You live here with your folks do you?" he asked Karen, glancing about the porch.

"For the time-being," she said. "In the summers, of course."

"You're from Boston I bet." He was following the lines of the door with his eyes in a way that made me a little nervous. I thought maybe he was figuring out how to break in. The whole Woolsey side of the river, untouched by housebreakers all these years, could be fertile new ground.

'The heart of Boston," Karen said. "A brownstone on Beacon Street. Between the frat houses and the Scientologists."

His look suggested that he knew more than he was letting on. "And *your* dad, what's *he* do?"

Silence, a long, painful silence, and then she said, "He developed techniques for gene splicing. But he's retired."

Robbie was studying the rough patch in the yard now, thinking about concealment before or after the break-in, I figured, and then his gaze came back to Karen. "I've been hearing about your dad," he said.

She held his look. "Oh, I'm not surprised. Would you like to meet him?"

That was a surprise. I thought it was a terrible idea, but who was I? In we went, with Robin smoking and glancing around the yard again in the fading light.

"Whoever does your garden does a proper job," he said, "except for that corner over there. It's as thickety as it was when I was a kid."

It did seem out of place, a wedge of saplings and bracken jutting from the woods to the arc of the driveway.

Karen smiled mysteriously. "It's supposed to be like that. My father insisted on it. I'm sure you know why. You have a whole island that way."

I expected Robin to make a face when he saw Walt's hair, but he acted as if spikes and sunbeams were just the most natural thing in the world. He leaned down and took Walt's big limp hand in his own and gave it a little shake. "So you're the master of the *Sea Clip*. I've heard a lot about you. Three-time winner of the Penobscot Regatta."

Walt looked up at him for a moment, actually looked into his eyes, and then dropped his gaze back down to the floor.

"She was a pretty boat in her time," Robin said.

"How could you have seen her?" Karen asked. "That was thirty years ago."

Robin seemed to be talking to Walt. "There's pictures in that tavern outside of Lubec. Walter Sterling standing at the helm of the *Sea Clip* the day he won the regatta in record time."

I thought that Walt must still have something of his old self if Robin could recognize him from a thirty-year-old picture on a tavern wall.

"He sailed the Cauldron too, didn't he?" Robin said, looking into Walt's vacant eyes.

Karen knelt down beside him. "Twice. The second time he took me."

"Now you want to sail it for yourself."

Karen's eyes flashed. "There are a lot of things I want to do."

Without taking his eyes from Walt, Robin smiled. "I have no doubt of it. That your mother?"

Geneva was approaching the French doors. As usual, she looked ready to step onto the first boat that came along. She was wearing a pink windbreaker, white slacks and spotless blue sneakers. "Karen, I was going— " When she saw Robin standing in the shadows she stiffened.

"Mother, this is Robin Dunning," Karen said. "He's a friend of Amber's."

"We went to grade school together," I added, to make sure that Geneva didn't get the wrong idea.

"From the other side of the river," Geneva said. "What brings you way over here?"

Robin came forward into the light. He smiled and said without hesitation, "I came to pay my respects to the man who won the Penobscot Regatta."

Geneva seemed to relax. "Well, thank goodness it's not because of this silliness that's going around. How did you get here? I didn't hear a car."

Robin motioned toward the river. "I do a little sailing myself."

"Isn't it rather calm out? And dark?"

Karen spoke for him. "Mother, if there's any wind at all, Robin can sail on it. And he knows how to sail that water out there, day or night."

Geneva patted Walt's shoulder. "Well, Robin, I'm sure that my husband has enjoyed meeting you, in his way, and we don't want to keep you from getting back home with a little light left. Or I can drive you and—"

Karen cut in. "Not likely, Mother. Robin lives on an island."

"I see." Geneva had her guard up again. "And what line of work are you in, Robin?"

He smiled and glanced toward the river with his dark eyes. "Some of this and some of that. The moving business I guess you could say."

"The moving business." Geneva seemed to be waiting for a punch line.

"With his boat," Karen said. "He's very handy with a boat."

"So that explains your interest in the Penobscot Regatta. Do you race?"

Again, the hint of a smile crossed his face. "Can't say as I do, exactly, except when I'm in a hurry."

Suddenly Geneva seemed to lose interest in him. It was as if Karen and I were the only ones in the living room. "One of your father's prescriptions has run out, so I've got to go into Eastport. It's getting late. I'd say that visiting hours are over."

Robin put a hand on Walt's forearm. "Maybe I'll see you again, Dr. Sterling. I hear you get around some." He bowed toward Geneva, smiled at Karen, and disappeared in the darkness on his way back down to the river.

Geneva put off the trip to Eastport. By the way she stood there with her hand on her hip I could tell that she was building up to a fight.

"Karen, this has gone far enough," she said, "quite far enough." Her lips went white.

Her daughter looked around the room as if to see what had set her off.

"It's bad enough that you hauled your father around in a boat that you hardly know how to sail and that you put him on display for the—for the locals. But when you bring all kinds of people into our house—"

"Do you mean *Robin*, Mother? Robin's not all kinds of people. He's *one* kind. He's one of our neighbors. Are you saying that our neighbors aren't good enough to come into this house?"

Geneva's hand was on the banister. Her knuckles blanched. "Don't go twisting what I say! You know very well what I mean. Your disrespect is inexcusable."

Karen took on an innocent look. "My disrespect for whom, Mother?"

"All right, all right, for *me*, of course. We already know how much you disrespect your father so let's talk about your disrespect for me. Just why it has always been so, I don't know. I suppose that's between you and your—your conscience. When it's just *your* disrespect I can deal with it, but when you bring people in to mock me that's something else again, something I won't tolerate."

I glanced past her to the kitchen, where Mrs. Conditt was busying herself at the sink, listening in but pretending not to.

"You don't know *anything*." Karen stood with one hand on her hip and the other on the back of the sofa. "First of all, you have no way of knowing what my feelings for my father are and, second, what makes you think I disrespect you when I hardly—"

I knew that she was about to say *when I hardly think about you at all* and I was extremely glad that she stopped short of it. She smoothed the back of the sofa and turned away. "Never mind. This has gone way too far. It's ludicrous really, laughable."

Sitting on the hassock, hands on his knees, Walt continued to stare at the floor.

Geneva let out a breath and released her grip on the banister. "All right. I think I've made my point. You know how I feel. I'm sure that the young man—"

Karen spun around. "Won't be back? My God, Mother, who in his right mind would come twice to this house anyway?"

I was beginning to wonder. Yet something held *me* there. I liked Karen, partly I guess because she seemed so vulnerable in her daring and stormy moments. But I was beginning to feel more sympathetic toward Geneva, too, because she seemed so hemmed in. Karen had her wildness as a kind of refuge. Geneva could only react to it. She had to run what was left of the household and try to keep her fragmented little family together. Karen had me as her confidante. Geneva had, so far as I knew, only the shadowy Jack Crystal.

Geneva came forward and put her hand up, the diamonds of her engagement ring sparkling gold and blue as they caught the light from the lamp. "Just one more thing." Her shoulders sagged. She sounded drained. "It may not always seem like it, but we have family pride at stake, a fragile pride to be sure. And this house is full of reminders of it. You have pride and you have a future. You *are* the future, the last of the Sterlings." She put her hands on Walt's shoulders. "Don't throw it away, for his sake if not for mine."

I felt sympathy for them, sure. But just then I wanted more than ever to get away, to go to Mount Desert and start all over, to meet new people who had no history.

CHAPTER 10

I suppose that beneath her desire to push everything to the limit, Karen also had a nurturing side because, a couple of days after the big blowup with Geneva, she was talking about doing something to help Robin. She was lying on a quilt in my yard, watching the water lap at the rocky shore on its way from the river to the bay. Karen was in a light pink halter top bikini and, sitting there beside her in cutoffs and a yellow polo shirt, I felt about as chic as a walrus. The fog was coming in again, quietly erasing everything beyond Dunning's Point. "Living out there alone like that," she sighed. "I think we ought to do something to cheer him up."

I looked down at her to make sure she was serious. "Oh, I think he's plenty cheerful already. He smiles a lot, don't you think?"

She sat up cross-legged and put her elbows on her knees and her chin in her palms. "Sure, he *seems* happy. But you know how stoical men are. He could have an arrow in his heart and press on and say it was nothing at all. They're raised that way, to make light of everything. I think it has to do with evolution, something about warfare and hunting woolly mammoths."

Once she got a notion into her head, she was not to be stopped. "Look," I said, "arrow or no, I don't think he needs any cheering up from us. He's out there on that island because he wants to be. You can be sure that if he wanted to live in town, he could do it. My mother says that his parents threw him out and disinherited him after he got busted a time or two, but there are plenty of empty houses around here. He could probably break into any one of them and live rent free—if he wanted to."

She swung her hands wide, like a cormorant flapping its wings before takeoff. "Oh, you have this mindset that everyone's in the spot they're in because they *want* to be, because they don't *want* to be helped."

"I don't know," I said, "but I have a pretty clear impression of Robbie—Robin if you want—that he's in control of what he's doing. Even in elementary school he seemed to know what he wanted and how to go after it."

She turned suddenly and asked, "Do you think he wants *me*?"

I was rolling a smooth granite pebble in my palms. I heaved it so hard that it clacked on the rocky shore. "Karen, *don't* even think about it. Sterling pride, remember? I mean, your mother was right about that much, wasn't she?"

She put her elbows back on her knees and looked at the fading bay. "She was talking in code, Amber. When she says pride, she really means *money*. Hey, it may be kind of rundown, but we *do* have a brownstone on Beacon Street. We may be on our way to the welfare rolls, but for now we are, as they say, a family of means. I suppose she's gotten over her concern for my virtue, but she won't ever get over her concern for my money."

I was a little concerned about money myself because, after getting off to a nice start with the Sterlings, I was pretty much frittering away my chance to make some summer income. Sure, I was a little lazy and I was enjoying unemployment, but time was slipping away and every day represented lost revenue. In the fall Karen would be off to who knows where enjoying her money in some glamorous way, but if I didn't sock away some cash, I would be spending another year right there in Ashton, and the very thought of more wreath-making made my eyes well up.

The sun disappeared behind the oncoming fog. Karen stood up and put on one of Walt's flannel shirts. "Look, I've got a great idea! Let's help Robin get set up in business."

I sat right where I was. "Are you out of your mind? I have a hunch that Robin's already in business—up to his pointy little ears. The last thing he needs is help from us."

"Oh, now come on." Karen stuffed her feet into a pair of topsiders. In that sloppy outfit, she looked even more ravishing somehow. "Where's your sense of social obligation? We can help set Robin up as a tour captain. There's plenty to see around here. He can take, what, five or six people at a time, charge fifty dollars a head and get it. All he'd have to do is clean up his boat a little. He could start tomorrow."

The morning sun burned off the fog and spread out a cloudless sky. I was weeding the window boxes when Karen came barreling up the driveway and stopped the Mustang with a scrccch. "Great day for a trip," she said, leaning around the windshield.

I came toward her with a handful of weeds and a stray geranium. "It sure is. Where would you like to go—St. Stephen's? Yarmouth?" I made a deliberate motion away from Robin Dunning's island.

"Don't be silly. This is the day we turn that boy around. Someday we'll be looking back at it with wonder. Move over. I'll give you a hand with that."

I tried to talk her out of it, of course. Pop had led me to believe that Robin would as soon cut our throats as go straight. But she was not to be turned around and I would've felt guilty letting her go out there by herself, which she surely would have done if I had balked. So the minute we got the window boxes weeded, there we were, on our way to the marina to crank up the *Sea Clip.*

Whatever Robin had done was quality work because that engine started up on the first try and purred from the minute we left the slip until we hoisted sail in the bay. The day was so soft that *I* could've taken the helm. The sunlight splashed across the chop like a scattering of brass buttons, and the jagged shoreline was so clear that you could count the cones on the pine trees. The wind was right and Karen was determined and confident and so we shot through the slot effortlessly and made straight for the lonely house of Robin Dunning. We tied up at the mooring on the ledge and took the *Sea*

Clip's inflatable to the shore path. I stepped out and secured the boat to a sapling as Karen hauled in the oars.

"If he's not here, we're not going into that house," I said.

Karen smiled as she climbed out of the dinghy. "You're not the least little bit curious about what's in that room?"

"No, not in the least." I nearly had myself convinced. "We may have caught him in a good mood that last time. Let's not press our luck."

My resolve was unnecessary because as we wound our way to the top of the path, I caught sight of his boat moored on the backside of the island. By the time we had a clear look at the house, he was slouching in the kitchen doorway, having a smoke as he watched us approach.

He took a pull on his cigarette and called out. "Don't tell me you ladies are stuck again."

Karen quickened her step. "We've got an idea! A business proposition."

He came down from the stone step, looking at her sidelong as if she might be rabid. "A proposition. What kind of proposition?"

Right there in the dooryard she started telling him her plan, and I was sure that he was going to cut her off, but she got through the whole thing while he just stood there by the kitchen step, his face breaking into a slow smile.

"Well, what do you think?" she asked when she had finished.

Still smiling, he rubbed the back of his head with the heel of his hand. "I think you're cracked—but I kind of like what you're saying."

I couldn't believe what I was hearing. At first, I thought they were playing a joke on me, but as she went on in detail about cleaning up his boat for the tourist trade and putting ads in the *Quoddy Tides* and flyers up around town, I could tell it was for real, and I realized that I didn't know as much as I thought about either of them.

"It's your boat, right?" Karen said as an afterthought.

He patted the peeling doorjamb. "My grandfather left it to me, along with this island."

"Good! And of course, we'll have to clean you up, too," Karen said, "just to make you look more, you know, professional."

"One thing at a time," he said. "You can't just go hauling people around the bay. You've got to have a skipper's license."

Her shoulders drooped. "A skipper's license?"

"Yuh. That's right." He winked at me.

She sounded crushed. "Well, how long does it take to get one?"

"To get mine? A minute or so I suppose if some girl hasn't broken into the house and ripped it off."

"Let me guess," I said. "You've already done charters."

Karen laughed. "Doesn't anybody talk straight on this side of the river?"

"Well, we're just kidding around, aren't we?" He looked at me to make sure that *we* weren't putting one over on *him*, but he could tell right away that I was even more surprised by her idea than he was. I had no idea how far Karen would go. Was she *trying* to push him until he pushed back?

Right there in that overgrown dooryard, I became the third wheel.

He *let* her cut his hair, his long, dark, curly locks. Docile as a lamb he perched on the kitchen step, draped in a striped bed sheet, as the rich crescents fell. He submitted meekly as she tilted his head with spread fingers. When she was done and she shook the sheet into the warm breeze, the shorn curls took to the air and scattered across that wild island.

"Beautiful!" she proclaimed, holding the black comb and bright scissors high. "A creation."

I was amazed. His features were sharper and stronger, making him look less boyish and more sophisticated, like an up-and-coming executive on vacation. I couldn't believe that it was all due to a simple backyard haircut. I also had a hunch that Karen would never be able to repeat what she had done. With the bright sun flooding the dooryard, the unstoppable tide heaving out to sea, and all the powers of the island flowing through his breath and his veins, Robin seemed to me a creature of the place and yet Karen the outsider had left her mark on him.

At least she hadn't tried to take him to Maurice.

But, splendid as he was on the island just then, Karen's creation wasn't so well suited to the tourist traffic that passed through Eastport, Maine. We had to work on him to make him suitably deferential to potential customers. Karen and I stayed close by to make sure that he didn't slouch, didn't have a cigarette hanging from his lips, didn't swear or spit, didn't rub his hands on his pants, which were freshly-creased khakis that were a great match for his new blue and beige checked dress shirt.

"Just stand straight and they'll think you can sail them all the way to Hawaii," Karen said, watching some tourists fiddle with their camera as they came onto the pier. "Even if it's only a jaunt to Downeast Ledge, they'll like that sense of the unlimited horizon."

"You do have a way," he said, smiling awkwardly and sticking his hands in his pockets.

With the first customer we hit disaster. He was trim, middle-aged, sporty, tall and tan and decked out in stuff from that mail order place in Wisconsin that sells the nautical preppy look. He pulled back the sleeve of his windbreaker and looked at one of those watches that have time zones on them.

"Look, I've got two hours before I have to be in Campobello. How far can that thing get me?"

Robin looked past the boat, out toward the sparkling water of the Western Passage. "It can get you out as far as you—"

Something in the man's windbreaker started playing "In-A-Gadda-Da-Vida." He pulled out a cell phone and started talking to somebody about a teleconference. He paced around the pier and gestured with his free hand, seemingly talking to a whole person and not just a voice. He had no idea where he was going or who was crossing his path. He hurried along in his own private world that had nothing to do with passing boats and swooping seagulls. Finally he snapped the phone shut and came back to us. He looked at his watch again. "All right. So we're down to an hour fifty-five. Where can you take me? I want some action."

He got some.

As we left the pier, Karen told the client a few safety rules having to do with coming about and floatation devices and man overboard procedures, but he wasn't interested, probably because he was so used to ignoring the canned spiels of flight attendants on airplanes. It wasn't all that windy, but since the client said that he wanted action, Robin sailed toward open water, and when we got there, he went on a beam reach and sheeted the sails in so tight so that the boat heeled over hard and white water came whirling over the rail and into the pockets of the man's windbreaker. He groped his way up to the high side and sat between Karen and me.

"Well, now. This is more like it," he said. He checked to make sure that his phone was still dry. Then he put an arm around each of us. He smiled as if posing for a picture in the catalogue of the nautical preppy people. "This is my kind of travel. So what are you girls' names?"

Our names didn't matter because he forgot them immediately. After we had scooted around for a while, our client got out the cell phone again and called somebody on Campobello. He hunched between Karen and me and started talking about the exchange rate of the Canadian dollar and how he had made thirteen thousand dollars on it in one afternoon while he was riding his exercise bike on the highest setting.

Then he lost his signal.

When Karen tripped over the tailings of a line, she somehow wound up in his lap.

"I'm really sorry," she said, prying herself from his hands.

"That makes one of us," he told her with a pat on the thigh. "Any time."

Robin watched him for a moment and looked up at the tall sail splashed with sunlight. I could tell that he had something in mind, and as our client clenched his phone and went forward trying to find a signal, Robin eased the boat back toward Ashton, tightened the sheet, and picked up speed.

Karen was so intent on listening in on the client's efforts to get his phone working that she didn't notice what Robin was up to. But by now I had guessed. I tried to make eye contact, but he just smiled and looked out into the bay.

Before long we were slicing along briskly. The wind was steady and the gulls plunged and dived on it, crisscrossing and shrieking over our wake. Robin asked Karen to get his sweatshirt from the cabin, and when she was on her way down the ladder, he asked me to free the jib from the rail, which required me to drop down to the low side of the boat. Up near the high side of the bow, the client had reconnected and was chatting about firewalls and secure servers and was really getting into it. He stood up and made a broad sweep with his arm to make a point about turnover, and that's when Robin yanked in the mainsheet. The boat heeled over so sharply that our client fell down and had to grab one of the wire shrouds to keep from going overboard as his precious cell phone glinted in the sunlight on its way into the cold waters of Cobscook Bay.

"Damn!" sputtered the man as he untangled his legs from the rail. "God damn!"

Karen went forward and helped him to his feet. "Of course we'll give you your money back."

"Or give you another ride," Robin said with a straight face. "Just give us a call."

We tried again. We took on a family of four. The kids were boy and girl twins about nine years old and they hated just about everything their parents wanted to do. The father was inclined to humor them, and the mother told him that he was being spineless.

"For God's sake," Karen muttered as we cast off, "doesn't *anyone* get along?"

It turned out that part of the problem was nausea. The father had talked the mother into taking the trip because he loved boat rides, but as soon as we left the pier, the mother's face turned the color of pea soup. She went below, but it was stuffy down there, and the smell of the wood polish Karen and I had slathered on to brighten up the cabin sent her right back topside with her hand clapped to her mouth. I waited for her husband or one of the twins to console her, but they were in the bow looking for marine mammals that were nowhere in sight. Despite all of our preparations, we hadn't thought to bring anything for seasickness, and so all we had to offer was advice—take in the fresh air and avoid looking at the horizon.

"We could go back," Robin offered from the tiller.

Shaking her head, the mother spoke through white fingers. "Not on your life. I'd never hear the end of it."

Robin sailed the boat flat and avoided the tight places where the water tended to get rough.

CHAPTER 11

For the next day or so he was so patient and such a gentleman that I almost forgot about his career of sacking and vandalism. I was fascinated by the way he submitted to Karen's ideas and adjusted his wild ways to the needs of his passengers. I wondered if Karen had worked some mysterious magic on him, just as her father was changing the lives of practically everyone who had crossed his path during the summer.

We had a couple of good days and made a little joke of setting up a company with the three of us as shareholders. Robin was the chairman of the board, Karen was the chief executive officer, and I was the mascot. We split the money four ways, a quarter for each of us and a quarter for the boat. Robin smoothed a wad of twenty-dollar bills and tucked it into the hip pocket of his khakis. Karen made some joke about our corporate treasurer and, still laughing, we were walking across the pier on our way to get ice cream cones when three guys converged on us. They were all about our age and I could tell at once that Robin knew them.

"We'll take some of that, Robbie. You owe us that and a lot more." The biggest of the three came up with his hand out. He was taller and heavier than Robin. His fingertips were black and he had a smudge on his jaw, an attempt at a beard apparently. His jeans were tucked into black rubber boots and the tail of his green flannel shirt hung out on one side. His slick dark hair was either wet or greasy.

Robin smiled and brought the bills out of his pocket. "Sure, Ted. Come on up and I'll give you what you've got coming."

The other two came closer but maintained their distance as Ted came toward us, his hand still extended.

Robin peeled off two twenties and started to hand them to him, but the bills dropped and fluttered to the pier. When Ted reached for them, Robin clamped both hands onto his arm, went into a crouch, and flipped him into the air. Waving his arms, Ted managed to land on his feet, but tottered backwards at the lip of the pier and took a long fall into the water.

"You see, I did the time," Robin said, chest heaving as he went toward the closer of the remaining two. "And I learned a lot more than how to make license plates in Thomaston. I did the time while you dirt bags ran loose. So, yeah, you've all got something coming, and if I see you again, I'll give it to you."

I scrambled after the twenties while Karen looked over the side to make sure that Ted was still alive.

"You should've taken swimming lessons when you had the chance," Robin said as he moved toward the second guy, who backed into the street and just missed being flattened by an SUV turning onto the pier. The third guy ran up the hill, toward a row of historic brick sea captains' houses.

Karen watched Ted haul himself onto the cement of a nearby boat ramp. "What were they talking about, Robin? What did they mean you owe them?"

He lit a cigarette without offering her one. He was impatient with the question. "Haven't you noticed that a lot of people around here say stupid stuff? It was just a shakedown. Forget it."

She looked back at the ramp. Ted had disappeared. "You knew them though. Who were they?"

He took out his cigarette and spoke through the smoke. "I told you, forget it. People around here are always trying to shake you down. Hell, my old man probably overcharged you for working on your yard."

I was relieved when a good rain came in the night and kept right on into the morning. I had slept badly, thinking about what might happen the next time we showed up at the pier, and it seemed to me that maybe this day of rain would break the spell, would somehow dissolve Ted and his friends, and that the whole dangerous, ugly scene would fade into fiction. I decided that if

Karen called or came over with another of her nerve-wracking schemes, I wouldn't be home. I put on my turquoise slicker and hiked over to see the mother of my high school friend, Cherie Gillespie. Even though Cherie had moved to Woodland determined to become a secretary, she was no damn good at writing, so in two months I'd received only one postcard—a picture of the fiberboard plant—and no emails, which was not surprising since our server was always going down. Somehow we had missed each other during her visits to Ashton, so I wanted to put our friendship back on track through a visit to Mrs. Gillespie, whose house was a mile toward town. I was hoping that Cherie's dad wouldn't be there because you never knew when that mean streak of his would surface.

I was still thinking about Robin and Karen though, wondering if they were good for each other or if Robin was playing along with Karen for the sake of getting his hands on her money. Karen wouldn't be the first highborn woman attracted to a wild and scheming man. So there I was, deep in thought and trudging along the shoulder of the road with the rain beating down on my turquoise hat when a familiar red pickup truck came splashing up behind me.

Fred reached over and rolled down the window enough to get a good look at me. "You're crazy walking around in this stuff. Get in, Amber. You're getting soaked."

I was wearing lace-up rubber boots, also turquoise, but he had managed to throw water over the tops of them. I could feel it running down my shins. I stepped away from the road. "I was fine until you came along. I'm sure you have someplace you need to be, so why don't you just go there?"

"Already been. I'm taking an IT course over in Machias. Prof says I have a knack for it."

"For information technology? Well, I have some information for you. Your stupid truck got me wet."

"Sorry, gorgeous. It's a lot drier in here."

I flapped the water from my sleeves. "Don't call me that!" It was the pet name he had used when we had been an *item*. It seemed okay at the time, but now it felt insulting, not to mention inaccurate.

He set the parking brake and slid over to the passenger side of the truck. "Aw, Amber, I didn't mean anything by it. We're going our separate ways. I can live with that. I was just trying to be friendly. I mean, damn, we grew up together, didn't we?"

The rain was awful, but I was not about to get into that truck. "That remains to be seen," I said. "You're getting your precious interior wet. Better roll up and move on."

For the first time in his life, Fred surprised me. He got out of the truck and stood there in the rain with the door open. "Look, if it's about the picnic, about Grandpa, I can explain."

I glared at him, which was hard to do with wet hair in my eyes. "Can you?"

He wiped the rain from his brows. "Well, no, on second thought, I can't. About the apples, I mean. Things just kept going one step further, you know. Taking him there was okay, I think. I'm pretty sure. After that, well, it seemed to make sense at the time."

I didn't even care about his grandfather at that particular moment. I was mad about practically everything else I could think of, including our breakup. Worst of all, of course, I was mad at myself for not handling it better.

"Very little around here makes sense," I said at last. I stepped to one side to get around him and sank ankle deep in mud. "You're getting your upholstery wet."

He blocked my way, "Then let it get wet until everybody comes to their senses."

I was impressed, but I had no patience for that kind of dramatics. I motioned toward the open door. "Just get in, will you?"

"Will *you?*" He had his hands on his hips. His black hair was plastered down the sides of his head. The rain ran down his nose, down mine, too.

"Yes, yes, you damn fool! Now get in before I get even wetter."

Arms folded, shoulder pressed against the door, I sat dripping on his sacred upholstery.

"God, it's a toad-strangler out there." He yanked his door shut and took off the brake.

His attempt at small talk annoyed me because it implied that suddenly we had slipped back into the same old routine.

"Who cares—if you're not out there standing in it like a dumb ox," I said. I figured that would put him in his place.

He reached across me and put the window up. Why did he reach across me? As a little attempt at intimacy or did the switch on the driver's side not work? Suddenly Fred had a little mystery about him, but I put that out of my mind.

He pulled onto the road. "So where you going?"

"To the Gillespies." I felt foolish saying it because by the time I got there I'd be too wet to go inside.

"How's Sherry doing?"

"Her name is pronounced *Cher-EE*," I said. "The French way. Beats me why you don't know that. We only went to school together for about twelve years."

"Okay, so how's she doing?"

He was so relentlessly cheerful and I had been trying so hard to be a pickle that I couldn't help laughing. "She's fine, fine! She's got a place in Woodland near the fiberboard factory."

He gave me a worried look, as if I might be losing my marbles, which of course, made me laugh all the more.

"Good. I'm glad she's doing all right. You two were real close, weren't you?"

I couldn't stop laughing. His concern just made everything funnier. He was sopping wet and I was sitting there in my turquoise witch hat with water running off the end of my nose. I thought back to all of those times when he had gotten annoyed with my being ticklish and all of it just seemed so funny, so terribly ridiculous, that I doubled over laughing.

He never did know how to deal with me when I had one of my spells. He always tried to ignore them. It was his old football player's philosophy: *You got a pain somewhere, you just work through it.* The flip side of which was, if somebody else is in pain, you just work through that too.

"I haven't seen you since the picnic," he said.

"Really? I don't recall," I said.

"That thing with Grandpa, it really was kinda wild."

I was looking for a piece of Kleenex. I found a damp clump in the pocket of my slicker, wrung it out, and touched it to the corners of my eyes. I had laughed myself to tears. For a moment I hovered at the edge of another breakdown, weighing the humorous and the serious. "I suppose it was," I said, "if you consider beaning a recently deceased relative with apples at a picnic wild."

The windshield was fogging up. He peered through the arcs of the wipers. "A bunch of us had been drinking, of course. I'm not sure if that makes it better or worse."

I stuck the wad back in my pocket. "I'm sure I wouldn't know."

"Of course, you could take just about anybody around here and find a little wild corner in them. Even over on the Woolsey side that's probably true, don't you suppose?"

I saw in my mind the untended wedge of the Sterlings' grounds, the patch that Walt had wanted that way, back when he was known as Dr. Sterling. Even then he had known something about the need for a wild patch. I tried to imagine him with his mind intact, talking to Fred about it, but I couldn't get the words to come together.

"So maybe that was it for us," Fred continued, "for the Archers I mean. That was the deepest part of the woods for us if you get what I mean." He swept his wet hair away from his forehead. "Aw, hell, I'm not making any sense."

I couldn't bring myself to tell him that he was making *perfect* sense, maybe for the first time in his life.

"Still, I'm not ashamed of it," he said. "I don't suppose Grandpa would've minded. I mean, hell, he was the center of attention and that's what it was all about, honoring Grandpa."

"*A-hmmm.*" I swallowed a laugh. Fred was just like a dinghy that Brian had built in junior high. From some angles the lines looked pretty good, and if you knew just how to balance it, you could go along gracefully. But it was so top-heavy that the least little puff of wind or the shift of a person's behind would capsize it and dump everyone in the drink. Fred was talking sense about something that mattered to him, and now I was doing my best to keep the conversation from tipping over.

"It's the Irish in us, maybe, or maybe the Penobscot blood."

Well, I thought. He *has* been thinking.

Somebody was coming at us, too fast, in a minivan. Fred leaned on the horn and pulled onto the shoulder to let them pass. "You know, speaking of Indians, I've got a great idea. We've got the bloodlines, both of us. We ought to start a casino."

Was I suddenly talking to a green alien from some doomed sulfurous planet? I gripped the door handle in an effort to maintain my composure.

"I mean," said the alien, possibly a three-headed one inhabiting Fred's body, "there's big money to be made, Amber, and all you've got to do to open one is have the tip of your big toe be Indian. I'm a sixteenth."

"Oh, good," I said. "But that means you'll probably need to put *all* of your toes in hock." I managed to keep a straight face.

"No, look. You're a sixteenth, aren't you? We could make a lot of money together."

"Except that there's already a casino in Maine. And I doubt if being one-sixteenth Penobscot would be worth a hill of beans anywhere else." I jerked off my rain hat, nearly strangling on the string. "Anyway, I don't care about making a lot of money. I'm going to go down to Mount Desert and make just enough to go to grad school, winter term maybe."

"Mount Desert? Catering to stuck-up summer people and tourists?"

"It's a funny thing," I said, "but their money spends just like anyone else's."

"Well, when are you going?"

I had been dragging my feet so long that I felt silly saying it, but I told him as soon as possible, in a week or two.

"Isn't the season already half over on Mount Desert?"

"Sure," I said, "but they *always* need help down there, especially late in the season."

"What about Hal? He's gonna have a big re-opening, you know."

"So I hear."

"Yeah, well, his plan gets bigger by the day. The Brogue 'n' Burr. He's borrowing big. He's all fired up."

Walt really *had* gotten to Hal. "I'd like to help him," I sniffed, "but I'll be gone by then. There are plenty of girls around here who can wait tables. He doesn't need me."

When the Gillespies' house came into view, their car was nowhere to be seen, and I felt more foolish than ever. They were *always* home—except for this one instance, apparently. Even the pop-up camper was gone from its weedy corner by the woodshed. So I was wet and limp with nowhere to go.

Eyeing the empty driveway, Fred stopped the truck. "You're not missing much. Her old man's been a bear ever since he kicked the sauce." He gave me one of his crooked smiles. "Want me to put you back where I found you?"

"Just take me home," I said.

"What about Sherry?"

I watched the rain streak down the window. "I'll send her a postcard," I said.

CHAPTER 12

Mrs. Townsend responded to Walt's touch in her own way. She took up painting.

"Always wanted to," she said, smiling as I tripped over the yapping Peach and his chew toys on my way across the living room. "My dear Paul—Paul the First—loved painting so and always wanted me to take it up, but I never had the patience. Now I do." With a broad brush she was whiting out the gaudy still life that had hung over her fireplace for as long as I could remember.

I had always thought of that painting as kind of a representation of Mrs. Townsend—something rather humdrum that did its best to present a fresh appearance. "I sort of thought of that painting as *you*," I ventured to say.

"Well, no *more!*" was her cheerful, raspy reply. "The real me is about to show herself!"

"What about Maurice?" Peach had finally worn himself out, allowing me to come within hailing distance. "It's ten-thirty. Shouldn't we be going? He'll be expecting you."

"Not anymore. I called and canceled." She was swathing what appeared to be exterior gloss on top of the bright pansies and petunias. They were disappearing as if in a spring snowstorm. "Oh, don't worry. Maurice is off on a jag of his own. He's in love! Couldn't care less about fluffing up this dreary old *do* of mine."

"In love? Maurice?"

"Oh, yes indeedy. Apparently he had been wanting to speak his mind for quite some time, but just didn't know if it was the right thing to do—until Walt."

I felt dizzy. The world seemed to be turning upside down. I curled the car keys around my ring finger. "Does that mean that you don't want to go into Eastport today?"

From top to bottom, Mrs. Townsend gave the flowers a swash of the brush. "Oh no. Quite the contrary. I want you to take me to the bookstore. They sell art supplies there."

"Are you sure?" I asked. "I don't remember seeing—"

"Sure I'm sure! I've been avoiding looking at them for about twenty years! Always had the urge, but never had the gumption. They're in the back, between the maps and the magazines."

What was it about Walt that made certain people follow through on their most deep-seated desires? My pop had met him, had shaken his hand, and *he* was still perfectly normal. He still shuffled around the house in a coffee-stained t-shirt, bellowing about misplaced pliers and swearing at the drive belt on the dryer.

Robin had met Walt, and he continued to haul his quarrelsome passengers back and forth across the bay, smiling in anticipation of little tricks he could play to call their attention to their surroundings. A surly teenage boy seeking solitude in the bow had been snapped into life by a wake that broke across his face. The boy's father, smug and dry in the cockpit, burst out laughing as the boy fumbled to dry off his iPod, and all the while, back at the tiller, Robin looked as innocent as an angel. Same old Robin.

But Hal was in the throes of creating the restaurant of his dreams. Out on Route 1 he had put down his last dime—and quite a few more besides--to transform his faltering eatery into a culinary nirvana.

"He's probably trying to come up with a fancy new name for Spam," Mom said with a smile.

"It's the real thing this time," Hal had told her. "Linen table cloths and candles and—" He kissed his bunched fingers— "recipes you wouldn't believe. Offer the best and the people will come. That's where I went wrong before, aiming too low. But most of all, I had no *focus*. Now I do."

Everyone seemed to know about Hal's big plan. I mean, even *Fred* knew.

Karen had grown resentful. While her mother was off on one of her all-day trips, she told Mrs. Conditt to wash the remaining sunbeam color out of Walt's hair. "He looks like his head caught fire," she said. "Everybody around here owns a piece of my father except me—and I want him back."

We were on the porch, hearing the hair dryer in the bathroom undo Maurice's artistry. "I hadn't thought of it that way," I said. "I just thought that Maurice wanted to give of himself."

Karen was not sympathetic. "Look, I've lost him twice—once when Alzheimer's got him and again now that he's become this— this *celebrity*. Those people out there have no idea who my father was. He was brilliant, sure, but he was basically ordinary. He was just *my father.* He put on his tie in the morning, sometimes crooked, and took it off at night. He remembered jokes for years, especially if they were dirty. He liked brandy when he was feeling mellow and Scotch on the rocks when he was uptight. Every time he had a book come out, he took us to dinner at this very middle class Italian restaurant on Boylston. I think he even pinched one of their silver forks one time. When I broke the school record for the breaststroke, he emptied a bottle of champagne into the pool. *That's* my father, not that—that mystic they're getting all glassy-eyed about."

I could hear Mrs. Conditt saying something to him. She spoke in that high, deliberate voice you'd use on a child or a dog.

"Okay, so after the Alzheimer's, I got used to that guy in there," Karen was saying. "I got used to leading him around like a two-year-old. I got used to the vacant stares and the swill that came out of the blender. I accepted it as the new normal. That's what I had. I learned to live with it. Now I'm losing him all over again. He's become—I don't know what, but he's not my father, not mine at all."

Sometimes we seem to do nothing at my house but hang up clothes to dry and take them back down. I was taking them down when a cream colored sports car with the top down came up the driveway, a scaled-down replica of some vintage model by the look of it. There was Mr. Jack Crystal in a camel hair touring cap and little round sunglasses that barely covered his eyes. He had on a tweed jacket with suede patches at the elbows, and I got the impression that this was his version of power dressing. I could tell that he was on a mission. When he came to a stop, I thought he was going to tip his cap, but instead he just raised it enough to scratch the top of his head.

"Karen isn't here," I told him. Absentmindedly I had brought over a bra and a handful of clothespins.

He took off the sunglasses and slipped them into his breast pocket. "I know. Thought you might like to go for a little ride. It's a sweet car."

It seemed to me that I had spent the whole summer going for rides. "I'm kind of busy," I said.

"Oh, yes, I know. Saving up for grad school. Come with me for a little spin and you might be able to save up quickly."

What did he mean by that? I had no idea, but I figured that he was harmless enough, and I was curious, so I went into the laundry room and told Mom where I was going and assured her that I'd be back extremely soon. "Strictly business," I said. "And not much of that, I'm sure."

The dips and potholes of the Dunning's Point Road were a test for his driving skills. While he was talking, he drifted onto the shoulder and threw gravel, and at the curves he slowed down and took his half out of the middle. I was a little worried about being creamed by an oncoming vehicle, of having to walk the eternal path with Jack Crystal and having people wonder forever what the hell we were doing together in the first place.

"I think it's grand the way you and Karen have come together," he said, crossing the center of the road as he looked over at me. His touring cap was so resistant to the wind that I thought he must have glued it on. "It's just grand, fabulous."

My hair was driving me crazy so I pulled it back hard. I wasn't sure if my eyes were actually slanting or if I was just squinting into the wind, but I knew the look couldn't be gorgeous and I didn't care. So there I was in the Chinese position, waiting to see what Jack Crystal would say next.

"She's a great girl, Karen is. I've known her all her life."

He looked over at me, waiting for me to say something no doubt, but I couldn't think of a single intelligent thing to say.

"She's very bright of course, very bright, very imaginative," he went on.

"No doubt about it," I said before the silence got too painful.

He looked over at me again. I imagined him lobbing tennis balls over a net and waiting for me to hit them back. "Very high strung though. She's always been high-strung."

He was right about that, but I wasn't about to agree with him.

"Well," he said, thumping the steering wheel with his sunburned hands, "so I think you've been good for her."

I shrugged. "I never thought of it that way. We were just having a good time."

"Oh, sure, of course." I thought I was in the clear, but then he zinged me. "Now tell me about this young fellow—Robin."

I stiffened. "He's lived all his life around here, pretty much does what the guys around here do. Gets around, has a boat."

Jack smiled as if I had just told a joke. He gave the wheel a little pull to avoid a pothole. "Just an ordinary guy, huh?"

"As far as I can tell. His family goes way back. This road and the point are named for them. In fact they say that on the old charts Downeast Ledge is called Dunning's Ledge. Word is that the Dunnings got here first, except for the Penobscots and the Passamaquoddy."

He took one hand off the wheel and gestured impatiently. "Well, what does he, you know, *do?* What's his profession?"

I spoke without great interest. "I don't know. Gets by somehow. I don't think his parents left him much, but he got a house from his grandparents, makes some money sailing tourists around."

"Oh, sure, the sailing. I guess you and Karen have been helping with that."

"Oh, not really. Robin sure doesn't need help to sail the boat."

"I guess not, he being one of the seafaring locals. But I guess it cost him something to get started."

"No, we helped him clean out his boat and he was all ready to go."

That seemed to satisfy him. Then I saw his jaw set and he said, "I guess some of the young fellows around here get into scrapes with the law. That sounds kind of romantic, doesn't it— *scrapes with the law.*"

Now I knew what he was getting at, but I didn't know how to steer clear of it. I tried to sound low-key. "There are guys getting into trouble all over Washington County," I said. "Most of them straighten up after a while, once they work through the wild patch."

"*The wild patch.*" He seemed to turn the phrase over in his mind a few times. "I guess for some it's bigger than for others."

I was starting to hate the way he kept saying *I guess.* It was like a stick that he poked at me.

"I guess so," I said.

As he shifted into fifth, the replica car snarled. "Well, let me get to the point. Geneva wants Karen to stop seeing the Dunning boy. Karen has this history of throwing herself at the least desirable people she can find. Her analyst has a name for it. I forget what, but we thought we might break her of it by coming up here for the summer. We had no idea that she would go to such lengths to humiliate herself all over again."

I felt as if I'd had the wind socked out of me. Suddenly the skin on my face felt stretched to the breaking point. He was making Karen sound like another person altogether. Sure, I could see some of what he was saying about her throwing herself at Robin, but the girl he was describing was sick. I wanted to get out of the car, but we were going too fast, way too fast. I watched familiar things shoot by, but I was seeing them in a strange new way. The first widening of the river fell back behind me and then the long disused Carpenter's Hall and the jumble of houses at the center of town.

At least now he had both hands on the wheel as he talked. "All I want to do—all *we* want to do—is to protect her from another unhappy experience. Since she's a friend of yours, I would think that you'd want to protect her too." He gave me a quick look, skimmed the shoulder of the road, and pulled back into the middle of the blacktop.

I felt sick to my stomach. He had said so many hard things that I didn't know where to begin an argument, especially since they had some truth to them. I was tempted to tell him that Karen's relationship with Robin was only a friendship, but I knew that it might already be progressing beyond that. I wanted to say that Robin wasn't necessarily *undesirable*, but I knew that plenty of people, my own parents included, would disagree.

"She's a grownup," I said finally. "Don't you suppose she entitled to make her own decisions—and mistakes?"

He smiled—at my naiveté, I suppose. "If only it were that simple. Karen is part of a family, a family that cares very much about her future."

I twisted around to face him. "And her money?"

"Well, we can get into the philosophy of money some other time if you like but, sure, money has something to do with it. Money is what makes families secure and it's also what attracts some people to those families. But this is really about Karen. Somebody needs to look after her without being too obvious." He gave me another of his looks.

I turned back around and glared through the windshield. "Oh, no. Count me out."

"Not an option. You're already *in*. Does Karen know that the boy's been to prison?"

So he and Geneva had been doing some snooping. It made me wonder what they knew about our get-togethers with Robin. It made me wonder what else they would do to separate him from Karen.

"He was imprisoned illegally," I said. I was pretty sure that Robin had been guilty, but I felt like defending him, and anyway, as far as the law was concerned, he was innocent.

"Let's not allow a few fine points obscure the facts, Amber. He got out on a technicality, but the next time he won't be so lucky, and you and I both know that there *will* be a next time. Look, all we're asking you to do for now is to stay with Karen and keep us informed. It's the sort of thing a friend would do—and right now

Karen needs a friend. Of course, we realize that you'll have certain expenses and we'll be glad to cover those—liberally."

We passed the lot where they had torn down the old high school. Nothing remained but a few granite foundation stones and some pretty lousy scrap lumber and shingles. Now we were out on Route 1, approaching the shuttered shell of the restaurant Hal had after the sandwich shop. Happy Hal's House of Fine Food. The manager had set fire to the place and run off to Skowhegan with most of the money. Word had it that the license plates he made were some of the best to come out of the correctional system. I thought about money and how I could build a future on it. The summer was slipping away, and all I had saved was a few dollars and this could be a chance to catch up while helping to keep Karen from hurting herself, but my face went hot when I thought of yielding to the temptation.

"Let's not go any further—or any faster," I said. "Whatever Robin may have done is history. He's making a respectable living and I've never seen the least indication that he's interested in Karen's money. To tell you the truth, I'm not even sure he's interested in *Karen*. Okay? Now I've said even more than I should've. So can we—"

He tried to take the turn back toward town, but he was going too fast and he slid into it. His touring cap went flying off and he hit the brakes so hard that my forehead smacked into the dashboard. I was furious. I shoved my door open and tumbled out of the car, unaware that I was pressing my hand to my eye.

He glanced back through the dust, looking for his cap in the road. "Oh, how awful! I'm terribly sorry. Damn place could use some signs." He came after me. "Here, let me—"

Half blind, I ran into the woods, leaving behind Jack Crystal and his replica car with both doors open, stopped in the middle of the road. I heard him call after me a couple of times, but I was so busy thrashing my way through low branches that I had no idea what he was saying. I had run off a little crazy and yet, as I slowed down and thought about it, I had probably done the right thing because the fewer people who knew that I had been out riding with Jack, the better, and the last thing I needed was for Karen to find out. He had won something, though, because he had wanted me to keep things from her and now I would be doing just that. Jack and I now had a secret between us and it would force me to lie to Karen.

Not long afterward, when Robin and Karen and I went out in the boat again, I had reason to be glad that I had spurned Jack's offer because our little knot got tighter. We'd had particularly good outings on the boat and a beautiful long summer evening with the surrounding pine woods going gold in the slanting sunlight and scenting the offshore breeze. I for one was slightly dizzy from all the fresh air and sunshine, and I suppose that none of us wanted to let go of the day. Robin tied up at Skipper Kip's to buy some gas, and we decided to pick up some groceries and have a picnic at Dunning's Point. All summer long and into the fall, kids would go out there to drink beer and hoot at the moon and I suppose we figured that this was our turn.

We had the place to ourselves and we went out onto the little spit of land that had been favored by the Archers since the dawn of time, not far from where Fred's grandfather had gotten beaned. Toward the end of the point there was an old wheel rim that you could build a fire in, and we decided to do it up brown, so we got some dry sticks and Robin peeled the bark from some larger damp pieces and started some shavings with his cigarette lighter. Before long, we were well into a weenie roast, complete with s'mores, apples baked in foil, and beer.

Karen watched the sparks float up into the night sky, which was still glowing pale blue in the northwest. "Do you know what I wish?"

Robin let a marshmallow ignite, blew it out, peeled off the black skin, and ate it. "You wish that we could be here forever."

She let out a painful little laugh. "How did *you* know? Is that what you were thinking?"

He seemed to wink at her from across the fire. "Who knows? Maybe we *will* be here forever. You know, haunting this place. Maybe a hundred years from now somebody's going to come out here and happen to look this way and here we'll be, forever tending this fire. That's how hauntings happen. Not so much from murders and accidents, just from everyday occurrences that make an impression in time."

Karen peered at him through the smoke. "Do you really believe that?"

Smiling, he put his marshmallow back over the fire. "I read it in a magazine I swiped from a gas station. I use it to keep my kitchen table from wobbling."

She snatched up a beer can and threw it at him.

He deflected it with his arm. "So tell us the truth about your shiner, Amber. I hope you weren't getting picked on in school again."

I wasn't used to drinking beer, so I felt slightly unbalanced. I stuck to the story I had been telling for several days. "I fell on the stairs in the dark. I didn't want to turn on the light and I *thought* I knew my way around the house. I've only been living there for twenty years. Goes to show you, even places you've known all your life can surprise you."

He looked over at Karen. "What do you think? Is she telling the truth?" His tone was playful and yet I felt uneasy. Somehow he knew that I was lying.

I looked down at my feet. "Don't be ridiculous. Why should I fib about a black eye?"

"It takes one to know one," Karen said. "What have *you* been lying about, Robin?"

The question didn't bother him in the least. He tilted his chin back, finished his beer, and cracked another. "Everything."

"Everything?" She leaned forward and the fire distorted her features. "You can't lie about *everything*. It's impossible because the minute you say you're a liar, you're telling the truth."

"Okay, just that one time then. Caught in the act."

"Lying or telling the truth?"

He had been sitting cross-legged. He unfolded and stood up. "That's as far as I go without my lawyer."

She looked up at him. "What about it? What about the robberies, the antiques missing from summer homes?"

"Ask the law, Karen. It's all we have to go by. What the law says, that's true. What did the law say?"

"What's in the room, Robin? The room at the top of the stairs?"

He took a long drink and dropped down on his haunches. "Nothing at all, dear. Nothing at all."

Now *she* was starting to feel uneasy. She shook her head as if to clear the smoke and start fresh. "Okay, okay. Never mind. I've got a great idea how we can make more money."

"We're doing all right," I said. "Let's not get too fancy."

She'd had I don't know how many beers and I had the impression that she was spilling an idea that she had been keeping to herself for a long time. "Listen now. This is what we can do. We can go down to Mount Desert and set up there. We can run trips two, three times a day all summer and through October. There's something like three million people who go through there in the summer. All we need is a tiny fraction of them and we'll make a fortune!"

He sat back down and took another swig of beer. "You mean, just rent a place somewhere and a slip and make a summer of it?"

"Sure! There are plenty of little places, cottages we could rent. Doesn't have to be anything fancy, just a couple of bedrooms and a kitchen."

As they faced each other over the fire, I shrank back into the shadows. I was getting in over my head. It seemed to me that sharing a house with Karen and Robin would be like lighting up at a gas pump. Jack Crystal's words came back to me. Maybe Karen *was* throwing herself at Robin, and I had no way of telling whether he cared for her or not. He was interested in her idea though. I could see him working on the details in his mind.

"We can have a good solid business going," she went on. "There's no way anyone could have any objection to you."

I wanted to stop her. I thought that the air and the beer were making her say things that she would regret later. I saw Robin's dark eyes watching her from across the fire. He was waiting to see how far she'd go.

She bit into a marshmallow. "I mean we could have a pretty good thing going, you and I—and Amber, of course. We couldn't do it without Amber." She touched me with a sticky fingertip. "Have you spent much time on the island?"

"Not since I was a kid," I said. I remembered visiting Pop's cousins at a place called Raggedy Ass Corner, but I didn't mention that. I said, "It has all those mountains, of course."

Karen waved her arm over the fire, scattering sparks and smoke. "You can be on top of any of them in half an hour. My favorite is Gorham. Climb Gorham for just a few minutes and you can get a sweeping view of the ocean, then go on up Champlain. In August there are blueberries up there like you wouldn't believe and paths that go on and on. Have you been there, Robin?"

He finished another beer. He was used to drinking. It didn't have any effect on him. "Just on that ocean drive," he said. "That road that goes around the eastern side. And to Bass Harbor. I had an uncle that fished out of there till the bank took his boat."

She licked her fingers. "Well, when we go, I'll take you up Gorham Mountain, my favorite place in the whole world, and to Jordan Pond for the sweetest view in the world—and popovers."

I had never seen her so happy, and I was sorry that she had to get that way by drinking too much. "One thing at a time," I suggested. "Maybe we should go down there and check it out, you know, see if we can make it work." I still had plenty of misgivings about the idea of getting more involved with the two of them, and I wanted to buy some time to think out the best thing to do. Robin was thinking, too. I could tell by the way he was watching her. She fell back and propped herself up on her elbows. He smiled and started to reach out to her, but at the sound of an approaching truck, he stood up and backed away from the fire.

The headlights broke into the clearing, swept across us, and then cut back and held us in their glare. Robin stepped into the shadow of a tall pine tree. Karen sat up, shielding her eyes from the light. I stood up, hoping that we could get our way out of whatever trouble was coming. The driver got out and swung a flashlight beam back and forth across the ground as he approached.

Karen struggled to her feet with the aid of a stick too long to put in the fire. When the man came into the light of the fire, I laughed.

"Winthorpe! What are you doing out here tonight?"

He smiled and rubbed the flashlight against his hip, throwing strange shadows into the trees. "I come out here every now and then to make sure we don't have any vandals tearing the place up." He trained his light on the toppled Porta Potty at the edge of the woods. "Last year they tried to set fire to it. Guess that was too much trouble, so they just pushed it over again. Sometimes they'll girdle the trees, stupid stuff like that. Just destructive and expensive. Makes me mad. There's a pack of them around here. We'll catch them and make them work it off if they don't just go to jail." He moved his beam through the shadows. "Hello, Robin. How you doing?"

He moved up to the fire. "I'm all right. The girls and I were just talking a little business."

Winthorpe smiled pleasantly. "I hear you've been doing day trips. Still doing night trips?"

Robin smiled self-consciously and ran his fingers through his wind-blown hair. "That's kind of a loaded question, isn't it? Wouldn't stand up in court."

Winthorpe remained amiable despite the edge he put on what he said. "You've made a study of the law lately, haven't you? Kind of from both sides."

"'Course! It's the law we live by."

"Some of us. But there are some folks around here, really pissed-off, who'd like to get their hands on the ones that see it different. You wouldn't have any information, would you? Stuff stopped disappearing for about six or seven months there, and then last spring it started up again all of a sudden."

Robin remained casual. "They don't usually get stuff in the winter, do they? It's kind of a pain getting in and out on those unplowed roads."

Winthorpe nodded. "And the water's too rough. You think that's all there was to it?"

"It's the simplest explanation. Isn't that the one to go with?"

"Until they get the guy that's doing it. And this time they'll do it right. No paper mistakes." Winthorpe made a motion of turning a key and throwing it away. He looked from Karen to me. She was standing up straight now, although she was still leaning on the stick. I realized that I was blinking a little too fast. "You girls okay?" Winthorpe asked. "You look like you might be more comfortable at home."

He was right about that. My stomach had gone sour and suddenly I felt very tired, even though I was overjoyed that it was Winthorpe who had come out to the point and not someone else.

CHAPTER 13

We continued the day trips on the *Paul D*, the three of us, but something had changed. Karen was edging away from me and moving toward Robin. The way a boat in a mooring field slowly shifts and points in a new direction with the changing wind, she changed toward me, and the boat we shared got smaller and smaller. I had known all along that they could handle the boat business between them, although I was the most creative and aggressive when it came to drumming up "clients" as we called them. I was best at smoothing over difficulties and at dealing with the locals, most of whom knew me or Pop or Brian. I was a sort of lubricant that kept down the friction between Robin and his surroundings—and between Robin and Karen.

That was the paradox—that the more interested they seemed in each other, the more tension there was between them. Maybe it came because they expected more of each other and relied on each other more and were more vulnerable because of each other. Tipsy or sober, Karen was in love with Robin and had lost her judgment where he was concerned. At the end of the day, sitting on her porch or gazing down the river from my yard, we talked about it, we argued about it, and the more I tried to reason with her, the more she defended him. He had become her cause. If he needed help, she'd give it. If he was self-sufficient, she needed him. If he was a thief, she'd reform him—or join him.

"You're crazy," I told her as we walked up from the pier in Eastport with the water darkening in the bay behind us. "You'd throw away your whole future just to tag around with a housebreaker. Karen, there's nothing glamorous in that. There's also the possibility that he'd get sick of you—isn't there?"

She gave me a long, lost look. "Thanks for your vote of confidence."

I held her by the wrist. "It's not about you. It's about *him*. We're talking about a guy who likes to ride with the wind, wherever it takes him. He's not into debutante balls and gallery shows. He's strictly one day at a time. He comes across like prince charming, but otherwise I doubt if he's much different from those other guys on the dock."

She patted my hand. "He's not prince charming. He's Blackbeard—remember? The pirate in my dream."

We had a good time in that boat when the weather was fair and the clients were reasonable. On the long summer afternoons, when the charters were done for the day, we'd go out for a last spin in the bay. Robin would unbutton his shirt, light up a cigarette, and go up into the bow while Karen and I did the sailing. He'd sit with his back to the windward rail and the waves shattering behind him, watching us work the tiller and the lines. When Karen had the helm, she'd do her best to douse him by slapping into the troughs broadside, but he had an uncanny knack for dodging the spray. "Let's see if we can put his cigarette out," she told me more than once as he sat smoking and scheming, but we never could. He was too fast for us.

Sometime after the Fourth of July, I hit upon an idea that had all kinds of promise. I convinced Happy Hal to team up with us for a big promotional campaign. Since his reborn restaurant was right on Route 1, he could advertise our charters and we'd advertise the Brogue 'n' Burr. We could put out a brochure together and offer package deals. Karen put up the money and supervised the layout of the brochure and Robin provided the mystique and adventure. For a discount, you could have lunch at Hal's and an evening cruise with us or take our afternoon trip and have dinner at the restaurant. Several days before opening night, Hal reported excitedly that the new place was already booked.

"Not a reservation to be had," he beamed. "I'm turning people away, if you can believe that. I tell you, I owe a lot to your dad, Karen. He's the one that gave me the inspiration."

She'd been hearing that kind of thing from plenty of other people too. "You'd think that he could cure the lame and make the blind see," she said as we walked to the car one night. "They're making him out to be whatever they want him to be."

"Maybe it's an easy thing to fall into," I said. The night was so warm that I swung my windbreaker in my hand as we walked. "Maybe the main thing is that he made them want *something*. Kind of got them off their own personal ledges."

Hal was so nervous about the big night that he talked me into helping out as a waitress. After the freedom of the water, I wasn't keen on jumping up and down to squeeze into pantyhose and arranging carrot and celery spears on a relish plate, but since it meant so much to him and it was only one night of being cinched in and painted up, I agreed to do it. The getups weren't bad as such things go. They were modeled after sailors' uniforms, white skirts and navy blue tops with white stripes bordering short sleeves and a square collar. Actually, on opening night, fresh and pressed, they looked pretty damn sharp. I had put my hair back with a couple of combs, not Chinese tight, but respectably trim. We looked good, the whole lot of us, six waitresses and Hal, who looked crisp as a crouton in a dark blue double breasted suit that he got at the Immaculate Conception resale in Calais. How deep he was in hock for all that décor I don't know, but he had moved fast, and it all looked classy and the spread looked scrumptious, right down to the last sprig of parsley. He may have been unlucky at business, but when it came to dining, Hal knew how things should be, even if not many of his customers did.

After quite a bit of fretting and scurrying around and last-minute straightening, he swung the doors open at six-thirty, the time when the first twenty-four people were supposed to show up. It was a beautiful evening, the kind that made you hungry, with the sky a pale cloudless blue and a breeze bringing the chilly salt air into the main dining room. Without quite being aware of it, we all stood at attention in our nautical attire that was practically still warm from the iron. I swear you could smell the linen tablecloths and the wax in the candles. After a while I became aware that the two busboys were standing at attention, too, back there by the swinging doors to the kitchen. The chefs were standing by the grill in their poofy white popover hats, as I called them. The salad girl, who was my friend Cherie's kid sister and a video game addict, was thumb-wrestling with the dishwasher. Together we stood there.

Six-thirty passed. You could hear cars passing on Route 1, but otherwise the place was so quiet that I could actually pick out the hissing of the gas jets in the broilers. At about ten minutes to seven, Hal had a look at one of the brochures, and there were plenty of them to look at, that's for sure. He checked the time, he checked the date, I'm sure that he checked to make sure we had put the right *state* on there. Then he tucked the brochure back into its little wooden rack by the front door, folded his arms and stared out at the empty parking lot.

"Maybe the road's blocked," one of the busboys said. The other one had drifted back into the kitchen, where he was now thumb-wrestling with the dishwasher. Cherie's sister was screwing around with her iPod.

"Maybe there's a storm coming," someone offered.

Hal did not bother to adjust his gaze. The clear blue sky was that obvious.

Back at the grill, the chef turned down the burners.

It costs a chunk of change to keep a restaurant open, even for one night. I wondered if Hal could feel himself sinking deeper into debt with every tick of the ship's wheel clock.

"Maybe there's some kind of bug going around," one of the girls suggested. She had been silent so long that her voice was scratchy. "Sometimes they...." Her theory trailed off.

I'd like to tell you that seven o'clock brought some remedy, but it did not. We were there, pressed and dressed and ready to serve, but nobody showed up, nobody.

One by one, the waitresses drifted away. I heard the little pops as the chef turned out one burner after another. One busboy took off his apron and hung it on a chair. The other took off with Cherie's sister.

I patted Hal on his broad, well-tailored shoulder. "I guess these things just happen," I said, and it was about the dumbest thing I ever *had* said, because—first of all—I had *never* heard of something like that happening, where an entire night's reservations disappeared into thin air. And second—I had picked up that phrase *I guess* from Jack Crystal, who had nearly knocked my head in with his goddam lousy driving. I hated that phrase to begin with and here I was saying it at the worst possible moment. What did that mean, *I guess?* In my case it meant that I was a bubble-headed booby lying down and accepting some kind of outrage that was *not* acceptable.

On my way home that night I figured out what had happened. Those scumbags that Robin had put to flight on the pier had done the whole thing to get revenge on Robin by striking at Hal. They'd seen our brochures and called in all of those reservations *themselves,* phoning at different times with different names, probably using stupid put-on voices that Hal was too sweet to suspect. They were clever enough to use names that were plausible, in some cases real last names from the area. Of course, poor Hal had done them no harm, but he was caught in the crossfire. I called him up and clued him in and he wondered why he hadn't thought of that himself, but I didn't. He was just too sunny to imagine that anyone would blow a whole night's business for a prank against somebody they didn't even know.

The next day, when I told Robin, he had no trouble believing it. After all, he knew the people involved.

"Just what do they have against you?" Karen asked as we eased the *Paul D* out of the slip at the marina. "And how far are they likely to go?"

"That was just a start," he said, "just a warning. They'll keep ramping things up till they get their asses thrown in jail." He steered with the tiller while the motor did a slow *puh-puh-puh* through the boatyard.

"Have they tried to get at you before?"

He didn't seem too interested in the question. "They've been around. We used to trash houses together. They haven't shaken the habit yet."

"Isn't that just a waste of time," Karen asked, "if nothing else?"

"They help themselves to a few things on the way out."

"So they're burglars you mean."

"You could say that."

"Were you?"

A sunburned man resting in an approaching rowboat raised a hand to his green cap in salute. Robin waved back. "You really want to know? If—"

I interrupted. "You don't think they'd do anything to Hal's place."

With his free hand Robin undid his top button. "Right on Route 1? No, they're through with him. Like any other joke, it's only good once. He'll be okay."

He was, too. One misty afternoon, Karen and I stopped over for a bowl of chowder and had to wait twenty minutes. Hal was almost too busy to apologize. He passed by, smiling, breathless, balancing plates of lobster salad rolls on each arm, and asked Karen about Walt. "I owe so much to him for just getting me off the dime," he told her. "Give him my best, will you?"

"Sure," she said, adding when he had gone, "maybe I'll bring him over for a little something from the blender."

She wasn't any more cheerful about the other testimonials. As a favor for Mrs. Townsend, we took Peach with us when we went to the bookstore to restock on art supplies. We ran into Maurice and was he ever happy. He had finally "made the move," as he put it, and put his social life in order by coming right out and professing his love for "the dear one," although he seemed to avoid revealing the gender of the object of his affection, which made for some kind of convoluted sentences in his rhapsody. "We have *moved* in together and made our lives one," he reported as Peach jumped up and tried to smell his crotch. "And I waited so long to make my feelings known! Now the object of my affections and I will share every night."

"Does the, uh, object of your affections also do hair?" I asked, trying not to wonder what Peach was finding so utterly fascinating about Maurice's pants.

"Oh, absolutely! Absolutely! We did each other's hair on the first night." He did a little pirouette and Peach dropped down and settled for sniffing his ankle. "Do you like mine?"

It was kind of layered and spiked with pale green highlights. I assured him that I did like it.

He told us to be sure to thank Walt for all the encouragement. When we parted, Peach went after him, thrusting his black nose into Maurice's ankles as if prodding him down the street.

"Nice guy," Karen said when we were finally free, "but he looks like a damn pineapple."

At first I figured that she was just annoyed with his complimenting her father, but the more I thought about it, the more I concluded that she was right, that Maurice *did* look like a pineapple. I have a rule that I never make fun of somebody who has his heart in the right place, which certainly applied to Maurice, but I couldn't shake the image of the talking pineapple. Despite myself I started snickering, then laughing outright.

"You're as wicked as I am," Karen giggled.

I straightened up and looked off toward the pier so as not to crack up completely, and the first thing I saw was the produce department of the little grocery store over there. I lost my composure completely. There was a whole stack of pineapples, several of whom were the spitting image of Maurice. Peach had become enthralled with a fire hydrant. I sank down onto it, wiping tears from my eyes.

Passers-by were starting to stare.

"It's okay," Karen assured them. "She has a vitamin deficiency."

Well, that got me going all over again, and I'm just glad that none of those onlookers knew me. Finally I hoisted myself back into a standing position, wiped my eyes and blew my nose. I let out a sigh. "You're a bad influence," I said.

"Just wait," Karen told me. "Just wait."

I suppose I broke down like that partly because I was worried. Maybe that's why I'm so ticklish in the first place, because it gives me a more or less pleasurable diversion from deeper emotions. I was worried about myself and I was worried about Karen and her family, afraid of what Robin's former friends might do to them—or me—to get back at him.

"So what *do* you think is in the locked room at the fortress?" she asked me one evening, quite out of the blue, as we lay on a quilt in my yard, looking at a hint of the northern lights that glowed green high above the river.

"Right now? Maybe nothing," I said, listening to the soft lapping of the water on the shore. "Maybe he moves stuff in and out of there—after a cooling-off period for each load."

"Do you think he's been getting stuff since, you know, since we've been doing the trips?"

I came up on one elbow. "Who knows, Karen? Why don't you ask him?"

She continued to lie on her back and study the sky. "Maybe that's what pirates are supposed to do."

"Even if it's *your* house that he visits some night and *your* family treasures that go sailing off to parts unknown?"

She looked over at me. "He already has a lot more than that."

I pulled my hair back and held it until my scalp hurt, then let it go. "Karen, have you ever been in love before?"

She seemed not to find the question very interesting. "I don't know, I—no, don't think so. Not until now. Is that good or bad?"

"I'm not sure. Bad I think. It seems to me a little perspective would be helpful here. People fall in and out of love all the time, don't they, without throwing their whole lives away?"

She looked back toward the vague green forms in the sky. "Oh, now you're starting to sound parental, so wise. I suppose you've been in love twenty times."

"No, as a matter of fact, I haven't. And I've never sailed into the Cauldron either because there's all that water out there in the bay that's perfectly good, so why risk everything to go into that one tight little place?"

She sat up, clasping her knees. "Why, why, *why?* Okay, let's play twenty *why* questions. Why did my father leave that part of the yard untouched?"

"Karen, we're not talking lawn care here."

"All right. Why did he come to Ashton in the first place—little old Ashton without so much as a Starbucks or a *New York Times*? Why? Not just to get away from little old Jack Crystal."

I had set something off and I tried to stop it. "All right, just forget it. We don't have to—"

"Little old Ashton. It's so *wild*, Amber. That's what he used to say to his friends down in Boston. 'You wouldn't believe Ashton. It's so *wild*. Not one thing stands quite straight,' he'd say. 'The people may cheat you, but it's worth the price for the entertainment. The people, with their country ways, are so *amusing.*' That's what my saint of a father used to say—that you people were *amusing*. What do you suppose his adoring fans would have to say about that? If they knew that he took them for rubes and dupes and hicks? Do you suppose they'd let him transform their lives?"

Jesus Christ. I could almost see her bitterness spilling out and running across the quilt in a scalding stream. "So you're saying that you're in love with Robin because—what—he amuses you?"

She stood up, brushing the grass from her legs. "No, just the opposite. He may be the first person I've ever met who *doesn't* amuse me."

I stood up too. I was starting to see flashes but they had nothing to do with the northern lights. "And what if *he* finds *you* amusing, Karen?"

She put a barrette between her teeth and her words came out hissing. "I suppose you might like that."

I couldn't believe what I was hearing. "You think *I'm* interested in Robbie?"

She arched a brow and clipped the barrette above her ear.

"Well, I'm not. You can be sure of that."

"You've spent as much time with him as I have."

"Big deal. It was business, mostly."

"Maybe *he's* interested in *you*, Amber. I'm serious."

"For one thing, no, he's not. And for another, I don't care. I don't need a man in my life just now. And I certainly don't need Robbie."

"Oh, you're just in it for the money then."

I picked up the quilt and started to fold it, but instead threw it back down on the ground. "I've been doing it because I *thought* we were friends—all of us. I don't care about the money."

"But you think Robin does."

"Okay—yeah." I had spoken the truth, but I had spoken it too quickly, and I wished at once that I hadn't been so impulsive. I also began to fear that I was wrong.

Karen crammed her feet into her topsiders and marched toward her car. "Okay then, let's just find out. Let's just go ahead and find out."

I stopped and watched her get into the Mustang, turn, and drive toward the road. Shielding my eyes from the headlights, I looked into the night sky one more time, trying to distinguish the dim, unfolding forms there.

CHAPTER 14

The next morning, when we met at the boatyard, it was almost as if our argument had never happened, except that Karen greeted me with a hug and a kiss on the cheek and asked me to forgive her "little flare-up," which she assured me was nothing but an irrational outburst. "Call it the influence of those wild northern lights," she said.

The sailing was routine, except that when we arrived back at the pier in Eastport, our last client of the day gave us a tip in the form of half a dozen lobsters in a bucket of seawater. "What do you say to a boil tonight?" Robin asked. "We can go over to my place and make an affair of it. Then come back by starlight."

We bought some corn on the cob and Waldorf salad and candy bars and beer and sailed back into the bay on a dying breeze. I'd been up by the mast, admiring the beads of light in the east as they came on against the darkening shoreline, and listening to the soft rush of the water against the hull, when I heard a distinct splash from the cockpit. Karen pulled back from the rail, smiling impishly. Robin was looking at her as if she had just lost her mind.

I turned around to face them. "What was that?"

Still smiling, Karen wiped her hands on her thighs. "The one that got away. There are only three of us. We hardly need to massacre six lobsters."

Robin didn't seem impressed. "I can tell you what *they'd* do to *you* if they had the chance."

Karen looked down into the bucket, which stood by the companionway. "Do you know how old a pound-and-a-quarter lobster is?"

Again, Robin didn't seem very interested. "About seven years. All of it spent eating garbage off the bottom, including the carcasses of any fool girls who end up down there."

Karen pulled out another lobster, carefully peeled the rubber bands from its claws, and tossed it into the sea. "Home again, home again."

Now Robin seemed annoyed. "You throw in one more and you might have to go in and get it back. Prices may be down, but those are still worth something, and I'm hungry, even if you aren't."

I wasn't sure what she was up to. Was she just trying to get some kind of response from him, even if it was unpleasant? Or was she edging into the irrational again? I didn't know what to expect, and I wouldn't have been surprised if Robin had tossed her over the side and towed her along on a line until she came to her senses. Instead, he did something completely cool and rational. He relied on the routine to break the spell. "Come back here and take the helm, Karen. I want to make sure the anchor line's clear."

He didn't leave any room for argument. He left the tiller and went forward. Before the boat could point into the wind, Karen took over and Robin hunched over the tangles of rope and chain in the bow. The rest of the ride to Dunning's Island was without incident, and I couldn't help thinking that even though Karen was steering the boat, Robin was steering *her*. I also concluded that while she seemed to enjoy testing him, she seemed downright happy when he took control. I preferred not to think about what the next test might be.

We got a driftwood fire going on the rocks at the foot of the path. Once the water began to boil, Robin put the lobsters in and Karen and I wrapped the corn in foil and arranged it beside the pot. Robin and Karen rolled a birch log against a block of granite and got comfortable and I sat on the overturned bucket across the fire from them. While we were waiting, Robin and Karen got into the candy bars and beer and I had some of the Waldorf salad.

When we were ready to pull out the lobsters, we realized that we had forgotten to get butter.

Karen put the lid back on the pot. "It's not the same without it. "Got any in the house?"

"Not sure," Robin told her. "I don't use it much. Might be some in the icebox." He started to get up.

Karen put a hand on his shoulder. "No, no. I can look. I'm already up." She took a flashlight and started up the winding path, leaving me alone with Robin.

I had plenty of questions for him—about the night raids, about the guys on the pier that were after him, about his feelings for Karen, but he seemed so at ease, sitting on a birch log, leaning back against a granite boulder, that I was reluctant to say anything that might stir him up. On the other hand, the silence was increasingly awkward, so I tried something harmless.

"You remember that boy you knocked over for pushing me down on the playground?"

He made himself more comfortable against the granite, leaned back a little farther. "I remember."

"What do you suppose ever happened to him?"

"He's probably been knocked down a few times since. He wasn't the kind to get the message."

I nodded. "That was very gallant of you since you hardly knew me." The lid to the lobster pot rattled and steamed. The bucket was getting uncomfortable, but I wasn't about to go over and perch on the birch log beside Robin.

"I knew who you were. You were that ticklish girl."

I blushed and lied. "Oh, I got over *that* years ago."

"You had a dog that was always following you to school."

I felt strangely excited that he remembered me at all, let alone those details. After all, I was three years younger.

"What was that dog's name? Something strange—Mixie."

Now I was flabbergasted. How could he possibly remember all of those details? "That's because he was such a mongrel," I said. "We couldn't even tell what breeds he had come from."

"He was crazy about salt, that dog."

"That's right!" I had almost forgotten.

"Whatever happened to him?"

"Oh, he got torn up in the woods," I said. "Tangled with something wild." I couldn't resist asking about the guys Robin had tangled with on the pier. "What do you think they'll do next?"

His eyes flashed white as he glanced up toward the house, where the kitchen light showed through a lace of leaves and needles. "Something to move them along toward Thomaston."

My next question spilled out before I knew what I was saying. "Did you break into those summer cottages? Are you still doing it?"

He came to my side of the fire, picked up a little wisp of bracken and touched it to my chin.

I grabbed it and threw it away.

"You're still ticklish, aren't you, Amber?"

"All right. Yes."

He smiled. "All right. Yes."

"Why, Robbie? We're doing okay with the charters, aren't we?"

He went back to his side of the fire and settled back in. "Everybody's doing okay."

"Oh, sure. Stealing from the rich. You going to tell Karen— or does she already know?"

He took a cigarette from his shirt pocket and lit it. "What do you think she's doing up there in the house—looking for butter?"

I touched the back of my hand. It was hot from the fire. "You *wanted* her to go up and look in that room?"

"I just let nature take its course. She's got quite an imagination, you know—and the curiosity to go with it."

He had her all figured out. He had never said anything until now, but he had her all figured out, right down to her little fits of irrationality. Of course, he knew also that she was in love with him, and now I knew the meaning of that cliché—*madly* in love. The remaining question was what were Robin's feelings toward her? If he threw her over, she might do something dangerous, and if he didn't, there was no telling what the two of them would do together.

Now I had *more* secrets from Karen, and the gap between us widened. I could tell her about Jack's trying to get me to spy on her, but I couldn't tell her what Robin had just said because she would accuse me of trying to keep them apart. I thought about Karen going upstairs, testing the door, finding it unlocked, and discovering a roomful of elegant antiques, stacked floor to ceiling, ill-suited to the rough timbers and cracking plaster of the smuggler's den. What would be her reaction to the proof that the adventurer she was giving herself to really *was* a pirate?

When I saw her coming down the path, I knew that this might be my last chance to ask Robin what he felt for her, but I let it slip, not wanting to be responsible for too much knowledge. What was between Karen and Robin would have to stay between them.

She was cheerful as she came back into the firelight with a stick of butter. "You two been catching up on old times?"

"Talking about dogs mostly," I said, eager to defuse any ideas that she might have gotten. The last thing I wanted was another jealous accusation.

The lobster was delicious, and we ate it shamelessly, with the hot butter running down our chins and forearms. The night air and the rich wash of salt and smoke tinged by the scent of the sea was almost as intoxicating as the beer. We picked up the short history we shared and passed it among us like a knotted cord, talking over the moments that stood out, good and bad, as we ran it through our hands from beginning to end. We laughed like children, without any deeper motive to please or impress. We were hardly more than three wolves baying at the speckled sky. We enjoyed the animal pleasures of the food and the fire until the coals burned low and the night turned black and cold. None of us wanted to make the long, grim trip back, and so it was easy for Karen and me to convince ourselves that to stay would be better, even though we'd have plenty of explaining to do when we got home.

We dragged ourselves up the path to the house. Karen and I shared the musty bed in the room stacked with old cardboard, huddled for warmth under a slippery gold comforter, and slept little, even after the house grew still.

Whether it was a dream or a disjointed sleepless thought I don't know. But as we sailed out in the morning I had this fuzzy image of people sneaking onto the island, shadowy forms creeping up the path, looking in the kitchen windows, testing the locks, and filtering noiselessly through the thick woods. My skin pricked when I thought of them moving down the long curving driveway to Karen's house, sliding past the screen door, and taking their pick of the prizes in the living room.

I was almost glad to call Mom from the marina and tell her about our little sleepover because it made me feel that I had some control.

"It would've been helpful to have some news earlier than this," she said with typical understatement. "Your father was ready to send out the Coast Guard to look for you, but I said you were probably just holed up somewhere having a picnic." In her day, my mother had pulled more than a few stunts. That's why she had an uncanny way of knowing what I was up to, and why she was slow to judge and quick to forgive.

Making the story as boring as possible, I explained what had happened.

"Probably just as well that you didn't try to come back after dark," Mom said. "There's a lot more things can happen once the sun goes down." Her voice had no irony in it, so I was sure that she was talking about sailing and nothing else.

"That's exactly it," I said, smiling at the phone. "I don't suppose you could sort of clear the way for me with Pop?"

"Yes, I can smooth his feathers for you, dear. But don't you go forming any bad habits."

As I hung up, I was looking forward to a successful day on the water, getting home in time for supper, and sleeping in my own bed.

But then, I was clueless.

CHAPTER 15

One benefit of being an apprentice sailor is getting to concentrate on the technical details instead of worrying about bigger issues. I suppose that most of the time Robin could run the *Paul D* in pretty heavy weather without giving much thought to it, but my mind was sunk into the smooth operation of the winches and keeping the lines free, so I wasn't able to dwell on my fear of shadowy men moving in the night. Karen and I hadn't spoken about the locked room, and I couldn't read her face to tell what she had found in it, although I was sure that she had found a key and looked. She went about the business of greeting the clients and giving them the rundown as if nothing had happened. But it was very likely that she knew about Robin now, and knowing seemed not to diminish her feelings for him.

The day was beautiful, our best, although I definitely had my hands full keeping up with the tacking and the rolling while keeping the clients relaxed. Knowing nothing of sailing, they were edgy when we heeled over in the big puffs, but they were also impressed by our seamanship, and they tipped generously, both of the first two sets of voyagers that we took out. As for the third, I'm afraid we were never to know.

Late in the afternoon, we were on our way back from the edge of the Atlantic, pounding along atilt on a brisk breeze. The client was a coin dealer from Littleton, New Hampshire, a slight, nervous little guy who had come to the sea to get his courage up. Whenever Karen bent over, he'd steal a look at her derriere, at least until the return trip, when she put on a windbreaker. He talked a lot about his investments, but it was all Greek to us. We had no idea what "walking liberties" or "bust halves" were and we didn't get around to asking. We just let him go on and nodded as if we were fascinated.

"Speaking of liberties," Karen whispered to me, "did you know that 'the client' has been eyeing your ass all afternoon?'"

I burst out laughing, barely able to whisper back, "I was going to tell you the same thing."

Her giggle was low and throaty. "Well, when he gets home he'll have some interesting pictures to show."

I made a face and laughed again, drawing his attention. "I think I'll go below and get my sweater," I told her. "To wear around my waist."

I was only halfway there, stepping over the cleated lines on the roof of the cabin, when I saw the smoke. It rose in gray wisps off to the south. I wasn't sure where it was coming from, but one look at Robin's face told me. Sensing something wrong, Karen turned around in the bow and stared at the distant disturbance.

"It's probably somebody thinning their woods or clearing a field," she said to no one in particular. "It's probably farther away than it looks."

The client asked what we were talking about, but nobody answered. Robin fell off the wind slightly and sheeted in the main. I dropped down and tightened the jib. I didn't have to look back to know that we were headed for the smoke. We were on a course that was new to me, and I was surprised at how fast we approached Dunning's Island, despite an array of rocks and ledges. When we rounded the last island blocking the view of Robin's house, we saw the flames fingering the window frames of the second story. Black smoke poured from the chimney and scattered in the wind. The ledge was clear, and without slowing down, Robin took us around to the other side of the island, where a jon boat wallowed in the waves just beyond the reach of Ted and his two frantic friends.

Robin took us in close, dangerously close, until he could reach down and grab the trailing painter of the drifting boat. Ted jumped into the water and floundered toward it, but Robin tied the painter to our transom and sailed away before he could catch up. The two on shore swore their lungs out at each other, at us and our ancestors, and most of all at Robin. Then they turned their ferocity toward Ted, who had failed to secure the getaway craft in the first place. When we were out a hundred yards or so, almost beyond hearing them, Robin gave Karen the helm and walked the runaway boat toward the bow. He tied it fore and aft to the *Paul D,* climbed into it, and got the outboard up to full throttle. Then he rejoined Karen and me, pointed the growling, bucking jon boat out to sea, and released the lines.

The thing shot through the curling waves like an aluminum torpedo.

"Holy mother," the man from Littleton said. "Where's that thing going?"

Karen watched it for a while and then said, "France."

"Do you want to drop the sails?" I asked Robin. "We can get to the boatyard faster if we motor in."

"There's no hurry," he said. "There's no hurry now."

I knew what he was up to, and Karen did too, and both of us knew what it was going to cost him. "If he'd have let them go, that might've been the end of it," I said as we went below for coffee and crackers. "What else could they take from him? This way, they'll probably go to jail, but they'll testify against him at every step, try to make another case against him."

"Do you think I was about to stop him?" Karen asked. "Even if I wanted to, do you think I could've stopped him back there?"

She was right, of course. The minute he saw that jon boat drifting loose, he knew that he had those three trapped and convicted of arson.

Before the sun had quite set, Winthorpe and the sheriff had gone over to Dunning's Island and hauled off Ted and his friends. We were watching with binoculars from well out on the water. Not until the threat was removed did Karen and I think to console Robin for the loss of his house.

She stroked his shoulder. "What are you going to do? If you want to rebuild, I can—"

To my surprise, he put his hand on hers and held it. "Actually, if you really want to help, there *is* something you can do—tomorrow night."

That moment became the great divide between us, but for a night I crossed over to their side. I could probably rationalize it by saying that, after all, he had already stolen the antiques locked in the cellar of his house and that I was just helping to move them to a safer place. I could say that I wasn't really sure where the antiques had come from or where they were going. Taking a step further, I could say that I was buying Robin and Karen some time to straighten their lives out when, in fact, I was doing it for Robin because I had fallen under his spell too. I could untangle my feelings for him and put names to them and lay them out to dry in the sunlight, but when I let go, they tangled right up again and led back to that island.

Once we got going, loading the antiques into Robin's boat was about as routine as any other moving job. Most of the downstairs was still standing, but the upstairs was burned stinking black, including the mysterious locked room, which had been *empty* because Robin had already stowed all of the goods in the cellar. Even in the cellar the burned smell gave me a headache, but once we got them outside, the goods seemed none the worse for wear. It was mostly small stuff, vases, mantel clocks, silver tea services, antique toys, china, and a particularly beautiful inlaid end table. As I helped carry it all down to the water's edge, I couldn't help thinking of the pleasure those things had given their owners and how the owners must have felt violated to have their houses broken into and ransacked. If there was any justice in what the guys from the pier had done to his house, it was in making Robin suffer the same way his victims had suffered.

I wanted to say, *we can take it all back, make amends,* but I knew that wasn't going to happen, so I rationalized some more: The treasures were already stolen. I hadn't stolen them. I was just helping to save them from harm, and at least *somebody* would be benefiting from them. Then I put it out of my mind and thought about other things as we marched up and down the path, juggling our flashlights with the valuables, but my mind kept going back to the beautiful inlaid end table, and I couldn't help wanting it even though I knew I couldn't have it and would never be able to enjoy it even if I could somehow squirrel it away in some remote shed. And that very end table is what Karen and I dropped on our way down the path. I let go of my flashlight in a last-second effort to save the table and, as the beam shot a zigzag into the clouds, I heard the sickening crack and splinter of the legs breaking. We both swore and scrambled around in the bracken and rocks trying to get a good look at the damage, but I knew right away that at least two legs had broken off and that the little table had lost its value forever. My first impulse was to take it into the garage and adopt it, to fix it as well as I could and take care of it always as penance for my crimes, but I knew what a damning piece of evidence it would be.

"Take it on down," Robin said without interest as he passed by with an elegant black vase painted with orchids. "We'll put it in the boat with the rest."

"You can't sell it," Karen told him as she scooped up the severed legs.

"Damn straight. Come on. Let's go. We don't have any time to waste."

I would have found his callousness annoying if it weren't for the urgency in his voice. He believed that the sheriff's deputies might already be on their way over to check out the claims made by the arsonists, claims that Dunning's Island was again a stopover for stolen goods and that this time Robin Dunning might well be clapped into prison without the benefit of a legal loophole.

It was tiring work, as much because of the anxiety as for the physical exertion of carrying things down to the rowboat, but Robin and Karen seemed tireless. Robin would climb into the rowboat and ferry the larger items, one or two per trip, to the *Paul D*, he and Karen would haul the items aboard, and he'd row back for the next load while I brought some of the smaller things down to the end of the path. For the bigger ones, we'd both go up to the cellar. I was always thinking that I heard a boat approaching and that we'd be caught with the goods. If that happened, no amount of explaining on my part would spare my family and me from the shame. I might even be implicated in Robin's earlier marauding and, worse still, linked to the thugs from the pier. I could imagine all kinds of rumors echoing through Ashton for years, even after my release from prison.

The closer we got to finishing, the faster I worked and the more impatient I became when Robin and Karen seemed to take too long loading the boat.

Robin stood up in the rowboat and waved me over. "Time to change positions. Come on, Amber. You and I will load while Karen brings stuff down."

When we got to the boat, she started to argue, but saw that it was pointless. I barked my shin on an oar as we traded places and, without breaking stride, helped Robin carry a handsome little cedar chest into the cabin while Karen began rowing for shore.

"Careful," Robin said as I backed down the cabin ladder, "this will fetch something pretty if we don't ding it up."

I thought, how nice that he was so concerned about other people's property. "Maybe you should've been a professional mover," I said.

Without looking up from the chest, he smiled. "Maybe I am."

We moved a few things around in the cabin and, as we came back out, I watched Karen on the shore, moving the flashlight over the treasures at the foot of the path. "How far are you going to go with this" I asked Robin.

His reply was casual, as if it were common knowledge. "There's a place just this side of Mount Desert. A guy that's got a dock on one of those roads that loops off of Route 1."

I found it charming that he shared the information so readily, but I had something else in mind. I nodded toward Karen. "I meant, how far with *her?*"

He looked at me as if I'd committed some breach of etiquette. "That's kind of up to her, isn't it?"

"Not entirely." It felt like a breach of confidence, but it seemed important to add, "She's a little out of control. I'm sure you've noticed that."

He backed down the ladder into the cabin and wrapped the black vase in a towel. "Whatever do you mean by that, Amber?"

I followed him down. "I mean, she can't resist this piracy crap any more than you can resist stringing her along with it, any more than you can resist *doing* it. Why not give her a break and leave her now? We've all had some fun."

With more strength than I thought he had, he picked up the cedar chest and carried it into the v-berth. He cleared a place for it with his foot and set it down. Slightly out of breath, he came back through the crowded cabin. "She can make her own decisions same as anyone else. If she makes a mistake, she'll learn from it. You've made mistakes, haven't you, Amber?"

Mistakes? More and more, I was thinking that tonight was the king daddy of them. I backed away as he went up the ladder. "Do you care about her, care what happens to her?" I asked. "Do you love her, Robin?"

He went straight for the rowboat. "With not more than two hours to dawn, we don't have the time to talk. If you see a little light coming this way fast, we'll all have *plenty* of time to talk—but we'll be in different cells."

He had made me nervous enough to put Karen's future out of my mind. I was more concerned about my own. Tired as I was, I moved faster and faster. We all did. We hauled and rowed and loaded without so much as a pause for water or any other comfort. When we wrestled the last box of Waterford crystal into the cockpit, the sky was already fading to gray above Eastport. The boat was so full that Karen and I had to sit forward of the mast. Robin had spread a couple of spare sails over the treasure. He fired up the motor, and we headed toward Karen's house because it was the safest place for him to drop off his accomplices. I was tired and cold and increasingly nervous, sitting up in the bow, watching boats trace across the bay in the early morning. I thought of various stories I could use if we were apprehended, but they became more and more far-fetched, and before we were halfway there, my imagination went numb, so that all I could do was admire the flat gray clouds tinged with pink and follow the flights of hungry gulls. Robin looked comfortable with the danger. He lounged against the transom, steering with a couple of fingers on the tiller. He was apparently unaffected by the cold because he was wearing one of his familiar Hawaiian shirts.

I wanted to talk to Karen, but I didn't want to raise my voice above the drone of the motor, didn't want to call attention to us, and didn't want to have my words carry across the water—or back to the stern. So I sat clasping my knees, staring toward the widening mouth of the river to the place where we would break free from our crimes.

When we had climbed into the rowboat and gotten to the stone steps, instead of throwing the painter back to Robin, Karen wrapped it around the upright. "Wait here," she told Robin, "I'll be back in five minutes."

"Five minutes," he repeated, making it sound like a guarantee that he would be gone in six. He sprawled back and folded his arms.

I wasn't sure what I was supposed to do, but I wanted to get as far as possible from that boatload of stolen goods, and so I followed her up the steep steps to the yard, glancing back once to make sure that Robin was still waiting. Ahead we could see the corner of the garage, enough to tell that the Mercedes was gone.

Karen hurried up the path. The wild patch was dim in the shadow of the woods. She picked up her pace on her way to the porch. "Damn her," she said. "Now she can't even wait till breakfast to take off with her lover."

Mrs. Conditt met us at the French doors. "Heavens, were we ever worried about *you*—both of you."

Karen brushed past her. "I suppose my mother is out, personally dragging the river."

I tried to be reassuring. "We were fine. Just had kind of a breakdown."

We swooped into the living room, which was strangely empty for the breakfast hour.

Karen glanced into the vacant kitchen. The familiar captain's chair was unoccupied. "Where's my father?"

"He went with your mother. They left about half an hour ago, for Bangor."

"Bangor." Karen was impatient and annoyed. "I suppose this is the day for his checkup."

"Yes, they were going down to Eastern Maine Medical Center, thought it would take most of the day. She was terribly worried about you."

Karen began pacing like a trapped cheetah. She was weighing a decision of some kind, and she knew that Robin would wait only so long. "All right. Things are screwed up good. So what else is new?" She was leaving fragmentary damp footprints on the Persian rug. "Damn. Why does everything always have to go to hell?"

I noticed for the first time that Mrs. Conditt had a dishtowel in her hand. She folded and unfolded it as she watched Karen make her rounds.

I was starting to ask if I could help somehow when Karen came to a conclusion. "All right. All right! I'll be the noble one." She motioned toward the screen door. "Come on. Let's go say good-bye."

We went back across the yard almost as fast as we had come up, only this time, instead of being in a hurry, Karen was simply mad. Somehow her parents, even in their absence, had gotten her worked up again, and I could only guess what had set her off. "Look, if there's anything I can do…." My voice trailed off as I waited for her to explain.

At the top of the stone steps she thumped the wooden rail with the heel of her hand. "You can put Walt right here—can you do that? Put him right here instead of in Bangor so I can say something to him. How about doing that for me, Amber?"

I put my hand on top of hers and stopped. Below, at the end of the rail, Robin waited in the rowboat. Beyond was his boatload of swag. My voice came out a shrill whisper. "You were going to go away with him, weren't you? You were going to say good-bye to Walt and go off with that *pirate* down there. Only Walt being in Bangor wrecked your plan. Does Robin know?"

She pulled her hand away. "Who cares? He would've found out soon enough."

"At least this way you have a little more time to think about it," I said, following her down the steps. "This may be the biggest favor Walt's ever done for you."

"Whose grandmother *are* you, Amber? Haven't you ever dared to think big?"

I got loud. "Big? Karen, *anybody* can think crazy. It's easy to throw everything away—not so easy to get it back later."

She didn't bother to look back. "I wouldn't know. I never had all that much to throw away. Is that so hard to believe? Trophies aren't everything."

She was more and more like that horse that had run away with me, blind, wild, self-destructive—and willing to knock over anything in her way.

"Looks like this is it," she told Robin as she reached the foot of the steps. "I suppose you'll be gone for a while."

Despite the danger, he looked sleepy. He was rumpled and unshaven, and his curly hair seemed to have grown a week longer during the night. In the golden morning light, with the water reflecting in his eyes, he was strangely beautiful, like some exotic sea creature caught in the glint of early morning and not likely to be seen again. He waited for her to cast off the painter and when she didn't, I loosened the loops and tossed the line to him. He shoved off with an oar and the rowboat floated free.

Karen had pulled her windbreaker about her. She stood at the foot of the steps, her arms crossed against her chest. "How long do you think?"

He dipped the oars into the water and settled into a rhythmic stroke. "Long as it takes."

The tide was going out and, with the help of the current he was soon tying on to the *Paul D*. By the time we got up to the yard, he had climbed aboard and started the motor. He didn't put it in gear, just drifted with the current and the tide as if defying Ashton for the last time.

Karen and I walked the edge of the yard. She stood so close to the edge that I thought a passing puff could throw her into the river. She was either unaware or unconcerned. Pretty patterns in the water played across her face. Her hands, still clasped to her shoulders, had gone to fists, and her strawberry blond hair fluttered across her forehead. She looked like the figurehead of some old sailing ship, jutting out over the waves at the outset of a grand enterprise. Only she was bound to this ledge at the mouth of the river as the ship ventured forth without her.

She dove, of course. For her whole life, she had been swimming as if to practice for this moment, and now she was surfacing and swimming as she had never swum before. She might have overtaken the boat even if Robin hadn't swung around to pick her up. The retrieval wasn't graceful or glamorous, but at least he didn't use a grappling hook to haul her in. I saw her wave and heard them laughing until distance and the increased pitch of the motor drowned them out. I watched them for a long time as they faded into the bay, watched them until I lost them in the crisscrossing of boats in the distance. Then I felt cold and tired. With a growing headache, I went back to the house and phoned my father to come pick me up.

CHAPTER 16

I don't mind telling you that during the next several days I spent plenty of time crying. I had this dream in which I was on Dunning's Island again, standing alone in the smoke of the burned-out house. I had no way to get off, and far ahead I could see a boat, no more than a silhouette gliding toward the rising sun, with Robin and Karen drinking champagne from a black vase. The boat got smaller and smaller, but it never disappeared completely. Behind me, through smoke and fog, I could barely make out Ashton, scattered along the mouth of the river and stretching out on the two necks of land on either side. I could see Mom and Pop and Brian working on the house. Mom was carrying clothespins in her mouth and Pop and Brian were sawing one-by-fours and taking them into the house. Somehow I was able to follow them as they went upstairs. The clothespins in Mom's mouth turned into nails that she handed to Pop and Brian as they laid the boards across my bedroom door and sealed it up.

For a few days I didn't know how to pull myself out of it. At least I had some diversions to take my mind off my troubles. Brian was supposed to have an interview with the yacht yard down on Mount Desert, but he had blown it off when he came home late from a fishing trip with some of his football friends. At first my parents didn't have anything to say about the setback, although you could tell that they weren't thrilled. But things heated up pretty quickly. "What did you catch?" Pop asked with folded arms. They were in the living room and, over Pop's shoulder, through the new picture window, you could see the river that had lured away Brian and his friends.

"Didn't get that far," Brian said vaguely.

"Didn't get to the fish?" Pop asked. "Wasn't that the idea? Isn't the river full of them?"

"Well, we had a problem with that new motor of yours."

Pop boomed. "What's *wrong* with my new motor?"

Brian put his hands in his pockets, pulled them out and wiped them on the hips of his jeans. "Nothing. Last time I saw it."

"The last time you *saw* it?"

"The motor was fine. It was the mounting bracket that was no good. We were most of the way to Eastport when I dropped the motor down to get a little more speed and it, uh, it kept going."

Pop jabbed his finger toward the front window. "My *new* motor is in the bottom of the goddam river?"

Brian was a little unsteady on his feet. "Well, that would be the place."

My mother couldn't help intruding. "Just be glad he wasn't hanging onto it, Frank."

I thought that Brian's transgressions would dwarf my own, so I picked that day to confess. It seemed to me that, even agitated as he was, Pop might be the more distracted of my parents, and so I made a point of tagging along when he went out to the garage to cut some new braces for the laundry room floor. "One of these days that damn washing machine's going to drop right through the planks," he said, sawing neatly along his pencil mark. "I just hope I'm not under there trying to prop it up when it does."

I couldn't think of a delicate way to get to the matter at hand, so I cut right to it. "Pop, I committed a crime the other night."

He looked up from his mark to see if I was kidding. "Wouldn't have anything to do with Master Robin Dunning, would it?"

He already knew or had guessed more than I realized. "I helped him move some stuff."

Pop stopped long enough to blow the sawdust from his mark. 'What kind of *stuff?*"

I shrugged. "Oh, all kinds. You know. Antiques."

Pop nodded. "I figured he had some."

I was hoping that he'd ask me more questions, but he was making me do all the talking.

"Karen and I helped him haul the stuff out of the cellar after his house burned down. We loaded it onto his boat."

"I suppose that was better than letting it sit there in the cellar hole. Lucky that he could catch the ones that burned the house down."

"Yeah, but he had to move those antiques fast, before word got out that they were there."

The end of the two-by-four clattered onto the cement floor. Pop picked up another board and put it on the sawhorses. "I suppose so, somewhere down the coast most likely."

"Karen went with him."

"Wanted to be helpful, huh?"

"Not exactly. She's in love with him, or something. When he left, she jumped off the ledge and swam after his boat."

Pop nodded. "Good swimmer, is she?"

"That's kind of beside the point, isn't it?"

"Not if she's going to be with Robbie. She might have to jump ship at any time."

I jumped back as the end of the second board clattered on the floor. "So what do you think my legal status is?"

He picked up the two-by-fours and propped them on the sawhorse. He put a hand on my shoulder. "Legal's one thing and ethical's another. You can get away with one and run afoul of the other. If you've been running with Robbie, you might consider retiring."

"You can be sure of that. I feel tainted, like that time on Rush Island that Cherie and I smoked all those cigarettes."

Pop blew the sawdust from the end of the two-by-four. "When was *that?*"

"What? Oh never mind." Was I losing it? I'd forgotten that I'd never told anyone.

"What are we going to do for excitement around here?" he asked. "Come September, it's going to be awful quiet. Now where the hell did I put that pencil?"

So much for my confession. I pulled it from behind his ear. "Oh, don't worry," I said. "At the rate I'm saving money, it's going to be years before I go off to grad school."

I did make a few dollars from Mrs. Townsend, but not in the usual way. For a good three weeks now, she hadn't given a hoot about having her hair done. All she wanted in Eastport was painting supplies, and so we went in and cleaned out the bookstore again.

The owner of the place smiled as he rang up her purchase. "You must have a wicked good collection by now. You can start your own art store."

"My own *gallery*," Mrs. Townsend assured him. Her hair was starting to lose some of the lacquered look Maurice had given it. I wasn't sure if I preferred the limp, more natural look.

Her pictures were something else again. They were portraits of various people, none of them recognizable, who bore a strange resemblance to prunes. I think she was trying to capture the look of faces creased by our Downeast weather, but their complexions were a little too dark and the creases were not exactly natural. Clearly Mrs. Townsend was following some inner muse, and there was no telling where the trail would end. She was productive, too. She had canvases stacked all over the house, framed, unframed, finished, unfinished—a whole gallery or produce department full of prune faces staring at you from the floor, the furniture, the walls. She even had one sitting on the toilet tank. At least, wherever she went, she wouldn't be lonely. She said she was building up to doing a portrait of her beloved Paul.

"Well, what do you think?" she asked me one day, her hand on her hip and Peach yipping his head off.

I was kind of stuck, but I blurted out something that surprised even me. "What if you were to make them a little more abstract," I suggested. It was a strange thing to say, but it seemed to me that Mrs. Townsend's faces fell into that gray area between realism and something else, making me wonder what would happen if she went for something that was an object in itself instead of a fruit-like representation of something else.

I swear, she and Peach both turned and stared at me. It was the craziest damn thing you ever saw, both heads swiveling around at the same time. I thought she was going to throw me out the window, but instead she said, "I think you've put your finger on it, dear. I think that's what the muse has been trying to tell me, but I just haven't been listening." She came right over and kissed me on the cheek, or tried to, but I turned at the last second and so she got me on my earlobe, which was very ticklish.

I wriggled free and said, "Then I suppose we'd better get into Eastport and pick up some materials for the new masterpieces."

On the way in, she gave me a little lecture. "Now, I know that you were only kidding, Amber, but don't go getting the idea that my art is going to be *recognized* for what it is. I mean, unless maybe if I cut an ear off to get a little attention. But I'm doing this just because it's *me.*" She made a vague gesture with her sinewy, marbled hands. "Most of the art in this world passes unrecognized and so what? What's recognition? It just means you make a few bucks, maybe a lot of bucks, from hawking your stuff to people who probably don't understand it anyway. It's all wide of the mark. God, what I wouldn't give for a cigarette. I don't suppose you—well, anyway, this is the real thing. This is straight from the muse. You can forget selling out—commercialism, licensing, that kind of selling out—because that's not what I'm about."

Peach went into one of his barking fits, prompting Mrs. Townsend to turn and quiet him with a slushy *shush!*

I couldn't find a place to park near the bookstore, so I doubled back and was presumptuous enough to pull into Maurice's "customers only" lot. What a disaster that was because he saw us coming and assumed at once that Mrs. Townsend had at last returned for a hair job. He hurried up to us, taking those funny little geisha steps of his, as if his platform shoes were pinching him.

"Mrs. Townsend, Mrs. Townsend, I thought that you had *croaked.*" He was out of breath, even though he had only gone about twenty feet. "Where have you *been*, dear?" He put his hand to his chest. "I would've called you if I had your number."

Peach became fascinated with the cuffs of Maurice's pants.
Mrs. Townsend wrapped the leash around her bony fist and
yanked him away. "I don't give my number to just anybody," she
said. She looked up at the hairdresser and batted her eyelashes.
"The men would never leave me alone. Of course, in *your* case I
ought to make an exception."

With a little flip of his hand he dismissed the flattery, if that's
what it was. "Well, I'm *so* glad you're here now! Come on in. I
want you to meet Reginald."

Mrs. Townsend stood her ground. "I'd love to, dear, but I'm
afraid I'm on my way to the bookstore—to buy art supplies."

His look of disappointment changed to one of excitement.
"No."

"Yes! Yes, indeed. I'm finally acting on the urge."

"Well, I certainly know how *that* is," he said, cocking a brow.
Maurice's eyebrows were so expressive that they could've had
their own names.

Mrs. Townsend's voice broke as she gave Peach another yank.
"I'm doing portraits, and I'm about to make a breakthrough."

"Me too!" Maurice pulled away from Peach's inquiring nose.
"And it's all because of Walt, isn't it? That wonderful, wonderful
Walt. When will you be bringing him back for a touchup?"

"That's a little complicated," I said. "Family issues."

Maurice looked pained. "Oh, and what a shame! Such a nice
man."

"His daughter is AWOL," Mrs. Townsend declared. "It's a
terrible thing."

"Oh, how *could* she—with such a wonderful dad?"

I could imagine Karen seething as they piled on the adulation.
They talked of others whose lives had been restarted by Walt's
magic. Hal, of course, practically owned the stretch of Route 1 at
the cutoff into Ashton. He was even thinking of opening a gift
shop where the sardine outlet store used to be. Hal swore
repeatedly that he owed everything to Walt for getting him off the
dime, out of the doldrums of business failure and into the business
of living his dreams.

Maurice and Mrs. Townsend shared other stories. She knew
of a real estate salesman somewhere around West Pembroke who

was in such a terrible slump that he couldn't sell a life ring to a man overboard. He went over to the Sterlings' and just sat next to Walt for fifteen minutes, didn't say a word. Then he got up and went out and started signing deals on property that didn't even have road access, sold boulder fields to farmers and bogs to homebuilders.

They spoke of the checkout girl at the home furnishing store outside of Eastport, how she had gotten up the gumption to move out of her parents' house at the age of thirty-seven and had met a plasterer and become engaged after a whirlwind courtship. The couple was planning to get married at the end of the construction season and restore the waterlogged Cape Cod out by the gas station, a place that just needed a good airing out and a few hundred pounds of plaster that could be bought at a discount by a person who knew the right place to get it.

Maurice and Mrs. Townsend could've stood there swapping marvelous stories all afternoon, but Peach was developing some urgent needs and was being none too subtle about them. "You know I'll be hurt if you don't come in for your usual," Maurice said.

Mrs. Townsend coughed and promised that, yes, she would be in as soon as she had her current canvas finished. "Then I'll be putty in your hands," she said. "In the meantime, you wouldn't have a smoke, would you?"

Peach was becoming quite embarrassing now and, with no further pretence of dignity, she jerked him away from Maurice's ankles and turned sharply toward the bookstore.

I looked back in time to see Maurice wave cheerfully. *"You ought to come in, Amber. I think we could do great things together."*

I nearly got myself run over by a chartreuse Volkswagen. "That'll be the day!" I called back. "My hair is just *there*— straight, streaky, stringy!" I wasn't being modest. It was the truth. I was just plain old brown-haired me no matter how you dressed me up. At the senior prom, when all the other girls were doodled up beyond recognition, I wore my hair the usual way, except for a few Bobbie pins to keep it out of my face when Fred and I danced. Well, I needn't have worried because for the fast dances

Fred moved to about every third beat of the music, shaking and jiggling like the agitator of a Maytag, and for the few slow dances he just kind of stood there and undulated like an aquatic weed.

The afternoon was pretty well shot by the time I got Mrs. Townsend back home. I was still coming down the front walk when I heard the phone ringing. Mom met me at the screen door and told me that Jack Crystal had been trying to get me for the last two hours.

"We've all talked to him," she said, "and I don't think he believed any of us when we told him we didn't know when you'd be back. Kind of a strange duck, isn't he?"

He was also nervous. "I would appreciate it very much if you could come over for a talk." He laughed awkwardly through the crackle in the line. "Don't worry. No car ride this time."

I asked why he wanted to see me, but he wouldn't say.

CHAPTER 17

Pop was overdue for a water district meeting in Eastport, so Brian volunteered to run me out to the cottage in the Whaler, whose new motor had been retrieved at considerable cost from the bottom of the river. I took him up on his offer because I had something I wanted to say to him. When we were about halfway across, I let him have it.

"I can't believe you blew off your interview with the yacht yard," I said.

He revved up the motor and drowned me out. "How's that?"

We slapped over the water so hard that I had to hang onto my back teeth. "Just forget it," I said, although I knew that I was completely inaudible. Then I got mad. I raised my voice, exaggerating the words so that if audio failed, he could read my lips. "It was *dumb* of you to be out fishing when you were supposed to be interviewing with the yacht yard! A lot of people around here would break a leg for a chance like that." He started to rev up some more, but I reached back and grabbed his arm. "Are you just thinking to hang around here all your life? Are you just going to play mud ball with your pals till you're fifty years old?"

"Aw, lay off," he said. "We lost the motor, that's all!"

He took his hand off the lever just long enough for me to reach over and drop our speed. The Whaler settled abruptly and the river swirled around us. I braced myself against the seat to keep from falling overboard. "I mean it, Brian. You got an appointment to see them again?"

"Of course I do!" He eased the speed back up.

I was encouraged. "Promise me you'll make it happen this time?"

He shrugged. "There's no guarantee that they'll hire me, you know. It's just a preliminary kind of thing."

"Are you worried that they'll look you over and turn you down?"

"I'm not worried about *anything*." He gave the lever another twist and we shot toward the far shore.

What if he should talk to Walt, I wondered, but I couldn't see it. Somehow it didn't seem right.

As we approached the Sterlings' mooring we could tell that something there wasn't quite right. The *Sea Clip* was on the mooring ball there for some reason, and riding so low in the water that at first I thought she'd sink like granite before we even got to her. We tied up and climbed aboard and went below to have a look. I was relieved to see that the cabin floor was dry, but the boat had a pungent smell about her, the reek of trapped seaweed and rotting fish.

From the foot of the ladder, I watched Brian poke around under cushions and compartment covers. "What's happened?"

"She's got a leak in her somewhere, but at least it hasn't come up here yet."

For the first time, I was struck by how much he sounded like Pop. "Well, what can we do?"

He didn't turn around, just stooped down and ran his hand along the seams in the deck. "Get her back to the marina, that's what. Then fix the leak before she goes to the bottom." Again, pure Pop.

I wasn't about to admit that I was aching with curiosity about Jack's urgent need to see me, so I just said that I was past due up at the house.

"I'll entertain myself down here," Brian said on his way back to the cabin. "Just don't be gone all day."

I got the Whaler started on the second try and motored over to the stone steps without incident. Jack came to the door almost before I set foot on the porch. I could tell he was very eager to see me. As he ushered me to a chair in the living room I saw Mrs. Conditt and Walt at the kitchen table. Walt was at his usual place at the end and she was bending over him trying to talk him into eating his blended lasagna.

"What's the matter?" I asked as we took our places in the oversized living room chairs. "Has something happened to Wal— to Dr. Sterling?"

Jack seemed to find my gaffe amusing, but he looked too drained to smile outright. His hair was dark against his pasty face. He looked like he needed sleep. He sat down at the edge of the couch. "Dr. Sterling is fine—as fine as ever anyway. We've called you here to talk about Karen. Can you tell us where she is?"

I thought it was strange for him to say *we* when Geneva was nowhere in sight, but I thought over an answer to his question, putting my mind back to Karen's dive into the river and her powerful strokes as she swam to Robin's boat. After too long a pause I said, "I haven't seen her since the last time we were here."

Jack nodded. "She went away with that boy—Robin."

I could hardly deny it, but I wasn't about to go into the details.

"And do you know where she—where *they* went?" Jack sat forward, crossed one knee over the other and clasped it with interlocked fingers as if to say that nobody was going anywhere until I had answered all of his questions.

Somewhere out on the river a kicker boat sped toward the bay. I decided to give Jack just about everything I had. "Robin was going toward Mount Desert. I suppose they went down that way."

I must have glanced toward the stairs just then because Jack explained that Geneva was feeling unwell and was resting in her room, leading me to wonder if she was distraught about Karen's disappearance.

"Mount Desert," he repeated, "any idea just where and for how long?"

"Mr. Crystal," I said, "I didn't even know Karen was going until she took off." I tried to imagine how that voyage had gone. Had it turned into a romantic sunset cruise or had the water beyond the bay thrown Karen into a fit of doubt or seasickness or—worse still—had Robin been the one throwing up over the transom? Sailing was one of those things that could look so glamorous from a distance, when up close it could be a matter of nausea, chills, leaks, the smell of sickening fumes, and bickering. Even if the trip had gone well, there was no telling where Karen had gone. If the trip had gone badly, she could be anywhere.

Jack seemed to be making his mind up about something. Back in the kitchen Mrs. Conditt had finally gotten Walt to drink some of his lasagna. She was saying something in a reassuring tone and washing the blender.

"Do you think that you could find Karen," Jack asked, "if you had to?"

"Around here do you mean?" I wondered if he was implying that she was hiding out at my house.

He sat even farther forward on the couch. *"Anywhere."*

I heard Brian whistling out on the *Sea Clip*, and I had the feeling that we needed to close this conversation before he started yelling for me to bring the Whaler back, but I was at a loss. "I really don't understand," I said.

Jack put his fingertips together. "It's very simple, Amber. We need to find Karen—not tomorrow or the day after—*today*. And we're willing to do whatever's necessary to find her. You've spent half the summer with her. You know something about her—her dreams, her desires. In fact, right now you probably know more about her than anyone else in the world— including her analyst." He glanced toward the yard and then looked steadily at me. "So we're asking you to find her, whatever it takes. I take it you're still saving money for grad school?"

"Trying to." I hadn't been doing a very good job of it.

Jack pulled a handkerchief from his coat pocket and wiped his hands with it. "Well, as the executor of more than a few estates, I know something about grad school expenses—tuition, books, room and board, travel. I believe you said you were hoping to attend at Orono?"

"Sure," I said. "Hoping to."

He put the handkerchief back in his pocket. "Find Karen for us within the next two weeks and we'll cover the first year for you. How's that?"

I started to go on about how I intended to go to Mount Desert to make some serious money before the season ended, and then I realized what he had said.

"Just give us an estimate and we'll cut a check the minute Karen comes into the house. If it turns out not to be enough, we'll make up the difference. If it's too much, you can keep the difference."

Suddenly, finding Karen seemed a lot more possible. In fact, I saw that finding Karen could *be* my summer job, whether it took a day or two weeks. But then the doubts came crowding in. *Why* did Jack want to find Karen? What if Karen didn't *want* to be found? What if she was actually trying to get away from Jack? Then I'd be betraying her. After all, if she came back to Ashton, there was a chance that she'd be arrested for helping Robin to sell stolen merchandise. That thought struck even closer to home. If she could be arrested for helping Robin, so could I because I had been on the island all night, moving those antiques from the burned house to Robin's boat.

From his wallet Jack took five hundred-dollar bills, about two weeks of shouldering trays at Happy Hal's. "You'll have some expenses," he said. "So this is to get you started. Bring her back, no questions asked, and you'll have a cashier's check for the rest." He stood up and put the money on the coffee table, bills so pristine that they stuck together. The generally bumbly Mr. Jack Crystal was in command of the situation now. He was on familiar ground, and I certainly was not, not being accustomed to having things happen by dint of cash on a coffee table.

I held the crisp bills tight in my fist, spoiling their newness before I realized what I was doing. They had the salty smell of a new deck of cards. "Wouldn't it be easier and cheaper just to have the police look for her?"

Jack had a ready answer. "Not if she's with a probable felon. Frankly, Amber, we want to avoid any legal problems Karen might have—at least for now. Also, we want her to be approached by someone she trusts. If she sees the police coming after her, she might well bolt and be out of our reach forever."

He said that word *forever* with a catch in his throat. I wanted to ask what was going on, but the money overwhelmed me, and anyway Brian broke the spell by rapping on the front door. I heard him telling Mrs. Conditt about *Sea Clip*.

Ever impatient, he had fished the little dinghy out of the v-berth and rowed himself to shore.

"If you leave her there like that for another week she'll go to the bottom," he said. I was kind of annoyed because I think he was mistaking Mrs. Conditt for Geneva.

She told him that Geneva had asked a man from the marina to bring it over to determine its seaworthiness, which proved to be not so great.

"And there it sits," she said, "until Mrs. Sterling decides what to do with it."

Jack got up and went to the door to talk to Brian, and I took the opportunity to go into the kitchen and see Walt. He was sitting in the same red-bottomed captain's chair, one hand on the edge of the table, the other trailing at his side. All of Maurice's magic had been washed from his hair, although Mrs. Conditt had left her mark. He had a lasagna stain on his collar and a little glob of meat sauce on his forehead. I sat down beside him and put my hand on his. I told him that I probably wouldn't be seeing him for a while. "I'm thinking that it's going to take me some time to find that daughter of yours," I said. "I just hope it's all for the best." I went over to the sink to get something to clean off the lasagna. "I'll be back just as soon as I can and maybe everything will come out okay, you know? Maybe everything will be the way it was. Who knows? Maybe better." I could hear Jack and Brian talking on the porch. I wondered if Brian had declined an invitation to come in or if Jack had just gone out there to talk to him. By the squeaking on the stairs I figured that Mrs. Conditt had gone up to talk to Geneva. "Looks like you have this town turned on its ear," I told Walt. "I don't know how it's happening, but it sure seems to be for the best. I just wish you could work your same magic on Karen, you know, get her off her ledge, but I don't think she believes in your powers. Maybe that's the way it tends to be, though. I mean, it seems to me that even Jesus had some problems with doubters in his family. Anyway, to tell the truth, I really don't know where to look for her, especially now that she's with Robin, but I've got to try. I don't know what's up, but I'll trust Jack that far, take his word for it that it's something important. I'm almost glad that you're not clued in on it, whatever it is. That way you can be the same old Walt. But I know that Karen wants to see you again."

He looked up at me. "I want to see *her*."

I dropped the dishtowel and looked around the kitchen to see who else had come into the house. I had heard a soft, determined, childlike voice that squeaked like an old swing. "Jesus Christ," I said, "you *talked*, Walt!" I came back to the table, sat down beside him and squeezed his warm, thick hand. I looked into his downcast blue eyes without seeing any flicker of meaning in them. Had he come out of his long dream enough to hear what I had said about Karen and respond to it or had he responded to some fragment of a conversation remembered from fifty years ago? Either way, I was excited and happy because I was one of those few that had heard him. Even though they weren't much to hang onto, I had those words as a kind of souvenir of Wal—no, of Walter Weston Sterling, the distinguished geneticist, physician, and author.

My rhapsody was cut short by dry rot. That was one of the things that Brian was telling Jack about, although he suspected more dire problems for the *Sea Clip*.

"Somewhere down below she's probably bubbling up like the spring on Route 1," he said. "Probably in the stuffing box for starters." He stopped just short of saying that the boat had been neglected for far too long, that the Sterlings and the marina had been remiss in their care of her. He didn't even know that Jack had done his part by running the kicker boat into her.

Suddenly everybody was in a hurry. I gave Walt a quick peck on the cheek, bellowed out a promise to call him often—by which I was telling Jack that I would give him regular progress reports on my search for Karen—and my brother and I dashed down to the boats, Brian to motor the *Sea Clip* to the marina while I tagged along in the Whaler.

I looked back at the house, at the glinting gabled windows upstairs, and thought for a moment that I had seen the pale face of Geneva.

CHAPTER 18

I was in a terrible spot. I had to explain to my parents that I was going to Mount Desert, but not to work—exactly. They grilled me good and got most of it out of me, but I wasn't about to tell them that I was going down there to find Karen for a vast sum of money. Of course, if I failed—which was likely—I'd come back after a week or two with nothing to show for all of the time spent. "I assume that borrowing the Dodge is out of the question," I said as Mom poked around with the vacuum cleaner. I made token swipes with the dust cloth, explaining that my mission for the Sterlings was urgent, although I couldn't explain why.

She jabbed the power head under Brian's bed and got it stuck down there. "They're a strange family," she said, tugging it free. "How do they expect you to drop everything and rush down to Mount Desert when they won't even tell you what it's for?"

"They don't exactly *talk* in that family," I said, not immediately aware of the understatement where Walt was concerned. "And I guess they don't exactly talk *out* of the family." I was still using Jack's phrase *I guess*. I seemed unable to stop.

Pop thought that the deal, as he called it, was the most peculiar thing he'd ever heard of. "Don't you suppose that if they can pay you, they can pay a professional—a private detective or something?" The vacuum cleaner had sucked up a sock and he was taking apart the power head to get it going again. The smell of hot rubber filled Brian's room.

I had already gone over that part with Mom, but I repeated it, stressing Geneva's desire not to scare Karen away by sending people with badges. "I'm the person she trusts most," I said with a mixture of pride and embarrassment. I still wasn't sure if I was doing Karen a favor or betraying her.

When the time came, they were wonderful. Pop and Brian figured out a way to let me take the Dodge. They were going to stay home and remodel the whole living room to do justice to the picture window that Mom had been wanting—and Pop had been resisting—for as long as I could remember. She liked her big view of the river, but Pop still grumbled that the picture window ruined the authenticity of the house. "Looking out of it might be perfectly lovely," he said, "but looking *at* it is plug-ugly."

"Well," she said, "what are you going to do more of—looking out or looking at? And do you really care what anybody else sees when they drive past this place? Don't even bother to answer because you and I both know the truth." Later she slipped me thirteen dollars from her stash behind the dryer sheets, saying, "You'd be surprised how much money there is to be made in washing men's pants. Just don't forget to call us every now and then."

Somehow word got out that I was going, and I had to give the same vague explanation to Mrs. Townsend and to Cherie's mother. "I sure wish I had gotten to see Cherie this summer," I told Mrs. Gillespie as Cherie's oversized dad slept in the armchair in the corner of the living room. All of the furniture in there had come from the Dennysville dump during its glory days, and Mrs. Gillespie had meticulously covered each piece with white sheets to keep it clean, so the dormant Mr. Gillespie looked like a pile of laundry. He and Pop used to drink and sing old Scottish songs all night long. He had sworn off the drinking, though, and for some reason, stopped singing too. "When he's on edge, Hershel can be such a bear," Cherie's mom explained as we observed him from the kitchen. "So whenever he can get some sleep I just leave him lay. About Cherie, I know she'll be sorry you missed her, but she's kind of moved on, you know."

I *didn't* know, unless she meant that short-term secretarial school in Woodland was some kind of life change, but I didn't have time to get into that. I went over to see Fred's parents because back when we were an item, I had lent Fred my copy of the high school yearbook and this seemed like a good time to get it back. Whenever I went on a trip, not very often I grant you, I had this little echo of concern that I'd meet with some fatal accident, and I tried to put my meager affairs in order before I left, which meant that I was usually up all night the night before and groggy the day of. So now I was getting the yearbook back, so if something happened to me, my parents would have it.

On the back burner was a faint hope that I'd see Fred and be able to tell him that I was off on an important mission.

Their house was one of the oldest in town, a peeling two-story Federal-style box with a bay window that had gone milky and a front door that had long since lost its steps to some other purpose. With open arms, Fred's mother received me on the porch that fronted the ruts that served as a driveway.

"Come in, come in and sit while I look for it," she said, nudging me into the front room. She wore wooden clogs that she'd bought at a resale years ago and in between rugs she clacked on the wooden floor.

Like the Gillespies, the Archers were big on covering furniture with sheets, but the Archers did it because of Blip. There he was in all his big black shiny glory, gnawing on something in the middle of the front room rug. It was the remains of one of those rawhide bones, I think, but back around the time Winthorpe's horse ran away with me, I had come into the Archers' yard and seen Blip chewing on what appeared to be a cat skull with little pointy gray ears still on it.

Blip dropped the object of his affections with a loud *snark* and came over to give my shins a tail-whipping. He was a noble dog who had guided a lost Archer child home back in the day, and now he was affection-starved, He plopped his giant head in my lap.

After I gave him a dutiful pat, he poked his nose under the sofa and came out with a baseball-sized object in his jaws.

"Blip, that's a rock," I said. "We can't play catch with that in the house."

He seemed to think otherwise and deposited it in my lap.

I picked it up with two fingers so as not to touch the drool and gave it a tentative roll on the floor. Blip came to life, ran slapdash over to it, came lolloping back, and dumped it on me again.

I really was afraid of damaging something, even in that ragtag mausoleum of a front room, and so I rolled the rock under the dust apron of the sagging sofa at the other end of the rug.

Blip did his best, rooting under there first with his nose and then with his paw, but it was hopeless. Or so I thought. Then he dug around a few feet farther over and came up with *another* rock. Clearly, this game had been going at the Archers' for a long time.

"You are so sloppy but so steadfast," I told him. "I can tell you're related to Fred." I began to get the feeling that I was reliving some dim, ancient ritual and that if I looked more closely at the walls I'd see the charcoal outlines of Neolithic bison on them.

This was the environment that had created Fred, and despite myself I felt a little tic of regret when I thought of leaving it behind.

Mrs. Archer came clattering back to inform me that the yearbook was nowhere to be found.

Under the sofa, I suspected.

After lunch the next day I crammed as much as I could into my backpack, set it beside me on the seat of the Dodge, and headed down the winding curves of Dunning's Point Road headed for Route 1.

I had everything planned out—what time I'd get to Mount Desert, the motel I'd stay in at Hull's Cove on Route 3, how much of the $513 I'd spend each day, how often I'd call home, where I'd look for Karen and Robbie, and when I'd admit defeat, turn around and go home. While I was planning, the Dodge got ideas of its own.

When the sway bar links gave up the ghost, I thought I had lost my two hind wheels. I was on a back road, most of the way to Mount Desert, just coming to this intersection where there's a round store that used to be painted like a huge piece of Swiss cheese with a giant gray mouse standing beside it. All of a sudden,

I thought that the Dodge must be dragging its under parts, screeching and sparking and ready to go up in a fireball that would be visible all the way back to Ashton.

When all was said and done—and paid for—I ended up spending several hours in Ellsworth, which is about a three-day walk from Mount Desert. The mechanic at the garage advised me that a hundred bucks *might* get the Dodge and me as far as Bar Harbor, though, so I made an executive decision and turned the car over to him and went looking for an eatery where I could stuff myself cheap. I found one of those chain places where two or three meals can probably clog your arteries for life and tried to look busy by fooling around with the menu, which was starting to come un-laminated. I say I *tried* to look busy because in the booth next to me there was this young girl, fourteen maybe, and chubby, with a big guy whose back was turned to me, who sounded old enough to be her father but wasn't talking like a father, not by a long shot. The girl had a bruise under one eye, and I was pretty sure that she hadn't gotten it playing Scrabble.

I tried to concentrate on my game plan, as Brian would call it, but when I went to the ladies' room, there was that girl again, leaning over the wash basin, looking at herself in the mirror, and her bruise looked even uglier under those fluorescent lights.

I tried not to stare. "There are a lot of hard things to bump into out there," I said. It was the best I could do for breaking the ice.

"Yeah," she said. She was rubbing some kind of face cream on it.

I couldn't help poking my nose in further. "Are you from around here or just passing through?"

"I'm from Wisconsin and getting as far away as I can go." She sounded nervous.

"Then you've about done it," I said. "You've pretty much run out of real estate. Go much farther and you hit water."

She tilted her face to get a better look at her bruise. The face cream looked kind of like spackling. "Really? What state are we in?"

When I told her she was in Maine, I got the impression that she'd never heard of it. I pretended to be touching up my eyebrows just so we'd have something in common. "Just out traveling then?"

She ran some water and daubed her eyes with it. "Pretty much. Kyle has this job he's going to and he picked me up in Indianapolis on his way." She made interstate flight sound like some kind of errand.

"Well, unless his job's in Canada, you must be about there," I said.

"I don't think so," she said, pressing her lips together, maybe to make them redder or fuller. "It's some kind of bar or club or something. He says I can work there and nobody will ask questions."

"If the two of you have traveled all this way," I said, "you must be old friends."

Now she was pinching her cheeks. I didn't know that anyone younger than Mrs. Townsend still resorted to pinching as a beauty aid. "Not really," she said. "We met last week, on the Internet. We hit it off right away though. But now he's getting kind of pushy, like he owns me or something."

I set my backpack on the counter and put my hands in my jeans pockets. "Is that where the decoration came from?"

My attempt to be tactful threw her at first. She gave my reflection in the mirror a puzzled look and then said, "Oh, this," and touched the corner of the bruise with her fingertip. "No, he was just kind of cranky from all the driving. He tried to teach me to do it, but I kept getting scared and over-steering, and he damn near peed himself." She pulled some Kleenex from the wall dispenser, stuffed it in her purse, and started to go.

I moved between her and the door, trying to be low-key so as not to appear threatening. I took a deep breath. "What if you could go back to Wisconsin tonight—or at least get a good start— would you do it?"

She slung her purse over her shoulder. "I don't know. I do kind of miss my in-line skating. It's too hilly around here, takes all the fun out of it."

One of Jack's hundred-dollar bills was starting to feel hot in my pocket. I pulled it out and offered it to her. "This is yours if you go out the back door of this place right now, just drop everything, leave your baggage or whatever behind, go to the bus station—which is that way—and head for Wisconsin. Promise me and it's yours." I dangled the money a little closer.

She stood there with her head tilted, trying to tell if the bill was real. She smiled. "That would be kind of fun, just to take off again." She giggled. "Wouldn't *that* be a joke on Kyle?"

I smiled back. "I bet he'll be sitting out there eating desserts for half the night before he figures out you're gone."

She snatched up the hundred, crammed it into her bra, and scooted out the back door, heading in the general direction of the bus station. I went back to my table and whiled away some time with a banana split. When I left, Kyle was still glued to his booth, glancing from his watch to the ladies' room door.

By the time I got back on the southbound road to Mount Desert, the sky had lost its luster and the scenery consisted mostly of dark woods and oncoming headlights. But from miles away, I could make out the gentle arcs of the island's mountains, rising from the sea like beached blue whales. I was still wondering about that girl in the ladies' room, wondering whether she was already on the bus west or if she had gone back to Kyle or taken up with someone else. I wondered if my hundred dollars had done good or harm and concluded that, despite the uncertainty of the outcome, I had no choice but to give it. Then I wondered if I should have done more, but I convinced myself that any more aggressive move might have scared that girl right back into that booth with Kyle. And that made me think of Karen and what Jack had said about not wanting to scare her off with any kind of authorities, which was where my part came in. Only now I was down to less than three hundred dollars to do the job, and the motel I was going to in Hull's Cove cost ninety-two a night.

Fortunately, the woman in the office there was in no hurry to collect since I had a three-night reservation. I signed in, threw my stuff in my little cabin toward the top of the hill, and drove down the winding road, four miles to the biggest town on the island, Bar Harbor.

The whole population of Ashton a couple of times over seemed to be on the sidewalks and driving down the streets. Only most of those people didn't *look* like the people of Ashton. They looked as if they were about to participate in a track meet, and in a way, maybe they were. They were wearing running shorts or striped nylon snap-away pants with matching windbreakers over designer t-shirts. Even though it was dusk, some of them still wore sunglasses perched atop their heads like horn buds. Some of them wore baseball caps embroidered with the names of exotic places. Most of them wore running shoes as striped and shiny as deep-sea fish. They crossed the street whenever and wherever they liked, not knowing that a certain green Dodge had one very frazzled and distracted female behind the wheel perched atop treacherous sway bar links.

After getting turned around a time or two, I got to Cottage Street, and after giving up on yielding the right-of-way, I edged into traffic on Main Street, turned left, and coasted downhill to a park. I found no place to pull over, though, even on the big stone pier, so I doubled back to the front of a music store where people were bonging away on this big marimba. I was thinking about the hopelessness of my situation when I chanced to see through the window of the store a pale-faced woman watching the musicians.

A wild idea popped into my head. I parked in the first opening on the town pier and fired up my pathetic relic of a cell phone to call Jack, failing to realize that the Dodge was blocking traffic. "This is about Geneva, isn't it?" I hollered into the failing phone. "That's why you're so eager to find Karen. That's why you've been gone with her all those days. That's why you went to Eastern Maine Medical Center. It wasn't for Walt, was it? It was for Geneva!" I raised my voice above the honking of the car behind me. I became aware of a parade forming behind the Dodge. "All those times when Karen thought that you and Geneva were off doing legal work or whatever, you were going to Bangor, to the medical center."

His answer came between complaints from the pier and blinked warnings that my phone was about to die. "She needs a kidney, Amber. And if she doesn't get it bloody soon, well, maybe there won't *be* any more Geneva."

I felt as if I had been kicked in the chest. They weren't looking for Karen just for the usual old parental reasons. They needed her to save her mother's life. "You want Karen to donate a *kidney?*" I asked. "Does *she* know any of this?"

Jack raised his voice. "About the kidney disease and the dialysis, no. As for the transplant, *we* didn't even know until last Friday. We don't even know if Karen's kidneys are a match."

A guy with New Jersey plates yelled something rude and physically impossible, but I ignored him. "Why haven't you told her, for crying out loud? Why hasn't Geneva told her? Isn't this something a daughter should know about her mother?"

His voice faded as I turned the phone. "Ordinarily I'd agree with you, but as you may have noticed, Geneva and Karen are no ordinary mother and daughter. Geneva was hoping they could smooth over their differences first, so that she wouldn't appear to be playing some kind of trump card in a quick grab to get Karen's sympathy. You can understand that, can't you? Look, whatever you do, do *not* tell Karen about this or all bets are off. Who knows how she would react. Just bring her back, will you?"

Or all bets are off. Meaning no grad school tuition if I told Karen about Geneva's predicament.

I moved the car over to a place in front of a mansion called the Seacoast Mission on West Street and walked back to the park. I sat on a bench, pondering what Jack had said about Geneva's illness and her not wanting to tell Karen about it. I didn't get too far. For one thing, the night was so pretty that I couldn't keep my eyes off the harbor and the chain of steep wooded islands called the Porcupines that bristled out of the water. The harbor itself was full of boats, pricey, well-kept fiberglass sailboats, most of them, and off at a pier by itself was a big four-masted schooner. Beyond it, a path followed the rocky shore, bounded by deep lawns at the feet of brightly-lit houses the size of hotels.

It was a magical, glorious place if you were with someone and achingly beautiful if you were alone.

A middle-aged man wearing a windbreaker, running shorts and shoes without socks sat down beside me and started a conversation. I began to reply before I realized that the conversation didn't involve me. The man was more or less singing along with some music plugged into his ear, bobbing his head and talking. I felt nervous sitting next to him, so I edged over to the end of the bench and then gave it up all together, thinking that I might start laughing. Boy was I in for a surprise because I had gone only a few yards, to a fountain strewn with coins, when I felt the tears come. I sat down on the edge of it, pressing my fingers to my nose to try to keep from crying. I didn't care if I got splashed. I just wanted to pull myself together and I wasn't even sure why I was coming apart.

It had something to do with Geneva and Karen. It had something to do with Robin and something to do with Walt and with Hal and even with Cherie, who was up there in Woodland at secretarial school. It had something to do with that dumb girl in the ladies' room. And, sure, it had something to do with me. I felt this overwhelming weakness and despair. I felt that everything I wanted was without any purpose, that even if I could make my dreams come true they would all come to nothing. At the age of twenty-three I wasn't sure that I wanted to go to grad school, wasn't sure that I would *ever* want to go to grad school, wasn't sure that I'd know what to do if I *did* go and got through it. I had been so mediocre with Walt that I wasn't sure I was cut out to take care of old people. But that big tailspin was quite beside the point right now because I was alone on a big island full of strangers, in a desperate search for two people who could be around the block or an ocean away.

My tears turned to laughter. The joke was on me, and it was a gem. I got up and left the fountain in a hurry. The last thing I needed was for someone to think I had lost my marbles. I walked back into the crowd on Main Street and consoled myself with a quart of mint chocolate chip ice cream and a small but dense piece of rum-coconut fudge. Then I returned to the shadows on West Street, stuffed my fat self into the car, and drove back toward Hull's Cove. I just wanted to sleep till morning and then start making phone calls to marinas to see if Robbie and Karen had turned up at one of them. Most likely useless, but something to do at least.

That mechanic in Ellsworth certainly knew his sway bar links. I was still about two miles from the motel when the Dodge went completely haywire. By the sound of it, all the ball bearings fell out and rolled around the road. The Dodge let out a mortal screech and there I sat. I was in no mood to deal with it at that hour. I just wanted to get back to the motel and lie down, but I had forgotten to tell Jack that I was already running low on money. So I would have to face that embarrassment in the morning, too.

I wasn't thrilled at the idea of just leaving the car and walking two miles. I'm kind of lazy anyway, and on top of that I was tired, so as soon as I saw some headlights coming, I stuck my thumb out. I figured that I was likely to connect with some nice family taking a leisurely route home at the end of their island vacation. Instead the first car to stop was occupied by three twenty-something guys who were passing around a can of beer, not their first of the evening by the looks of them.

"Thanks just the same," I said to the one who stuck his head out of the passenger side window. "I thought you were someone else."

"I'm someone else," said the guy in the backseat. He had dark eyes and a mustache and his upper lip didn't quite cover his teeth. I like rats. They're smart and playful, but I had a bad feeling about this two-legged one.

I looked around and contemplated a quick retreat into the woods, but I resented having to thrash around in there when all I wanted to do was go two miles down a public highway. I made a secret vow to myself that I would never hitchhike again, and considered flagging down a passing car, but everybody was moving pretty fast. And anyway, my luck had already gone sour once. How could I be sure that the next encounter would be any prettier?

I stood my ground, planted my feet on the shoulder of the road, and put my hands on my hips. My heart was not participating in my attempt to remain calm. Remembering a yoga course I had given up on after three weeks, I took a deep cleansing breath. "I'm staying here," I said, "and you're going—there." I pointed down the road.

The rat got out of the car, a dusty dark green thing with one headlight held in by duct tape. I memorized the license plate. It was from Massachusetts. "Where you going?" he wanted to know. He wasn't much taller than I was, but he was built like a tank. He'd been using those biceps of his, probably for nothing good. The guy on the passenger side got out. He had crumpled the beer can and the foam ran through his fingers. He was moving toward me when he stopped suddenly at the sight of something behind me. I glanced back just long enough to see a red pickup truck veering across the road.

"Oh, great," I mumbled. "Let's have a party."

CHAPTER 19

Behind me, the driver of the truck got out and started walking toward us. "Hey, Jonelle," he called, "we're gonna be late for graduation at the kick boxing school."

I nearly fell over. It was *Fred,* standing there, casting a giant shadow in the truck's headlights. He came up and hooked an arm around my neck and pushed his cap back. He had a toothpick in his mouth. It seemed to me that rat face and his friends weren't so different from some of the characters that Fred associated with back home, but the gentlemen from the green machine seemed none too eager to prolong the acquaintance. With the foam still dripping from their fingers, they backed off, folded themselves up in the car, and squealed onto the highway to the tune of a rattling muffler.

I wriggled free of Fred's arm. "Jonelle? Where did you come up with *that?*"

He took the toothpick from his mouth. "She was my mom's aunt. The one that lost her panties during the jitterbug contest."

My palms were moist. I wiped them on my hips. "Really. You sure they didn't come off while she was kick boxing?"

Fred smiled. He was a day or so behind on shaving, and I suppose that had made him look all the more fierce to my would-be abductors. "I thought that part was pure genius," he said. "And they must've liked it, too, the way they took off to tell all their friends. You shouldn't hitchhike, you know, even down here on Mount Desert. It only takes one crud on wheels to spoil your day."

"Or my life," I said. "Would you mind telling me what in the world you're doing here anyway?"

"I was coming down to look for work. I thought I'd make the rounds of the boatyards."

"And you just happened to come along at this particular time?"

"Well, the island isn't all that big and I've been up and down this stretch a few times on my way from one place to another."

"Is that so?"

"Just what are you doing down here?"

"I'm looking for somebody, that's what."

"Yeah, well no doubt *that* pays big money."

I wanted to tell him that, yes, it did. It paid quite nicely if I succeeded, but I didn't want to go blabbing the Sterlings' business and have him spreading it all over northern Maine, so I got catty and said, "There are worse places for making money."

"You were going somewhere," he said. "Do you want to walk or ride?"

We got the Dodge towed into a garage in Bar Harbor and when we got to the motel in Hull's Cove, I thanked Fred for giving me a lift, but I didn't mention being rescued. I had already convinced myself that I could've gotten out of the squeeze somehow.

He got out of the truck and tagged along as I went toward my cabin at the top of the hill, Number 18. "So tell me what you think of this idea."

"Not the casino again I hope." I wondered how far he was going to follow me.

"Forget that. Bad idea. No. I could use a place to stay on the island for a few nights and we can save some money if we share."

I stopped and gave him a hard look. "I *knew* I should've just taken off for the woods when those idiots came along. Fred, I'm not here to mess around. I really do have serious business here, and spending the night with you in a motel—ooh-la-la—is not part of it."

He came between the cabin and me and stopped. "Look, Amber, I've got no designs on your—*whatever*. I'd just as soon throw myself off Otter Cliffs as try to get through your defenses.

All I'm after is a place to stay until I can find work, preferably in a boatyard or construction. Three days, max. I'll sleep on the floor. I'll sleep in the closet. I just don't want to sleep in the truck. I need a place to clean up and get a good night's sleep. I'll pay my part and we can both come out ahead. That's fair, isn't it?"

He sounded so sincere and so desperate that I melted. "All right, all right. But it's by *my* rules. This arrangement will *not* be cozy."

His hands went up. "I'm not after cozy. I'm after *sleep*. If I can find a job and a place to stay *before* the three nights, I'll be out of there."

Suddenly I felt much better. Maybe without realizing it, I had been so depressed about being
lost and alone that even the companionship of a slob was heartening. Fred *was* a slob, too. He brought a bag of Cheetos in from the truck and trailed them all over the floor of the cabin. While I was gazing down the hill, admiring the long view of the deep blue cove, he was sprawled on the sleeper sofa, cracking his knuckles and trimming his fingernails with his teeth. When I went into the bathroom, he was sitting on the bedroom floor, using a hand towel to clean his shoes. When I went to the sink, I felt a wet washcloth squirt up through my toes. For some reason he had left his t-shirt wadded up in the bathtub. I tried to imagine the room without him, clean and quiet and spacious and private and decided that being with Fred still beat being alone.

Brushing my hair, I came out and asked him what his plan was.

He lay there watching me for a minute as if entranced by what I was doing, ordinary as it was.

I tossed the brush onto the bed and repeated the question.

"Drive around until I find somebody who'll give me a job," he said.

His plan was almost as brilliant as mine.

Time was slipping away and I needed every break I could get, so I made him an offer. "Look, you're bound to have some luck with the marinas and boatyards. They don't care if there are bugs in your hair, and there are several of them—boatyards, I mean— here on the island. Tell you what," I said, acting like I was doing him a big favor. "I'll go along with you. That way I can check those places out for Brian, you know, to see if they might hire him, too."

He looked puzzled. "What about this job of yours? Aren't you supposed to be finding somebody?"

"Yeah, and I'll look while you drive. As soon as I get the Dodge out of hock, we can go our separate ways."

I was so tired that I don't even remember the rest of that first night, except that I fell asleep on the bed while Fred wrestled with the scratchy sleeper sofa. In the morning, after a breakfast of Cheetos—extra spicy, I'm sorry to say—and ice water, we took off, and it felt good to have wheels again even if Fred was overprotective of them. For someone who inclined toward piggish personal habits when he was sitting still, he sure was a stickler about what went on in his truck. It got to the point that I'd kid him about how he had bonded with it. As we headed for the western side of the island I said, "Don't look, Fred. Quick, how many miles are on the odometer?"

He took me seriously and got it within fifty miles. "I just had the oil changed," he explained.

When we finally got to the boatyard over near Bass Harbor, I put my plan into action. While Fred was asking about work, I poked around looking for the *Paul D.* When I didn't see it, I asked the assistant manager if the boat had been there. She'd never heard of it and I spent a restless half hour walking the slips of the marina next door while I waited for Fred to find out that he was unqualified for every position they had, none of which were open.

I tried to bolster his spirits. "You think a tree puts down one acorn and makes an oak?" I said. "You've got to keep plugging along. It's nature's way." In almost the same breath, I suggested a scenic detour to the harbor, where I discreetly asked the harbormaster about the *Paul D.* He had no record of it. We checked a couple other places way over on the west side of the island with similar results. Despite my cheerful advice to Fred, I was starting to get discouraged. It was one thing to realize that you'd be traipsing all over the island looking for someone who probably wasn't there. It was another to actually drag your behind from one place to another without success. I couldn't help feeling hopeless. Fred had already given up on finding employment.

"Look," I said, settling back against the seat in the truck, which smelled like vinyl cleaner, "we're all worn out. Let's get something to eat and go back to the motel and crash. Tomorrow's bound to be better."

It was dark by the time we got back to Bar Harbor, and the place was really coming to life. Tired as I was, I wanted to cheer myself up with some window-shopping, but Fred was agitating for supper, so we went to a pizza place on Mount Desert Street. It was packed upstairs and down, but we got a fast deal on a large pepperoni that someone had failed to pick up. Fred had eaten a third of it before we even got it to the table.

"If you don't slow down you're going to barf, or maybe I will," I whispered, glancing around to see if anyone else was getting grossed out.

He gazed at me over an arc of crust oozing cheese. "I need a fill-up, Amber. We worked hard today."

"I think that we could use some organization for...." My thought petered out as I noticed a man at the next table. His face was familiar and he was looking at me.

Fred licked some cheese from his wrist. "Why don't we just *call* the boatyards and marinas? We'd save a lot of wear and tear on the truck—and me."

"Because it's educational to see these places firsthand," I said. Of course, I had my own agenda. I wanted to make sure that I wasn't getting the brush-off from some yo-yo on the phone. I had to see for myself that the *Paul D* wasn't there.

Fred was starting to get suspicious again. "Well, just what kind of work is it you're doing, Amber, that takes you to all these marinas and boatyards?"

"No offence, but that is N.O.Y.B., my friend. If it works out, I'll let you know."

"It's not like you to be so...."

"Diaphanous?"

"Um, yeah. I think so."

Shame on me. Diaphanous had nothing to do with it. It was a word from the GRE study guide. I was anything but diaphanous. I was opaque.

"I'm just being discreet," I said. "I'm maintaining a professional attitude."

"Well, you don't look very professional with cheese on your chin."

I couldn't believe it. I had a string hanging there like cow slobber. I stole a look at the guy a table over and he smiled, *smiled* at my chin drool, and turned away. I tried to regain my dignity. "Anyway, tomorrow we're going to hit these places early," I said. "We'll go right down the map from one to the next until we've talked to every boatyard, marina, and harbormaster on the island."

Fred tossed back his Dr. Pepper and put his elbows on the table. He crushed the can. "Okay with me. You're looking for Karen, aren't you?"

I choked.

He waited to make sure that I wasn't going to die. "You shouldn't eat so fast, you know."

I glared, but a cough spoiled the effect. "What in the world makes you think I'm looking for Karen?"

He pushed his cap back. He was wearing his favorite, the one awarded to the first place winner at the Aroostook County tractor pull. "Come on, Amber. Everybody knows she took off with Robbie Dunning. And a fair number of people know that he fences his goods over near Hancock. Next stop, Mount Desert to blow off some dough. After that, who knows?"

I chewed very slowly for a moment. Fred was smarter than I had realized, smarter by far. "All right," I said. "I'm looking for Karen. Big deal."

"And her mother's offered you some sweetheart deal for finding her."

I toasted him with my Diet Coke. "Okay, what else have you figured out?"

"That's about it. What's so urgent about finding Karen?"

"That's N.O.Y.—"

"Okay, okay. Who cares? You want to look at marinas tomorrow, we'll look at marinas."

"You know what *I* can't figure out?" I said. "How you just happened to come along when I was stuck on the highway."

He frowned and snagged a strand of cheese stuck to the bottom of the box. "There's such a thing as a coincidence, you know, especially down here. You never know who you're going to run into. Like that guy over there, the guy that was just looking at you."

I tried not to turn around. "Yeah? What about him?"

"He ran for president and he has a boat you could hold drag races on."

I turned my chair away to avoid the temptation to look. *"That's* who that is? He's here? I'm face to face with a possible future President of the United States and he sees me with slime hanging off my chin?"

After a good chuckle, Fred stuck the cheese in his mouth. "He's here all right, and so are plenty of others like him. It's that kind of place. Anybody can turn up."

"Well, I don't care about *anybody*," I said, rubbing my chin red. "I just hope that Karen and Robin are here."

In the morning Fred was having back problems. He made a face when he climbed into the truck. He wriggled around behind the wheel before he pulled the door shut. "I hope the bed was comfy," he said.

I winced as I watched him. "Yeah, it was fine."

"Well, I'm glad to hear that."

"Was the sleeper sofa all that painful"

"It may be a sofa, but it's no sleeper. It doesn't pull out."

"It's supposed to."

"Maybe if a gorilla's yanking on it, but otherwise it doesn't, Amber. I ought to know. I threw my back out trying to get it to."

"Well I'm sorry, Fred."

"And on top of that, it smells like somebody left egg salad in it, a long time ago."

"Oh, come on."

"You want to swap tonight?"

"Maybe we'll get lucky today and finish our mission. Get to go home."

"And maybe *I'll* get lucky *tonight,* but I don't think so."

"You may be crude, but you're a good judge of character."

We bought maps and drove all over that island—Pretty Marsh, Southwest Harbor, Somesville, Northeast Harbor, Seal Harbor—and looked at boats until I was seeing them with my eyes shut. The day was so clear that I sometimes forgot my purpose. From Southwest Harbor you could see across the Somes Sound to the whale-backed mountains rising above the spruce woods on the east side of the island. Sailboats bent beneath a stiff northeast breeze and you could see the occasional lobster boat patrolling its line of traps. A ferry streamed toward the outer islands.

Fred scanned the southern horizon. "They could be way out there somewhere. Down in the Cranberries or over at Swans Island."

We drove over to Northeast Harbor and took the mail boat to Islesford. It was an off-chance at best, so I allowed myself to relax and enjoy being on the water. In the summer the mail carrier doubled as a tour boat, and all the while, sitting back-to-back on the top deck, we heard about seals and cormorants and ospreys, lighthouses and mariners. I was so swept up in it that I forgot about Karen and grad school and basked in the warm sunshine and the chilly salt breeze, wishing that the trip would go on and on.

It didn't take long to determine that the *Paul D* wasn't in Islesford. We could see just about every boat in the harbor as we approached the wharf. But we had an hour-and-a-half layover, so we sat at a picnic table, looking across the water at Mount Desert. "We could be seeing them right now," I said, watching a little flash of light, the reflection of a car high on the tallest of the mountains, Cadillac.

Fred trimmed a piece of driftwood with his penknife. "And they could be back in Ashton by now. Not to be discouraging."

I propped my elbows on the table and put my chin on my palm. "We're kind of running out of places to look, realistically speaking I mean."

"There's always Swans Island."

"Sure. But it would take us most of a day to get out there and back on the ferry."

Fred took out his wallet and counted his money. "Can if you want. As long as you don't care about eating."

I gazed across the water to Mount Desert and a huge long yellow house that spread across the brow of the hill overlooking Seal Harbor. "That's very sweet," I said, "but let's eat once at least." We had chicken salad sandwiches at the restaurant on the wharf and then took the mail boat back to Northeast Harbor. Fred insisted on standing in the bow, hat in hand, with the wind slapping his hair every which way. "I've about run out of ideas," I told him, "and time. I wish I knew if they were even on the island."

An uncomfortable night, sun, wind, and the gentle rocking of the boat had taken their toll on him. He looked at me with sleepy eyes. "What does your woman's intuition tell you?"

I swept my hair back from my mouth. "I'm not sure that woman's intuition works that way. It's not like I'm clairvoyant."

He held my hair as I tied it back. "But you know Karen. Isn't that why they hired you to go after her? You think she's down here?"

"Well, I'll bet they came down here at least. You say that Robin sold the antiques in Hancock. And Karen told me more than once how much she loves it down here. She was happy here when she was a little girl. Yeah, I'm sure they'd come down here. I'm just not sure how long they'd stay."

"Okay. And there's no sense in their coming down here for just a couple of days, especially if they've got some money to blow. What do you think—four, five days maybe? Chances are we still have a day or so before they take off."

I wasn't convinced, but I appreciated his attempt to be encouraging and I needed some kind of direction, so I set that as my goal. Find Karen by tomorrow night or go back to Ashton. Our money wouldn't last any longer than that anyway.

We spent the rest of the afternoon driving around in mist that made the windshield wipers squeak and drag. Fred fussed and fiddled, trying to keep them from rubbing themselves into oblivion, and while he was distracted, we hit a pothole that threw me at the dashboard and made Fred sound the horn with his chest. "Aw, *hell*," he said as we got going again.

Somehow I had hit the dashboard with my elbow. I was flapping around like a killdeer doing the broken wing trick. I assumed that Fred was expressing concern about me and told him that I would be okay.

He hadn't heard me. He was intent on his beloved mode of transportation. "I think we screwed up the alignment," he told the ruby object of his affections. We were on a straight stretch and he let go of the wheel for a moment. "Yuh, we sure did," he said. "We're pulling to the right."

"I'm *so* sorry," I said, patting the dashboard. "I hope you're okay."

"First thing in the morning we're getting this looked at," Fred declared. Never mind that the Dodge was languishing with screaming sway bar links behind a garage in Bar Harbor. He let go of the wheel again and the truck obligingly drifted off to the right.

"Tomorrow is Sunday," I said.

"Well, we can't go driving all over the place with the alignment off."

"All right," I said, "I guess I'll just have to get around without the Dodge until I can get it fixed again. You really have done more than enough, Fred. Sleeping on that broken-down sofa, burning up gas and running up the miles." I couldn't resist adding, "I'll bet the odometer's all the way up to thirty-five two-fifty by now."

"Thirty-five three hundred," he said without looking at it. "And just how are you going to get around without your car?"

"Hitchhiking of course. I've only got to do it for one day."

"No way, babe. You want me to tell you some hitchhiking stories?"

"You want *me* to tell *you* some horror stories about people who drove around with *faulty alignment?*"

"Look, Amber, you don't have to get all sarcastic." Fred thumped the wheel with both hands and the truck jerked to the right. "I'll drive you wherever you want to go tomorrow, and on Monday we'll haul your sorry-ass car out of that garage in Bar Harbor and beat it back to Ashton."

I burst into tears. For the life of me, I have no idea why.

He looked at me like I was some kind of whack job, and maybe I was. "What gives, Amber? Didn't I just say I'd take you around tomorrow? I mean what else can I do?"

"Just forget it," I said through my tears. "You've done everything you can do. Everybody's done everything they can do." I wiped my eyes with the back of my hand, folded my arms, and slumped back against the clammy vinyl seat. "Tomorrow we'll finish up. I've had enough of this anyway. I'm ready to go back and work for Happy Hal for the rest of my life—if he still needs someone."

"What about working here on the island? What about all the great places to make money for grad school? Hal's going to start losing business by Labor Day. These places down here will still be going strong till the middle of October. Or maybe they've stretched the season all the way to Christmas."

"I don't care," I said. "I've had enough of this island. I feel like a complete idiot, chasing after a vapor trail."

"We'll give it tomorrow," he repeated, making me unsure as to who had convinced whom.

CHAPTER 20

During the next night neither of us got much sleep. Full of fried clams and beer, Fred was snoring and flopping around on the smelly sofa and I was alert and a little chilly in the bed, even though I was wearing everything but my hiking shoes and windbreaker. I began to think that the coldness was within, brought on by my frustration and misgivings, and that no comforter was going to warm me up. I missed my parents and Brian, of course, and I wondered how Walt was doing, wondered if he ever thought about me, but I didn't want to settle back down in Ashton. This expedition to Mount Desert, farcical as it had been, had made me want to venture out into the broader world, "the world beyond the jetties" as Pop called it. As I lay listening to soft rain dripping on the cabin roof, I wondered if I had what it took to carve a niche for myself in the world out there and concluded that so far it was looking very bleak since I was relying upon my ex-boyfriend to haul me around. I thought for a moment that I should've just kept Jack's money and made a show of pursuing what I knew to be a hopeless cause. That way at least I'd have something to show for my trouble. But when my thinking sank that low I was saved by something Brian used to say through the wall when I talked to myself at bedtime: "Shut up and go to sleep."

In the morning we were both wrecks. Fred had fallen off the sofa and was sprawled among a scattering of Cheetos on the throw rug beside it. At first I thought he had died during the night because he was wearing his baseball cap and he still had one foot on the sofa. How could any living person remain in that position all night? I slipped out of bed with the blanket wrapped around me and padded up to what looked like a crime scene. His mouth was open so wide that the sunshine pouring under the window shade lit up the fillings in his back teeth. His fly was at half-staff. In my effort to approach him silently I knocked over a can of Moxie and startled him awake.

He dropped his foot from the sofa and sat up on the rug. "Jesus and Joseph, Amber. What are you doing sneaking around?"

"Trying not to wake you up—assuming you were still alive. It's no wonder your back hurts. Do you always sleep like that?"

"Like what?" His joints popped as he stretched.

"Never mind. The rain's passed. It's a pretty day out. We ought to be going."

He yawned and stretched some more, turned around and zipped up his fly. "Oh, yeah, last day." He swiveled his shoulders and, I swear, every bone in his back crackled. "You know, I think the beer helps. I'm feeling pretty limber."

"Well, I'm surprised that you didn't catch pneumonia." I pulled my blanket tighter.

He smiled and put his hand toward me, fingers outstretched. "Damn, Amber, you look just like a princess—a Penobscot princess."

It was the sweetest thing he had ever said and he had said it because I was standing there in a linty blanket with my hair hanging in my face. I concluded that during the night we had *both* lost our marbles. But of course, as a male, he was prone to occasional fits of hormone-driven dementia. I brushed away his fingertips. "And the princess is eager to make the most of the day," I said. "I do appreciate everything you've done for me, Fred."

He seemed embarrassed. "Let's get going. We can get something to eat on the way."

We made tracks, all right, but after a while my heart wasn't in it and I settled into a tourist's frame of mind. Sure, we went to the marinas and boatyards and made phone calls and stared out at the sun-flecked water, looking all the while for the elusive Karen or Robin or the dark hull of the *Paul D*, but gradually I began to see the sweeping harbors and gliding boats for their own beauty, not as reference points in my stupid search. Time and again, I let my eyes be drawn away to the gentle arcs of the mountains, the steep spruce woods, and the receding blue Atlantic.

"Look, Fred, I've had enough," I announced as we wound our way yet again past the clear rocky pond that served as a reservoir for Northeast Harbor. "Let's call it a day. Let's blow off the rest of our money having fun and then get the hell out of here. What do you say?"

He had gotten used to cocking the wheel to the left to keep the truck going straight, but now he forgot and we wobbled when he let go for a second. "Well, what about finding Karen? We've still got a few more hours."

I couldn't believe it. He had actually come to care more about the search than I did. "Aren't you hungry?" I asked. "We can at least get something to eat and then decide what to do."

"We could go back to that clam place," Fred suggested. "That's a pretty good deal for—"

"Fred, this is *me* talking. As long as we're down here, let's live it up just a little."

We went to a place that both Karen and Jack had mentioned, the Jordan Pond House. It looked down a mile-and-a-half sliver of clear water framed by two of those whale-backed mountains, Penobscot and Pemetic, to rounded twin peaks that probably gave guys fantasies. Out on the lawn that sloped toward the pond were rows of rustic green-topped tables where you could have tea and popovers when the weather was decent. We had a good long wait, but I didn't care because the view was so gorgeous.

A hostess in a floral print cotton-and-silk dress and espadrilles led us to one of the green-topped cedar tables, and I stared at the rough-edged pond and the wooded mountains that plunged into it. When I thought about it, Ashton was pretty, too, but in a kind of scattered way, something here, something there, and the overpowering presence of the water. This was focused, as if some titan of a landscape architect had designed it to funnel your attention right down that pond to those twin mountains.

Nonetheless, I was quickly diverted by the arrival of the popovers. We broke them open and dropped butter into them and watched them steam, added strawberry jam, and let the creaminess stream down our hands as we took big piggish bites. I warmed my hands on the stout green china teapot and forgot everything but the here and now.

Fred emptied a packet of sugar into his hand. "Seems like we've had a good run. I kind of hate to see it end."

With closed eyes, I smelled the scent of lemon rising from my teacup. I had a vague sense that he was talking about our broken relationship, which now seemed an eon in the past. I heard him say something to the waitress, a tall thin blonde in a green polo shirt, khaki skirt, and bright new running shoes. She went to a nearby table, picked up a green ceramic sugar holder, and put it down in front of me.

"I kind of thought we'd find her" Fred told me, "but it's as if Karen Sterling doesn't even exist—and I'm starting to wish that she doesn't."

"You and me both," I said, dumping one and then another packet of sugar substitute into my tea. "Or at least that I'd never gone over to the Woolsey side of the river."

Out of the corner of my eye, I saw the waitress turn and come back toward us. I figured she was going to replenish the sweetener. Instead she said, "Excuse me. Did you say you were looking for somebody named Karen Sterling?"

The tea was awfully good, especially with plenty of additive, and I took a long, sweet sip. It obliterated the meaning of the words.

"We sure are," Fred told her. "Or we *were* anyway."

The waitress motioned toward the table where the sweetener had come from. "She was sitting right over there just about an hour ago."

I jumped up, knocking my teacup off the saucer. "Karen was *here?*"

In the air the waitress measured height with her hand. "A tall girl, kind of broad shoulders? Blondish hair? The reservation was under the name Sterling and the guy with her called her Karen. Good-looking guy. Dreamy eyes, dark, wavy hair, very self-assured and graceful somehow."

"They were *here,* an hour ago?" I repeated. My knee hurt for some reason.

The waitress looked a little embarrassed by my outburst. "That's their sweetener you're using."

Fred was standing up now too. "You got any idea where they were going?"

The waitress tried to remember. "They said that this was their last afternoon on the island." Her face brightened. "The girl, Karen, said something about picking blueberries on Gorham Mountain, someplace you could get to—"

"—in just a few minutes." I all but knocked the bench over to get clear of it. "Gorham! Karen mentioned Gorham to me as a place she loved! I'm such an idiot. I forgot all about it!"

My excitement made the waitress eager to get away from us. She started to say something about bringing us the check, but I pressed some cash into her hand and told her to keep the change. "Quick, how do we get to Gorham?"

She had to think about it for a moment. "Let's see. If you go down to Seal Harbor and take a sharp left onto Route 3, then— on the other hand, it might be better to go back toward Bar Harbor and pick up the Park Loop Road. Except you have to pay for Ocean Drive. You go past Sand Beach and Thunder Hole and Otter Cliffs and Gorham will be on your right. Just look for the sign." As we rushed away we heard her say, "You can be up and down it in no time."

I couldn't believe our luck. In my despair, I had been ready to throw myself into Somes Sound and now, all of a sudden, we were so close to Karen that we were using her sugar substitute. Our progress was painfully slow though. The parking lot was crowded. One of those monster campers was jockeying back and forth trying to get into a tight space. I wanted to get out and run screaming all the way to Gorham, even though the distance had to be several miles.

"Well, which way?" Fred asked when we finally got to the road. The traffic was so thick that it looked like a parade going both ways. While I got out our creased map of the island and tried to make sense of it, Fred turned right.

I looked up from the map. "What did you do that for?"

"We had to go *somewhere*. We had traffic backing up behind us. There wasn't any break on the left. She said you could go either way."

"She did not, Fred. She changed her mind. Weren't you listening?"

"Hey, at least we're going *somewhere*."

"Fred, we are going the wrong direction. You've got to turn around."

His hands left the wheel and we lurched to the right. "Okay, okay. We'll turn around as soon as there's a place."

The first place we came to was about a mile farther and it was very confusing. Three roads came together at strange angles with cars coming at us from all directions. Fred let the alignment make the decision and angled off to the right.

"Now what are we doing?" I smacked the map with the back of my hand.

We were going downhill on a wet, narrow winding road with a twenty-five mile-an-hour speed limit that was maybe a little too high, especially when your alignment was off. Under ordinary circumstances it would've been a very pretty route. It was lined in places with cedar rails and it threaded through the graceful arch of a great gray granite bridge. But since I didn't know how long this scenic meandering would go on, I was intent on finding a place to turn around. After about a mile, we came to a road that brought us crawling back through Seal Harbor.

Fred nodded to the right. "There's Route 3. Want to take it?"

"No, no, a thousand times no!" I declared. I had the map turned upside down in an effort to follow our actual progress through the tangle of underpasses and loops. I pointed at the straight road ahead. "Just get us up that way as fast as you can."

"Speed limit's thirty-five, Amber. There's hikers, bikers, everybody but the damn Stay-Puft Marshmallow Man is on this road."

"Well, until he shows up, try doing thirty-six. I'm not asking you to run over little kids, just get going."

We went back past Jordan Pond and plodded through curves clogged with dawdling tourists. At some of the tightest places, people on bicycles passed us going uphill. I wanted to knock one of them over, grab his bike, and pedal like hell for Gorham. I could see myself running up the mountain, catching up with Karen and tagging her on the shoulder as lights went on all over Maine. Instead I was nosing along with Fred. "When we get to the loop road, it's a right turn," I said. "That ought to be easy."

An instant later, I looked up from the map in horror as he turned right. "Not here! What is this? It's Cadillac Mountain for godssake! Turn around!"

There was a turnout on the left, but we had already missed it. We were going up the mountain.

Fred glanced around. "Where are we?"

I read from the map. "Well, we are on the highest point on the eastern seaboard of the United States. We are going all the way to the top apparently. We are going to see approximately sixty miles in all directions. And somewhere in there will be Karen Sterling and Robin Dunning—about *fifty frigging miles away*." I gritted my teeth and screamed.

"Okay, okay, but didn't you say turn right?"

I propped my elbow on the window frame and stared at him to make sure that he hadn't sprouted three green heads. "Do we have some kind of language problem here, Fred? I said not this turn, the next turn. It's about three miles from here."

"Well, you could've been more explicit, Amber. When you're navigating, you've got to be explicit. I can't have any of these soft, mushy, you know, kind of half-baked directions about what it means to turn right or somewhere on this island there's a right turn and maybe we should take it. You say *turn* right and—"

We'd had one phenomenal piece of luck and we had thrown it away.

I pulled my sweater up and wrapped it around my head so I wouldn't have to hear any more. I would've holed up in there all day, I think, if the bright blue sunlight hadn't burst through the rather tired weave of the sweater and lured me out with its irrepressible optimism. The broad mountain spread out around us and, with each switchback, more and more of the island opened up below us in a procession of lakes and islands, lesser mountains, and the blue hills of the distant mainland. I had very mixed feelings at the sight of it all because the more beautiful and broad the view, the farther I fell away from my purpose.

At the summit of Cadillac, most of Mount Desert showed itself, from the prickly islands poking up in Bar Harbor to the boundless blue ocean with its scattering of sails, to the rugged mountains that tapered off in the south, to the deep sound that split the island almost in two, to the parallel ridges of the western side and the islands that went on and on beyond. It was as if the teeming outdoor world converged here, and yet the glory of it was wasted on me because Karen and my future were slipping away from me.

"Let's go back down," I said when Fred came to a stop in the parking lot. "Let's get going."

Fortunately, once we did get back down from the mountain, there were no more wrong turns to make. We got onto the Park Loop Drive, which was nineteen miles long, all one way. "Just don't overshoot Gorham," I said, "or I swear I'll throw myself into the sea."

"It won't happen," he told me. "You and me, we've got it together now."

The sunlight showed pale green through the leaves of young birch trees, and I felt better until we came to the Ocean Drive entrance. We were a dollar and ten cents short of having enough for the entrance fee. The ranger pushed back her Mountie hat and waited patiently as Fred and I rifled through the truck looking for the difference. Of course, Fred had kept his vehicle so clean that there was not a dime to be made from plumbing the seats. We got nothing. We were still several miles from Gorham.

Fred saw that I was about to come apart at the seams and so he made a suggestion. "Get out and do what you do best."

I looked up from the palm of my hand. "What?"

"Get out there and do what you do best—emote. You know, plead your case. Break her heart. Get her to let us in."

I gave him a dirty look as I got out of the truck and went to talk to the ranger. I explained to her vaguely that we were on an urgent mission, possibly a matter of life and death, but she was unmoved. Apparently she didn't believe me, so I said, "All right. I'll level with you. My girlfriend went through there with my car keys. That's all. It's just so embarrassing that I didn't want to say it out loud. We came down here for a good time and we had this cat fight about a guy we met on the whale watch boat—not the one in the truck, by the way—and she ran off with my keys. Can you believe that? Have you ever heard of such a spiteful thing— over a *guy?* I just want to go in there and get my keys and I promise I will not wring her neck when—"

I started coughing. I could feel my face going purple.

Back in the truck, Fred was making a point of looking the other way.

The ranger took a black wallet from her purse and put a dollar and a dime into the drawer. "Not the best I've heard," she said, "but it was worth a buck ten." She gave me a windshield sticker and a couple of pamphlets and waved us on.

CHAPTER 21

"I think *I* could've done better than that," Fred told me when I got back into the truck.

"Just do better at getting us where we're going," I said. "As fast as possible without causing an accident."

Even though Ocean Drive was one-way, it was two-lane, so Fred was able to weave through the cars parked on the shoulder at the big attractions down there, Sand Beach and Thunder Hole. When we got to Gorham, there was no place to pull over, so I talked Fred into parking behind a Mercury Cougar at the far end of the lot. "Chances are they'll be up there all day," I said. "They'll never know we were here."

I hit the trail and bounded toward the granite spine of the mountain as Fred hurried to catch up. I was passing clusters of people talking strange languages, kids chafing under packs and cameras, lean brown couples in designer sportswear and pricey hiking boots. Fred came running up behind me and set his cap low on his forehead. "I hope there's only one way up this thing."

"We'll find them," I said. "I know it. I *feel* it."

We hurried up the meandering path, past a bronze plaque mounted in a granite outcropping, and stopped to take stock. People were scattered all up and down the trail, many of them pausing to pick the blueberries that seemed to be everywhere. I studied them all and convinced myself that none of them were Karen and Robin. "If they're this far ahead of us," I said, "they must be long since at the top of the mountain. Don't you suppose the best picking would be up there, where there's the most sunlight?"

Fred pushed his cap back off his forehead. "Maybe, but how many blueberries do you need? Why not just pick them here and go back down, save a lot of time?"

I had already continued up the path. "Because you get a kind of satisfaction from going to the top. Isn't that obvious?"

"Then there's just another one. And one after that. You going to climb them all?"

"One thing at a time," I said.

The path split. I wasted no time scrambling down the rocks of one fork and told Fred to take the other. He hesitated. "What if it splits again?"

I was moving quickly. "Pick one—they all go to the top, I'm sure. I'll meet you there." My path followed a cliff face and went up a set of more or less natural steps. When I arrived, panting, at the top, the first person I saw was Fred.

He took off his cap and wiped his forehead with the back of his hand. "By the looks of you, I think the path I took was easier." He motioned toward a stack of rocks. "Summit's up there."

When we got to the top I sat down beside a wooden marker sticking out of the rocks and caught my breath.

"Five hundred and twenty-two feet—is that all?" I looked at the people bent over picking and eating berries on the side of the mountain. "Well, do you see Karen and Robbie?"

"No. Maybe they went down the other side."

Ahead of us loomed a taller, steeper mountain, Champlain. "I'm licked," I said. "Driving around all day was bad enough. Guess what. I'm not about to climb every peak on the island." I waited for some kind of response, but Fred was walking down into the blueberry bushes. As it turned out, though, he wasn't after berries. He was asking people if they had seen anyone matching Karen's description. I wanted to hug him. It was such a sweet, hopeless thing to do. Instead I went down, too, and started asking around. People picking blueberries on a mountaintop under an open sky with the sea spreading all around are about as relaxed as you'll find, and nobody resented the interruption. They listened patiently as we spoke of Karen's broad shoulders and Robin's sinewy good looks, but with dozens of people wandering all over the mountain, all of them intent on their own picking, who would notice another fit young couple out for a hike in the air?

Someone did though. A family of four was picnicking just past the summit. They had been there for most of the afternoon, and about an hour and a half ago they had asked an athletic, attractive woman to take their picture. "We showed her how to use our D600," the mother said between bites of a tuna fish sandwich, "then she called over this guy—*charming* guy—and asked us to take a picture of them with their camera. They said they were on their way down the mountain. They were going to hike all the way to Bar Harbor and sail out at sunset."

Fred took off his cap again and wiped his brow with his sleeve. "You realize that we've got a problem, don't you? If they went down the far side of this mountain and on to Bar Harbor, they're walking against the one-way road. We'll have to drive all the way around the loop to come back at them. We sure can't catch up to them on foot."

The husband was playing with the zoom on the camera. The lens whirred in and out as he scanned the rocky summit of the mountain ahead. "As a matter of fact," he said. "I think that's them up there."

I think I gave him rope burn helping him to get that camera off his neck. There they were, unmistakably. They were talking as they ambled along the distant path. Robin was wearing his usual khaki pants and one of his loud Hawaiian shirts. Karen's hair had lightened almost to blond and she had it up in coiled braids. She was fanning herself with an elegant straw hat. If they were walking the mountains all the way to Bar Harbor, it would be sunset before they got there.

We ran until our wind gave out. Yelling wasn't an option. They were way too far ahead. I bent over and put my hands on my knees. "Look, Fred, what if we split up again? You go back down and take the truck and see if you can intercept them on the road and I'll try to catch up to them from here."

Fred wasn't in much better shape than I was. "No way," he puffed. "Then you'll get lost, too. We're in this thing together, Amber, sink or swim."

I was too pooped to argue. My only hope was that they'd stop again. I took out the trail map and satisfied myself that they were most likely to take the hardest route to Bar Harbor—the one that would lead us to the top of Cadillac Mountain and then down to the road just south of town. I caught my breath, stretched my arms and legs, and continued on the path. "Come on." I said. "Unless they're complete mountain goats, we must've gained on them a little just now. If they stop at all to rest or admire the view, we might catch up enough to shout at them."

Fools that we were, we kept believing that as soon as we got around the next bump on the mountain, we'd see them. Those mountains are deceiving though. As soon as you're on the back of the whale, you think you're about to reach the summit, but those bumps go on and on, and so did we. Naively, I thought that we would get within hailing distance when Karen and Robbie started up the steep trail to Champlain, but if we did, we couldn't see them for the trees because we were down in the dip between the two summits. I thought that we'd come upon them relaxing at some scenic overlook, that I would clasp Karen and Robin, too, and that the long walk back to the truck would melt away because we'd be laughing and joking as we walked, and we'd smooth over everything between poor Geneva and her wayward daughter. I completely forgot how far ahead they were and how strong. By the time I had seen them, they had been up and down Gorham and covered a stretch of trail beyond, and they looked as fresh as if they had just stepped off the boat. Fred and I were on the verge of collapse. When I'm winded my cheeks flush like a hothouse tomato. If I ever got back to a road, drivers would probably screech to a stop at the sight of me, mistaking my face for a red light. Fred was sweating through the crown of his cap, which was clearly the worse for wear now. We were not your typical crisp, casual hikers. We were a mop and a sponge wrung out by those wretched mountains.

We stopped talking about what we would see as soon as we rounded each curve. Talking made us too crabby. We just trudged on lamely, eyes fixed on the next hundred yards of trail as we dodged the occasional loitering photographer or dawdling kid, all of whom seemed to be having a lot more fun than we were.

Finally Fred deigned to speak. "Doesn't look like we're going to catch them."

I stopped just long enough to put my hands to the small of my back. "Well, thanks for the news flash. But I did *not* come all the way up here to let them slip through my fingers."

The path was too narrow for us to go side by side, so he contented himself with plodding along behind me. "Amber," he said, "why can't Karen's mother just wait till she comes home? Why are we killing ourselves like this?"

I ignored the question. We had reached the bottom of Gorham. Now we were beginning the ascent of Champlain and it was steep. The trail went up quickly on uneven granite steps and the flat, slanted backs of boulders. I was already starting to get winded again. I was also talking to myself. "If they had any sense they would've headed straight for the road instead of hacking their way up this fool mountain," I said. Hiking was one thing, hiking endlessly, desperately—and failing—was something else. I was beginning to re-think my joyous reunion scenario.

"What are you going to do," Fred was asking, "if we ever catch up with them?"

"Probably go right up to Karen and knock her over," I said, suddenly aware that my fists were already doubled. "You can take care of Robbie."

"I need to take care of my truck is what I need to do. It's how many miles back that way? How are we going to get it, except by walking all the way back?"

I was pulling myself onto a broad, flat rock. I paused long enough to turn and glare. "Don't say that. Don't even think it."

"Well, doesn't she just have a cell phone?"

I didn't bother to turn around and glare at him. "You don't get it, Fred. Robbie hates cell phones, and I'm sure Karen does too by now. If I know Karen and Robbie, they're in the process of dropping off the radar screen. We may need bloodhounds to find them."

When it came to delusions, Champlain was way worse than Gorham. Time and again, we quickened our pace when we saw what we thought was the summit, only to find that the trail took a turn and continued to rise through the rocks and stunted trees. It was like walking the bladed back of a giant stegosaurus and, after a while, about as comfortable. As we got more and more tired, we got clumsier. We turned our ankles and bruised our knees. Beside us, behind us, and below us, the Atlantic floated, a limitless deepening blue beneath a clear sky, but we were unaware of it, just as we had become blind to the berries thick in splashes of sunlight, the carpet of ancient moss, and the heady scent of pitch.

I came to a halt and sat down on an outcropping well short the summit. "I've got to rest for just a minute," I said, "or I swear I'll fall over backwards."

Fred dropped down beside me, trying to be subtle about catching his breath. "This would be a real bad place to do that," he said. Below us, the side of the mountain dropped sharply. It was thick with young trees so, while a fall might not be fatal, it would be damn ugly.

I pulled my hair back and fanned my face with a hunk of birch branch that rattled with dead leaves. "Does it occur to you that we were kind of unprepared for this little jaunt?"

"You mean life in general?" Fred asked, squatting with his elbows on his knees. He looked more like a frog than a philosopher.

"I can see your point," I said, "but actually I was thinking about our assault on Champlain. We didn't even bring any water—and I could sure use some."

"Tell you what. As soon as we get to town, I'll get you all you want." He tapped me on the shoulder. "In the meantime, if you want to catch those birds, let's get going."

And he was off, bounding from boulder to branch with new energy.

By the time we finally got to the elusive summit of Champlain, the afternoon was pretty well shot, and we had the place to ourselves. Karen and Robin had been there, of course, might even have lounged on the warm rocks and spoken of their good old friend Amber without having the least idea that she was wearing herself to a nub beating a path to them. I thought back to the day when Karen had dived into the river and swum to Robin's boat, and I began to wish that I had jumped in after her.

The trip down Champlain was madness, partly because we started on something called the Precipice Trail that turned into a series of iron rungs poking out of a cliff. "We can make up some time," Fred told me as he felt for the first rung with his foot. "This'll take us straight down and then we can cut across the face of the mountain and catch up to them if they took the Bear Brook Trail because it's a lot longer."

I was impressed. He was quick to get his bearings. I clung to a spindly poplar tree that had no more business up there than I did. "You're crazy if you think I'm going down there," I said.

He looked up at me, even though I couldn't see any more than the top of his cap. "Amber, this is the quickest way down. If Robin and Karen took it, it's our only chance of catching up with them. If they didn't, then we've got a good crack at beating them to the finish line."

I wasn't about to let go of the tree. "Fred, let me just tell you that I have this very reasonable fear of heights."

"Amber, you've got to work through your fears. That's what life is all about. If you hadn't pushed the envelope, you'd still be crawling around on your hands and knees."

"Not a bad idea in this particular place," I said.

He let go of the rung with one hand while picking up one foot.

"Do *not* do that!" I had visions of him cascading down the cliff, leaving me to pick up the pieces. It was a selfish concern, of course. I couldn't stand the thought of walking, or perhaps crawling, down that mountain alone.

With his free hand, he pointed toward the distant road. "That's where they're going, Amber. If you're ever going to catch them, you've got to go this way."

I moved my feet and a few pebbles rolled over the edge, showered Fred, and bounced into oblivion.

The visor of his baseball cap turned up abruptly. "Cut that out, will you? You might shake something big loose. Now are you coming down here or not?"

Still hanging onto the tree, I dropped to a crouch. "I'd kill myself. I just know it. Maybe you can go and—"

"Jesus and Joseph, woman! We've already been through all that. We're *not* splitting up."

"And I'm not going down there. I feel sick just at the sight of it."

"If you don't let go and come down, I'm going to come up there and *tickle* you."

"Are you nuts? Do you want to kill us both?"

Hand over hand, he came back up the rungs. When he got to the top, he sat down beside me and pushed back his cap. "All right, what do you say we split the difference? We won't take this way and we won't take the long way down. We'll bushwhack our own way in between." He pointed off in a new direction. "That way. We'll still have a shot at beating them to the bottom of the mountain."

I thought he was out of his mind, but I couldn't veto *all* of his ideas. So we went back up to the summit and started thrashing through the trees.

Fred charged along cheerfully. "You know, one advantage of doing it this way is you don't have to waste all that time looking for trail markers."

"Oh, that's nice," I said over the racket of snapping sticks and cascading rocks. "And we're having a pleasant little stroll in the wilderness."

Ahead of me he made an expansive gesture. "Limber Amber claims no pain climbing Gorham and Champlain."

I did a quickstep and caught him by the arm. "What? When did you write *that*?"

"Never. I just made it up."

"You're kidding. Just now?"

"Want to hear another one?"

"No. No more, please."

"Oh, come on now, Amber! It's a beautiful afternoon—"

"Getting very close to evening—"

"We're together and—"

Suddenly we *were* together. I slipped on the smooth slope of a rock, knocked Fred's feet out from under him, scooped him up like a runaway toboggan, and propelled him down the mountain. When we landed in a whorl of dust and pebbles, he was on his back on top of me. He sat up between my legs and set his elbows on my knees, making me feel like some kind of lounge chair.

"Damn! We never did *that* in Ashton!"

I untangled myself and got up, resisting the temptation to lean on his shoulder. "Well, forget that you did it here. What a dumb idea. I can't believe I let you talk me into your stupid shortcut."

Fred was looking around for his cap. "What do you mean? You can be sure that we're moving faster than Robbie and Karen. A few more of those and we'll shoot right past them." He winked. "Next time I'll even let you ride on top."

I gave him a shove, but he managed to maintain his balance.

"Oh, come on, Amber. Lighten up. It's not like somebody's dying."

For some reason, I was tempted to tell him about Geneva, but I held back. "You can forget your cap," I said, "because we don't have time to go poking around for it. You can come back for it."

He dropped to a crouch and began groping his way back up the drop-off. "Not on your life."

I started walking. "Me or the hat, Fred, because once I get going, you'll probably never find *me* again." I was becoming desperate. I would've said almost anything just to get him going.

He raked his fingers through a patch of leaves. "Amber, it's not just a hat."

I stopped and kicked a spindly birch tree. "You can always go back to Presque Isle and win the tractor pull next—"

He stopped his raking and looked up at me. "What are you talking about? I didn't win that tractor pull."

"Then what's the big—"

"The hat belonged to Danny."

Danny Burgess was Fred's cousin. He was about the sweetest guy you could imagine. He was so easy-going. When the bank took his car, he got around by hitchhiking. One night he accepted the wrong ride and died beside a drunk driver at the age of twenty-three.

"Fred, I—"

"Forget it. The sun's going to go down." He went crashing through the undergrowth and I followed, making enough noise for a herd of deer. As we got down into the taller woods, the light was failing. If Robbie and Karen really were sailing out at sunset, time was getting short, very short, and this compromise trail wasn't the great shortcut it was supposed to be because we wound up making our own path down the mountain, which required frequent stops to figure out how to work around bone-breaking drops and dangerous slides. At times the ground seemed simply to fall away beneath our feet. When the trees were close enough together, I kind of swung from one to the next, branch to branch, until I got to more or less level ground.

Finally we got to what looked like a dry streambed and we picked up the pace. "It's about time," I told Fred. "I've got to admit, until now I thought your idea was completely hare-brained."

"You weren't far off," he said. He pointed to what looked like a bright red leaf. It was a red metal square stuck in a tree trunk, a trail marker. "We're just about where we would've been if we'd gone the long, easy way."

By the time we got to the road, my backside was beginning to stiffen. Robin and Karen, of course, were nowhere to be seen. Toward town the sky had gone a pale blue-white. Traffic was picking up. Bar Harbor was quickening its pace for another summer night. We tried hitchhiking, but for some reason nobody slowed down for a sweaty buck with a five o'clock shadow and a wilted female with a tomato face.

Fred began walking backward with his thumb stuck out. "If we split up—"

I ran up to him and pulled his arm down. "It's only a mile or two. We'll be there before anybody in their right mind gives us a ride. *I* wouldn't even give us a ride."

He put his hands in his pockets, turned around, and picked up his pace. "What part of sunset do you suppose they meant—the beginning or the end? I mean, at this time of year it goes on for quite a while."

We were so close to town now that I was getting my second wind. We raced along the shoulder of the road, past walled estates and darkening woods. The gravel shoulder turned to a worn path, the path to an asphalt track that became a sidewalk. Now we were hurrying past pedestrians, window shoppers, idlers, and the just plain dazed. We dodged and ducked our way down Main Street, broke free at the hillside harbor park, and sprinted to the broad stone pier. The big four-master was already well out in the harbor, its russet sails brilliant in the crimson light from the west. As we ran, we scanned the rippling water for the familiar curves and angles of the *Paul D,* and when we got to the end of the pier, *there* it was, gliding elegantly past the last of the harbor islands.

That wrong turn up Cadillac Mountain had made all the difference.

I sank to my knees, sobbing.

Fred knew that we were beaten, but he tried to offer a few hopeful suggestions. "We could pay somebody to scoot us out there in a kicker boat."

With red eyes I looked up at him. "How? We have *no* money."

"We could try to raise them on the radio."

"Fat chance. I've never seen him turn on his radio."

Fred sat down beside me and stared out to sea. "Looks like that's it then. Sorry, Amber. We sure gave it our best shot."

CHAPTER 22

Back at the motel we licked our wounds and I called Jack at the mobile number he had given me. "I'm sorry," I said. "We were *that* close three times." When Jack failed to respond, I continued. "Sorry to be calling so late. It took us quite a while to get back to the truck, and once we did, we had a very irate Mercury Cougar owner to contend with. We had kind of blocked him in the parking lot for a few hours. We'll be coming home tomorrow."

He sounded frazzled and testy. "You didn't by any chance ask around at the harbor to see where they were going?"

"Sure, but they weren't moored or berthed in the harbor. They must've found a private hook somewhere. That's why none of the harbormasters had seen them. So now the only question is where were they going? Is Karen attracted to any other place that you know of?"

He started to speak and then turned away from the phone and sneezed. When he came back he sounded stuffy. "Sorry. I seem to be coming down with something. Guess I'm kind of strung out."

I got another idea. "If she was going to show Robbie around, within sailing distance I mean, where would she take him? You know, someplace that means a lot to her."

Even though Jack was blowing his nose, he managed to hear the question. "I don't know. I suppose she might take him to the place in Boston. With Geneva and Walt here in Maine, she knows she'd have the house to herself." After a long pause I thought he was going to sneeze again, but he came back on and asked if I would be willing to go to Boston to look for her. "You can even stay in the house for a few days if you like. It would take them a day or so to get down there by boat. I can give you the name of a man who can give you some spending money and a key."

I balked. "I don't know Boston worth beans, and I can't see sitting in a house all day and night waiting for someone that might never show, and I sure wouldn't know where to look for her—or even how to get around."

He sounded hopeful. "Oh, I can give you some ideas as to where she might go if she's not at the house. And as for getting around, the public transportation is marvelous."

He said *marvelous* with such enthusiasm that I doubted his sincerity. "Look," I said, "I'm going to have to think about it. Boston's a long way off."

Fred was standing beside me now. He had washed his face and slicked back his hair. He looked neat that way, but a lot older. He was daubing his forehead with a bath towel. "Tell him we'll do it," he whispered. He bent over and drank out of the bathroom faucet.

I put my hand over the receiver. "Stay out of this, Fred. You're not going anywhere."

He stuck a corner of the towel in his ear. "What do you mean? I'm your ticket to Boston. Drive you anywhere you want to go."

"Fred, that's ridiculous."

"Listen," Jack continued, "you might also try around Faneuil Hall, but that's a lot of space with a lot of people. I don't know. There's a restaurant called Thoreau's on the Harvard campus where the family used to go to celebrate after winning trophies and there's that place on the top floor of the Prudential Building. You might ask if anyone's seen them up there."

"It's not ridiculous at all," Fred was saying. "If Boston's our last crack at finishing the job, let's go. You really want to sit by yourself in that house all day and then hit the nightspots by yourself? Does that sound like a good time?"

"Ask around," Jack was saying. "If she's still in town, she'll have to come back to the house sooner or later. But the sooner you can find her, the better."

When Jack hung up, I bore down on Fred. "I'm not in this for a good time," I reminded him. "This is business."

"Then let's finish it."

"I was trying to talk on the phone. And you don't know Boston any better than I do."

He tossed the towel at me, forcing me to catch it to keep from getting hit by whatever he had rubbed off on it. "You kidding? I've been all over that place. Anyway, that's what smart phones are for, Amber. Ever heard of GPS?"

We finished off the spicy Cheetos for supper, split a frothy, lukewarm Moxie that had been rolling around in the back of the truck, and settled in for the night. I sat cross-legged on the bed while Fred stretched out on the alleged sleeper sofa. Maybe it was all the exercise and fresh air and being so hungry that made me light-headed. Much as I wanted to fall back on the bed and sleep, I also felt like talking, even if Fred was his usual monosyllabic self.

"I'm so messed up," I said. "I've made such a botch of everything. Here I thought I was going to start grad school at U-Maine in the fall and instead I've frittered away the time! I mean, I made some money with Walt and running the boat with Karen and Robbie and a few bucks at Happy Hal's, but not nearly enough."

From the sleeper sofa: "Yuh."

"And now I've spent the better part of a week running myself ragged chasing after those two—and for what? Nothing has happened, absolutely nothing. It's been a pure waste of time, you know?"

"Um-hmm."

"I mean it's been for a worthy cause, not for Karen really. Not even for Walt. Poor Walt. Even if Karen did come back, I wonder if he'd know the difference. Oh, sure he'd know the difference. I wonder how he's doing. I wonder what he's thinking. A mind like that, a genius, really, you'd think he had some idea of what's going on, wouldn't you? I mean there's that smile of his. That's got to mean something, doesn't it? And he talked to me—to *me*."

"Uh-yuh."

My head was spinning as if I'd had three or four beers instead of half a Moxie. The pain from landing on my rear end was gone. I felt pleasantly numb. "I don't know what he'd do if anything happened to Geneva," I said, "if she can't get a kidney, I mean.

You're not supposed to know that, by the way. Even Karen doesn't know. That's what this whole thing is about. I suppose it's only fair for you to know since you've insisted on getting mixed up in this mess. I wonder if they expect me to tell Karen that her mother needs a kidney—from *her*."

I thought that Fred must have been shocked by what I was saying because he was taking so long to reply. I felt like a dolt for having let the secret slip, and when he still hadn't said anything, I started to get mad. I listened to the room for a minute, to the slow dripping of the shower, and the distant departure of a car. Then I sat up and said, "By the way, I've taken off every stitch of my clothes. I'm lying here on the bed absolutely naked except for a large ruby in my navel and I'm waiting for you to arise and take it with your teeth and make me throb with passion."

From the sleeper sofa came, soft and high, the sound of snoring.

The next morning, as we sped down the Interstate, I was poking at his smart phone, feeling crabby. "Take it easy on that GPS," Fred told me. "It might come in handy."

"Handy for what?" I said, not looking up from the web of converging roads on the phone. "I thought you said you'd been all over Boston."

"I have. But there's a lot of roads in there."

"Do tell. Well, we'll certainly rely on your experience and expertise to get us through."

"Damn straight."

"So why are you getting off the Interstate?"

"Gotta get gas."

I hadn't thought about that. "And just how are we going to get it if we don't have any money?"

"Stick with me, babe, and find out."

Our quest for fuel led us to Freeport and the biggest traffic jam I had ever seen, far bigger than the backup at the border when the exchange rate favors a drive up to St. Stephen. "What's going on?" I asked. "Some kind of parade?"

Fred gave me a knowing look. "Just business as usual in Freeport. They've got about every outlet store in the world here now. Haven't you ever left Ashton, Amber?"

"Well, we never come down here," I said.

"You have now," Fred told me. "Welcome to the real world."

"And it looks like we'll be here for a while," I said.

When we finally found a gas station, it was quite a squeeze getting into it. Fred wedged the truck between two minivans, gassed up, and pulled a wad of bills from the hip pocket of his jeans.

"What's with that?" I asked as we walked toward the convenience store. "I thought you were out of money."

He peeled off three twenties and stuffed the rest of the bills back in his pocket as a green minivan jockeyed out of a tight spot behind us "You didn't notice, did you?"

"Notice what?"

"I sold the hubcaps to the guy at the garage in Bar Harbor."

"What!" There they were—all those ugly exposed lug nuts and I had been too caught up in my own troubles to see them. I was at a loss to come up with an articulate response. "Well," I said, "as soon as this business is over, I'll pay you back—with interest."

He hadn't heard me. He was watching the minivan squeeze past the pickup. We heard the rasping of hard-turned wheels, a screech, and the shrill scraping of metal. The hood of the pickup shuddered. The tires of the minivan squealed as it sped from the pumps and jumped into traffic.

The money crumpled in Fred's fist. "Did you see that? That idiot just sideswiped my damn truck! It's a damn hit and run! Wait'll I get my hands on that piece of—"

I held him back. "Fred, you can't. We've got to pay and then get to Boston." In a burst of inspiration I added, "Maybe they got his name from his credit card."

They didn't. The idiot had paid cash and he was long gone by the time we got back out to the truck. Then Fred took his time walking around and around it, looking at it from every angle.

"If you look at it hard enough, you'll blister the finish," I said as he got down on his hands and knees right there on the greasy cement.

"First the alignment and now this," he said. The front passenger side of the truck had a dent the size of a grapefruit. And Fred didn't look quite right without the ever-present hat. He had lost that too, for me.

I hunched down beside him. "You've already done too much. Just leave me here and—"

He stood up so abruptly that before I knew it, he was towering over me. "Once and for all, bag it, Amber! I'm not about to run home with my tail between my legs. Not now. I'm not going to let this thing lick me. I don't care if Karen and Robbie are in frigging Ethiopia! We're going to find them and root them out and bring them back—dead or alive!"

Ethiopia? I had no idea he'd ever heard of Ethiopia.

The drive into Boston did not improve our mood. Somehow we got sidetracked onto a six-lane road that paralleled the Interstate and we wound up in the scenic if formless town of Newburyport, Massachusetts. I pinched the bridge of my nose and looked at the map to see what our options were.

Fred glared at the road, which was thick with traffic. "It's okay. We can take this all the way into Boston. It's not that far. Didn't you say the house was on Beacon Street?"

"Yeah." I repeated the address.

"Well, that's right on the Charles, isn't it? Right on the river?"

"Absolutely."

"Piece of cake. Just tell me how to get from this thing to Mass Ave and bingo! We cross the Harvard Bridge and hit Beacon. Right?"

"According to the GPS."

I seem to recall that we went wrong on Highway 16. While I was looking at the map, we shunted off and suddenly we were on some vast fast-moving concrete artery heading for God-knows-where. "We were supposed to stay on 16," I said. "Can't I ever take my eyes off the road?"

Fred gestured with a hand on top of the wheel. "Amber, there was a sign that said 16 that way. I went *that* way. Then there was some damn sign behind a tree! I don't know what it said, but I've got a good idea."

The next hour was a terror of rotaries, befuddling traffic signals, and kamikaze drivers. At one point we wound up on Route 2, hauling ass for Newport, which suddenly seemed the urgent destination of everyone else in New England. "Get us off," I droned. "Just get us off and turn us around." While we were seeing the same little park for the third time, somebody in a bright red Mazda knocked into us from behind. Fred's knuckles were white on the wheel. "Just a tap," I said. "No point in stopping. We'd probably just get rear-ended but good. And anyway, the color's a pretty good match."

Fred was getting chipped away one piece at a time—first his precious baseball cap, then his truck, and I wondered why he was putting up with it. Maybe his original desire to be helpful had hardened into sheer determination to succeed. Maybe he had become even more hell-bent on finding Karen than I was. In a last-second decision, he changed lanes and cut someone off. The offended driver laid on the horn, swerved, and sped past us, honking and swearing at us as the lanes diverged. Hunched over the wheel, Fred looked over and shook his fist. I could tell that he was thinking of going after the offender.

"Forget it," I said. "We're almost there. Let's not blow it. How many miles on the odometer, Fred? Without looking."

He made a point of looking up at the rearview mirror. "Who cares, Amber? Pretty soon there won't be anything left anyway."

"Come on, Fred. How many?"

His grudging guess was off by a good three hundred miles.

"Do you have any idea where we are?" he asked.

"Give me a street name."

"All right. Magazine. We just passed it."

I thought we must be completely lost again. I scoured the map from the airport all the way over to Newport and then found Magazine. "Fred, what street are we on?"

He looked back at a sign, just missing a daring pedestrian who sprinted in front of us. "We're on Mass Ave."

The pedestrian somehow eluded another car and made it across the four lanes to safety. "We're on Massachusetts Avenue?"

"That's what I said. That's what they call it. Mass Ave. Now where the hell are we?"

"We're *there*, Fred. I mean, practically. Can you believe it? We just kind of blundered our way there. Don't you *love* Boston?"

"Dunno. We're still in Cambridge."

I motioned toward a big stone building with pillars and a domed roof. "All of that stuff over there is MIT. Can you imagine all the brain power that must be packed into there?"

He shrugged. "Not really."

"Now just stay on this and go right over the bridge. I mean *straight* over the bridge. Isn't it great? We're starting to communicate. There it is—the Charles River."

To our left, a cluster of dinghies sailed in circles. In the distance to the right, the river narrowed and the skyline flattened. Ahead, the jutting skyline of Boston crowded the edge of the river.

As we got onto the Harvard Bridge, I tried to get Fred to relax a little at last. "What do you suppose those marks mean?" I asked. All along the sidewalk on the left side of the bridge someone had measured off something called *Smoots*.

He loosed his grip on the wheel and sniffed. "Probably one of those nerdy metric things that didn't catch on."

A few turns later, we were parked on Beacon Street.

Fred peered up through the windshield. "You sure *this* is it?"

CHAPTER 23

It was a huge brownstone. Fred crouched and looked up through the windshield, trying to see the top of the place. "Looks like a damn post office."

Most of the block was taken up with fraternity houses. "We'll find out soon enough," I said. "The guy with the key is just over on Newberry Street, about three blocks that way."

We walked. I began to feel the tension drain from my shoulders. The guy with the key was a slightly befuddled retiree named Hedgepath who, with his fretful wife, ran a handsome house that had been converted into an upscale bed-and-breakfast. As we waited for Mr. Hedgepath to return with the keys and expense money, Fred leafed through a brochure and tossed it back onto a coffee table. "It's a wonder they didn't charge us admission."

I squeezed his arm. "Will you keep it down? It does cost some money to run—"

We waited, eavesdropping on the Hedgepaths as they tapped away at a keyboard in an effort to remember a password. They debated: Was it case sensitive or was that before the latest update? I had visions of Karen and Robin taking a leisurely departure from the brownstone back on Beacon Street as Mr. Hedgepath tried to convince Mrs. Hedgepath that they had added some numbers to the name of their first cat, in order to come up with a password acceptable to the system. Mr. Hedgepath was starting to say some colorful things about the computer, the software designers, and the cat. Mrs. Hedgepath was having none of his plan to start writing all of the pus-bucket—his word—passwords down on a goddam legal pad or else throw this whole insolent piece of garbage out the window.

Despite my advice, Fred went barging in and offered his services as an IT expert. I expected to smell smoke, but at length, a rather winded Mr. Hedgepath re-entered the lobby, reading over a pair of half-glasses riding low on his nose. "Here's the key and a cashier's check with the amount specified by Mr. Crystal and instructions having to do with the house." He handed me a manila envelope. "You're a friend of Karen's he tells me."

"That's right." I could feel the key inside the envelope.

"Well, more power to you. I've known her almost her entire life, and she can be hard on her friends. Of course, I thought the world of her father." He patted Fred on the shoulder. "And thanks again, my friend, for winning the battle with that beast of a machine."

I looked the other way, not wanting to admit that I had misjudged my ex.

It turned out that the brownstone was subdivided, but the Sterlings' part was still overwhelming. The rooms were big and tall and u-shaped with a broad view of the Charles. There were varnished panels and molding and knee-high baseboards and chandeliers that hung down like giant thistles. The furniture was worn, but massive and leathery. The herringbone hardwood floors were covered with large, frayed carpets that looked like they could fly with Ali Baba. Two walls, floor to ceiling, were lined with books, leather-bound mostly. Fred and I drifted around and gawked for quite a while before either of us spoke.

Fred concluded that there had been some mistake.

I went up the carpeted stairs and gently pushed on the first door I came to. The bedroom hadn't been used for a long time. The shade was drawn and the air smelled stale. On the bedside table I drew a question mark in the dust. On one wall a matted photograph showed a familiar view of Jordan Pond and its twin domes framed by the whale-backed mountains—the place where Fred and I had lingered for tea and popovers and learned by chance that Karen and Robin were nearby. In the foreground, sitting on the grass, was a young woman gazing toward the water. Looking closely at her wistful face, I recognized Geneva, hardly more than a girl.

"Must've inherited," Fred was saying on his way up the stairs. "Most of this stuff is too old for Walt to have picked it up himself." I heard him go into the bathroom and avail himself of the plumbing, about as subtle as a rhinoceros. "Hey, Amber," he said in mid-operation. "Somebody's been here recently. The toothbrushes are still wet."

I ignored him and went into the other bedroom. It was a tangle of clothes and sheets. A bit of bright color made me flip over the bedspread. It was a shirt, a Hawaiian shirt.

"Fred, they're here!"

He came out of the bathroom so fast that he banged his head on the door.

"Well, not right now," I explained, "but they're staying here." I held up the shirt.

He batted it with the back of his hand. "If only he was still in it. They could be on their way to Senegal by now. Could've left in a hurry for some reason, possibly with somebody chasing after them. So what do we do--just sit here forever waiting for them to come back—or not?"

My grip on the shirt tightened. "Do you have a better suggestion? I'm not going to let them slip through my fingers again."

His brows came together in concentration. "What do you say to a two-pronged attack? We leave a note saying we want to see them and then go looking for them in some of those places Jack told you about."

"You just don't like sitting around."

"Yuh, but I'm also starving. We can go up to one of those places, ask some questions, and get something to eat quick and then continue the hunt."

I shook the shirt at him. "You know, it's no wonder men die younger than women. You're always so hyper. Can't sit still. Gotta be eating or risking your neck or trying to you-know-what all the time. Can't you just settle down and wait, ever?"

He smiled proudly. "We idle high, Amber. We burn hot and we idle high. That's the way God made us. Now what's the name of that place up near Harvard? Thoreau's?"

I found a piece of notebook paper and a mechanical pencil and left Karen a note about as long and fervent as the Declaration of Independence, explaining everything except the forbidden reason for Geneva's needing to see her. I left it under a brass paperweight on the herringbone just inside the door where she'd probably stub her toe on it if she did come home. Then we found the nearest stop for the subway, the T, and went up to Harvard to get Fred something to eat.

"If Karen comes and goes while we're out, I'll murder you," I said as we sat down in a booth in the dark and crowded restaurant.

"Go ahead and do it, Amber, as long as it's with an excess of affection."

"Don't be disgusting. Put your napkin in your lap and get your elbows off the table. This is Harvard. This is high class. I'm surprised they even let us in here."

He compromised by dropping the napkin in his lap and taking one elbow off the table. "Hey, at least my feet are on the floor," he said. "Look, if Karen is half the pal you think she is, she'll wait for you. Now relax."

The napkins were linen, even better than Hal's. "It is kind of exciting, isn't it?" I said. "Harvard. Very glamorous. I can see why Karen would like this place."

I ordered sushi, which I hadn't had since college, and Fred ordered a Reuben on white bread.

I crinkled my nose. "White bread? Isn't that kind of gauche?"

He shrugged. "Not if that's what I like, Am-brr." He said it that way. Am-*brr*.

Was he making a statement about my—well, never mind. Every time the door opened, I looked for Karen, even though I didn't seriously expect to see her. I mentioned her name and described her to the waiter and the guy who had seated us, who said, "Yeah, I've seen somebody just like that."

"Really?" I almost fell off my chair.

"Sure. Just about everybody who walks in here. Harvard's full of them."

Fred sneered at him as he walked away. "Nobody said we got a comedian with lunch."

"Never mind," I said. "Let's just enjoy being in this classy place then go back to—"

He put up his hand. "Amber, do you see what I see?"

I turned my head so fast that my neck popped. "Don't tell me she *is* here?"

"No, look at that. There's something classy for you—a damn cockroach on the wall."

"Don't be ridiculous," I said, shrinking back. "This is Harvard."

"Well, maybe he goes to MIT, but there he is. Ain't he a beauty?"

I looked at the flocked wallpaper crowded with old sports photographs and felt my sushi flop over in my stomach.

Fred shuffled his feet under the table and looked down. "What the hell?"

I felt something skitter across my knees. A brown mouse jumped onto the table, ran a broken path from one end to the other of it, and dove toward the door.

Fred laughed. "Jesus and Joseph! It's the cavalry to the rescue. Go get that roach, boy! Sic him!"

Hearing the commotion, our waiter arrived with a flyswatter, but he was too late to paste the cockroach. And I was in the corner of the booth, pressing myself into the tufted vinyl upholstery.

Fred laughed. "Is that part of the show? It's the first time I've ever seen a mouse chasing a roach. It's like goddam Wild Kingdom."

"They were fumigating in the kitchen," the waiter explained without interest, "and all the pests are heading for the hills. Your lunch is on us, of course."

It was a free meal, so we stuck with it, speculating endlessly about where we might find Karen and Robbie. Fred had some good, sensible ideas, and I was beginning to enjoy myself again, beginning to be impressed, beginning to feel as if I fit in at

Harvard, beginning to feel that *Fred* fit in, until he helped himself to a fat spoonful of my guacamole, which, since I was having sushi, was actually wasabi.

Suddenly we did *not* fit in anymore, and as soon as he had gulped down all of our water and some snatched from the adjoining booth, we were out of there like a rocket, turning heads as we went.

"Anywhere else you'd like to go?" I asked, tripping over the forgotten paperweight as we re-entered the place on Beacon Street.

Fred stepped on my note to Karen. "I don't know. After Harvard, how much class I can stand in one day. Guess they haven't been here, huh?"

We played gin rummy until the spots wore off the cards. I won three games of Clue, one of them while playing a dummy hand. We paced and helped ourselves to a couple of cans of Moxie from the truck, even though it tasted like cough syrup and the ice from the refrigerator was freezer burned.

"Ah, the good life." Fred suppressed a belch.

I was beginning to bloat up. "Look," I said, "You're getting sick of sitting here, aren't you? What's that other place that Jack mentioned?"

"Dunno. But it's on top of the Prudential Building."

I tossed down my cards. "Come on."

We walked, learning quickly how to dodge traffic. Nonetheless, I was glad when we got to the Prudential in one piece. "Any roach that comes up here would get a nosebleed," Fred announced as the elevator shot up toward the fifty-second floor.

Pretending not to know him, I stared up at the rapidly changing numbers above the doors.

Fred looked up at the paneled ceiling. "Hey, I wonder what kind of cable's holding this thing up. What a hell of a ride that would be. Freefalling to the bottom."

I looked down at the floor, trying not to think about what might be unraveling overhead.

The top floor had a lot of glass, and the lights of Boston's night skyline scattered away from us like the Milky Way.

Somewhere out of sight, a trio played soft, drowsy jazz—piano, sax, and a meandering *tunk-tunk-tunk* on a string bass. I was relieved to see that formal attire was unnecessary since the best I had was clean blue jeans and an off-white wool-acrylic blend sweater. Fred was wearing jeans with a horrendously wide leather belt and a faded green Henley, but I suspected that there were people in the place with million-dollar wardrobes who weren't dressed any better than we were. I asked the host if anyone named Sterling or Dunning had been there or was expected tonight.

"As a matter of fact," he said, "we did have a reservation for a two-party under the name of Sterling for the alcove." He looked at his watch. "It was for half an hour ago."

I pressed against his maitre d' stand. "Are you *kidding?*" At nearby tables, heads turned to see who the loudmouth was.

He backed away. "Don't I wish. They've had a reservation every night for the past three nights and they haven't kept any of them. It's gotten to be kind of a joke."

I felt my knees buckle. "They've *got* to come sooner or later."

The host looked at me over his stand light. "You would think so, wouldn't you?"

We wound up sitting near the trio. Fred was optimistic. "Amber, we know that they're here in Boston now. This just might be the night."

"All the same, we're splitting a salad," I said. "We could be here another couple of days and we still need money to get us back to Ashton, so we're not going to blow it all on appetizers at five dollars a shrimp."

By the time the waiter came to take our order, Fred had fogged up the window by gazing out at the sights. I sat with my chin in my hand, staring at the glass doors as people came and went— groups of businessmen, couples dressed for an evening out, foreigners, the occasional family taking in the town. All of them seemed so relaxed and content, and I wondered what they saw if they noticed us—the small-town girl with the worried frown and the oversized lout with his nose stuck to the glass like a snail.

"I'm starting to think you were right in the first place," I said as we picked through the salad. Fred was setting aside the olives and rolling them over to me.

"About the casino? 'Course I am. We can make heaps of money."

"About Karen and Robin. I'll bet they took off in a hurry and left that shirt and stuff. They could be a thousand miles away by now. Finish this and let's get out of here."

As I turned my chair, I happened to see the entrance. My heart jumped. Walking through the doors were Karen and Robbie.

CHAPTER 24

When I looked again I thought she was someone else, someone older and more sophisticated. She was wearing a black cocktail dress and a pearl necklace and her hair was down and waved. She was wearing a slender bracelet that sparkled with diamonds. She had slimmed down a little, tweezed her brows and changed to a redder shade of lipstick that made her mouth even more full and voluptuous, and I wondered if this look was the whim of a night, a new direction, or a return to a former look. Some things remained the same though—her broad shoulders and the distant, preoccupied look in her eyes.

Robin had let his dark, curly hair grow out again, and was dressed in a tailored Navy blue blazer that accentuated his trim build. It was almost too expensive for the black t-shirt and gray chinos he was wearing, but he made all of it look good and right. He was wearing beige slip-on sneakers without socks and he followed Karen into the restaurant with the easy self-assurance of an owner.

Karen was less steady on her feet. She had been drinking.

"My God, look who's here!" She stumbled forward and threw her arms around me. "It's Amber, our own Amber!" Her breath suggested that she had a weakness for martinis with cocktail onions.

Despite all I had been through and was about to go through, I smiled. Even tipsy she was irresistible. I hugged her before untangling myself. "I imagine you remember Fred."

"Oh, sure!" She startled him by draping herself over him and kissing his ear. "The *apples*. Of course I remember Fred."

Fred looked wary as he shook Robin's hand. "How you been, Robbie?"

Karen steadied herself with a hand on Fred's shoulder. "You two know each other?"

"It's been a long time but, yeah," Fred told her. "Junior high or something."

"Sixth grade," Robin said.

Fred pretty much ignored Karen's clinging. "But I've been hearing about you. You sail all the way down here?"

If Robin had been drinking, he was bearing up well. "Just to Newburyport," he said. "We found a mooring up there then took a cab down and got Karen's BMW out of storage" He seemed amused by this unexpected encounter.

Karen insisted that we join them at their table in the alcove, so Fred transferred the remains of our salad over there while I tried to think of the best time and way to break the news to Karen. I was so intent on telling her about her mother that I wasn't quite aware of having won an entire year's tuition and expenses. It didn't quite sink in that I was finally making the transition from Ashton to grad school.

But then, was the deal for *finding* her or for delivering her to Ashton?

Limber and glowing, Karen pointed at the salad. "I hope that's not all you're having, Amber. I've never known you to be the dieting type."

Fred squeezed in and sat down and began admiring the view from the new vantage point.

"We eat light when we travel, don't we, Amber?"

"Oh, come on, let us get you something. How about a drink for starters?"

As if by magic, a waiter appeared and asked for our drink orders. For the sake of keeping Karen happy, I requested an old fashioned, only because I'd heard the name. I had no idea what was in one.

"Just the thing for an old fashioned girl." Karen said, seemingly all elbows as she propped herself on the table. It was a wonder that she wasn't knocking over the water goblets. Smiling sleepily, she looked from me to Fred and back. "What brings you two down here anyway?"

The time wasn't right. She was too happy and Fred didn't even know the real reason for our breakneck chase. I had been so intent on finding Karen that I hadn't thought out how I would break the news when the big moment finally came. I couldn't just say casually that Karen's mother wanted to see her. That would hardly explain the two of us coming all the way down to Boston. I sputtered for a moment and then said something about how much I had missed the two of them and wondered how things had worked out. That was true enough and flattering enough to be believable.

Karen straightened and took in a breath. "Well, *damn!* I'm *honored! We're* honored. Aren't we, Robbie?"

I wondered what course of affection had brought her to call him by the nickname that he had supposedly outgrown. "Your mother invited us to stay at your place on Beacon Street," I said, stretching the truth just a bit. I wasn't sure how much Geneva knew about what Jack had put us up to. "I hope it's okay."

The waiter came with the drinks, brightening Karen's mood even more. She had a whiskey sour, complete with a cherry and orange slice skewered with a plastic sword. How appropriate for a pirate's girl, I thought.

She threw away the miniature straw, took a sloppy gulp, and made a dismissive gesture. "Whatever Geneva wants is fine with me!"

I was tempted to say *does that include one of your kidneys?*

"So tell me," she continued between swallows, "how *are* Walt and Geneva?"

I hedged. "About the same as they have been." I smiled pleasantly. "They'd be happy to see you of course."

She rocked a little as she sat with her forearms on the table. "Well, I suppose they could come down here to see us."

Fred seemed ready to catch her if she fell over. "Yeah, well, you're kind of hard to find."

"Yes, yes we are, aren't we, Robbie?"

"We're off the grid," he explained. "Did you know that just about every move you make gets picked up in some database?

Every call you make or receive on your cell phone is tracked. You use a discount card at the IGA and suddenly you're getting mail—"

"Or email," Karen chirped.

"—about some deal connected to what you bought. They know what you eat and who you talk to and where you are every minute of the day. I knew a guy in Thomaston whose credit card statements got subpoenaed so his ex could prove he drank too much to have custody of his kids."

"And God help you if you use Facebook," Karen said, "because the gatekeepers watch it all the time for what they think is criminal activity."

Her expression when she said *Facebook* reminded me of Cherie when she discovered a pair of her grandmother's disposable underpants in her dresser drawer.

"So we're bailing on all of it," Robbie said. "Going under the radar all the way."

Fred chose that moment to be irrelevant. "How's the *Paul D* doing? She was a nice little boat in her day."

"She does what she needs to do," Robin said, meeting his look.

Karen leaned over and laid a limp hand on his tailored forearm. "First time I ever saw her—and *him*—they went right up to the Cauldron. Remember, Amber? That seems like years ago."

"It sure does," I said, trying to keep upbeat for the sake of the cause.

"*To,* not into," Robin said. "Nobody goes into it."

Karen gazed at him over her half-empty glass. "Except for my father, in the good old *Sea Clip.*"

I always felt a tug of sympathy for her when she called him *my father* instead of Walt. I hated to do it, but I told her about Brian's prediction that without drastic repairs the *Sea Clip* would soon be on the bottom of the river.

Her eyes took on their distant look as the news sank in. She tossed back her whiskey sour and her face lit up again. "Well, then, we'll just have to put up the money and see to it. See to it! In the meantime, let us buy you dinner." She raised her hand and snapped her fingers to bring the waiter.

"No, no," I insisted. "We're fine, really, aren't we, Fred?"

She reached across the table and put her hand on mine. She looked at me with smoky eyes. "It's okay, Amber. It's not *all* ill-gotten gains."

We played along. We ate. Fred finagled a hotdog, an item that wasn't even on the menu, wrapped it in white bread and squirted ketchup on it while I tried to distract Karen. We laughed about our crazy chase across Mount Desert and the near misses on Gorham and in Bar Harbor. When Karen rose unsteadily to go to the ladies' room, I got up too.

Fred snorted into his beer. "It always takes a pair. Whatever they do in there, it always takes two of them."

"Try to think of something more original to say while we're gone," I told him, doing my best to sound chipper, even though my insides felt as if they'd been wrung like a dishrag.

She was re-applying her lipstick when I told her that her mother wanted to, *needed* to see her.

She had her lips rounded anyway, so her answer wasn't surprising. "Oh?" It was as if I had told her that her hem was crooked. She dabbed at a place where she had colored outside the lines, perfecting her smile. "She had practically all summer to see me in Ashton. I'm down here now."

"Karen, it's not so simple."

Someone else came into the room. Karen touched up her lips and started to go.

I had no way of knowing if I would get a better chance and I'd already started, so I wasn't about to give up now, even if we did have an audience. This might be as private as our confrontation would get. I blocked the way. "She needs to see you as soon as possible."

Some of the smoke and congeniality left her eyes, but she was still loose and unsteady. "She can call me up. She knows where to find me—" she smiled and touched the tip of my nose—"or at least I'm sure she soon will."

"Calling you won't cut it, Karen." That was an unfortunate choice of words, but at least she didn't know it—yet.

She was starting to get annoyed. "Then let her come down here. There's no reason why I should jump every time she crooks her finger. I've done enough of that." She started to move around me.

I wanted to tell her everything then, but I couldn't bring myself to go against Geneva's wishes. For an instant I considered knocking her out somehow, throwing her into the truck, and hauling her back to Ashton in ropes. Instead I asked her to trust me, to believe that she had to go back as soon as possible.

She stopped, let out a breath, and glanced around the room before looking me in the eyes. "Amber, sweetie, I believe that *you* believe, but you don't know my mother, do you? You don't know what she's capable of. Tell me this. Is Jack Crystal involved in this little charade?"

"Only in—" I couldn't minimize it. Never once had I talked to Geneva about the danger she was in. The whole story had come from Jack. For all I knew, he was making it all up for some self-serving purpose. He was devious enough to do it, and right now—even in her limber condition—Karen seemed more real and believable than he did. I wasn't even thinking of the money now. I just wanted to do the right thing, but dealing with Karen and her mother, how could I possibly figure out what that was?

I caved and went back to the table with her, hoping that a better opportunity would come up so that I could get her to listen to me, even if I had to get her rollicking drunk to do it. At dinner I did everything I could to smooth over our relationship. I accepted all the drinks she pressed on me and got damn near drunk on my ass doing it. Plugging along with his beers, Fred eyed me as if he thought I had given myself up completely to the corruptions of the city and the company. I held onto my self-control as well as I could. I may have been a little clumsy with my table manners and not so good at getting out a straight sentence, but my inner mind was running the show the whole time and it was telling me that I owed it to Geneva, to Karen, and to myself to persist and to break down Karen's defenses as soon as I got the chance, and in the meantime to be her reliable old friend from a summer's diversion in Ashton.

After dinner we crowded into her BMW. Karen wanted to go dancing. She handled the wheel like it was a toy, and we were going fast enough to make me nervous before we were even out of the parking garage. She went smoking through the crowded streets, narrowly missing the more foolish jaywalkers who dared to cross in front of her. Robin sat beside her without showing any fear, and I was a little too dazed to understand what was going on, but Fred crouched behind her, bracing himself for the inevitable shattering impact, and when she hopped the curb cutting a corner, he wanted out.

"You're too goddam drunk to drive this car," he said over squealing tires and honking horns. "Stop this thing and let us out right now. You can kill yourself if you want to, but you're not going to kill us."

When she failed to respond, Robin caught her by the wrist. "Let them out, Karen. They're not into our game."

She pulled the car over and looked at him innocently. "Game?"

He continued to hold her wrist. "Yeah. Chicken."

She gave him a sleepy smile. "Oh, *that* game."

I fell to my hands and knees getting out of the backseat. "You guys going to be okay?"

Robin seemed unconcerned. "We'll see you at the house."

With all my heart, I hoped it was true. I imagined them disappearing at the end of a streak of flaming rubber, never to be seen again. How would I explain to Geneva that I had let Karen and her kidney slip away? I stood beside Fred on an unfamiliar street corner and watched the cars shoot past—cars that seemed to be driven by Sunday sightseers compared to the one we had just escaped.

"Now what?" I grabbed at my purse to keep from dropping it.

Fred pushed it close to me. "Hang onto that. There could be purse snatchers around here."

I tucked it under my arm. "How nice to have an urban guide. Now that we're standing here with no idea where we are, what are we supposed to do?"

He put his fingers between his teeth, let out a piercing whistle, and ran toward a halting taxi, waving his arms. He motioned to me. "Come on, Amber, come on! He's not going to wait all night."

By the time I made my way across the street, he was still arguing with the taxi driver. The conversation appeared to be going on in two different languages. As I tried to sort out what was going on, traffic streamed around us. Finally the cabbie said, "Okay. Get in."

We piled onto the backseat. Fred gave the address through the webbed glass partition and sprawled comfortably. "He wasn't going to let us in. Some rule. You just have to know how to talk to these big city people. Don't take no for an answer."

"I sure hope Karen doesn't take off on us," I said. I couldn't think about anything else.

The cabbie also had his mind elsewhere. He was talking on a cell phone, and we were going back across the Charles into Cambridge.

Fred banged on the glass. "Where the hell you going, man? You're supposed to be taking us to Beacon Street!"

I began to think of wild, improbable conspiracies, a scheme to kidnap us to prevent Karen from going back to Maine. Something to do with vast amounts of money and a secret will.

Fred and the cabbie conversed through the glass for a while. The cabbie had misunderstood and was heading for some far-flung suburb. As if we had lived in Boston all our lives, we told him to get onto Memorial Drive and take us to the Harvard Bridge. He went through the whole maneuver while talking on the phone. Still chatting away, he drove through a variety of tricky intersections and a red light.

From two sides, tires and horns shrieked within inches of the cab. Fred banged on the glass again. "Get off the phone and drive this car, you damn nut-sack!"

"The light was green," said the cabbie over his shoulder.

"It was red," I told him, suddenly sober.

He looked back at us, oblivious to the road. "It was green, wasn't it?"

Fred leaned forward and jabbed his finger toward the road. "Yeah, as green as a goddam cherry, Now put away the cell phone and get us there in one piece, will you?"

I was beginning to think that when your time comes, it comes, whether at the hands of a drunken free spirit or a chatty cab driver. Maybe Boston was out to get us. Suddenly I was desperate to get on the road back to Ashton, with or without Karen.

CHAPTER 25

When we reached the house on Beacon Street, Karen's BMW was nowhere to be seen. Fred gave my hand a quick squeeze. "Before you freak out, why don't we go inside?"

They were there. Still in her black dress, Karen was spread out on the sofa, her head resting on the arm as her raised hand followed the ornate tracings around the chandelier. Robin had thrown his blazer over the back of a wing chair. He sat balanced on the other arm of the sofa with his bare ankles crossed and his feet balanced on the corner of the coffee table. He perched like a sailor guiding a dinghy through shifty winds and, in a broader sense, maybe he was.

Karen dropped her hand and regarded us with sleepy eyes. "Hello, travelers. I suppose you feel lucky to be alive."

"You got it," Fred told her. "A cousin of mine got killed riding with a drunk. His only fault was being too trusting."

Karen wriggled on the sofa and her black dress tightened and rode up, showing her firm thighs. "Too trusting? Which one—the drunk or your cousin?"

The last thing I wanted was for Fred to lace into her, so I said, "If you don't mind, guys, Karen and I have a little catching up to do."

Robin got the hint. He dropped his feet from the corner of the coffee table. "Tell you what, Fred, I could use a smoke and a stretch. What do you say we leave them to it?" He picked up his blazer and slung it over his arm.

Fred let his shoulders go slack. "Sure. Why not? A stretch would do me good—and some fresh air."

When they were gone, Karen sat up and straightened her dress. "Doesn't have much of a sense of humor, does he?"

"The thing with his cousin, he took it hard," I said.

"So you two are an item again."

I sat down at the other end of the sofa. "No, we're—we're just a couple of people from Ashton, Maine, away from home and in over our heads."

Karen's lips formed a pout. "Not just because of me I hope. I mean I hope at least you got over to the Fine Arts Museum. They have a gem of a collection of American oils. It was one of Walt's favorite places in the world."

"And yours?" I said. "Like Mount Desert?" My eyes took in the polished panels of the walls and the dark leather of rows of books. "And this place?"

"Mmm, yes. My *places. Our* places."

"Wasn't it good? Weren't they loving parents?"

She laughed. "Loving? Sure they were loving. Of course they were loving. Sometimes I suppose they even loved each other. But you see, my father loved his work—and why not, he was damn good at it—the best. A *Sterling*. Excellent in all ways."

I wanted to be patient, not to lose sight of my purpose, however selfish or false it turned out to be, so I followed her. "Are you saying he wasn't there for you? Didn't see you take your first steps?" My mind went back to the shattered photograph under the dresser at the house in Ashton. "He didn't see you win your first trophy?"

She got up and walked to the wing chair, put her hands around the back of it as if to touch the shoulders of someone who made a habit of sitting there. "So after all, Amber, you really do think I'm just another spoiled rich girl who had ponies instead of parents."

I became aware of gripping the arm of the sofa. It was true. Without quite knowing it, I *had* come to think of her that way, but I wasn't about to admit it because the rift between us had already widened and I didn't want to make it worse. So I sat back and asked, "What is it then? What is it between you and your parents? Everybody loves Walt. Why shouldn't you?"

She pressed her fingers into the wings of the chair. "You don't get it. They don't *love* Walt any more than they love their lucky rabbits' feet. He's a talisman for them, a charm, an inanimate object, like a teddy bear or a favorite doll. They make what they want of him."

"But what about you, Karen? You knew him."

She came back around and sat in the chair. "He was handsome when he dressed up, despite the bow ties. He smoked too much, occasionally drank too much when he was excited. He sailed like he was trying to kill himself. He was a competitor! And he taught me to compete. We used to play croquet in the yard in Maine until the time he knocked my ball into the river. He and my mother had such a terrible row that he swore never to play the game again—and didn't. That's where the wild patch came from. That was our croquet field. Now it's a monument to the competitive Sterlings. It's a memento of our beloved family's unyielding drive to surpass."

I told her about the time I beat Brian at Monopoly. He got so mad at me that he ran the board through the circular saw—with my straight-A report card sandwiched inside it.

Despite herself, she smiled. "Amber, dear Amber, you're just not getting it. Walt didn't think of me as a daughter. He thought of me as a *competitor*. First I was to compete with him and then I was supposed to compete *for* him, to take on the world! Whatever I did, whether it was swimming or sailing or seeing the capitals of the world, I was supposed to compete. Not that it was ever spelled out, of course, but that's what rode on every breath the Sterlings took. We competed—with each other and then with everyone else. Now I suppose he has it somewhere in the back of his mind to be a model Alzheimer's victim. I'm sure there's some kind of award for that somewhere."

It was hard for me to believe that such a sweet, harmless guy could've been such a cutthroat, but I wasn't about to argue with her. "Okay, but didn't you say your mother came down on him for being so hard on you?"

"Oh, that one time, that one time that I remember, during a croquet game of all things. Not during the soccer games and the swim meets and the science fairs. There we were full tilt. There we won big, even if it cost us a few friends. You notice I'm talking collective. *We* lost a few friends for being too competitive—but that was the cost of being better than everyone else. That was the cost of greatness. And they wondered why I threw myself at the most outrageous men that came along—a Nigerian mama's boy and a pirate."

She was so bitter that I thought it best to let her spill, to let her pour out her resentment like a summer squall spending its violence. Having no idea how big the storm would be, I backed off. I got up and went to the window. The Charles glittered with lights, so different from the wild rustic river that divided Ashton. "What about the pirate?" I asked. "Is Robbie just along for the ride?"

"For the money, you mean? Isn't that what it always comes down to?"

I thought of Jack's offer to pay me for spying on Karen and then of the money he had promised if only I would bring Karen back to Ashton. For the Sterlings maybe everything did stem from money—including my relationship with the family. I imagined that if Karen found out about my arrangement with Jack she would throw me out of the house at once and swear off my friendship. I had entered into the arrangement with the best intentions, but now I felt two-faced and money-grubbing. "Look," I said at last, "during all that time we spent together I got the impression that Robbie cares for you, that's all. I was just hoping that the feeling was mutual."

With an odd lopsided smile, she watched me fidget. "How do you know it wasn't *you* he cared for all along?"

"What?" Coming back toward her, I tripped on the fringed corner of the rug. "Give me a break."

"You care for him, don't you? Isn't that why you came chasing down here? Out with it, Amber."

I thought of him standing at the helm of the *Paul D*, one hand on the boom as he bullied the boat about, thought of the boy who had defended me on the playground all those years ago, and I had to admit to myself that I *had* been drawn to him, and yet I was glad to have Karen come between us. "There's all kinds of caring," I said.

She was still smiling. "Now don't go platonic on me. We're talking primal urges here, not the brotherhood of man. 'Fess up."

With my foot I straightened the rug. "If you're talking about plain old lust, I think I'd have to say *no*. Robbie's very attractive I guess, but that doesn't mean I want to fling myself down in the v-berth with him and make babies. There's more to love than that."

She pursed her lips. "Now don't get your back up. I was just making a point about competition. There was an attraction between you and Robbie, but the old Sterling competitiveness kicked in. Now I have him."

In an effort to look calm I put my hands in my pockets. "Karen, you're welcome to him."

"You can honestly say that you'd rather have Fred, white bread Fred?"

"I've already told you. There's nothing between us. We're just traveling together."

She settled back in the chair and crossed her legs. "Oh, yeah. You just never told me why."

"We ran into one another on Mount Desert. He was looking for a boatyard job and I was looking for you. We decided to make a little vacation of it, that's all."

"It's not like you to get snippy, Amber."

I'd had enough. I came to the point, the terrible point. "Guess what? Your mother needs a *kidney*, Karen, and she's not going to get one unless *you* give it to her. That's why I came looking for you. To bring you back to Ashton."

She laughed, not like a drunk, but like someone who's heard a first grader let slip something unintentionally funny. Her face reddened and she put her finger to the tip of her nose. "I swear, she gets more imaginative all the time!"

I sat on the arm of the sofa. "Karen, she's been going to the Eastern Maine Medical Center. All that time we thought she was in Eastport doing legal work or whatever, she was going to Bangor. Jack was taking her down for dialysis."

"Is that what she told you?"

I couldn't begin to tell her about my deal with Jack, so I settled for less. "You've got to believe her sometime, don't you? Why should she lie about something like that?"

"To make me jump to her tune, that's why. She's done it before. When I was going out with Maturin she was having heart palpitations. I came home for that, but not for this."

I pressed my fingertips to my forehead. I didn't care about the money anymore. I just wanted everyone to do the right thing. I swept my hair back. "Okay. Suppose she's *not* lying. The least you can do is go up to see her before she flat out croaks, Karen. And if she is lying, all you have to lose is a little pride. You can cover that up by claiming that you're coming home to see Walt. Isn't that reasonable?"

She frowned. "Poor Amber. Always so reasonable. The Sterlings must be driving you crazy. You don't know who to believe. I suppose you think that Jack is just an old family friend trying to be helpful."

"I'm not crazy about him, but is that so farfetched?"

She got up, put her hands on my knees, and looked into my eyes. "Amber, remember—he's Geneva's lover."

"Karen, under the circumstances—"

She shook her head. "No, no, not under the circumstances— always." She held her hand low to the floor. "Since I was that high. One time, during a party, when I was all of about five, I came into the kitchen and there were my mother and Jack in the middle of a very heartfelt conversation. Geneva was crying. Turned out she had never wanted to marry Walt in the first place, but had to for some reason—money I suppose. Remember? It all comes down to that. Anyway, there they were. She was bending over the stove, stirring the hell out of some hot cider and I swear her tears were falling into it. He had his hand on her shoulder. Of course, when they caught sight of me the tender scene came to a halt."

I got up and stood with my hand on the chair. "If you were only five—"

"And six and seven and eight, when I won my first medal for freestyle. My father wasn't there but Jack was—not for me, of course, for Geneva. It got so brazen that even Walt found out about it. And you know what he did? *Nothing*. Oh, we spent more time up in Ashton, but then Jack just happened to rent a house in the neighborhood—*every summer*—and there we were all over again. Walt threw himself even more into his work and Geneva threw herself even more into *Jack*. Funny thing was, the Alzheimer's didn't make that much difference."

I was gripping the furniture again, wringing the back of the wing chair. "Karen, what a horrible thing to say."

She shrugged and turned away. "Oh, chill out. I was only talking about the love triangle, that's all." She turned around and pinned me with her hazel eyes. "Too bad *Jack* can't donate a kidney."

I couldn't help saying, "At least he's standing by her."

She took my hand and squeezed it. "What's in it for you, Amber? If I do go back, what's in it for you?"

"Nothing!" I answered at once. I meant it, too. I didn't care about the money anymore. "I just want everything to come out for the best, for everyone."

She turned at the sound of Fred and Robin coming into the outside entrance and then asked me point blank, "Do you think I should give Geneva a kidney—one of *my* kidneys?"

"I don't know, Karen. Just go up and talk to her though, will you? Go back and see Walt. Go tell Jack what you think of him. Get it all out. Hook Robbie on your arm and show him off, flaunt him. It'd feel good, wouldn't it?"

She ran her hands over her hair. *"God, yes!"*

"Then you'll go?"

"Amber, we'll go up tonight if you want to. We'll roust them all out of bed and I'll lay it on the line, even if it's the last time I ever see any of them."

Robin and Fred clattered into the foyer. "We're screwed," Fred announced. "The truck's been trashed."

"The *truck*?" I wanted to rush up and hug him, but I didn't dare. I was afraid he was blaming everything on me.

"They were pretty good," Robin said. "Disabled the alarm, broke the lock, cleaned out all the stereo stuff, and pinched the trailer hitch for good measure." He clapped Fred on the shoulder. "You've still had a better night than we have."

I looked at Karen. "What does he mean?"

"A little smack-up en route to the cabaret," Robin said. "A streetlight took on the BMW and won hands down. We left the carcass over on Newberry Street. "

Only then did I see the red mark on his cheek.

Karen giggled. "Oh, yeah. I forgot to mention that. It all happened so fast. Robbie was very brave."

Fred dropped into the wing chair and propped his feet on the coffee table. "God damn."

I knelt beside him and pressed his hand in mine. "I am *so* sorry. I'm afraid it's all my fault."

He pulled his hand away. "Forget it. Nobody made me come down here."

Karen sat down on the arm of the chair. "Amber and I were just talking about going back to Ashton tonight, weren't we, Amber? Do you suppose we could all go in your truck—what's left of it, I mean?"

"Drop me off in Newburyport," Robin said. "I'll take the boat up and meet you there in a couple of days."

"Will you?" Karen asked.

He put his hands in his pockets and smiled. "Sure."

"Why tonight?" Fred complained, "I'm beat."

Karen pulled her hair back in the old familiar way. "Something to do with momentum, I think. Anyway, Amber's homesick, aren't you, Amber?"

I stood up. "You wouldn't believe how homesick."

Fred drummed his fingers for a moment. "All right. If you want. As long as they haven't stolen the damn engine."

And so, somewhat the worse for wear, we left Boston. Karen and Robbie insisted on riding in the bed of the truck, which was particularly dangerous on those quirky streets coursing with death-defying drivers, but Karen seemed to welcome another chance to put her life on the line, and Fred was keeping the speed down anyway. At some bleary-eyed hour of the night we dropped Robbie off in Newburyport. He and Karen had a brief discussion in the shadows of the marina and then we were off again, the three of us wedged into the cab of the truck as if we were the best of friends.

Sometime after we left the broad pipeline of I-95 for a quiet country four-lane highway, I dozed off and dreamed that I was on Mount Desert again, climbing Gorham Mountain in the fog with Karen. We were looking for Walt, who was somewhere ahead of us. We kept calling his name but we heard no reply, just the steady crunching of our feet on the trail.

"Maybe he can't hear us," I said.

"And maybe he's not listening," Karen answered.

When I woke up, Karen was asleep with her head on my shoulder. Fred was staring into the twin tunnels of the high beams that pushed back the blackness.

"You okay?" I murmured.

"I'm fine," he said, blinking back the sleep.

"I believe you are," I said, thinking at the time that it made no sense.

CHAPTER 26

By the time we arrived dazed and numb in Ashton, I still had no idea what Karen was going to do, but I think she had been awake most of the night putting her plan together, and apparently I was going to get a front row seat for its unveiling because she insisted that I accompany her for her homecoming. More than anything else, I wanted to go home and go to bed because I get crabby when I haven't had enough sleep. I get crabby and I feel ugly, self-conscious, and dumb. And I say things I don't mean. I avoided looking in a mirror but I still felt like a dog. My hair was greasy and tangled and my left foot hurt for some reason. Also I seemed to be coming down with a sinus headache. I was in no condition to throw myself into a rematch between Karen and her mother.

There we were though, Karen and I, traipsing into the kitchen as if this were just another summer morning. Mrs. Conditt was giving Walt his post-breakfast cleanup. Karen kissed him on the top of the head, sat down beside him, and tried to read something into his expression.

"Are you happy to see me, Dad? Are you ready to spend some time together?"

"He's still quite the celebrity," Mrs. Conditt said, clicking as she savored her first atomic fireball of the day. "We have more people all the time, coming over every day. The Eastport newspaper even did a story on him. They hardly even mentioned all of his achievements, just *the phenomenon* as we've come to call it."

Karen didn't look up. I wasn't sure that she had even heard. "Is my mother here?"

Discreetly, Mrs. Conditt removed the fireball. "Yes, but she got up late. She's been in bed a lot lately. Mr. Crystal's coming over shortly. They'll be going to—"

"Yes, I'm sure he is and I'm sure they will." Karen said. She stood up. "Well, we'd better get to this then. Come on, Amber."

I heard a car in the driveway, and for once I was glad to see the familiar replica and Mr. Jack Crystal. Now, whatever happened, I would probably be able to stay clear of it. Karen looked around as if trying to find a way out of the house. I had the strange notion that she was afraid of killing him. She stiffened, smoothed her hair, took a deep breath, and faced the door.

Suddenly I was afraid, afraid that he would spill the beans about his offer to me, afraid that Karen would turn her fury against me—and that I would deserve it. Now *I* wanted to get away too, but the only way out was the river, and no boat waited to spirit me away.

He let himself in. He was wearing one of those gray tweed sports coats with patched elbows, brushed denim pants, and a pale blue knit shirt with a couple of picks just below the collar. His face lit up at the sight of us. He glanced from Karen to me and back. I could almost hear his mind shifting gears. "My God, look who's here!" he said, overacting just a little. "How were your travels?"

Karen continued to stand very straight. She rubbed one hand on the back of a chair. "Not as important as yours. Off to Eastport—or is it Bangor again today?"

He knew at once that I had told Karen about her mother. I could feel the room temperature drop. "We've got a few minutes," he said, not looking at me. "Why don't we go into the living room and have a chat?"

"I like it here," Karen said, "but maybe we should wait for my mother."

He pulled at his jacket cuffs. "I'm sorry, Karen. I—we wanted you to find out in the right way, from your mother, face to face." He still avoided looking at me. "Obviously it hasn't worked out that way. But at least now you're here and you know the score.

Your mother's a very sick woman. I suppose you also know that there's hope for her though."

Mrs. Conditt became aware of outstaying her welcome. She stood Walt up, put a jacket around his shoulders and, with gentle encouragement, guided him out to the porch.

"And you know," Jack continued, "that the hope depends on compatibility. If there's no match, there's no transplant and—"

Karen cut him off. "And even if there *is* a match, but for some reason there's no transplant…"

His brows went up. "Then the same, of course."

"So simple."

"I guess it is, in the long run. The next move is up to you, of course. What are your plans?"

It was such a strange, open question that I wasn't sure what he meant. I suppose he left it vague on purpose to give Karen room to steer the conversation. She avoided the real subject and said that she planned to do some sailing, perhaps as far as New York, assuming that the *Sea Clip* could be set right.

"A lovely idea," he said, "but the boat's dangerous."

Her chin went out. "I can handle it."

"I hope you'll act responsibly."

She laughed. "It's *my* boat—and my kidneys. And I want to use them for a while."

The silence that followed filled with the slow creaking of the stairs as Geneva came down. She looked thin and tired. Her white ankle-length notch pants looked loose at the waist and the pale blue silk blouse hung limp. She moved slowly, like a sleepwalker. Her voice was soft. She looked at each of us. "Hello, everyone." She embraced Karen and kissed her on the cheek. "How have you been, baby?"

"Same old same old," Karen said, looking at Jack and me rather than at her mother. "Jack tells me that you're off to Bangor this morning."

Her mother took her by the hands. "Now, look. I didn't want to make a big deal about this. That's why I didn't tell you."

Karen slipped her hands away. "When were you planning to, Mother?"

"As soon as I saw you again. It didn't seem like the kind of thing to discuss over the telephone or by postcard."

"How did you know I'd be coming back?"

"I only hoped."

"She's talking about sailing that boat again," Jack said. "I told her it would be a risky thing to do. She won't respond to the tiller."

I wondered if he was talking about the boat or Karen.

Geneva sounded too tired to argue. "Can we talk about it when I get back? Will you be around this evening, dear?"

Karen shrugged. "Of course, Mother."

For the next couple of days Karen had plenty to think about, and so did I. Foremost on her mind, no doubt, was her kidney. Until she went to Bangor for testing, nobody knew whether hers was even a match for her mother's, and she didn't want to go to Bangor until Robin came back. She didn't sit there waiting for the phone to ring, but we did spend hours on the porch, talking and staring toward the bay.

Walt was more popular than ever. He sat on the rattan throne in the corner of the porch as people filed in, knelt down, took his hand, and tried to read his eyes. Most of them swore that they had seen something meaningful in them, whether it was guidance for a lifetime or just a momentary warmth and glow. For my part, I couldn't tell that he was doing much of anything except gazing toward the river as he usually did, but when he favored somebody with one of his occasional smiles it was as if chimes had gone off, and people were coming from as far away as St. Stephen and Presque Isle to see it happen. On misty days they dripped their way across the porch. In fair weather they waited in the backyard, talking in small groups, discussing the news of the day—the lobster catch, the rummage sale at Holy Redeemer By-the-Sea, the price of gasoline on one side of the border or the other, that sort of thing. But the conversation always drifted back to the man sitting in the rattan chair on the porch, the man who conferred some kind of legitimacy on their hopes and schemes.

I have to admit that at times I shared Karen's misgivings about her father because at times he seemed an unlikely source of confidence. When the afternoons grew chilly, we'd put a wrap on him and, since wrestling him into his cardigan could be a major production, Karen liked to wrap his shoulders in one of Geneva's old mink coats, and there he sat, his head slightly inclined, his sinewy hands on his knees, looking like Queen for a Day. I was just glad that Maurice hadn't worked Walt's hair into a kind of crown but, from what I heard, he and Reginald were way too busy at the refurbished salon to come over and minister to the man on the rattan throne.

Fred came over once, rattling up in his picked-over shell of a truck. He was very good-natured about the setback and spurned my offers to pay for the damage, which would've taken years anyway. "I bought it in the first place," he said. "Don't you suppose I can come up with the money to fix it? Anyway, I was kind of enjoying myself for a while there."

"Me too," I said, trying to figure out just what he meant. "Sorry the job search didn't work out."

"To hell with the job search," he said. "I can get a job when I want one bad enough."

I had to give him a little squeeze. "Sure you can."

"Damn straight. What are *you* going to do though? Summer's about shot. You saved up enough for grad school?"

"Not hardly," I said. I hadn't seen a penny from Jack and wouldn't have felt right taking the money anyhow. I kept telling myself that.

The next morning I had an unexpected encounter with Jack. I was walking down the point road to see Cherie's mother, and along came the replica car. "I wouldn't presume to offer you a ride," he said. "Once burned."

It was windy and I looked at him sidelong through strands of hair. "I'm not expecting any money if that's what you're thinking. Just don't ever tell Karen that we talked."

He stopped with a slight squeaking of the brakes. He wasn't taking good care of his replica.

"I guess that's fair on both counts. You did kind of spill the beans about Geneva's kidney condition."

"Regardless," I said, "it wouldn't've been right to take money for something like that. I don't know what I was thinking."

He took off his cap and smoothed his hair. "Did Karen tell you the news? The kidneys match. She's going to be able to save Geneva."

I hadn't seen Karen for a few days. She had been down to Bangor and back and hadn't even told me the outcome. I was hurt. I was miffed. I walked on. "Good," I said. "Now she just has to decide if she's going to go through with it."

"Oh, don't you think she'll do the right thing?" Jack sounded upbeat and confident, like he was trying to sell me a used car. "Especially if you—"

I kept my eyes on the road. "But I *won't*. She's got to make that decision all by herself."

She had a strange way of making up her mind. I was pinning some sheets on the line when she pulled into the driveway in the red Mustang. She was about as cheerful as I'd ever seen her. She stuck her head out and smiled. "Don't you do anything but hang up clothes when you're home?"

I stuck a clothespin behind my ear. "Not really."

"I hope you're not ticked off that I didn't tell you the news."

"Oh, that's all right," I said. "I found out from Jack. We're all friends, right?"

"Oh, now settle down. When I found out, I was a mess. I still am."

"But I suppose at least you have Robin to help you think it through."

Her smile was bright. "He's back, yes! And camping out on his island. He's decided to rebuild."

She hadn't even shared *that* news with me. I felt that more than a river had opened between us. At the same time, though, I was relieved that I hadn't been caught up in the storm of her reunion because I was jealous, jealous of Robin for taking Karen away from me, and envious of their togetherness. I glanced back toward the clothesline. Mom was struggling with a sheet that was trying to take flight. "Should I ask what you've decided or should I get it from Jack?"

She remained sunny. "I haven't decided yet. Is that awful of me?"

"My God, Karen, she's only your mother. What does Robin say?"

"That he'll love me even if I give away half a dozen parts as long as we can still go sailing and make love. Isn't that sweet?"

I tried to picture him saying it, one hand on the boom as he leaned down to tell her, behind him the sea a deepening gray flecked red with the last rays of the setting sun, and Karen's face tilted up to his as the boat rose and fell like a mother's breast. In my mind, I scribbled out the touching scene with a black crayon. "So what are you waiting for?" I asked.

She was still wearing her hair down. She swept it back from her forehead. "For the nightmares to stop. In my subconscious I seem to be very touchy about my kidneys. I'm even afraid of the anesthesia. This isn't like getting a broken arm set. This is permanent."

"Even more permanent for your mother if you *don't* do it," I said. "But don't let that stop you. How long does she have without it?"

Karen seemed not to have heard me. She was looking past the house to the river and the distant bay. "Don't worry," she said suddenly, "I'll have an answer soon enough, in a couple of days— an answer that will make everyone happy." Her face brightened again. "Say, how'd you like to join me for lunch tomorrow? There's that nice place near the marina in Eastport. When the wind is right it's nice to sit outside and watch the boats come and go. What do you say?"

I warmed to the idea at once. "Sounds great. Just the two of us?"

She smiled mysteriously as she put the Mustang into reverse. "Well, eventually."

I thought she meant that Robin would be joining us, but once again I had misjudged her. When we arrived at the pier-side restaurant, Jack was waiting for us at a four-table. Even though he smiled when he looked up and saw us, I could tell that he was as surprised to see me as I was to see him. "Amber, how nice to see you! I hope you're joining us for lunch."

Karen laughed. "Sure she is. She can be a witness."

Jack smoothed the linen napkin by his plate. "Oh, that won't be necessary. The business part of our get-together is pretty cut and dried. This just seemed like a good time to take stock."

Karen sat down across from him, leaving me to choose the seat next to her. She hung her purse on the back of her chair. "Okay, we're here. Shoot."

CHAPTER 27

The place was crammed. Without success, he tried to get the attention of a waitress. "Some days it's hard even to get a menu in here."

I got up and got three menus from the hostess stand. "If need be, I can take the orders, too," I said. "That's one thing I have experience with."

Jack chuckled. "Very good, very good. A handy person to have around."

Karen left her menu on her plate. "I suppose we're here about the money. Eventually life as we know it always comes down to that, doesn't it?"

"I just wanted you to be aware of the situation," Jack said, unfolding his menu. It was one of those laminated things with pictures, more suited to a burger joint than to one of the finer restaurants in Eastport. Hal wouldn't have been caught dead with that kind of thing in his place. "As you know, " Jack continued, "your father's will stipulates that two years after his death you are to begin receiving an annuity in monthly payments, derived from interest accrued by the estate."

Karen frowned as if he had just told a bad joke. "I've only known that for about two years. Is there something new you have to report?"

Patiently, he continued. Maybe his courtroom experience had hardened him to hostility. "Of course, the will takes effect only after your father's death. In the meantime, his resources are to go on providing for the family's ongoing needs—maintaining the houses, supporting you and your mother and your father."

She stared at him over his menu. "So what are you saying, that the money's drying up?"

He laid his menu down and met her glare. "As you now know, in addition to the expense of caring for your father, your mother has had some considerable medical expenses lately. Her insurance will cover part of it, but kidney disease is an expensive proposition. If she has a long recovery, the care for her and your father will put a considerable strain on the resources of the estate."

"For God's sake, Jack, let's just call it *money,* okay?"

"I simply want you to be aware that between those two events and low interest rates, it's been necessary to draw down the principle, so that in the event of your father's death, the annuity will be diminished considerably. In fact, the estate may be forced to liquidate one property or another just to meet its expenses— depending upon how long the current situation continues, that is. Of course, we wouldn't want to lower the level of care your father has been receiving."

Karen looked at me. "My God. Mrs. Conditt must be making out like a bandit. She'll be supplied with fireballs for life."

Jack was not amused. "It adds up. Over time, it adds up."

A waitress appeared and asked if we'd like to order our beverages. I opted for iced tea with lemon. Jack wanted coffee.

"Just water for me," Karen said, without taking her eyes off Jack. "Ice water. Bring a pitcher, will you?"

When the waitress had gone, Jack summarized. "I don't want to trouble your mother with all of this right now. She's under enough stress as it is. Of course, it's not the sort of thing I like to tell anybody, but then it's my job."

"Oh, yes," Karen said, "there's always the expense of administering the estate. That's going to eat into the resources, too, isn't it?"

She wasn't cutting him any slack, but he was as cool as ever. "Take my word for it," he said, "that's the least of it. Because I'm a friend of the family, I've never charged a nickel for my time, just for the travel and office expenses."

I thought that she would be shamed, but she wasn't. "So just what are you suggesting?" she asked. "How am I supposed to manage this financial crisis, Jack?"

Now the waitress was picking up speed. She set down our beverages and asked if we were ready to order. Karen declined. I went for the club sandwich and Jack decided to support the local economy via a lobster salad.

"You can have some of mine if you get hungry," I told Karen.

She took a sip of water from her goblet and patted the pitcher. "I'm fine. Really."

When the waitress had put the menus under her arm, tucked her pencil behind her ear, and departed, Jack placed his hands on the table. "Look, Karen, I'm not about to tell you what to do and I'm not sure I even have any advice to offer, except to maybe—how do I say this—settle down a little? Regardless of how this business with the kidney turns out, your parents are going to need you. Somebody has to be around to hold things together."

She put her elbows on the table and leaned toward him. "Why not you, Jack? You've got all that experience at it."

He patted the table. "Karen, I'm not in any position to—"

"How about this then? You and Geneva have my father declared incompetent. You get power of attorney. Maybe the two of you even—you know?"

He patted the table a little faster. "This conversation really has gotten far afield of what I had in mind. All I'm saying is, if you could settle down a little and—"

"There's that word again, Jack. What do you mean, *settle?*"

He struggled for words. "Let me put it this way. If you could get past the risk-taking—"

"What do you mean, *risk-taking,* Jack?"

He planted his hands on the table. "It's the company you keep and—taking chances with your life and the lives of others. I guess that's what I mean."

He was using *I guess* again. I wondered if it bugged Karen as much as it bugged me.

She started to press him further but he put his hand up to stop her. "No, no. Let me go on. Just from what I've seen this summer it seems to me that you've put your father's life on the line by sailing him around in that godforsaken tub, the *Sea Clip*. I suppose you might survive a disaster in it, but I doubt if he could."

"Why should there be a disaster in it, Jack?"

"Because, if I may say so, you're not a capable enough sailor to avoid one. That water out there is full of rocks and ledges and riptides, and even a man such as your father had his hands full with it back when the boat was in better shape. You're nothing but courting disaster taking him out there."

Her jaw hardened and her fingers went white around the stem of her water goblet.

"Then there's your disregard for your mother. You may not have known about the kidney disease—until Amber went ahead and told you—but you knew that she was unwell, and it was precisely at that time that you chose to run off with that—that waterborne burglar. His kind turns up in the penal system every day and, mark my word, he's going to go right back into it because he'll go one step too far. And for the likes of him you abandoned your mother. I'm just glad that we could retain Amber to find you and bring you back."

Karen's fingers went slack. She set the goblet aside.

I felt sick. I was glad, at least, that she kept her eyes on Jack.

"And then," he said, "therapy notwithstanding, there's your own self-destructiveness, Karen—the reckless driving, the procession of parasitic men. Does this current one, Dunning, think he's going to get his hands on six or seven million dollars? If so, I guess he's in for a disappointment."

Jack was looming over the table now, so close that I could smell Listerine.

Karen jumped up, snatched the pitcher, and threw the ice water in his face. As he fell back, she threw the pitcher, catching him square in the chest, and over he went, crashing into his chair on his way to the floor. She grabbed the goblet and sent it crashing after him. She had her hands on the table and would have upended it on him, dishes and all, if I hadn't pulled her away.

She broke loose and bolted for the door. Ignoring all the shrieks and rubbernecking, I scooped up her purse and ran after her.

She swore all the way to the car and left a streak of burning rubber clear to the highway. I'm not sure how I had gotten in, but there I was, and even though I was afraid for my life, I knew that I had to go with her. She drove with one hand while brushing tears from her eyes with the other.

"Tell me what he meant, Amber. Tell me what he meant about *hiring* you to bring me back. Tell me about that."

I told her everything. I told her about spurning Jack's offer to pay me for spying on her and about his offer of a year's tuition if I could bring her back to test her suitability as a kidney donor for her mother and how I had renounced the money when I saw how complicated the whole situation was. I even told her how Fred had turned up by chance on Mount Desert, but she didn't hear that. She was still thinking about my treachery as the woods and the traffic flashed past.

She cleared her throat and glanced over at me. "I suppose I should be glad at least that my mother doesn't need a *heart* transplant."

That broke the tension and I laughed, but then—I don't know why—I started crying. I put my elbows on my knees and my face in my hands and wept with shaking shoulders.

She took a hand off the wheel long enough to pat my back. "Good thing I'm the one doing the driving."

I shook my head and brushed the tears with the back of my hand. "I don't know why I'm such a mess."

"I've got the name of an analyst if you want one. But to tell you the truth, I think he's even more screwed up than I am. I don't think he ever did me much good. Not as much good as you have. Good old reliable Amber, always trying to do the right thing." She picked up speed to pass a bread truck. "There's something I want to show you."

She drove to the cottage, taking the rutted driveway without any regard for its blind curves and granite bumps.

Mrs. Conditt was on her way downstairs. "Your mother's asleep."

Karen all but bowled her over on the way up. "Don't worry. I'm not about to wake her up now." She went into the room that had been mine, which now was Mrs. Conditt's. I felt awkward barging in like that, with Mrs. Conditt's oversized underwear strung out on the backs of chairs and a large bag of atomic fireballs spilled across the middle of the floor. Apparently her urge to clean up didn't include her own space.

Karen rolled back the rug and picked up a large key. "You see, Robin's not the only one with a secret room." She unlocked the closet and we were bombarded by trophies—loving cups, figurines, plaques, certificates—a shower of recognition. She nudged a gold archer statuette with her toe. "The bookshelves downstairs—and in Boston—used to be loaded with this crap until I slipped going off a diving board and lost a meet for my entire team. That's when I really went off the deep end and rounded it all up and stuffed it in here and hid the key. That's when they set me up with the analyst. I've only been back in here one time since."

I felt sick to my stomach. "Karen, I had no idea. I—"

She went into the closet and pulled out a shoebox. "Wait. There's more. When I was in boarding school they wouldn't let me have a cell phone and no Internet access. It was *that* kind of place. I was supposed to write *letters* to my parents. Same when I was in Paris. Would you like to see those letters?" She dropped the box on the bed, not bothering to move a pair of very large inside-out pantyhose. "Go ahead. Have a look."

I opened the box as if it had a cobra in it.

"Go ahead. It kind of sucks, but it won't bite."

Inside were two bundles of letters tied with cotton string. The postmarks on the top letters went back several years. The addresses were written in a willowy cursive, some in green ink, some in purple.

Karen picked up the top bundle and broke the string. "Go ahead. Read one."

I turned over the first letter. "It's still sealed."

She dumped the lot of them on the bed. None of them had ever been opened.

I fanned through the other bundle with the same result. "Jesus Christ, Karen."

"So you see, in a way, my parents have been asleep for a long time, at least as far as *I* was concerned. Walt could write his books and win his awards and Geneva could give of her great legal talents and do God knows what with Jack, but where I was concerned, they were sleepwalking. Now she wants my goddam kidney."

I fought the impulse to sit down on the bed and have another cry. "I'm so sorry, Karen. I wish I had a good reason for you. I wish I could even make something up, but I'm—How long have you known?"

"Since just before Maturin. Not a coincidence, I suppose, that I threw myself into an empty fling after discovering that my parents didn't give a—" She crammed the letters back into the shoebox. "Look, let's get out of here. We've got places to go and things to do."

I should have stopped her, should've tied her to the bed to keep her from leaving the cottage, but then, regarding Karen, I still had a lot to learn.

CHAPTER 28

I should've seen the handwriting on the wall when we took Walt with us. Mrs. Conditt could tell that Karen was upset and tried to come up with convincing excuses to keep him home, but Karen wasn't buying any of it. "According to our attorney," she said, "I'm in charge now and I say Walt comes with us. Or do you want to wake up Geneva and ask her about it?"

Her attorney had said no such thing, of course, and would probably not even be available for comment until he dried himself off.

Mrs. Conditt stood aside, sputtering. If she'd been sucking on a fireball just then, we might well have had to perform the Heimlich maneuver on her.

"Let's get out of here," Karen said, helping me to guide her father out to the car.

I thought that Walt looked paler than usual, although maybe that was just in contrast to the blues and greens of an unusually bright day. Even for Ashton the air was cool, considering that we were only about halfway through August. The sky was clear and the wind was scuffing up whitecaps in the bay. When I looked back to make sure that Walt was belted in good and saw him gazing toward the bright water, it seemed to me that his blue eyes had lost some of their luster. I tried to read something into them, tried to fathom the magic that so many others had found, but I came up empty.

I watched Karen scoot up to the tailgate of a van, cut over, and surge past it the second the road was clear. I envied her confidence. It always took me about two years to get up the nerve to pass on a two-lane highway, and right after I finally did, the bothersome vehicle usually turned off. She was passing two or three cars at a time and shoehorning back in with just inches to spare, parallel parking at sixty as Pop calls it.

I could tell that we were headed back toward Eastport, but other than that I had no idea what she was up to until my mind drifted back to our disastrous lunch with Jack. He had set her off by accusing her of risk-taking—with her parents' lives and her own—and her knuckles had gone white when he told her that she wasn't sailor enough to master the *Sea Clip*. Now she was throwing more than water back at him. She was going to put Walt's life and her own in that leaky boat and take the biggest risk of all. A few days ago, hadn't she said something about making everyone happy? How could she do that without proving herself to Walt, proving herself to everyone, before she made her final decision about whether to donate her kidney?

"Brian says that boat's dangerous," I reminded her. "You won't prove anything by taking it out now."

Her hair streamed across her face as she looked over at me. "So that's why you've been so quiet. You've been putting two and two together."

"Yeah. And however many go out in that boat, the number coming back could be zero. Look, Karen, at least take the time to get it fixed up, and then if you want to take Walt for a ride while the weather's still warm, fine. But right now it's so waterlogged that it'll roll like a pig. It'll be slow to come about and grist for every rock and ledge that's out there. What's to be gained by taking it out today?"

She looked very pretty just then, with her chin set and her hair flying. "Call it a handicap. Walt took me in under the best of circumstances—seasoned skipper, well-tuned boat, dead high tide. I'll have none of those advantages, except for a calm and steady crew. His crew was terrified and damn near useless."

She had confirmed my worst suspicion. She was determined to sail the *Sea Clip* into the Cauldron.

"You're going to kill yourself and him too," I said. Even now it felt strange to talk about Walt like he wasn't there. "What's that going to accomplish?"

A crosswind roared through the convertible and her voice went shrill as she shouted above it. "Thanks for the vote of confidence! Okay, let's say I *do* get us both killed! Everyone's happy! Walt's not going to know the difference, and as long as they can get their hands on my corpse fast enough, Jack and Geneva can help themselves not to one, but to *two* kidneys! How's that for a deal? But guess what! Hard as it may be to believe, I'm not suicidal, so I just might get us through, in which case I'll have proven that I'm as much a sailor as Walt ever was, and then I'll gladly go under the knife! That's right! Once I get through the Cauldron—dead or alive—I'm going to give Geneva a kidney! Now how can you beat *that* for generosity?"

My God, I thought, I wonder what part Robin has in all of this, and I bet I won't be long in finding out.

Karen told the men at the marina that we were just taking the *Sea Clip* out for a few maneuvers for some insurance documentation and, since it was her boat, they weren't about to stop her. But when people saw Walt, they came out of the woodwork to get a close look at him, to shake his limp hands, and to share warmed-over testimonials to his powers, to take phone pictures of him. Karen smiled obligingly and then set about getting ready to cast off. The smell of the boat was worse than ever, a kind of rotten devil's-apron-strings aroma that wafted up from its bowels. As I helped settle Walt into his place in the cockpit, Karen started the engine and we got going as quickly as possible to dissipate the reek of the leak.

Even though she was intent on adjusting the throttle, Karen was aware of my move toward the pier. "I suppose you'll not be coming with us."

Was it a dare? From the get-go, she had assumed that I was going to run home screaming, which, of course, would've been the intelligent thing to do, but I was fed up with being pushed around. I wasn't thinking about what water and rocks can do to skin and bone and brains, I was just mad and cantankerous. I spat into the water, oblivious to the people watching "I *am* coming!

What made you assume that I'm not? You shouldn't make assumptions about me, Karen."

She straightened and smiled. "It's damn stupid of you."

'Yeah, well, stupidity rules."

By the time we got into the bay I was feeling better. The afternoon was pretty and the air was fresh and I thought that Karen would come to her senses, flirt with a rock or two, and steer the leaky old hulk back to Eastport. I had one of my longer conversations with Walt, one-sided, of course. I went on and on about the weather, how cool it was and how tropical Mount Desert seemed after a person had been trotting up and down its mountain trails for most of a day. I secured a canvas hat to his head, tightened the string at his sagging throat, and blabbed on about whatever came to mind, not realizing until well into my monologue that I was yakking up a storm because I was so nervous. I was hanging my hope on the Cauldron itself—on the wind and the tide conspiring to make entering it impossible. I was wishing that its sheer contrariness would bring Karen to her senses.

We were a good team. As usual, she worked the tiller and the mainsheet and I winched the jib and kept an eye out ahead. I watched a cormorant shooting toward the water, its long black neck stretched forward even as its beak broke the water. I never did see it return to the surface. Fortunately, I was not a believer in omens, much.

Karen didn't slow down until we came to Downeast Ledge, and then I knew where Robin had been since his return from Boston. The outline of a new top story had replaced the charred timbers of the old, and he stood high above the front door, hammer in hand, tapping at the new frame of the window that faced the river. When Karen hove to beside the *Paul D*, he raised his hammer in salute and propped his elbows on a crossbeam.

"Hello the house!" roared Karen.

"Hello yourself!" he shouted back. He climbed down a wooden ladder and came to the edge of the drop-off. "Come to pound some nails?"

Karen steadied the tiller with her foot. "Maybe later! We're on our way to the Cauldron!"

If he was surprised or concerned, he didn't show it. He stood at the edge of the cliff, so close that I thought it would surely give way and hurl him into the foam. "You've missed the tide!"

"It'll still be high enough by the time we get there!"

'You'll be fighting it going in!"

"That much faster getting out!"

"You're riding low, Karen!"

"There's still plenty of water where we're going!"

"How's the steering?"

"I got here, didn't I?"

"It's a lot tighter in there!"

"Come and watch if you want!"

I wished that he would offer to take her through it himself, but I knew that even if he did, she'd never stand for it. She'd have to do it herself or it wouldn't count because she wouldn't have bested her father's accomplishment. As we swung into deeper water again, I looked back from the jib winch, and there he was, rowing out to the *Paul D.* Maybe he wouldn't be there to help us through, but he cared enough to watch and, if necessary, to pick up the pieces. Again and again, I looked back to follow his progress as he started up the motor and trailed after us without taking the time to raise a sail, and the sick feeling came back to the pit of my stomach as I thought again of the words that had brought us to this point of no return. Jack had all but told Karen that she *couldn't* sail the *Sea Clip,* had practically *forbidden* her to take Walt out in it, and yet he must have known that Karen would rebel. Was it possible that he *wanted* her to take risks, to gamble with her life and Walt's—and lose? If so, he had manipulated her just right because now she was about to take the biggest risk of all.

I told her what was on my mind. It's true that I was afraid of the Cauldron, and my basic fear of sailing grew stronger now every time the boat pitched on the tossing water. It was true that I welcomed an excuse to turn back. But this was a *good* reason! If Karen wanted to take on the Cauldron, she had a lifetime to do it under better conditions than today's and of her own free will, not because she had been tricked into it by a schemer who had something to gain if she and her father didn't come back.

Was it possible that his ambition stretched even further? No Karen meant no Geneva. Could Jack possibly have something to gain from that?

She wouldn't hear any of it, wouldn't admit that Jack was playing her like a puppet. As she saw it, she was going to meet her destiny, and it was far older than any lunchtime confrontation. Her voice rose above the slapping of waves against the hull. "If you want to get out, it's not too late! Robbie can come and pick you up and Walt and I can do it alone—if that's what you want!"

I dug my heels into the listing deck and took hold of a cleat. "All I'm saying is, you don't have to do this now! You can do it on tomorrow's high tide, on your own terms, not because Jack goaded you into it!"

I looked back across the bow. Dunning's Point took shape, showing the leaning cedars at the edge of the Cauldron and the picnic ground where yellow afternoon sunlight filtered through the thinned-out woods. I could see the thin floating line of foam at the mouth of the Cauldron, where wind and tide and rocks had whipped the water to foam. I saw a piece of driftwood, bleached and sinewy, tossed high and hurled against some unseen barrier, pounded until it shattered and vanished. I saw boils of water form and break as the rapidly dropping tide brought granite fists punching through the chop, and only the look of concentration on Karen's face convinced me that she hadn't lost her mind.

In the few minutes of calm remaining, I made sure that Walt's life vest was secure and saw to my own. I pitched one to Karen, but she let it fall at her feet. She called a jibe and eased us into it so that the heavy boom merely drifted across until it was all the way out on the opposite side, and then the sails blocked the view of my one source of comfort—the picnic ground. With the wind dead behind us now, the *Sea Clip* seemed to slow down and wallow in the waves that smashed into each other from all directions. I could see gray flashes of the rocks that formed the mouth of the Cauldron and, novice that I was, I knew that a wind shift could catch the boom, throw it back across, and crush us against those rocks; and I knew that the wind, funneled through narrows and slots, could pivot on a whim. I allowed myself one last look back at Robin and saw the *Paul D* waiting at the edge of the white water, its bare mast stuck to the sky and Robin standing at the helm, with one raised hand propped on the boom.

"We're in it now," I said too softly for Karen to hear. "We're on our own."

I swear I could feel the water drop two or three feet when we went through those rocks. The *Sea Clip* settled on her stern, and the water swirled around us until I thought we had come into a whirlpool. We needed more speed and, to get it, Karen steered a little toward the wind and tightened the mainsheet and we plunged forward. Now we were seeing what Robin had seen when we had first caught sight of him at the picnic, just before he had turned back—the broken cliffs of the park grounds blocked by the bending canvas of the main and jib; on the other side, a jagged wall of granite rising out of the pounding sea and, all along the way, rock after rock emerging from those erupting domes of water. From land I had watched it a hundred times in my twenty-three years without ever imagining how fearfully fast the tide dropped in the heart of the Cauldron.

The decks were slippery, soaked with spray and waves that channeled into the cockpit from the low side of the boat. Karen was fighting to maintain her stance at the tiller when the worst happened. A wayward puff hooked the end of the boom and threw it across so hard that we went into a spin. Tumbling into the rail, I caught myself on the jib as it tried to cross and stuck, still held in place by the opposite sheet. I grabbed at whatever I could get—cleats, lines, canvas—and looked back to make sure that she had regained control, but with the tilt of the boat what I saw first was Walt flipping over the rail, shoulder first, into the tossing water. Karen threw the stern line overboard, pointed to the tiller, yelled something I couldn't quite hear, and jumped in after him. Hanging there with the water washing over me, I gaped at the empty stern and the swinging tiller and felt a stinging in my heart. The rock wall rose above me so high now that it blocked the sky. The *Sea Clip* was trying to point into the wind and in the process was going broadside to it and heeling so hard that water was swirling into the cockpit and pouring into the cabin. I half climbed and half fell into the cockpit and laid hold of the tiller, knowing only that I couldn't let the boat stay on her beam and fill up, knowing that if I pointed her too far into the wind, she'd stall out and crash into the rocks, and if I turned and ran again with the wind behind me, a shift could jibe her again and knock her over. For the first time, I had come to think of the boat as a woman, a woman fighting for her life.

Behind me, drowning in the wash, Karen's voice was telling me what to do, and I realized that my hand had frozen on the tiller as wave after wave hit the heeling hull broadside. "Go downwind! Downwind! We'll take her straight out the back way!"

I yanked on the tiller, and the mainsail swung far out to the side. The jib was still fouled up and flapping wildly, but the boat seemed to slow down again, and I looked back just long enough to see Karen dragging behind me with one arm wrapped around the stern line and the other hooked across Walt's chest. "Straight through!" she shouted, "Straight through!" And then the water crashed into her so hard that she almost lost the line.

The back of the Cauldron was even more terrifying than the front. I had never seen it before. It was shaped to kill, with high rock walls that narrowed into a kind of funnel at a break not more than fifteen feet wide. Most of the time, with a wavering crosswind, it would be impossible. You wouldn't have room to zigzag through it, so your only hope would be to turn around and go back out the way you came in. But now, with the wind dead behind us, we had a chance to shoot right out the back—as long as the wind didn't shift and the rocks stayed out of the way. I wanted to turn around and head toward the wind, where a sudden shift would be less catastrophic, even
though new rocks were rising behind me all the time, jutting their frothy heads out of the water as the tide continued to drop.

I came to my senses as Karen yelled again. "Straight through!" I had frozen at the tiller, unable to fall away from the wind to pursue the dangerous, unstable course. She rose head and shoulders out of the water, Walt still with her in one crooked arm, and shouted the command, so loud that my hand moved on the tiller of its own will, and the *Sea Clip* surged toward the rock slot, apparently bent on self-destruction. Now there would be no turning back because the pounding water allowed no room for it. To turn around would be to lose momentum and smash into the jagged walls, not once, but again and again, as the wind-driven water thundered against them. My knees were shaking from cold and fear and my arm had gone as rigid and numb as a stick, pulling the tiller back each time it tried to turn us toward the wind. As we approached the slot, which was howling fury with the wind cutting through it, I could tell that I'd have to make a slight correction because the thing wasn't truly straight but diagonal to the left, and that would mean steering perilously close to a murderous jibe. I wanted to look back to Karen for directions, but there was no time, and I could see that holding course would surely slam us into the overhanging wall, so I made myself give the tiller a proper yank that lined us up with the slot. As the rock walls blocked the light, we hit on the starboard side, scraped and banged, nearly knocking me off my feet. Then the *Sea Clip* hit again and bounced, struck a rock with her keel, bucked and shuddered and broke into the prettiest open water I had ever seen.

Then came the jibe, and it threw us around hard, freeing the jib, which popped out wide. I let out the main and we leveled off. Finally free of the slot, we were in the lee of Dunning's Point, plodding along in a soft breeze. For once I could turn into the wind, put the boat in irons, and let her drift slowly backward while I helped Karen aboard. She had tied Walt to the stern line, and between the two of us we hoisted him up by his life vest without fear that we would lose him.

I looked over my shoulder to the rock wall at the back of the Cauldron. The slot had disappeared as if by magic.

"Jesus, Joseph, and Mary," I whispered, "why weren't we all killed?"

Karen had tied the stern line around Walt's waist. She undid it and sat him on the floor of the cockpit. He didn't look much the worse for wear, although one cheek was going red. She went below and came back with a couple of blankets, took off his life vest, and wrapped him up good. She was strangely calm. "We were improvising, but it worked out okay," she said, putting a hand on Walt's shoulder. "We did it. We threaded the needle with the *Sea Clip*, didn't we, Dad?"

I was sailing us into the bay without even being aware of it. I had trimmed the mainsail and set the tiller without giving it the least thought. The Cauldron had given me some reflexes. "Is that what they call it?" I asked. "Threading the needle?"

Karen wrapped the second blanket around her shoulders. "I've heard of people doing it in kayaks when the tide is dead high, but until now, never in a sailboat—and never when the tide was running out."

"Well, if they talk to me, nobody will ever try it again," I said. I ached all over. My arms and legs were sore to the point of cramping. I stretched them as best I could. "You did this," I said. "I froze up back there. We'd have gone over if you hadn't kept telling me to fall off and head for the slot."

She smiled as she thought about that for a moment. She pulled the blanket tighter and pressed the water from her hair. "Maybe that's a first, too, skippering a boat from a trailing stern line. Once you got going, you did fine, Amber. Don't ever doubt that."

"That was my own personal Downeast Ledge," I said, scanning the sun-glazed whitecaps of the bay. "And you got me off it. I don't think I'll ever be afraid of sailing again."

Far to the east, Robin was coming toward us now, still bare-masted and under power. By the time he caught up with us, we were most of the way back to Eastport.

He brought the *Paul D* within a boat length and paralleled our course. He smiled as he adjusted the motor to match our speed. "You sure have a style all your own!"

Karen turned, smiling and waving. I had never seen her look so happy and relaxed. It was as if she had finally removed some great splinter from her heart. "Well, I doubt if anyone will ever do it that way again!"

By the time we slogged back into the marina, it was apparent that the *Sea Clip* had paid a price for her passage through the Cauldron. She was leaking worse than ever. I remember Brian telling me that a hole two inches square a foot below the waterline of a boat would let in 4,760 gallons of water per hour, and considering the beating we had taken, I was surprised that we weren't already rotting on the bottom. At the marina they hooked up a couple of pumps, and when we left, the *Sea Clip* she was squirting from both sides.

"Life support," Karen said as we walked to the car, looking like a tribe of Indians in our blanket robes.

She was already thinking about her promise and what it would be like to be lying in the hospital minus a kidney.

CHAPTER 29

Aside from the bruise on his cheek, which skipped all of the preliminary colors and turned a banana yellow, Walt seemed unfazed by his swim through the Cauldron and, sitting on the porch watching him gaze out toward the river, I decided that, either way, he probably would have survived it gracefully. In his prime, before the Alzheimer's, he would've had the presence of mind to make one fast move after another to get through the ordeal. And in his "unplugged state," as Fred called it, he was probably so relaxed that he wasn't even aware of the danger. For him, getting sucked through a rock hazard in life-sapping cold water was probably not much different from sitting on the porch listening to the words of admirers tumble through his head. He may not have been all there, but what *was* there was rock solid. That's what I thought as I watched him sit on the rattan throne in the corner of the porch. He was solid.

Fred, Robin, and I went to the Boston transplant center with Karen. She let Fred drive the Mustang because it amused her to see him, resplendent in a frayed brown henley and aviator sunglasses, behind the wheel of the bright red sports car.

"You might consider getting one of these with the insurance money from the truck," she suggested with a wry smile.

Robin and I were in the backseat not saying much. In unguarded moments I was still reliving my experience in the Cauldron and coming out of it feeling at something of a loss. I wasn't sure that I could ever return to waiting tables. I was ready to move on to something new, but I wasn't sure what.

"Have you ever thought about going to college?" I asked Robin.

We were going down a stretch of Route 1 where you could get glimpses of the ocean, and he had been looking over that way. His black curly hair danced about his forehead. He turned and studied me with those dark blue eyes of his. "Can't say as I have. What could I learn there that I need to know?"

He had a way of putting the cap on a subject with just a few words. I wondered if he and Karen had ever exchanged paragraph-sized thoughts. "Oh, I don't know," I said. "Maybe you'd want to go to law school."

He laughed. "Why would I want do a crazy thing like that?"

"Maybe for the love of learning—or maybe because lawyers generally make more money than antique thieves."

He settled back against the seat and looked up into a scattering of benign clouds. "Especially once all the antiques in the neighborhood have been hauled off—or locked up."

"So?"

He looked over at me. "How many guys do you suppose have gotten into law school after doing time in Thomaston?"

"What difference does it make? You used the law to get yourself out. What's done is done. You can't change it, but you can go on to the next thing."

He went back to his cloud survey. "Reading up to get myself out was one thing. Don't know as I'd have the patience for it long term. Sitting still isn't for me, Amber."

"Then what about boats? You could go to work at one of the places that build and design them."

"Now you're trying to cast me in the same mould as Brian. I'm a pirate, remember?"

I was starting to lose patience. "Well, who would know best how to make a boat go than somebody who'd been using one to avoid arrest?"

He looked over at me again, trying to figure out just what I was after. "Maybe you're onto something there. Maybe Brian and I should open a boatyard."

"Well, why not? It would beat living from day to day and season to season, wouldn't it?"

Geneva and Jack had arrived at the hospital before us, and the farther we walked down the long waxed corridors, the more out of place I felt. Once Karen checked in, she seemed to belong to the place and not to us. I asked her if she was going to see her mother before the operation.

She gave her hair a little flip as she sat down on the bed with the hospital gown in her lap. "Count on it. I want to make sure my kidney's going to a good home."

Robin, Fred, and I went back to the house on Beacon Street, had a few beers, and played a strange variety of three-handed cribbage. I couldn't tell if Robin or Fred was particularly concerned about the operation, but I was on pins and needles. I kept thinking about the scalpel cutting into the tender part of Karen's beautiful back, tools like needle-nosed pliers separating her skin and muscle, various sharp instruments going in and snipping all of the ducts and vessels that connected the kidney to her, and then the organ itself lifting out like a giant gray bean, limp and glistening and slipped into some kind of shiny high-tech bag, slithering into a corner and waiting there until the surgeons reversed the whole process with Geneva. Only somewhere in the course of the imagining, *I* had replaced Karen as the donor, and I felt an ache where I supposed one of my own kidneys to have been whittled out of me.

I felt a surge of sympathy for Karen, and I wished I could be in the hospital room, holding her hand and comforting her, telling her stories to keep her mind away from what she was going through. I thought of her bravely sailing into the Cauldron, jumping in to save Walt, and then commanding our escape from the end of a rope, and I wondered if what she was going through now was any easier.

As the night went on, I got more and more on edge and increasingly less patient with Robin and Fred. Between them they had put down a six-pack of tall Narragansetts. They were getting slap-happy, and their cribbage rules got wilder all the time. I wanted to tell them that I thought they were disgusting, that they should be thinking about what Karen was going through and the sacrifice she was making for her mother. But I didn't. I wondered if either of them would make such a sacrifice—Fred who showed his respect for his forebears by throwing apples at them, and Robin, who had crossed some local roughnecks and gotten his grandparents' house burned down for it.

I wanted to think that they were showing their concern in some strange masculine way, denying it by engaging in juvenile behavior—they had taken to slapping their cards down and betting swigs of beer each time the pegs moved—but I couldn't convince myself that they were concerned about Karen at all, rather than just putting her out of their minds and taking their pleasure where they could find it. I wasn't likely to see them jumping up at dawn—around nine o'clock for them—to rush to the nearest florist for a get-well bouquet.

Around midnight Fred knocked over the cribbage board with his knee. They finished off the beer and Robin went to bed. Fred was pretty well glazed but still conscious for some reason. He fell back against the sofa cushions, smiling. "This sure beats that other trip down here, doesn't it? That little car of hers is fun to drive."

I made a point of frowning. "Fun, Fred? By this time tomorrow, Karen will be minus one kidney."

"That might be a little rough," he conceded, "but she'll get through it. I mean, she's in one of the best hospitals in the country, isn't she, and *she* made the choice to go through with it, didn't she?"

I was sprawled in the wing chair with my legs thrown over the arm. I sat up, planted my feet on the floor, and gave him a hard look. "*None* of it's been easy, Fred. In case you hadn't noticed, Karen does not exactly get along with her mother, and now she's giving her a kidney. I wonder how you'd hold up if you faced a decision like that."

"Why hell, Amber, I don't like her mother that much either. She's kind of a cold fish."

My eyes narrowed. "You know what I mean. You wouldn't give up one of your kidneys to anyone. You need them too much for filtering beer."

Putting on a hurt look, he stirred in the embrace of the sofa. "Oh, now that's not fair. I only have beer when the company calls for it. How many times did I have beer when you and I were going out together? None."

"Big whoop, Fred. The point is, I don't think you or Robin either one is quite tuned in to what's going on here. You think this is some kind of party. You don't really care about Karen or anything else."

His foot fell off the coffee table. He started to pick it up but apparently decided that he didn't want to make the effort. "Now don't give me that, Amber. There's plenty I care about. I came all the way down here, didn't I? I could've been looking for work Downeast somewhere."

"Give it another month or two and it'll be wreath season again."

"Not for me it won't. I've had it with that seasonal stuff. I'm ready for something real and solid. I'm ready to settle down."

"Sure, Fred, for the night maybe."

He sat up and gave the nearest beer can a shake. Finding it empty, he set it back down. "No, I'm serious. I've had it with living out of a truck and going from one make-do thing to another. Another winter's coming and I want something steady." He was surprisingly sober.

"Well, good for you," I said. "As soon as we get back, you can start looking."

"It'd be a lot better if we were looking together again."

"Fred, we've had some good times and things have worked out pretty well, finding Karen I mean. But that was just chance that we ran into each other on Mount Desert. Let's leave it at that."

He got up and came closer, cleared a place on the coffee table and sat down. "You haven't figured that out yet?"

"Figured out what?"

"Stopping for you on Route 3."

"You said you'd been driving that stretch a lot."

He leaned closer, rattling the beer cans on the table. "Amber, I saw you because I went down there looking for you."

"You *what?*"

"When I heard you were going down to Mount Desert, I went looking for you. I didn't know what was going to be happening to you down there. *Somebody* had to look out for you."

"You were, like, *stalking* me?"

"Well, in the good sense, yeah."

I tried to get past the meaning of what he had said. "If that stupid car of ours hadn't broken down again, everything would've been fine. It was just those stupid sway bar—"

"Amber, I went down there looking for *you*. Now doesn't that say something about caring?"

I felt trapped in that wing chair. I tried to think of something to say.

He spoke deliberately, using his hands like he was trying to get through to a deaf person. "The job hunt was for real, but it's not why I was down there. Running up and down those mountains, busted broke, going hungry, even what happened to the truck— that was okay because I was down there with you. It was always about you."

I got up and went to the window with the vague notion that it was a way out. I wondered how far I might go on the Charles if I had a racing shell—or was I more likely to have one of those little cat-rigged boats that just sailed in circles all day?

Fred came and stood behind me. "That's just the way it is, Amber. For the life of me, I can't take it apart and put it back together. It's the way the sun brightens up your face when the morning fog burns off or that little catch in your voice before you laugh or the way you smell after you've been caught in the rain."

I turned around, pressing my hands into the wall behind me. "Fred, you're making this so difficult, and I'm confused enough as it is. Let's just get through tomorrow and go back to Ashton and put our lives in order."

He put his hands on my shoulders, but I wriggled away before my ticklishness kicked in.

"Amber," he said, "wherever I go, I want you there. Without you Ashton's just an empty shell, a place to drive around aimlessly. I can't do that forever. Let's go somewhere and make a fresh start. We don't have to rush into a, you know, relationship or whatever. Let's just find a place where we can have something to look forward to at the end of the day, where we can make the most of ourselves, and whatever else comes, let it come."

I kissed my fingertip and pressed it to his lips. "Don't think about those things right now. You can get yourself all turned around thinking like that. Give it a rest. Give yourself a rest and give me a rest. Your thinking might be different in the morning."

He looked lost and out of place in that room full of paneling and leather-bound books. He put his hands in his jeans pockets. "I haven't had that much to drink."

"In the morning," I repeated, "in the morning."

CHAPTER 30

We camped in Boston for two more days, the three of us, playing cards and driving to the hospital. The surgery took place in the early afternoon, and Karen was dead to the world for the rest of the day. We tiptoed in to see her as the sky was going dark through the blinds. She was on her back with the head of the bed raised slightly. With tubes coming out of her nose and tubes coming out of her arms, she reminded me of the poor old *Sea Clip*, hooked up in the berth with pumps pouring out of both sides. Her face was the gray of weathered cedar, and her hair looked dark and damp against her forehead. The room smelled faintly of adhesive tape and warm linen. She looked delicate in the broad bed with its steel rails and, despite her claylike look, she appeared almost stylish in a cotton hospital gown with an intricate floral pattern.

She looked so vulnerable, so helpless. With the tip of one finger, I touched the back of her hand and knew that I loved her.

On the way out of the room, Fred summed it up poetically. "She doesn't look half bad for a girl knocked flat on her buns."

In the morning, when we came to see her again, she looked a lot better. She was sitting up, brushing her hair and humming.

"Maybe we should all give up a kidney," I said as we entered the room. "It seems to agree with you." I bent down and gave her a gentle hug.

Smiling, she put down the brush and held her hand out to Robin, who knelt and kissed it. "Always the pirate," she said. "So gallant."

Fred—*Fred*—-presented her with a bouquet that must have cost a fortune down in the hospital gift shop.

"This is a racket we ought to go into," he told me. "There's gotta be a hell of a markup on
this baby's breath crap."

"Well, how did it go?" I asked Karen. "You don't even look tired today."

"I shouldn't," she said. "I've been sacked out most of the time since yesterday afternoon. I want to take this bed home with me. Speaking of which, they're letting me out of here tomorrow. They're no more eager to have me than I am to be had. Something about insurance, no doubt."

I glanced toward the hallway. "How's your mother?"

"A lot better than she was, I suppose. In no time, she and Jack will be able to dance the polka."

"You haven't seen her yet."

"No, I'll hobble over there today. They want me to move around so the stitches set right. Thank God they took out the NG thingee this morning." She flapped her arms, rattling several feet of plastic tubing. "After lunch they're going to haul away the IV and the PCA, I think it's called—a morphine drip. Some of the funny smokes we had on the *Paul D* would've been welcome, too, but no such luck. You have to be dying before they'll let you have that stuff. I hear that Jack spent quite a while in my mother's room last night. And you know what? I'm sick of hating his guts. I think I'm just going to let it go. He and my mother can have sex in Fenway Park for all I care. I'm not going to burn myself out on it. And I'm through arguing with my mother." She straightened her gown and smiled. "After all, now it would be kind of like arguing with myself. If more people shared body parts there might be less strife in the world."

Robin looked askance at Fred, no doubt putting a risqué spin on what she had said.

About a week later, as we rode through a light rain on the way back to Ashton, I asked her which had been worse, the Cauldron or the kidney operation. We were in the backseat of the Mustang. Robin was driving and Fred was up front with him, talking carburetors.

"All the operation required was trust," she said. "Then, before you know it, they've knocked you out and the whole thing was over. One minute I was talking to the anesthesiologist and the next I was staring at the ceiling in the recovery room. They could use a little paint up there."

"And the Cauldron?"

"Well, sweetie, that was *you* I was trusting. As soon as I saw my father go overboard and I knew I had to go in, I was trusting you because I wasn't about to try to *swim* us out of there." She laughed. "Maybe I was thinking that Walt and I could act as a kind of sea anchor to keep the boat slowed down to help you steer us through."

"Some steering," I said. "I was just holding on for dear life. If I didn't have to hang onto the tiller, I would've been on my knees praying."

With the heel of her hand, she smoothed her brows. "Oh, don't you suppose God has enough people pestering Him as it is? Save divine intervention for the big things. We handled the Cauldron okay on our own."

When we got back to Ashton, the rain was coming down again, and I had this strange urge to go on to Woodland to see Cherie. I needed to talk to someone who wasn't neck deep in the Sterling family. But I wasn't about to take my chances with our old wreck of a car, even though Brian said the new links were fine. So I contented myself with helping my mother go through clothes for the Holy Redeemer-By-the-Sea rummage sale.

"They feel they didn't get it right the last time," she said. "So they're going to have another go at it. Your dad says they've seen the error of their ways and so they're inviting us infidels to donate too."

We had plenty of clothes to contribute, that's for sure—years' worth. I held up a shirt that I remembered from about sixth grade. "If I didn't know better," I said, "I'd think that you and Pop were saving some of these things for their sentimental value."

Mom folded a cowgirl skirt and laid it in the donation box. "Well, maybe we were, but you know something? After a while you just run out of room and you figure somebody may as well be using these things." She smiled at the next item, one of Brian's t-shirts from his superhero phase. "And it's too long to wait to save them for our grandchildren. Brian was supposed to have another interview the other day."

That sounded ominous. "What happened this time?"

"He was all dressed up. You should've seen him. You wouldn't have recognized him. He even had his hair slicked back. Your father and I were just hoping that the car would hold up for the trip to Mount Desert."

I found my spelling bee medal from third grade and put it in my lap. "After what happened to me, I can see why."

"Well, as it turned out, the car wasn't the issue. Brian's friends were. He drove by where they were playing football and—"

"Oh, no."

She nodded. "They started throwing clumps of dirt at him, and before he knew it they were up to their old tricks, roughhousing in the mud until Brian looked like the wrath of God. Where they went after that I wouldn't know. He came home about six o'clock in borrowed clothes."

"He blew it off? Couldn't he have called and said he was sick or something?"

"Could have, maybe." She gave me a knowing look. "But, of course, it wasn't going to be that way. He just doesn't have the ambition. He'll be one of those that just hangs around Ashton until he makes up his mind to do something better, if ever."

"Maybe he *should* go see Walt. You know, let some of the magic rub off."

"I don't know as that would be for Brian, but it sure seems to have worked for some others. Mrs. Townsend's paintings have become popular with the tourists. I can't imagine why, but they have. The less they look like something, the more popular they are. Now she's doing these things that she calls *MainEscapes*, with the two words run together liker that, kind of cute. If you use your imagination her pictures look like lighthouses and lobster boats. She's been putting them up at Hal's restaurant and they're buying them just as fast as he can get them on the walls. She says she owes it all to Walt. Just for herself she even did a portrait of him, but if you ask me, it looks like a fried egg over easy. She's done two or three of her first husband, at least she says he's in the picture somewhere."

"Maybe it's like one of those ink blotches. Different people see different things."

Mom laughed. "Sure, maybe it depends on how hungry you are! Maurice has been doing quite well, too. He and Reginald have the salon fixed up very nicely. They have some of Mrs. Townsend's things up, too. That way she gets to see them when she's in the chair."

"Well, Mom, why don't you have your hair done sometime? It could be the beginning of the new you."

She dropped one of Brian's junior high football jerseys and bent over to pick it up. "God, Amber! That would be like sewing pearls on a boot. What would your father say if I came home with sunbeams shooting out of my head?"

"We could go in and get a two-for-one," I suggested. "Wait till he's been into the Scotch and then burst in on him."

She snickered. "Or wait till he's had a few more and then let Maurice go to work on *him*. Your father still has enough to work up some pretty good spikes. It might start a whole new fashion around town." She put her palms in front of her forehead and extended her fingers to look like moose antlers. "Can you see everyone all spiked up? Winthorpe and all of his kids and Fred's mother and—no, his old man's too bald. We'd have to paste something on." She laughed until she all but fell over, then sat up and wiped away a tear. "Oh, dear, I'm going to miss you all over again when you go off to grad school."

In all the laughing, I had lost the spelling bee medal and I was poking around in my chair for it. "I don't know where I'm going, Mom, or what I'm going to do. The summer's pretty well shot and I've hardly saved anything. What little I had I blew down to Boston."

"Your father and I have been talking about it, and he says we can try to dig up some jars in the yard."

"It wouldn't be worth it if I don't even know what I want to do."

"Except that by now you probably know what you *don't* want to do. Maybe grad school will help you to find out what you *do* want to do." She found the spelling bee medal under my chair and put it on my lap. "Then there's always the possibility that if you go to grad school, you'll actually get an education. You've probably learned just about everything you can around here."

The screen door opened just then and Pop banged through the kitchen looking for a screwdriver. "You're always using them for chisels and digging up dandelions and God knows what," he said. He jerked open a couple of drawers and then came into the living room to repeat his accusation. He took off his canvas hat and, unbeknownst to him, a sweaty strand of hair followed it, sticking straight up like one of Maurice's spikes. Mom and I took one look and laughed ourselves silly.

He stood there in his sweaty t-shirt, twirling his hat on his finger as he tried to figure out what the hell was wrong with us.

Mom got up, smoothed his hair down, and kissed him on the cheek. "We could explain, dear, but I don't think you'd get it."

When I went over to the Woolsey side to see Karen, she was out in the yard with Robin. They were playing croquet in what had been the wild patch, now cleared smooth, although a few rocks remained.

"No point in making it any easier than the original," Karen said. "Walt always liked banking off the hazards." She tapped her ball and watched it bounce off the side of a wicket. She was wearing a pair of her mother's loose-fitting slacks and one of Robin's Hawaiian shirts, but she looked fresh and chic, especially for someone just a few days past giving up a kidney.

I looked toward the woods. "But what about the wild place? What about always needing a wild place?"

With her mallet, Karen pointed toward the sea. "We always have that out there. We don't need it at our doorstep anymore."

Was it falling in love with Robin or conquering her fear of the Cauldron that had brought this change in her? Or was it what she had done for her mother? The Karen I had gotten to know and like, despite her faults, was slipping away from me, just as she had moved beyond previous lovers and friends. She had somehow been set free, perhaps back when Robin had come along and fulfilled her dream by tugging us off the ledge. I was happy for her, but at the same time I couldn't help feeling a little lonely as I watched Robin and her rapping away at their croquet balls, apparently without a care in the world.

I left them and went inside to see Walt. He was upstairs lying down, so I settled for shooting the breeze with Mrs. Conditt, and before long I realized, to my shame, that she was every bit as much a person as Walt, so that I wasn't *settling* for anything at all in taking the time to talk with her. She was sitting at the kitchen table with her feet up on a chair.

"My back is killing me," she said, bending over and rubbing the base of her spine. "After a couple million years of evolution, you'd think that people would be put together better."

I pulled up a chair and sat down beside her. "My friend Winthorpe tells me that pigs are even worse. Their joints only last about a year and a half before they get arthritis."

Mrs. Conditt made a face and sat back suddenly. Something popped under her gray uniform dress. "Is that so? Well, I'm sure that if they had to lug Dr. Sterling up and down those stairs, their joints wouldn't last that long. And all this business about failing organs. If you ask me, we should all be stuffed with cotton. It would save a lot of bother." She reached into her apron pocket and offered me a fireball.

I thanked her and started to tuck it away for another time, but reconsidered and stuck it in my cheek where it stuck out like a bubble. "It must be hard keeping up with Wal—with Dr. Sterling, especially now that Geneva has been so sick. It's too bad you can't take a vacation." Like her, I clacked when I talked.

"Dear, this *is* my vacation," Mrs. Conditt said. "You've been to the house in Boston. You can imagine what it's like down there, tripping over him every five minutes. I'll keep right on working until I've put enough aside to have somebody take care of *me.*"

"Maybe you can stay with your family," I said.

"Fat chance! The mister and I parted ways when he couldn't stop betting on the ponies, and my daughter's husband can't stand the sight of me. Whenever I'm around, he drinks something fierce. When he gets plastered, he tries to use the TV remote for a cell phone. God, what a ruckus that raises! So I do my girl a favor and stay away. No, it'll be the old folks home for me, if I live that long. It's depressing, but I'm facing up to it. I've even been around to a few of those places here in Maine and in New Hampshire. Have you ever seen the inside of one?"

I couldn't remember that I had. I could only think of Fred's grandfather, kept in the lap of his loving family, until the final picnic and bombardment.

"Well, let me tell you," Mrs. Conditt said, "I've worked in more than a few of them and even the ritzy ones are just fleabags in ways that you notice right off the bat. The poor old dears with the walkers lining up at mealtime no, I mean well before mealtime, like a chrome parade, drooping ladies and befuddled gents, until someone shuffles them into the dining room. Oh, the better places try to fluff things up, don't you know, with bright paper cutouts tacked to the walls and little entertainments to perk up the spirits, but God didn't intend for all the tired gray folks to be thrown together like that any more than He intended for whole herds of young folks to live together always, don't you think? Don't you think He intended for folks to live in families with babies and geezers and everyone in between so they can learn from each other, and when the old ones bite the dust, well, the family goes on and new ones come in as the old ones go out. Those homes, they're so depressing just to visit. Think what it must be like to live in one."

"Of course it's wonderful," I said, "that Dr. Sterling has been able to live at home. It's wonderful that you've been able to care for him here."

Without acknowledging the compliment, she went on to make another point. "And the help in those places. Sometimes you'll come across somebody who gives a rat's ass, but most of them, the pay is so paltry that the help is sloppy. They'll double or triple the medications and then wonder why the poor dears are seeing purple frogs leaping out of the lampshades."

My eyes widened. "How perfectly terrible."

Mrs. Conditt crunched down on her fireball and chewed it for a moment. "So that's why I'm working day and night even as my back screams murder. Because when I go in the bin, I want the place with the fewest *purple frogs*."

CHAPTER 31

Iwas glad when the phone rang and interrupted us. It was someone at the marina wanting to talk to Dr. Sterling, even though the *Sea Clip* was in Karen's name, and now, with Geneva still in Boston, it was up to Karen to take the call. Mrs. Conditt and I listened from the kitchen as she responded to the news that the boat was leaking badly and would cost an arm and a leg to repair.

"Just keep it resting comfortably," Karen said, no doubt confusing the man at the marina, because she had to re-state her intention in less poetic terms. "Keep pumping it out for now. Don't put it in dry dock and don't let it sink."

The man at the marina apparently told her that the boat could be maintained that way only so long because she came back more emphatic. "I know that. Just keep it as it is for now. We'll have an answer for you in a couple of days. How's that?"

Before he could reply, she hung up.

Robin had come onto the porch. She called him into the house. "Crisis. How much do you think for putting the *Sea Clip* back on its feet?"

He shrugged. "More than anyone in their right mind would want to pay. A boat has a life like any woman, child, or man. Sooner or later the day comes."

She threw out her hands. "What am I supposed to do, let it sink to the bottom right there in the marina?"

Robin had no doubts. "Get what you can off it and let them have the rest for salvage. Then it's their problem."

"Some pirate," she said. "Whatever happened to the romance of the sea? That's the boat that took us through the Cauldron."

He was unimpressed. "Well, all right, Karen. Turn it into one of those yard shrines."

She touched me on the shoulder. "What do *you* think? Should we just let her go?"

I tried to imagine what Pop would say, or Brian, and it didn't take me long to decide that they'd vote with Robin. A boat wants to be sailed, and once it's no good for that anymore, why put more money into it? "I think you should sleep on it," I said. "Wait till things settle down. Maybe even ask your mother. She might welcome the distraction."

Two days later, Geneva came home. She had been thin going into the hospital and now she looked downright wasted but her color had improved. She refused to let us make too much of a fuss over her. Maybe she wanted to maintain her independence. I happened to be at the house when the replica car pulled into the driveway because I thought that Mrs. Conditt could use some help with Walt while Karen and Robin went off to Dunning's Island to work on the house. I must have been tired that afternoon, though, because when I saw her, all I could think about was how she and Jack would look if Maurice got his hands on them. So while they were speaking in subdued tones of the hospital experience, I was seeing them with Maurice's sunbeams shooting out of their heads, and I had to twist my mouth something fierce to keep from laughing.

It was easy for me just to hang around, to sleep on the living room sofa at night, and to help Mrs. Conditt with Walt—and Geneva—by day. The place had become a hospital. Geneva couldn't get up and down the stairs without help. Mrs. Conditt was more and more bothered by her back and would make all kinds of faces in her effort to stave off the pain. She took three kinds of medication for it, but mostly relied on great quantities of fireballs. Karen was doing very well, but we all worried about her overdoing it, and I could picture her out there on the island, swinging a two-by-four and splitting her sutures. And then, of

course, there was Walt, unfazed by the chaos, the man who had
dined with Nobel laureates and been through the Cauldron three
times—once alone, once with his terrified daughter, and once at
the end of a rope, in some ways the steadiest person in the house.

With Karen gone so long, Jack came over often. He never
mentioned the money, the offer of grad school tuition, probably
still figuring that since I had broken my part of the contract, he
was no longer bound to his. So when Labor Day rolled around,
there he was for most of the three-day weekend, shooting the
breeze with Geneva, trying to get her to eat more, trying to cheer
her up with chipper observations about the weather, fluffing the
sofa cushions for her until most people would be throwing up just
from all the coddling. I had a feeling that Karen was staying away
partly to be with Robin and partly to be away from Jack, though
when he wasn't around she seemed to have mended her fences
with Geneva. And the more I saw of him the more convinced I
became that by all but forbidding her to go out in the *Sea Clip*,
Jack really had been trying to trick Karen into harming herself
with it. The more I saw of him, the more I concluded that he was
shrewder than he pretended to be, and I wondered if Geneva
knew how devious he could be, if she had even the faintest idea of
what he might have in mind for Karen.

One afternoon, when Mrs. Conditt went to the garage to look
for a magazine article about the Isle of Capri, I was upstairs
getting some pictures I had left on Karen's bed, and I heard
Geneva talking in the master bedroom. I could tell from the tone
of her voice that she wasn't just muttering to herself the way Mrs.
Conditt was always doing. She was asking questions—and not just
casually either. She was really hoping to come up with some
answers, and the only person she could be talking to was Walt.
She was asking him for advice. "What should I do?" she asked.
"Can you tell me? At this point, any idea you have would be
welcome—even a bad one if it had your old certainty and
insistence behind it. In a blizzard, any way down the mountain
beats freezing to death. That's what you used to say, isn't it? And
any port in a storm. You seem to have helped everyone else in
town with your magical power, whatever it is, so why not me?
Can't you send some of it my way? What do you think I should

do? We've lost Karen to her sailor or—I don't know—before that I guess. We weren't very good parents, were we? We only had one chance to get it right and we fluffed it. But don't you suppose she must care for me—for us—considering what she did for me?"

Suddenly I felt about as welcome as a cold sore on prom night. I wanted to go downstairs, to leave Geneva alone with her husband, but I couldn't go now because she'd hear me, which would be awkward for both of us, so I had to stay there and eavesdrop.

In the next room the bed creaked. Geneva had sat down beside Walt. "Do you understand how I feel, just a little?" she asked. "We're running out of money because our income has dwindled and what we saved we have managed badly as it turns out. We're just lucky that Mrs. Conditt is so loyal or she would long ago have thrown us over for a family who could pay better. I just don't know what we're going to do."

I couldn't believe it. They had a brownstone on Beacon Street and one of the most desirable pieces of coastal property in the county, and yet they really were running out of money. The difference between them and me was that, for them, making wreaths was not an option.

"Have you used it all up?" she asked. "Have you given away all of your magic? Can't you even give me some suggestion?" The bed creaked again as she got up. As she moved toward the door I flattened myself against the wall of Karen's room so she wouldn't see me as she passed by.

She was most of the way downstairs when I heard Walt say in a high, rusty voice "That's all I have."

It was selfish, of course, but I felt slighted, felt that I had lost another relationship when I heard him speak to someone else.

A few days later, Geneva called and asked if I could come over the next afternoon because Jack had to drive her and Mrs. Conditt down to Bangor. I welcomed the opportunity. I had Mom drop me off at the cottage, which was kind of a pain for her because on that narrow road she had to squeeze past a crew working on the phone lines. But suddenly it was as if the summer had started all over again because there I was, alone with Walt. I enjoyed it. I was much more in control of things than I had been back in May. I knew how to blend his food and I had some pretty decent dinner recipes under my fingertips, too. I didn't have to worry about keeping up with him because I knew what he was likely to do in any given situation and I was ready for him. There would be no more wrestling around in the bathtub and no more suicidal sailing with Karen. I had even gotten over my initial nervousness with Geneva. After all, she was just as confused as I was and, in her way, just as poor. You wouldn't have known it to see us side by side, but we had plenty in common—probably more than Karen and I did.

I put his LP of Welsh songs on the turntable and got ready to settle in for the afternoon.

At one end of the porch we had the jigsaw puzzle we had begun early in the summer, the fuzzy picture of a ballerina up on one toe. We had installed most of the pink tutu—or at least I had, with moral support from Walt—but we still had most of the swirling blue background to put in, having saved the hard part for last. So we plunked down at the card table and went to work, although when Walt shifted around in his chair, he invariably bumped a table leg, causing some of the pieces to fall on the floor. My main concern was that some of the pieces were missing entirely, and that we'd painstakingly connect 990 pieces and come up ten short, with part of the ballerina's head missing, which would make for a very unsatisfying puzzle experience.

As the sun began to angle down beyond the mouth of the river, and the shadows of the pines and cedars began to lengthen on the far side, I was thinking about those missing pieces and I said something funny about how maybe this could be a new direction for Mrs. Townsend to pursue with her paintings—fuzzy pictures of girls with holes in their heads. One faucet-shaped piece was driving me crazy because it had the ballerina's ear on it, and I was sure that it had long since hit the deck, so I bent over to take inventory down there when Walt bumped into me with his chin. I started to tell him not to bother, that I could do the picking up, but I realized that something was wrong. He kept right on going, knocking over the card table. Puzzle pieces flew all over the place and he landed face up on the floor.

"Jesus," I said, "Jesus Christ," as his arms flopped down and his head turned to one side. He had stopped breathing. He had stopped doing anything. I forgot what I was supposed to do for a moment. I knelt beside him, pressed my mouth to his and blew, watching his chest rise and drop back down. So far as I can remember I tried everything. I straddled his hips and, with stiff arms, pushed hard on his breastbone, over and over. I rolled him on his side, limp as a Raggedy Ann. I talked to him, I cried, I called for help that was nowhere within earshot. I tried the house phone, but the lines were still down for repairs. I tried my cell phone but it roamed endlessly. I swiped Geneva's car keys from the kitchen wall and tried to drive the Mercedes to find someone, but in that treacherous driveway I ran it into a rock and stalled it before I realized that I was just running crazy. I walked until I could get my phone to work, called my mother, and went back into the cottage, where I sat down cross-legged beside Walt to wait.

CHAPTER 32

I remember making my mind go back to the Cauldron. Instead of letting my eyes rest on the dead man beside me, I followed the distant shore of the river out to the bay, past Dunning's Point, and out to the ragged islands where Robin and Karen were surely fleshing out the frame of the house and dreaming of their future together. In my mind I sailed, low to the water, past Downeast Ledge and on to the Cauldron, which set my heart to racing—even in an imaginary trip that could come to no grief. I sailed again over that foaming lip of rock and into the dangerous confusion of waves and granite and I thought how much that Cauldron was like Karen, with her clashing moods and sudden, capricious shifts. I saw Walt fall into the water again, saw her jump in after him, leaving me to make my way through the storm and wreckage that was the Sterling family.

No one was to blame for Walt's death—not Karen for dragging him through the Cauldron at the end of a rope, not me for botching my effort to revive him, not his Boston doctor for failing to predict the fatal stroke. Walt was dead before he even hit the floor, they said, killed in an instant by a piece of plaque in his heart. Nothing had brought it on and nothing could have prevented it. As Robin would say, he had his life, like any woman, child, or man.

Mrs. Townsend brought me the obituary from the *Boston Globe*. Maurice framed the one in the *New York Times* and hung it behind the counter in the salon. Both write-ups were short—one column and not much longer than my thumb—and chronicled Walt's achievements in genetic engineering. Neither mentioned

Geneva, Karen or Maine. I read them dry-eyed. For the time being I was all cried out.

Geneva, Jack, and Mrs. Conditt attended the memorial service in Boston. Karen and Robin stayed on Dunning's Island to get as far as possible with the house before fall set in. And I must say, it seemed strange not to have to go over and take care of Walt in their absence. As I had done most of my life, I stayed away from the Woolsey side of the river, but this time it wasn't because I had no dealings with the people there. I just didn't want to see the empty house, the empty croquet field, and the sinking boat. I stayed home and hung laundry with a vengeance. Pop and Brian got busy, too, and cut the trim to go around the picture window that faced the river.

The service in Ashton took place in the Carpenter's Hall, one of the more solid structures in town, even though the carpenters had long since moved on to a brick and glass building in Eastport that was less ornate and a lot easier to keep up. In fact, word had it that the present hall required no carpentry whatsoever, which was said to be part of the attraction since whatever carpenters were left in the neighborhood congregated in the hall not to pound nails but to drink beer and talk about politics and women. The Carpenter's Hall in Ashton, on the other hand, was a looming hulk of hewn six-by-sixes and scrolled lintels built by local craftsmen in the heyday of the town more than a century ago. Most of the time it sat empty, shuttered and padlocked. Every now and then someone would bring up the idea of putting it to ongoing use, but after a few minutes of breathing in the mustiness of the place, they always gave it up. On the day of the service, Carpenter's Hall was so crowded that there wouldn't have been room for Walt if he *had* been there, which he was not since he had been cremated in Eastport several days previously.

"Ah, a common question nowadays," said the Methodist minister from Machias who officiated. He was an acquaintance of Walt's by dint of having competed against him in a regatta once upon a time. Mrs. Townsend had asked him where the ashes were to be buried.

"Folks aren't quite as rooted as they used to be," the minister went on, "and so it sometimes takes the survivors a while to decide where to inter them."

He was right. Cherie's grandmother was still reposing under the kitchen sink in a mayonnaise jar. After long indecision, Cherie's mother had gotten used to having the remains there in the house—or some of them, since Cherie's father had come home tipsy last winter, slipped in the icy driveway, and sprinkled out much of the grandmother to make a skid-free surface.

Karen looked pretty in a black crepe short-sleeved dress and pearl necklace. She sat beside Geneva in the front row. Jack was nowhere to be seen. I attended with Fred, who was wearing a charcoal gray sport coat over a navy blue cotton sweater and black Levis, and his black hair, still wet from the shower, added an even more formal, funereal effect. I twisted around, and there was Robin in a back corner, leaning forward slightly to catch every word of the proceedings. He had on loose blue slacks and a black leather jacket over a new striped dress shirt. His wild hair and dark complexion made him all the more the pirate.

The minister gave a little speech about Walt, saying that he was now free of his recent restraints, and then invited comments from the crowd, which several provided in halting, timid voices, and then the collective urge seemed to be to get back out into some fresh air.

Just when Karen came up with her idea, I don't know, but I'm sure that it was *her* idea because she had to convince Robin to go along with it. After all, it was dangerous and probably illegal, too. But the more I thought about it, the more logical her idea seemed, logical and downright inevitable. Above all, it was a loving thing to do.

Curiously, nobody at the marina questioned us when we disconnected the bilge pumps from the *Sea Clip* and slipped out of the berth. That crazy engine started right up, as if protesting that it was too good for what was about to happen. Karen had chosen sunset, not so much for its beauty as for the privacy offered by the coming darkness. The boat was hell to sail, even under power. It was so low in the water and sluggish that it bobbed like a bottle. Robin kept alongside us with the *Paul D,* under sail the whole way and luffing to keep from leaving us behind. We had the *Sea Clip's* little pump going all the time, slowly losing to the leaks in the hull. By the time we got into open water, the sun was touching the treetops in the west and I was starting to worry about getting back. On and on we went toward the darkening sky, with the water so calm that it was eerie, not waves but low glassy swells such as you might find in the eye of a hurricane.

"It's time," Robin said from the helm of the *Paul D.* The evening was so calm and we were so alone that even though he was thirty feet away, he sounded like he was standing beside me. Karen brought the engine down to idle and Robin brought the *Paul D* over to pick us up. When the two boats kissed, Karen and I climbed aboard the *Paul D* and Robin took our place on the *Sea Clip.* "Damn Chinese fire drill, isn't it?" he said. He went down into the cabin of the sinking boat.

I wet my fingertip and raised it toward the darkening sky in the east. "We may yet get some wind."

Karen watched Robin emerge from the cabin with an armload of rags. "We can take all night getting back for all I care. It's beautiful out here."

Venus was already bright in the sunset. I wondered if Mom and Pop and Brian were watching the emerging stars through the picture window. Before the sun came up in the morning, maybe we'd be able to sit in the living room and watch Venus rise.

Aboard the *Sea Clip* Robin shut down the engine. He tied the tiller to the boom. With a rippling of canvas, he raised the jib and the main, which hung limp, flapping as his movements rocked the boat. The boom drifted back and forth in a short arc. After he had tied a bunch of the rags together and poured gasoline over them, he gestured for us to come back over and pick him up.

It was all so gentle and matter-of-fact that you would think people torched boats every day.

Karen reached out and helped him climb back onto the *Paul D.* "So handy to have the acquaintance of an arsonist," she said.

He looked back and watched the *Sea Clip* drift farther out to sea. "You've got to do what you're good at," he answered. When we were downwind of the Sterlings' boat I smelled gasoline.

I also smelled pitch. Karen had brought out her archery set. With his lighter, Robin got the first arrow going. She steadied herself, flexed her broad shoulders, drew the bowstring to her ear, and let the flaming missile fly. At the end of its broad arc, it hit the *Sea Clip* high, caught in the tied-off loops of the main halyard, and fizzled out.

Robin sheeted in the main, picked up a little speed, and closed the gap by a few yards. Then he brought us around to the windward side of the *Sea Clip* so that Karen had a better target. "Land one in the cockpit and you're home free," he said.

Her second shot grazed the coping over the companionway and skittered into the water.

Robin powered up the mainsail again. "It's just rotten luck. We'll get it this time. I'm going back aboard."

She caught him by the sleeve. "That boat's full of gasoline, Robbie. One spark and it's all over."

He squeezed her hand. "Well, we're not lighting her up now, even though we're trying to. Don't you suppose I'll be safe on there for a few more minutes?"

"Robbie, I don't like it. I've got a bad feeling. We can just sink the damn thing, knock some holes in her. She's contrary to the end. First she won't stay afloat and now she won't go down."

As we came up to the *Sea Clip*, he turned the tiller over to Karen. "She'll go down all right. Don't you worry about that. She'll go down in glory." When the hulls touched, he climbed back aboard the derelict and emptied most of a can of gasoline into the cockpit, making the air reek so of danger that I was afraid the *Paul D* would go up too.

He climbed onto the deck and watched as the boats drifted apart on the swells. By the time Karen and I knew what was going on, it was too late for us to grab hold.

"What are you doing?" she yelled.

He ran his hand along the side stay as if to play it like a harp. "Just waiting for you!"

"To shoot? Are you crazy?"

"Just want to get a good close look."

"The whole thing's going to go off like a bomb!"

"You shoot—I'll jump."

"Robbie, this has gone far enough!"

It was their game of chicken. He was daring her to set the *Sea Clip* on fire while he was on it. "Don't wait all night," he said as the boats continued to drift apart.

"I won't do it!" She looked at me, expecting me to chime in.

Still leaning against the stay, he made a casual gesture, a flip of his hand. "Won't or *can't*, Karen?"

She took a deep breath. Her hand was tight on the tiller, even though the boat was floating powerless. "It's gone too far, Robbie!"

He shrugged, took out a cigarette and put it to his lips.

"Robbie, don't!"

He reached into his hip pocket, for his lighter, I suppose.

Karen dropped, hung onto the tiller. "Robbie, stop! I give up—*whatever*!"

He rode the gentle swells. "Do it, Karen. Do it."

Lips pressed white, she let go of the tiller and steadied herself. This time the *Sea Clip* forced her to go forward, and she stood in the curve of the curling jib, waiting a good long time for the angle she wanted. Then she shot her last arrow into the heart of her father's boat.

The cabin erupted in fire and Robin dove, swimming to us with strong strokes as the cockpit burst into flame, then the sails. The floating inferno slowed, tilted on a rising swell, and turned back toward the low line of the land. Robin brought us around until the *Sea Clip* seemed to touch the red ball of the dropping sun. She tilted again, then righted herself and went on to the west.

Watching the reflection of the flames play across the water, I said, "You'd think she was trying to go home."

The bow of the *Sea Clip* dropped abruptly and plowed into a swell, and then she rolled over on her side and disappeared behind a curtain of smoke and steam. Robin joined me at the tiller and watched with us as the smoke lifted and the white water knit together where she had gone down with Walt's ashes.

After saying good-bye to Walt, I had to get away for a while, so I took my chances with our old beater of a car and drove up to Woodland to see Cherie. Up until April, she had been my best friend, and I wanted to know why she had taken off so suddenly to go to secretary school and why she had been avoiding me ever since. I figured that after spending a summer with someone as complicated as Karen, I'd be able to get along fine with Cherie, get everything straightened out, and return to normal. I might even make up my mind about what I wanted to do with the rest of my life.

I made a point of getting to her house at suppertime because she was most likely to be home by then. I wasn't expecting to stay over, but I would've been happy to do it. I thought maybe we'd have a couple of beers, get silly, and lay all our cards on the table. We might touch on some sore spots in our relationship, but we'd come out better friends for it.

When I found the house I could see why she hadn't called me up to tell me about it. It was a mobile home that had outgrown its walls with make-do carpentry and spread out on a wooded hillside on the far edge of town. Cherie was outgrowing her walls too, being about six months pregnant by the look of her through the screen door.

We hugged and she invited me in, apologizing for the mess, which was spectacular even by Cherie's standards. The kitchen, the living room, and the bedroom seemed to flow from one to the other, back and forth, in a swirl of spillage. The bedroom, which looked like it had been hit by a bomb, had what appeared to be breakfast dishes on the floor. Lying next to a stack of dishes by the kitchen sink was a black push-up bra hooked together with what looked like a diaper pin. The round kitchen table was buried under piles of mail and tabloid newspapers and half a dozen wreath forms. Gracing the living room sofa was a bag of fat-free potato chips and a dozen cans of generic diet soda still stuck together with their plastic yoke. A silent TV that took up an entire corner of the room flickered like a strobe light, showing a young couple looking at million-dollar condos in Maui. In front of the screen sat a red plastic basket overloaded with laundry. The predominant *odeur* was of week-old cat litter.

"Sit down, sit down, Amber." Cherie brushed some crumbs from the slipcovers. "Sorry I've been out of touch. It's just been so hectic."

Trying not to look too long at her belly or the furniture, I positioned myself on the sofa. Without delay, the cat, a small black thing with oversized green eyes, started rubbing against my ankles.

"Yeah, it's been kind of a hectic summer," I said. "I can't quite believe it's almost over."

Cherie ran a hand over her short, dark flipped-up hair and nodded. "Ain't that the truth."

I didn't know where to begin without being obvious. I reached down and petted the cat, which responded by growling.

Cherie ran it off and came back to the sofa. "He's a crazy little turd. I can't believe I took him in, let alone put up with him all the time. He's always doing that. Rubbing up against people and then swiping at them when they're trying to be friendly. Maybe I'm crazy, too. Being pregnant can do that to you—if you weren't already crazy to *get* pregnant in the first place."

I plunged right in and asked, "So who's the lucky dad?"

Cherie adjusted herself against the arm of the sofa, brushed some more crumbs from the folds of the slipcover, and patted her round belly with both hands. "Robin Dunning. He sure is hard to resist when he's on a roll."

CHAPTER 33

I felt my stomach tighten. "Tell me you're kidding, Cherie."
She found an open can of her diet soda on the floor and swigged it down. "Oh, it's all ancient history now. You know how it is around Ashton along about March or April. You'll do anything for a little excitement. I suppose I would've turned to drugs if there were some around. Well, anyway, suddenly there was Robbie fresh out of Thomaston, smelling like smoke and thrills and away we went. I knew he'd been taking stuff out of the summer homes, but I let that pass right over me. I mean, after all, he'd beaten the rap, so he was free and clear as far as the law was concerned." Thinking back, she smiled. "I must say he sure does have a way about him. The way we were going I was bound to get knocked up."

I let out a breath. "Are you sure it's Robin?"

She looked at me as if I had lost my marbles. "Amber dear, we did it in every room of my parents' house, even the upstairs closet, and believe you me, *that* took some effort."

Suddenly I felt sorry for Karen, throwing herself at another male without any idea of what he was really like. In a switching of the cat's tail, my sympathies careened back and forth. On the one hand, Jack Crystal had been right in opposing Karen's relationship with Robin. On the other, he had done his best to bring her to grief by goading her into risking her life   and Walt's and mine—in the Cauldron.   On the one hand, Robin was devious and double-dealing. On the other, his fling with Cherie *had* taken place before he had even met Karen. And for that matter, maybe the whole mess was none of my business. I couldn't help asking though, "So what about you and Robbie?" I used his childhood nickname because I couldn't help being mad at him. "Are you going to be seeing him again?"

Without much luck, Cherie was looking around for another open can of diet soda. She found a little sprinkle in one, took a swig, and dropped it on the floor. "You want to know something? Once I found out I was expecting, I didn't much care if I saw him again. Isn't that strange? I always thought that those girls who wanted to be single mothers were whackjobs, but suddenly I can see where they're coming from. All those candlelight smiles with Robin were just Mother Nature's trick to bring another baby into the world. That's all she cares about is babies. The rest of it's just smoke and mirrors. Aren't you proud of me? I figured that out all on my own."

I asked her how her parents felt about it.

Cherie flounced her maternity top, a pink rose pattern that she wouldn't have been caught dead in a year ago. "Well, you'll notice that I haven't been back all summer. Mom's sends me clothes and some spending money every now and then, but apparently the old man spends a lot of time frothing at the mouth. If you ask me, he's a lot easier to live with when he's drinking. So I say, let him drink."

"Do they know who the father is?"

Her hand went out like a stop sign. "Hell, no! And promise you won't tell them. Promise me that, Amber."

"Sure, Cherie, I promise."

"Good! Because if word gets out, we'll have murder and mayhem right in the streets of Ashton. It won't be just a matter of getting Winthorpe to clap Robin back in jail. It'll be a whole lot messier than that."

I felt my stomach tightening up again. I was ready for a change of subject. I asked how secretarial school was going.

Cherie lit up a Virginia Slims and smiled through the smoke. "I might get through it, but I might not. They're so damn old-fashioned that they still make you learn shorthand. Fat lot of good that does when you can work a damn iPad. Anyway, I want to do what's best for the baby, and I'm not sure that being shut up in a school and then in an office is the best thing. I don't know. I'm just taking it one day at a time." She blew a stream of smoke through her fingers. "The guy who runs the school is kind of cute and I think he likes me. What about you, dear? How've you been?"

I told her about the excursions with Robin and Karen. To make it sound unimportant I added, "We were making pretty good money for a while there."

As I expected, she had already heard about the trips on the *Paul D*, probably from her mother, although I had no idea just what she had heard. Her mother had a knack for embroidery, and I'm not just talking about needlework. "So how's Robin doing?" she asked in a way that sounded kind of suspicious.

I got right to the business at hand. "Cherie, it wasn't like that, not between Robin and me. He helped me out after I got pushed down in third grade, so I feel gratitude toward him, but that's all."

Cherie smiled and tapped her ashes into one of the diet soda cans. "I never thought otherwise, dear, but you know how people like to talk."

"And what else do people talk about?" I asked, glad that the major matter was settled.

She looked puzzled or else bothered by the smoke. "Something about some summer girl that's taken up with him. How he ever— Screw it. I've got a pretty good idea how. For her sake, I just hope she has her wits about her or we can start a little daycare center with descendents of Robin Dunning. It kind of pisses me off to think about it though. Him doing me and then running off like that with someone else. It seems kind of irresponsible."

The room was getting stuffy and I was feeling flushed. The cat came back and rubbed against my ankle again, but I wasn't about to touch him this time. He went over to Cherie and she ignored him, too. I asked her what her plans were.

"My bed is pretty much made," she said, patting her belly again.

Through a half-open accordion door I could tell that her bed definitely was *not* made. In fact it was strewn all over the room. The mattress wasn't even on straight. "You're going to stay up here and raise the baby and be a secretary or something like that?"

She nodded. "And get a head start on the wreath season. Or marry money." She laughed and coughed. "Know anybody who's got some?"

She walked me out to the car and we had a good long hug. A beater of a Chevrolet came splashing through some muddy potholes and went on down the track that curved through the trailers squatting in the woods. Cherie gave it a thumbs up and pointed to the satellite dish sprouting from her roof.

"We're all getting 'em," she said. "Nothing down."

A few days after my trip to Woodland, Karen came over breathless with news. "Jack's out of the picture. Can you believe it?"

From my usual position at the clothesline I had seen the familiar red Mustang turning into the driveway, so I was waiting for her. She hadn't even gotten out of the car yet. I had never seen her so upbeat. She had her sunglasses pushed back like a hair band. Her face glowed from sun, wind, and excitement.

I was afraid she had done something drastic, even more drastic than throwing a pitcher of ice water in his face. "How?" I asked. "Is everything okay?"

She climbed out of the car. "You bet! I think something about my father's death just changed the whole chemistry between my mother and Jack. He came over and started talking business and she ran him out of the house. I'd like to think it was my kidney that gave her the strength to do it."

So much for burying the hatchet with Jack, I thought. But no more scary car rides.

Beaming, Karen hugged me. "I just feel so *different*. It's already changed things between my mother and Robbie. She's much more accepting now." She must have felt me stiffen because she pulled back. "What's the matter?"

I lied. I flat-out lied. "Nothing at all. Everything's happened so fast, that's all, and I'm just so happy for you."

She held me by the shoulders and gave me an inquiring look. "You sure?"

"Of course I'm sure. It's like a cloud has lifted."

"It sure is." She took me by the arm and walked me toward the house. "And that's not all."

I was expecting her to tell me that she had decided to go back to Paris and finish school or maybe that she would transfer to some respectable school in New England, so I wasn't ready for what came next:

"Robbie and I are getting *married*. Isn't that wild? We're going to go down to Portland to pick out a ring and get married at Dunning's Point."

I felt as if I had been smacked by the boom. I felt light-headed. My feet seemed to have been knocked out from under me. My stomach went sour. It was as if Robbie—and Karen with him—had started playing chicken with the whole town.

Karen squeezed my arm. "Can you believe it? Robin and me. Watch out, world!"

The sights and smells of Cherie's trailer rushed back to me. I saw her sunk into the sofa in her pink rose print maternity top, sitting under the satellite dish she couldn't afford. "Watch out, world, is right," I said with as much enthusiasm as I could muster. "Every time I think I've got you figured out you throw me a curve."

She batted her eyelashes. "It was Robbie's idea. Well, maybe he was kidding or blowing a little too much weed when he said it, but I could tell that he was serious underneath. I could tell that he wanted me to pick up on it."

We came to the screen door and I stopped at the step. "If anyone ought to know him by now, it would be you." I was never good at smiling for pictures, but I clamped a clothespin on my fingertip and managed a good one now. "That's great. That's just great."

A day or so later, I was helping Pop level the picture window. One of the original old square nails had lost its head and Pop was trying to pull it out with a pair of pliers. Thinking about what I knew of Robin and Cherie, I knew just how that nail felt. Here I was supposed to be Karen's best friend and I wasn't telling her something she should know about the man she was going to marry. But if I *did* tell—breaking my promise to Cherie—and word got out, there'd be hell to pay with Cherie's dad and somebody might get hurt. Plus there was no telling how Karen might react. As Pop was telling me to stop daydreaming and hold the light higher, Mom came into the room with the Eastport newspaper in her hand.

"They're doing it real official," she said, handing me the paper.

Frowning, Pop straightened his back. "Jean, we're trying to get something done here and you've just taken away my light."

"I'll hold your light for you," she said, taking the pin lamp from me. "She's got to read this. Doris Townsend told me about it. She thinks it's hysterical."

Robin and Karen had put a wedding announcement in the paper. It was a proper old-fashioned, conventional declaration of the coming nuptials. By the wry tone I could tell that Karen had written it. She described herself as a "seasoned student of several Continental

institutions" while Robin came off as "the sole surviving son of Ashton's founding family, involved in various transport enterprises."

Mom laughed. "Isn't that a riot? Don't look so worried, Amber. It's best to have a sense of humor if you're going to get married."

Pop got a good grip on the nail and pulled it squeaking from the wall.

I was thinking about Cherie up there in Woodland, coming across that announcement and weighing her options.

Karen had everything figured out, from the flowers in the bridal bouquet to the career plans of the groom. She had chosen me as the maid of honor, and out at the picnic ground she walked me through the entire ceremony. It struck me as a strange place for her wedding since her only experience out there had involved a pig that had gone thermonuclear and the apple bombing of a dead man, but of course it was where she had first seen Robin as he sailed to the edge of the Cauldron and, even then, she must have decided that he would play a part in her destiny. Also the point was named for Robin's family, and the only other venues around Ashton would've been Karen's house—a beautiful but rather forlorn spot now—and that reeking old Carpenter's Hall.

As we walked through the comings and goings of the ceremony, she told me about their plans. "We're going to finish up the house enough to button it up for the winter, then take the boat south, all the way to Fort Lauderdale. We'll do some chartering there, maybe teach some lessons, maybe take a couple of trips to the Keys. Then come back up here in May or June and finish the house."

The sweep of her thinking took my breath away. It encompassed the entire east coast of the United States, and here I was, still trying to figure out if I was going to go back to work for Happy Hal or try to squeak into a job on Mount Desert at the last minute. I got that familiar ache in my stomach as I thought of spending the rest of my life making do in Ashton. Nosey me, though, I kept wondering how much difference Robin's recent past would make to her, or if she already knew about it and didn't care.

As it turned out, it made a difference to Cherie because she came down to Ashton and paid her parents a little visit. I was helping Pop and Brian do the finishing work on the picture window when Mom answered the phone and came in with the news that Cherie's father was on the warpath to get Robin.

She watched us struggle with the new window, which was too narrow at the top by about a sixteenth of an inch, so Mom's remarks were accompanied by Pop's colorful verbiage.

"They must've known that they were throwing the fat in the fire with that wedding announcement," she said. "There's enough people around here that suspect Robbie of plundering their homes to keep him on guard for the rest of his life, and now Betty's saying he's the father of Cherie's child—which I didn't even know she was going to have."

That last was aimed directly at me, so I explained that my silence had been an attempt to avoid this very catastrophe.

"Well, anyway," Mom said, "up to now her dad didn't know who was responsible, but that wedding announcement set Cherie off, so the cat's out of the bag, and Hershel knows right where he can find Robin—out on that point on Saturday afternoon. Don't you suppose we ought to do something?"

Pop was usually annoyed when Mom asked that question because he invariably had his mind on something else. He straightened his back and put his hand on the window frame. "Yuh, we ought to do something. We ought to hold the goddam light straight so I can see to measure."

She put her hand next to his. "I'm serious, Frank. There's no telling what might happen if Cherie's dad gets his hands on Robin."

He stooped down to look at something else, the corner where the discrepancy was more like an eighth of an inch. He tapped Brian on the elbow. "There's something screwed up somewhere. This thing's off kilter."

"Well, the damn window's straight," Brian said. "It's the *house* that's crooked."

Mom started to speak again, but Pop cut her off. "If you want to stick your nose in it, call Winthorpe. It's his job to take care of that kind of stuff."

She put her hands on her hips and threw back her head. "Winthorpe! What's he going to do—throw a flaming pig at him?"

Pop thumped his chest. "And what do you expect *me* to do about it? Go over there and shoot one or the other of them?"

Now Mom was getting impatient. She set her chin and pecked the air with her finger. "Look, Frank, alls you've got to do is keep him away from that wedding. You know he's not going to try anything before then, and once it's over, they're going to take off." She turned to me. "Aren't they?"

I nodded, not wanting to give too much information. "They'll be gone for months."

"So there you are," Mom said. "Just keep him away from that wedding Saturday and we'll all be better off."

"An eighth of an inch," Pop said to himself. "One way or the other, we're going to set this damn thing straight."

CHAPTER 34

As Saturday approached, we didn't know what to expect. If Pop had a plan to control Cherie's dad, he wasn't letting us in on it. At Mom's prodding, I went over to see Cherie, but was relieved to hear that she had already gone back to Woodland, possibly because she thought that a confrontation with Robin might be bad for the baby. Talking to her mother at the door to the screen porch, I listened for the sound of her father's voice, but heard only the TV and a Mixmaster. Cherie's mother was making snickerdoodles, a family favorite. She always made them without self-rising flour, but now she was at her wits' end because she couldn't find her cream of tartar.

"As if things weren't already going to hell in a handcart," she said. "This is not the way I wanted to become a grandmother."

I couldn't help wondering if Cherie's project of "doing it" in every room of the house had included the junked up screen porch. I offered to rush home and get some cream of tartar.

Mrs. Gillespie wrung her hands in her apron. "Did she tell you about what was going on, Amber?"

"No, ma'am, she sure did not. I was as surprised as you."

"I thought girls always told girls everything."

"Well, maybe they do. But sometimes it just takes a while."

"All those years of Sunday school and only the best TV shows."

Cherie's parents had a satellite dish, too, but it had been malfunctioning back in March and April, when alternative forms of entertainment had become irresistible. "Maybe everything will turn out for the best," I said. "Cherie seems pretty happy."

"Well, she didn't seem very happy when she was here the other day. The news about this wedding really set her off."

'Oh, but she'll get over that, don't you think? Once everybody has, you know, taken off?"

"As long as Herschel doesn't get to them before they *can* take off."

I couldn't help sticking my nose in a little further. "I know my pop's been looking for him about something. Is he—is he around by any chance?"

Even through the screen door I could see Cherie's mom's eyes get big. "Are you kidding? He's been like a caged tiger ever since the news. The last I heard he was off buying a chain saw."

I swallowed. "A chain saw?"

She gestured toward the yard. "As you can see, we've got quite a lot of dead wood around the place. He's been putting it off for years, but now he's suddenly fired up to cut it all."

They did have quite a number of fallen trees on their property, including one that had leaned against the barn roof for as long as I could remember. After being that way for so long, the place wouldn't look right without it.

On Friday, the day before the wedding, I was over at Karen's to consult about my bridesmaid's dress, which was nothing but a slightly altered version of this green satin number with spaghetti straps that I had worn to the senior prom. I was feeling insecure about it because it was six years old, maybe a little long, and the bodice was kind of tight. I hauled it over to Karen's one more time so she could have a good look at it and reassure me that I wouldn't make a fool out of myself wearing it. Mrs. Conditt said she liked it. Geneva said she liked it. Karen wanted to raise the hem an inch.

"It's your wedding," I said, folding it on the kitchen table. "I might look like some kind of fertility goddess, but it's your wedding."

"Are you okay with it?" Karen was more gracious than I had ever seen her.

"Sure, sure. If you want me to, I'll even get a cupid tattooed between my boobs."

Karen and Mrs. Conditt had a good laugh. Even Geneva smiled.

"Look," Karen said, "why don't we go for a drive, you know, to clear our heads a little, a last drive for a while."

At first I thought that she might be whisking me off on another of her adventures, but it soon became apparent that she just wanted to feel the cool, woodsy Maine air in her hair. We didn't talk about the upcoming trip to Florida and the Bahamas. Oh, yes. She had added the Bahamas now. We didn't talk about the wedding and we certainly didn't talk about Cherie's dad, wherever he might be at the moment. It was pretty clear to me that even if Karen had heard about Robin and Cherie, she hadn't heard about the vendetta, and she seemed so happy and I was so chicken-hearted that I wanted to leave it that way. Anyhow, I concluded that Karen was very controlled when it came to her emotions. Never once had I seen her cry during the proceedings for Walt, not during the memorial service in Carpenter's Hall and not during the awkward aquatic committal of the ashes.

She surprised me again though. It was dusk, and we were on our way back to the house with the wind starting to get chilly as we sped along one of the back roads. I wasn't thinking about anything in particular except the ballerina jigsaw puzzle that Walt and I had never finished, so I'm not sure exactly what happened except that suddenly Karen hit the brakes and there was a moose lying in the road, a cow. We hadn't hit it, but somebody else sure had, and recently. We could have gone around her easily enough, and yet there we were, kneeling down beside her, trying to read the last flicker of light in her glazing eyes.

Karen burst into tears. She sat down right there in the road, put her face in her hands, and wept. I had been traveling those roads all my life and I had seen I don't know how much road kill, so I was used to it, but seeing Karen so utterly reduced, I cried too. It was the craziest damn thing, the two of us sitting there for I don't know how long as the woods went dark, crying for a fallen moose.

When we got back to the house, Geneva and Mrs. Conditt were boxing up some of Walt's clothes—pairs of those formless gray pants, flannel shirts, and some dressier stuff that smelled like mothballs. The sight of the cardboard boxes on the living room floor would've hit me hard if I hadn't spent an eternity sitting beside his body, getting very used to the idea that he was dead.

Like the rest of us, Mrs. Conditt was subdued but businesslike. "It's been a strange, empty house without him," she said. "You might not expect to miss someone who was so quiet, and yet I feel his absence everywhere. I feel like I've lost my shadow."

Geneva was folding linen handkerchiefs. "As soon as we take these things off to the second wind store," she said, "it'll be time to turn around and pack everything up." Apparently Walt had gone through quite a few hankies during his prime because she kept folding and folding. All of them had his monogram on them

"I wish you'd reconsider putting the cottage on the market," Karen said.

Her mother grasped a handkerchief like she intended to use it. "We've been through all of that. We simply can't afford to keep this place empty eight months a year."

"I'll have my money—in a year plus a couple of weeks, Mother."

"That's going to be too long to wait. The house in Boston isn't getting any cheaper to keep up, you know, and property values up here are on the rise right now. We can do pretty well despite the capital gains taxes."

Looking at the empty chair on the porch I decided that she was right. Maybe one day Karen would come back and reclaim the property with what was left of her inheritance, but for now it was hard to imagine the house as anything but bait for the next generation of vandals and firebugs. Better to sell it and let someone take care of it.

"Oh, I almost forgot," Geneva said. "Walt would've wanted you to have this." She went to the bookcase and came back with the LP of Welsh songs. "You know, he was sort of old-fashioned in some ways. He said he liked LPs because they demonstrated the principle that it takes friction to make music."

I didn't tell Karen about Cherie's dad. I had to trust Pop to keep him occupied long enough for the newlyweds to get away, and I was plenty nervous when Saturday came around. I was upstairs having a tug of war with that green dress when I heard the owner of the new chainsaw come to the door. How Pop lured him over I don't know, but suddenly there he was at the formal front door, as if he meant business.

I slipped downstairs, trying not to rustle too much, and nearly bumped into Mom sneaking in from the living room. For the first time in about two years, she was wearing a skirt and it looked a little too feminine for her. "What are you laughing at?" she whispered as we squeezed into the dim foyer that smelled of Cherie's father's sweat and cigarette. "We'd better be able to run if all hell breaks loose."

Mom had put my hair up in kind of a twist and my neck seemed so long that I felt like a damn swan. I couldn't help measuring it with spread fingers. "Where's Brian?"

"He's gone over to Fred's to borrow a tie. I'm making him wear one and he didn't like any of the ones here."

"I'm glad," I said. "It's probably better to let Pop handle this."

Pop had closed the door between the foyer and the kitchen, but I edged it open just enough to see what was going on. Mom sneaked it out a little farther. Cherie's father was in no mood for a social visit. Our kitchen has an island in it, and he was coming around one side while Pop was doing something with the drawers on the other side. Herschel's big voice boomed through the house. "Don't hold me up, Frank. I'm on my way to fix something."

Pop remained cordial. I heard him moving one of the kitchen stools. "Hershel, I've about had it with these goddam cabinets and I want you to tell me if I should rip them all out and start from scratch."

"How the hell should I care, Frank? You can knock the whole place down and start from scratch as far as I'm concerned."

From the far side of the kitchen came the clinking of bottles. Mom and I looked at each other, trying to figure out what Pop was up to.

"The point is, Hershel, I'm running out of room for all of this booze, and I've either got to get rid of it or fix this place up somehow. What do you think?"

Hershel's big hands slapped the counter. "So what's under the cloth, Frank? Am I supposed to ask?" He came around to Pop's side of the island and we heard clinking again as he pulled away a tablecloth, apparently revealing a good sample of Pop's liquor supply. "You know I'm off of this stuff, Frank. What the hell are you up to?"

I missed something through the crack of the door because suddenly Hershel was holding a bottle of Pop's coveted Scotch and Pop was going into the living room. "If you're scheming against me, Frank, here's what I think of your drink!"

He threw the bottle right at the new picture window.

Mom and I jumped, but Pop caught the bottle, snatched it right out of the air. As Mom and I checked to make sure our hearts were still beating, he took the bottle back into the kitchen. "Damn, Hershel, there's better things to do with *this*."

I don't know what happened next, but the bottle crashed to the floor and suddenly the whole place reeked of single malt Scotch. Pop yelled at Mom to "go get the mop and dustpan from the garage."

"It's right there in the kitchen," she yelled back, missing completely the point that he wanted us to make ourselves scarce. I tugged at her organdy sleeve and we bumped our way through the front door and tumbled into the yard, leaving Pop to handle whatever came next.

We waited out by the driveway and intercepted Brian. He was wearing the black-and-white diamond pattern tie that Fred had worn to the senior prom. "Don't you suppose I ought to go in and help?" he asked, pulling toward the house.

To my surprise, Mom let him go. "It'll probably take at least two of you to handle him before it's over," she said. As he hurried toward the screen door, she called out, "Just do what your dad says, you hear?"

We waited a while longer, staring at the house, which was strangely quiet. Then we decided to go and have a peek through the kitchen window, which faced the eternal clothesline and the river. Unfortunately it was on a slope and too high to get to without climbing onto something, so we hauled the stepstool out of the garage.

There was no level ground to put in on though. So I took off my high heels and Mom climbed onto my shoulders. "Jesus and Joseph," I said, "you're killing my shoulders and my feet are on a rock." Also my twist was unraveling. I was one droopy swan.

"Hold still," Mom whispered. She had planted a knee on each side of my neck and put her hands on the window ledge. Her hem was coming down over my eyes.

"What do you see? What do you see, Mom?"

She gouged my ear with her knee for the sake of a better view. "Oh my God. They're drinking—all three of them. Wait'll I get my hands on that man."

"Which one?"

"Oh, hell, he *saw* me." Suddenly we were falling over backwards. We sprawled on the rocky ground and stared up at the window. Mom collected herself and ran around the corner of the house, out of sight. I grabbed up my shoes and went after her in sagging pantyhose. She was leaning up against the wall, trying not to laugh out loud. "He saw me. You should've seen the look on his face."

"Who?"

"Hershel. His eyes practically popped out of his head!"

"He's probably not used to seeing overdressed women falling out of windows."

She came away from the wall. "Do you really think I'm overdressed?"

I brushed some of the wall's white powder from her shoulders. "No, I'm just jealous."

She laughed again. "Let's go. If they start crooning, they'll be dead to the world in no time."

As we passed the screen door, I thought I heard singing, fine old Scottish songs seasoned with good old Scotch whiskey.

CHAPTER 35

I was nervous all the way to the point because I didn't know
what to expect. Ordinarily, weddings can be nerve-wracking
enough what with all the details that can go wrong. This one
was something else. If Herschel got loose, he could cause a
lot of damage. Or maybe Ted and some of his bunch, facing a
year each for arson, had gotten out on bail and were plotting
some kind of revenge against Robin. Even Mrs. Gillespie might
decide to come out and muck up the proceedings at the part
where the minister says, "If anyone knows why this man and this
woman should not be joined…." She sure had plenty of reasons to
speak up. I could hear her again, protesting, "This is not the way I
wanted to become a grandmother!"

Karen and Robin arrived in the red Mustang. Geneva and
Mrs. Conditt followed in the rasping yellow Mercedes. We had
quite a little crowd out there on the point, many of them
beneficiaries of Walt's special powers. Some of them, no doubt,
were just curious onlookers. Some had probably showed up
because the weather was so fair. The late September sun glinted
off the waves that crowded past the point on their way to the
Cauldron, which was again at high tide, making me shudder at
the memory of going in there.

The bride wore a white tulle ankle-length dress with a beaded
bodice and a floral pattern on the skirt, scooped so low in the back
that I thought she might be trying to show off her incision. She
had none of the other traditional wedding dress fripperies, as
Mom called them. Her strawberry blond hair was pulled back in a

long ponytail, just as it was when I had first seen her, and her lipstick and nails were the same mauve.

The park looked great. The Porta Potty, scrubbed free of graffiti, stood at attention.

Fred of all people was Robin's best man, chosen, I suppose, because he was the only local with whom Robin had recently enjoyed a pleasant moment. That was the price of being a pirate, I decided. It was hard to find true and trustworthy friends. Fred was wearing his old black prom jacket and tight fitting pants, giving me flashbacks to those sweet, romantic, waning days of high school. When he saw my dress he smiled and said, "We couldn't have done it better if we'd planned it."

Hal was there as a guest and official caterer, spreading finger food on the picnic tables, which led me to hope that the reception would be snappy, enabling the bride and groom to get the hell out of there before Mr. Herschel Gillespie came to his senses. Maurice and Reginald showed up looking like something out of the *Gentleman's Quarterly*. Instead of spikes and sunbeams, Maurice had his hair going straight up and then kind of erupting with green highlights. Reginald's was layered with something of a pinecone effect. Maurice was in a shiny black suit coat worn over a black t-shirt and pleated charcoal pants. Reginald was all in black except for a powder blue blazer. When the wind shifted, it became apparent that the two of them were very fragrant. Reginald was a former wrestler and had this compulsion to have his hands on somebody all the time. He was using Maurice to demonstrate the hammerlock.

Fred's parents were there, and I was relieved to see that they appeared to be completely without apples. It occurred to me that if apples were their custom at funerals, something similar might be their tradition for weddings, but I figured that they were probably there just to see Fred perform. I happened to know that Mrs. Archer had a weakness for gussying up, and she never missed a chance to see Fred dressed to the nines.

At the last minute, Winthorpe arrived with his youngest boy in tow. Mom found out that he was planning to head Mr. Gillespie off in case it became necessary, but so far the boy was giving him plenty to keep up with. The little terror kicked a shoe off and glared.

"Well, what's the matter with him?" Mom asked. A streak of white from the house still chalked her shoulders.

Winthorpe smiled as his boy wriggled like a fish. "I sold that parlor organ that was left on the porch. Got a hundred and sixty for it from a man that came all the way from Cherryfield. Fixing up some historic house I suppose. Anyway Carlyle's been climbing the walls ever since."

Mrs. Townsend was about the last person to show up, and she arrived with Peach. She had taped a red felt ribbon to his head and hung a little silver bell from his collar. "Very festive, wouldn't you say?" she asked, giving the leash a yank to keep him in line.

"Just keep him away from these tables," Hal said, assuming a defensive position between the dog and the hors d'oeuvres.

"No leg in the crowd will be safe if he's feeling frisky," Mr. Archer warned, to his wife's embarrassment. She'd brag about pinching grafts in plant stores all day long, but whenever her husband told one of his off-color jokes, she'd clam right up.

The ceremony was perfectly charming, except that most of us were blinded by the reflection of the sun on the water. Robin was very dashing in tails of all things, an ancient outfit by the looks of the vast lapels and slightly frayed piping on the pants. The Methodist minister who had put Walt away went straight by the book, and when he got to the part about "speak now or forever hold your peace," everybody twisted around to see if somebody would come running up with a whole list of grievances. I held my breath and stared straight ahead during what seemed an unnecessarily long pause, and then we were through it. Robin and Karen exchanged rings, kissed, and cut the cake, which Geneva had commissioned from a one-armed baker in Lubec.

"Now tell us about your plans," somebody said as the crowd pressed up against the picnic tables.

Smiling, Karen wiped a glob of frosting from her cheek. "Well, we're going to sail down to Florida for the fall, then maybe cross to the Bahamas when the weather lightens up."

I felt so envious. The freedom, the togetherness.

"Sounds very glamorous," Mrs. Townsend was saying, "but shouldn't you consult the owner of the boat first?"

Karen looked startled. She turned to Robin for an explanation, but she could tell that he was just as puzzled as she was. "What do you mean? Robbie's the owner of the boat. He got it from his grandfather."

Suddenly all you could hear was the quiet munching of celery that Reginald was feeding to Maurice.

The crowd parted as Mrs. Townsend hauled Peach up to the table. She stopped and caught her breath. "I beg to differ because a good forty years ago his grandfather sold that boat—to me."

We all gasped. How could Mrs. Townsend, who never went near the water, own the boat that had raided half the summer homes in Ashton?

Frowning, she pulled at something under her brocade belt. "Like most things around here, it all comes down to money. Once upon a time the grandfather of the groom was strapped for cash, and I being a young and foolish widow and more than a little in love with the damn crook, bought his boat but let him continue to do God knows what with it. I marvel that he didn't rob me in my own bed. Heaven knows he ripped off everybody else around here somewhere along the line. Anyway, there were only two stipulations. First, that our little deal would remain secret. I mean, I wanted to help, but I didn't want to die of embarrassment."

Robin shook his tails and started to say something, but Mrs. Townsend put up a jeweled hand to stop him. "The other stipulation was that the boat be renamed the *Paul D* to remind me that I was, after all, married to a rather dear and understanding man—my first husband, Paul D. Grieve, may he rest in peace."

Karen's took Robbie's hand. "Is that true?"

He drew her close. "Knowing my grandpa, I don't doubt it."

Mrs. Townsend tightened her grip on the leash to keep Peach from jumping at the goodies on the table. "Don't despair, dear. While painting I've had plenty of time to work everything out in my head, and if you want to take the *Paul D* off to some crazy place, go ahead! However I'll hear no more rumors of my boat being used for shady purposes."

Robin smiled. "Shady purposes? Whatever do you mean?"

Mrs. Townsend had more. "In order to verify that the *Paul D* is put to good use, I have one more stipulation. You will take with you a passenger, a watchdog you might say."

Karen didn't like what she was hearing. "A passenger? On our *honeymoon*? You've got to be kidding. Who?"

Mrs. Townsend yanked on the leash and Peach lurched forward. *"This* is who. I've had him for seven years and he's the most cantankerous little crab there ever was. I think a nice long voyage on my boat might soften him up." She handed Robin the leash and Peach bared his teeth. Mrs. Townsend continued. "And all I require is a little documentation emailed to me each day—a photograph of my former dog enjoying himself on my boat. I think we'll all benefit no end from this little arrangement, don't you?"

"Email?" I blurted. "Since when do you know anything about email?

She was dismissive. "I learned all about if from your friend there, the best man. He's got quite a knack with such things."

Fred cleared his throat and glanced my way. "So I'm told."

Perhaps detecting some urgency in the proceedings, Robin passed the leash to Karen and raised his hands toward the crowd. "Well, thanks, everybody! Looks like we'll be in touch."

And then they were gone, the two of them—or three—in the red Mustang, and that was that. No throwing of the bouquet, no tossing of the garter, no bubble blowing, no dancing. It was as if a fast escape had been part of the plan.

Mrs. Townsend had also made some plans. After the newlyweds and their companion had left for warmer waters, we asked her about being lonely with Peach gone, and she said that she was upgrading her companionship. What she had in mind was Mrs. Conditt, who had been cast adrift by Walt's death and Geneva's declining fortune. "Do you by any chance like painting?" Mrs. Townsend had asked her, and Mrs. Conditt had replied, "I'm sure I *can*. Care for a fireball?"

Geneva had plans to go back to Boston and use her legal skills to establish the Walter Weston Sterling Foundation, a non-profit corporation for the support of budding medical students. She sighed. "Maybe I can get one of them to explain some of Walt's books to me."

A day or so later, the fog came in from the bay, and sat for what seemed like a week. Mrs. Conditt drove Mrs. Townsend over to talk to Pop for some reason, and when they were through she asked me why I was still hanging around Ashton when the summer was clearly over and all of the grad schools must have started.

"Not for another week," I said, "but that would be for last-minute admission. I'd have to put the money right in the bursar's hand and hit the ground running."

She hauled out one of the stools and sat down at the kitchen counter. "Then why don't you just do it for pity's sake? You shouldn't be wasting away up here in the fog like this."

I glanced at Mom and Pop. "Well, I didn't manage to save much money this summer."

She put her elbows on the counter. "What about your parents? Can't they help you out?"

I frowned. "Not this year. Maybe next fall."

Pop slid a piece of paper toward me. I turned it over. It was a cashier's check made out for the estimated amount of a year's tuition and expenses at Orono.

I stared at it, pinched it to make sure it was really there.

"Well, Amber? What do you say?" Suddenly I was a child again, with Mom prompting me.

"Thanks. I mean, thank you! But where did this come from?"

"You can't tell through the fog," Pop said, "but Mrs. Townsend just bought herself another boat."

I looked toward the new picture window, but the yard was murky. I couldn't see a thing. "You bought *our* boat?"

Mrs. Townsend got up and shrugged. "Well, I thought it was about time to name one after my *second* husband, Paul R. Townsend. The more I think about it, the more I think he was a pretty fine gentleman, too. I seem to have this thing about men named Paul."

I came around the island and gave her such a big hug that we almost fell over.

When she had regained her balance, Mrs. Townsend patted my hand and said, "Just put that education to good use. For some of them around here it's too late, but not for you."

"I already know what I want to do," I said. I had been thinking about it ever since Walt's funeral, maybe a lot longer. "I want to take care of people who don't have anyone else to take care of them. I want to do it the best it's ever been done."

She headed toward the door with Mrs. Conditt in her wake. "I'm glad to hear that because, if you're fast, you may be in time to make *me* your first customer—and I want quality geezer care. Shirley here is fine company, but she's a hell of a painter. She's got great talent. So I'm sure that before long she'll be heading off to some art colony."

A few days later, Pop reported that another instrument had turned up on Winthrop's porch—an ugly upright piano with chipped keys and a surprisingly pretty tone. This appearance was even stranger than the last because the piano had Carlyle's name on it. My money from Hal's had just about covered it.

Even though time was tight before classes started, I agreed to a day trip to Mount Desert. Fred and I went under a flimsy pretext—looking for the beloved cap that he had left behind on Champlain Mountain for my sake. I felt that the trip was the least I could do in return for his putting up with me for so long and, now that I was leaving home, we could finally *be* friends and not have to worry about sliding back into our old dead-end affection-free relationship, especially after he told me that he was leaving Ashton to pursue a career in IT.

"I still like pounding nails into boards," he told me, "but the future's in information, and it turns out I'm pretty good at it. I can always pound nails for a hobby."

We quickly reached the summit of Gorham, where we had first caught sight of Karen and Robin during our desperate dash to bring them back to Ashton. We stopped and turned into the chilly wind to see how far we had come, and it seemed as if the whole island spread out below us, its thick woods now streaked with autumn orange and rust, framed by the deep blue gray of the spreading sea.

My breath caught at the sight of a familiar shape showing gold against the horizon. I pointed at the approaching sail. "Is that the *Paul D?*"

Gently, Fred pulled down my hand. "No, they're gone, long gone. You won't see them again until next summer." As we watched the boat move toward us and then turn to the south, floating like a spark on the bright water, I became aware of his warm arms around me. We had the mountaintop to ourselves, and we watched as the boat moved toward the rugged islands at the edge of the open sea.

"What do you think?" I asked. "Did Walt really have the magic to turn people's lives around?"

Fred watched the boat disappear on the horizon. "He turned *ours* around, didn't he? I'm finally ready to do something with my life—and you're not ticklish anymore."

And I wasn't, not even when he tilted my chin up and kissed me.

I settled back into his arms. The path down, with all its twists, could wait a little longer. For now, the top of the mountain belonged to us.

Acknowledgements

Thanks to everyone who helped to make *Downeast Ledge* the book it is: James A. Brown, Jr., Herb Gilliland, Patricia Gilliland, Ross Gilliland, Kelly Harms, Jim Haselden, Jean Hill, Vicki Nonn, Ken and Claudette Potter, and Susan R. Sweeney all brought their experience and expertise to bear on the story to its betterment.

A longtime summer visitor to Maine, Norman Gilliland is a producer at Wisconsin Public Radio. He's the author of two books about classical music—*Grace Notes for a Year* and *Scores to Settle*—and two previous novels, *Sand Mansions* and *Midnight Catch*. In 2006 he produced the first complete dramatized audio version of *Beowulf*. He was one of seven cast members in the film *A Note of Triumph: The Golden Age of Norman Corwin,* which won the Oscar for Best Short Documentary in 2006. He and his wife Amanda have two sons and live in Middleton, Wisconsin.

Made in the USA
Charleston, SC
06 May 2014